# BEHIND THE DAM

## A NOVEL

*Joanne - Remember the Sippo Book Club. Enjoy the book!*
*— Dave*

## DAVID GRINSTEAD

A TRIBUTE TO THE REAL BUILDERS AND THE PEOPLE WHO GAVE UP THEIR LAND FOR THE DAM.

*Behind the Dam*
Copyright © 2017, David R. Grinstead. All rights reserved.

No part of this publication may be reproduced, stored in a retrieval system or transmitted in any way by any means, electronic, mechanical, photocopy, recording or otherwise without the prior permission of the author except as provided by USA copyright law.

This is a work of fiction. It is not intended as an exposé. Any similarity to actual persons, living or dead, and places real or imagined is coincidental. Names, places, time, events, people, and happenings are fictitious or enhanced for the sake of the story. Some of the incidents and events actually happened, and some of the locations, names, and times actually exist but are taken out of context from many sources and construction projects and are combined solely for the purpose of entertaining and captivating the reader.

Foremost, in telling this story, is my intention to enlighten the reader about the unsung workers, inner workings, events, sacrifices, and toil that go into construction projects and facilities that we take for granted. As a Methodist minister once told me about a big rock on the church property, "It must be granite because it's been there for so long we take it for granite."

Second Paperback Edition: July 2017

Cover and Interior Design by D. Robert Pease
www.walkingstickbooks.com

*Published in the United States of America*

*Dedicated to
Heather
We wish you could have stayed longer. God bless you.*

# BEHIND THE DAM

# PREFACE

In 1970 the US Army Corps of Engineers and a large construction company set about to build a controversial flood control project in Southwestern Ohio. To resolve many setbacks, problems, and challenges the Corps' resident engineer and the contractor's project manager had to set aside different motives. Through all the adversity they had the same goal, build the dam. This is the story behind the building of the dam and the formation of the lake resulting from the damming of the Trout River.

Environmentalists objected to the project before and during the building of the dam. They claimed the cost was excessive and the dam was not needed. Opponents accused the government of being uncaring about 185 families who lost their homes to make way for the dam. The opponents would fight to stop construction of the project from its start to the filling of the lake behind the dam.

The government kept the project going despite anti-dam devices that included protests, injunctions, lawsuits, camp-ins, and newspaper editorials. One deranged old woman exemplified the opposition as she fought to save the home where she was born and where she planned to die.

Weather, floods, labor unrest, and accidents beset the

builders during the six years it took to build the dam. Union disputes and personal tragedies complicated the already challenging and ominous task. The rural location and lack of supplies and workers exacerbated the builders' problems. Building the project was made more difficult by the ulterior motives of a rogue government inspector.

A politician and some realtors took advantage of hapless owners who wanted to sell. Another owner resorted to deception to enhance the value of his property.

Hardships and perils were part of the worker's assignments. Without tribute, they put a portion of their lives into the Trout River Dam. Their efforts made the project a beautiful and useful reality. In the final stages, a financial crisis threatened the contractor's business life.

Every building project requires a place for it to exist, a parcel on which to build. Incidents in this book recognize the people forced from their beloved homes and land, which in many cases had been in their families for generations. Before they left their land, these people endured hardships and unknowns and made sacrifices to make way for a facility that would be used and enjoyed by strangers. There is more than just water behind the dam. There is a trail of broken lives, hard work, and, ultimately, satisfaction of a job well done.

This book is a tribute to the men and women who toil in the construction industry. Their sacrifices, dedication, and skill make life more comfortable while surrounding us with pleasing and useful structures.

# CHAPTER 1

Seated in his three-sided cubicle in the archaic building that was home to the US Army Corps of Engineers, Louisville District, the young engineer's desk phone chimed announcing an internal call, he answered, "Hello, Wayne Henderson here."

"Wayne, this is Jordan Lipper. Please come up to my office. We need to discuss something with you."

During ten years with the Corps, Wayne had never received a call from chief engineer Lipper directed solely at him. His first thought was that he had gravely erred on one of his former projects and was being called to answer for the resulting problem he may have caused. He put those thoughts aside and answered, "Yes sir, I'll be right up." Becoming more concerned he thought, "Who the hell is 'we'?"

An answer to the "we" question occurred when Wayne entered Lipper's large corner office, and he saw the district's deputy commander, Lieutenant Colonel Chad Ramsey, whose presence alarmed him.

Lipper said, "Have a seat. We have a matter to discuss with you." Wayne nervously sat as directed.

Lipper went right to the point, "In February 1966 Congress mandated the building of five flood control and recreational dams in Ohio, Indiana, and Kentucky. We want you to manage construction of the thirty-six million dollar Trout River Dam in Southwest Ohio, Clearfield County. Today is March 15, 1968. We want planning and design work on this project to begin no later than April first. That gives you two weeks to get things rolling. Actual construction has to begin no later than April 1970."

Lieutenant Colonel Ramsey explained, "Your responsibility will be all encompassing. You will be in charge of planning, design, land acquisition, and construction; even the dedication ceremony. You're our first choice because of your excellent work designing several dams and your talent for solving problems outside the normal realm of construction."

Lipper added, "You will be expected to reside at the project until completion. We anticipate construction will take six to seven years. The government will provide nearby housing for you and your family. Your title will be the resident engineer." Lipper looked directly at Wayne and told him, "We need to know by Monday if you accept the challenge."

In a more reasonable voice, Lipper said, "I've asked Joan Schroeder from our public information office to fill you in on what's been going on until now. She'll be over to your office in a few minutes. Thanks for your time, give this opportunity serious consideration."

\*\*\*

Wayne returned to his office to find Joan waiting for him. Joan's appearance and attire evoked a conservative business attitude. She was attractive despite having her bright brunette hair tucked into a no-nonsense bun.

After introducing herself, she went right to work, "For

the past year and a half the public information office has been working to inform the residents of Clearfield County about the benefits of the Trout River flood control dam. Our public relations staff went through a tedious process of public meetings and hearings. The meetings were well attended and sometimes adverse. Our public relations personnel utilized hundreds of well spent hours answering questions, addressing concerns, and providing information about the project. Unfortunately, most of our time was used trying to appease opponents of the project. We have completed our work. As of last month, February 1968, we've informed the interested residents of Clearfield County about all aspects of the dam and lake."

"The site selected is on the Trout River in Clearfield County, Ohio," Joan explained. "It's about ten miles southwest of Stanton, the county seat. The Trout River and the proposed dam and lake occupy a beautiful valley running southeast to northwest in the western section of the county. The impoundment that will be created by the dam includes several small tributaries in valleys leading into the Trout River."

Wayne thought Joan seemed like she wanted to add to her message but was reluctant to proceed. "Do you have more to say?" asked Wayne.

Finally, she said, "I must warn you there are a lot of opponents to the dam and all that it represents. Some opponents are dangerous. Be alert, it will get worse as the project progresses until they realize the futility of their actions."

Wayne, after a moment to absorb the briefing, said to

Joan, "Thanks for taking time to bring me up to date about your activities. But most of all thanks for the heads up."

After Joan had left, Wayne sat there trying to imagine the task before him. Soon a man from a nearby office entered his work space and said, "Wayne, congratulations, word is going around the office about you going to Trout River as the resident engineer. I'm Lloyd Timmerman. I just came back from the same position at a similar project in Indiana. Do you have a few minutes for me to share my experience on that project?"

Wayne replied, "Sure, I'm all ears."

Lloyd settled into a chair and began telling his story. "Let me start by saying I know, and so does everyone here, that the primary purpose of these projects is flood control. Eventually, they save lives and prevent the loss of millions of dollars in property damage."

"Some of our coworkers relocated to new places with little impact on their lives and family. However, more than a few families had disastrous repercussions, including divorce and family divisions."

Lloyd continued, "When you get there you'll find that a lot of people affected by the project don't share the 'do good' aspect. People you've never met are going to hate you, the Corps, and the U.S. Government. To build the project the government will have to take property, forcibly if necessary, from about two hundred families and compel their relocation to new and unfamiliar surroundings. You will be a very visible government employee to whom they will have direct access." Wayne was becoming uncomfortable as Lloyd's story unfolded. "The environmentalists consider that the dams are unnecessary, expensive, a danger to the environment and just more pork barrel spending. Litigation to stop the work will spring from all sides and when least expected. Farmers who have held their land for generations, only to have the government flood it in the name of progress; will fight until the water is lapping at their outbuildings. You and your family will be right in the middle when controversies occur."

Wayne started to say something but was interrupted by Lloyd's raised hand. "Give me another minute. The contractors are there to earn a profit. Your job is to oversee the building of a dam and lake that will last more than a hundred years. The contractor is not your enemy, but there will be disagreements and conflicting goals that have to be satisfied."

Timmerman continued with advice. "There is one major justification to accept the challenge. It's the feeling you'll have of overseeing the building of something that thousands will enjoy year after year. About eight years from now you will look at the finished dam and lake, and you will say, "We did it, and it's beautiful."

As he was leaving Timmerman said, "Gratification will come as a result of the challenge. But there will be sacrifices and anguish in store for you. Good luck."

Two hours later, sitting at his desk, Wayne was coming off the high and beginning to realize the assignment's potential impact on him and his family.

\*\*\*

Wayne intended to leave work early so he could tell his wife, Melissa, about the opportunity that would change their lives. Just as he was gathering up the things he wanted to take with him, a man entered his cubicle. The man wore a suit and tie. He had an imposing aura about him.

The man extended his hand and introduced himself. "I'm Richard Albert. I'm an attorney and general counsel for the Corps. May I have a few minutes of your time?"

Wayne, wondering what the hell this was about, stammered, "Sure, of course, have a seat."

Albert explained, "Chief engineer Lipper asked me to bring you up to date on some issues that affect the Trout River Dam project. What I have to tell you is beyond what Miss Schroeder said earlier."

Wayne put the things he had in his arms back down and said, "I'm interested. Educate me."

Attorney Albert began, "As soon as the five projects were known to the public, opposition began to grow on the belief they are unneeded and environmentally unsound. A major concern for the opponents is the anticipated acquisition process and the subsequent impact on people's lives caused by forced relocation."

The topic Albert was talking about caused Wayne to become more uneasy, this topic was beyond his comfort zone. Albert continued, "Congressional mandates passed into law on January 11, 1966, provided federal funding for all five projects, dictating that land acquisition and construction go forward despite the opposition."

"Federal budget cuts began with the Nixon administration. Political haggling is delaying full funding until at least 1969. Then we can resume activity on the five flood control projects, including Trout River. In the interim, we are ignoring increasingly more intense and biased stories and subterfuge intended to dismantle the projects. Only construction funds are affected. We have to provide support for planning, design, and property acquisition. The message I'm giving you is, we'll continue as planned for as long as our limited funding lasts. We're hopeful the next Congress will restore full funding. Do you have any questions?"

Wayne answered, "No, thanks for the information." He wondered, "What are they asking me to do?"

# CHAPTER 2

Wayne Henderson graduated cum laude from Purdue University in 1954 with a degree in civil engineering. After graduating, he accepted a position as a structural design engineer with Melchior and Anniston Engineering, a highly regarded design and construction firm located in Indianapolis, Indiana. After four years Wayne was disillusioned with the job. He prepared and saw the construction drawings, but he seldom saw the steel and concrete results of his design efforts.

In 1958 he saw a Corps of Engineers ad in a trade magazine seeking civil engineers. Wayne responded to the ad and three weeks later the U.S. Government employed him at the US Army Corps of Engineers, Louisville, Kentucky District Office. Wayne was average size, five-ten and 180 pounds. He stayed fit mostly because of his love for the outdoors. He liked to hike, hunt, and fish. Intense and focused on his work, he was well liked by coworkers and management. Despite his relative youth, Wayne quickly had a reputation as the go-to engineer for solving difficult and unusual engineering problems. More important to Jordan Lipper, his boss, and others in the chain of command was his ability to intuitively grasp and solve situations outside the realm of academic engineering.

## BEHIND THE DAM

A year before going to work for the Corps, in May 1957, Wayne met Melissa, a local girl who taught third grade in the Indianapolis Public School System; he was 25, she was 24. Wayne and Melissa were married three months later, and a year after that their son John David was born. John David became simply JD.

When the resident engineer position became available, Wayne and Melissa were married eleven years. Wayne, Melissa, and ten-year-old son John David (JD) lived in La Grange, Kentucky, a suburb east of Louisville. They were active in the community, their church, and JD's school. They knew that moving to rural Clearfield County in Southwest Ohio would require sacrifices and adjustments to a new, rural, social environment.

When Wayne arrived home from work on that auspicious day in March 1968, he immediately told Melissa about the new assignment. Wayne explained to Melissa, "My mind is a jumble. I've been asked to be the resident engineer on a massive dam project in Southwest Ohio. I want the job but taking it will affect all of us. It will change our lives. I'm not sure the change will be good."

Melissa shook Wayne's arm and exclaimed, "Wayne settle down! You're talking so fast I can't understand you. Let's sit at the kitchen table. You need to calm yourself."

Wayne asked himself, *"How can I do this? How can I tell her what I want to do? This opportunity will change our lives. Well, here goes."*

"Mr. Lipper the district chief engineer and my boss asked me to be the resident engineer on a flood control project in Ohio. The catch is; by the time the construction phase begins in late

1969 I'm expected to be full time at the site. I can turn down the assignment, and it'll go to someone else. If I accept it, we'll have to move to Ohio. Turning down this assignment will not jeopardize my present position. It may affect my chance for future opportunity. That's just the way things work, especially with the government. What I'm concerned about is how this assignment and moving to Ohio will affect you and our son."

Wayne was trying to keep his outward demeanor calm but also serious. Inside he felt excited about the opportunity. Wayne's excitement was brief when he saw tears flowing down Melissa's cheeks. Tearfully she said, "I'm concerned about our son. She sobbed, "JD will have to attend a rural school that might not have the quality teachers and programs he has access to here in La Grange. As an outsider, he'll have to make new friends and earn acceptance. I'll have to give up my teaching job. You can't expect us to give up our home and friends. Our parents are close by, my sister and your two brothers are just across the river in Indiana."

Melissa tearfully continued to voice her objection, "We'll have to find a new church. JD will leave a lot of church and school friends. He'll have to find a new scout troop."

Wayne moved to Melissa's side and put his arm around her. "You know I don't want to be uncaring and do anything to cause a situation that disrupts our lives. This job is an opportunity that I've got to consider, an opportunity that we must both consider."

Melissa erupted, "You talk about caring for your family! But in the same breath, you allude to a so-called 'opportunity' that will rip us from our home and plop us down in some godforsaken hick town in Ohio! I can't do that."

Wayne was trying to be sympathetic to Melissa's feelings. When she settled down after her outburst, he told her, "Let's let this simmer for a day or so. I'll admit I'm excited about the challenge this presents. There are also monetary considerations. Managers make more money than designers. This opportunity can open a new path to promotion."

Melissa put her head on Wayne's shoulder and more calmly said, "Yeah, you're right, I have become too emotional. Let's put this aside for a while."

During a tense Saturday, they avoided talking about the "damn dam", as Melissa labeled it. Saturday night when they went to bed, Wayne felt the two people in the bed seemed like strangers to each other.

Sunday morning Melissa was the first to speak, "I don't want to spend another night like that. We didn't even say 'good night; I love you' to each other. We've never ended the day by not saying I love you to each other. Even when we disagree during the day, we always make up. After church, we need to talk until we decide. One way or the other, do we go to Ohio or not?"

The discussion resumed Sunday afternoon. Wayne told Melissa, "Accepting this assignment will have a significant and possibly negative impact on our lives. I have to consider that being away from the office for a long time might cause me to lose my place in the promotion pecking order. We might be embarking on a life of moving from one project to another. Regardless, there's no guarantee that this will lead to better opportunities."

Melissa sat across from Wayne at the kitchen table. She came around and sat touching Wayne. Once again tears were streaming down her face. But holding Wayne's hand she suggested, "Let's include JD in our decision. I know he is only ten, but he should be part of this."

Wayne thought a moment before answering, "You're very upset. Let's take a minute to calm down before involving him." Melissa toweled her face dry. Squeezing Wayne's hand, she said, "I know this is important to you. I know you want to do what is right for you at work. I know we both want to do what is good for JD. But I am concerned you will turn down the new job because of me and how I feel about staying here."

Melissa, as her voice became less tearful continued, "I'm scared to death, but I think we should go to the job in Ohio. It'll be a challenge. We might regret it, but let's do it!"

Later that afternoon they explained the decision to JD. At first, he was very upset. He cried as he told them, "I won't go." To Wayne he screamed, "I hate you! I'm gonna' lose all my friends. I won't know anybody over there."

Melissa saved the day by explaining to JD about the new job his dad was getting, that his dad would be in charge of having a big dam built. But what won JD over was when she told him, "We'll be living near a river, and there are lots of wild animals nearby."

JD exclaimed, "You mean dad, and I could go fishing every day?"

Melissa answered, "Well, not every day. But yes, you and dad can go fishing."

After they had made the decision to go to Ohio, Wayne, concerned about their home in La Grange, asked Melissa, "Should we sell it, close it up, or lease it?"

Melissa quickly answered, "We should sell it. We don't want to worry about collecting rent and paying for repairs while it's occupied by strangers."

Wayne immediately agreed, "Most of our furniture and other stuff should fit in the new house. Having our furniture will make the surroundings more familiar. Since the government is providing a house and we have a place to move to, we should put this house on the market and stay here until it sells."

Wayne hugged Melissa and JD," I don't know what the heck we're doing. But we'll be doing it together."

Melissa, still reluctant concluded, "We're going, but I'm frightened about the realities."

Wayne said, "Looking on the positive side, we all enjoy being outdoors. Hiking and exploring new places are some of our favorite activities." They didn't speak of it, but they were both looking forward to 'country living.'

On Monday, March 18, 1968, Wayne was promoted to his new assignment as resident engineer in charge of all the difficult and complex activities required for construction of the Trout River Dam and Lake. From talks with other past and present resident engineers, Wayne knew the challenging assignment would lead to many personal and job incidents in which construction glitches, forces of nature, and acrimonious opponents will test his abilities.

Wayne told Melissa, "I don't think of myself as being an aggressive person, but I don't back down from confrontation and disagreement. I hope I'm right for this job."

# CHAPTER 3

Less than a year before Wayne became the resident engineer an event occurred that would affect the Corps property acquisition effort.

A local politician conceived a scheme that would adversely impact the cost of the government's land acquisition process. Prior to October 1967 residents of the county knew of the proposed dam. However the exact location of the planned dam and lake was only known to a select few in Clearfield County. One of the insiders was Bert Halgren, the president of the three-person Clearfield County Commissioners. Halgren was among the first to know because the Corps of Engineers Deputy Commander, Lieutenant Colonel Chad Ramsey, in an honest attempt to be open, made a courtesy call informing Halgren of the location of the planned dam and lake. Ramsey had no idea Halgren would conceal the information and use it for his benefit.

Halgren, 62 years old, gray hair and mustache, short and overweight, but still active, was known for his public charm but private deviousness. He was not about to let anything happen in his county unless it had his blessing and, directly or indirectly, rewarded him. He was recently reelected to the county commissioners and was serving his third term in office. Halgren did not share the insider information about the proposed dam with the other two commissioners.

From the insider information he received, Bert knew that sooner or later the federal government would have to start buying land within the impoundment formed by the dam. Unknown to anyone, using a county map, he outlined the approximate area to be covered by the new lake. He intended to take advantage of knowing the location of the affected area before anyone else.

Bert's scheme was to secretly buy up some of the affected properties before the general public knew about the dam and its location. He selected a small circle of like-minded real estate professionals that he believed would agree with his plan and keep it secret. The other two commissioners, vice president Richard Walling and member at large Charles Langley, had no inkling about Halgren's plan nor did Halgren include them.

Bert was no stranger to 'under the table' county transactions. During his reign as a Clearfield County Commissioner Bert occasionally profited by using his position to move questionable projects through zoning and building permit approval.

On October 19, 1967, Bert met with his three realtor friends who, after swearing secrecy, gave their enthusiastic reaction to his greedily conceived plan. They met at Bert's mini-farm just outside Stanton.

Bert shared the secret, "Gentlemen, I have some news that is good for our county. The Corps of Engineers is going to build a dam and lake on the Trout River." He allowed their excitement die down before he continued, "There is a land buying opportunity, but we'll have to move quickly before news about the dam becomes public. As you know real estate values, especially in rural parts of the county, have been weak."

Harvey Barnes, one of the realtors and a known opportunist, asked, "What's your plan, Bert?"

Bert confided to his three co-conspirators, "First I want to know how you'll feel about buying some of this land now before the government acquires it. Then when they begin buying you'll sell to the government for more than you paid. I'll guarantee when they start buying the prices they pay will be more than they are now. We'll have to hold on to the properties for up to three years."

Vincent Osgood and John Cooper, two of the realtors in the room, both eagerly acknowledged their willingness to take part in the scheme. Osgood and Cooper were successful and wealthy, but their acquiescence confirmed their greediness. Apart from their commonality of greediness they had differing personalities.

Osgood, 46, of medium stature, was the country club type, had an inflated ego, was domineering, and a community leader. His attractive wife and two adult children usually went along with whatever he said and did. He was adept at manipulating people.

Cooper, 50, at six feet tall and one hundred fifty pounds, was known in the community as a string bean. He was unmarried and kept to his self. He was not socially active in the community and enjoyed things he could do by himself such as hunting and fishing. He was rumored to have a nasty temper. His real estate business was a one man enterprise. He liked to list and sell. He didn't like to share commissions.

The third realtor was Harvey Barnes, 44, on the chunky side, a heavy drinker and ne'er-do-well whose real estate business was barely paying his light bill. He would eventually be employed by the U.S. Government to assist with a few dam related property acquisitions. He was divorced from his wife of five years. She dumped him more than twelve years ago. She opted for more stability, money, and better looks. Harvey would grab a piece of any transaction, so long as he didn't have to do any of the advertising and listing work.

Before the meeting ended Osgood asked Bert, "Do you think we are entering into a situation that will create a conflict of interest?"

Bert answered, "How could that happen? All you are doing is buying some real estate for investment purposes. Here is my plan. On Monday the three of you will go to the county assessor's office and quietly, don't draw attention to what you are doing, go through public records, real estate listings, and pending foreclosures and put together a list of potentially distressed properties within the impoundment area. Don't disclose your findings to anyone but me."

Bert promised, "If this goes as planned we will buy some easily available properties. We'll split the profits from each property you individually acquire sixty percent to each of you and forty percent to me."

Before the meeting ended Bert admonished the three, "You'll have to keep the purchases to six or seven properties by each of you. If you do more than that, you'll attract attention at the assessor's office."

The meeting ended with everyone upbeat about the plan and the potential profits.

Several days later, on October 24, all three of the conspirators were back in Bert's office with a list containing twenty-nine distressed properties lying within the lake area.

Osgood, speaking for himself and Cooper; told Halgren, "John and I have enough stocks, bonds, and cash to pay for the properties we anticipate buying."

Barnes said, "I have no idea how I can buy any of the properties."

To keep Barnes in the plan, Bert realized he would have to front Harvey cash for him to participate. He regretted he included Harvey but told him, "Harvey I'll loan you enough money to hold up your end of the program. But anything I do will be top secret. If you mess up and word gets out, I'll destroy you. You won't be able to buy a candy bar or walk on the sidewalks of this town. You won't be able to sell an outhouse. Do you understand?"

Harvey responded with a croak in his voice that he understood.

Bert ordered him, "Now get the hell out of here."

The illegal purchases began immediately. During the next two months, by December 23, 1967, sixteen residences and five dormant farms were acquired by the three insider realtors. They were not able to buy eight other potential properties without divulging the essence of their scheme.

Osgood bought six residences and two dormant farms. Cooper bought seven dwellings and two dormant farms. Barnes finished off the buying using Bert's money to pay for the remaining three residences and one inactive farm.

By the end of February 1968, they closed all the deals and paid the money to the sellers. The deeds to all twenty-one homes and farms were surreptitiously transferred into the names of Osgood, Cooper, or Barnes. The three conspirator realtors, with Walgren's help, had bought twenty-one of the many properties needed by the government to build the dam and lake.

# CHAPTER 4

On Monday morning, March 25, 1968, Wayne met with the Trout River team. He began the meeting by telling the assembled group of thirty-one people, "We have a daunting task ahead and an even bigger challenge. We are going to build a flood control dam and lake in Clearfield County, Ohio. The dam lies within a rural but potentially hostile environment. People living and farming within the impoundment area will be forced to relocate. By working together we will put all the elements of this project together and give the residents of Clearfield County and Ohio a facility they, and the Corps can be proud to say it's ours and it is good." At the end of the meeting, Wayne told the team, "To succeed, we'll all have to put our best efforts into this project."

Later that day Wayne reported to Lipper, "This morning I had a three-hour meeting with the Trout River team. With only a week of preparation I met with the planners, designers, surveyors, environmental engineers, real estate acquisition specialists, and construction compliance technicians. Activity for building the Trout River Dam and Lake has begun."

As an afterthought, Wayne said, "By the way, I found out that the government completed the necessary and relevant environmental impact study, it is two-hundred pages long. We're not going to redo that already completed study."

Lipper replied, "That's a good start. Report your team's progress as necessary. Let me know if I can assist you."

While Wayne and his team were planning the construction of the dam, another force was working to stop the dam. Wayne and his family were still in their La Grange home. After church, he was reading the Sunday, March 31, 1968, edition of the Cincinnati Daily News. He shouted to Melissa, "You have to see this. In the editorial section, there is a column length condemnation of the Trout River Dam. The writer is a guy named Roger Wilkins. He sounds like our enemy." Together they read the article.

## CLEARFIELD COUNTY PROJECT TO ADVERSELY AFFECT THOUSANDS OF PRISTINE ACRES

*The Trout River Dam and Lake, a so-called flood control endeavor by the Corps of Engineers, is in the planning stages. The dam will stretch across the pristine Trout River in Clearfield County, Ohio.*

*In addition to damming the crystal clear waters of the Trout River, the Corps of Engineers, Louisville District, is already building four other misguided flood control dams and lakes, one in Ohio, one in Indiana, and two in Kentucky.*

*The leadership at the Louisville District Corps of Engineers is environmentally weak and uncaring about the adverse effect on people who have been or will be ripped from their homes and forced to relocate to make way for these dam and lake projects. The projects are ill-advised, environmentally unsound, and wasteful. They do not address water conservation and wilderness preservation.*

*Members of the Cincinnati City Council, other local newspapers, and those who care for the environment have stated their opposition to the planned projects. We need to bombard the Corps of Engineers and local, state, and federal government officials with our concerns. Tell them to stop this waste of our money.*

*All of the planned projects are unneeded, environmental dangers, and show a lack of caring for those displaced by the impoundments.*

*The Clearfield County dam alone will waste thirty-six million dollars of tax payer money. Together the five unneeded dams will waste more than two hundred million public dollars. Money wasted on the dams is needed for social programs.*

*The U.S. Government, Congress, and the Corps should hang their heads in shame over this woeful waste of money.*

Roger Wilkins, Special Projects Writer

Wayne told Melissa, "I bet that guy will become my nemesis for the next seven years."

## BEHIND THE DAM

\*\*\*

After Wayne, with Melissa's and JD's help, made the decision to accept the assignment to be the resident engineer at the Trout River Dam, he spoke freely with Melissa about the team and their work.

One such conversation on April 6, 1968, happened during their Saturday evening meal. Wayne explained to the family about how the Louisville office was addressing the projects. "The district has committed nearly a hundred talented people to the building of the Trout River Dam and four other flood control projects. One of the challenging aspects of my job is staying involved with the other four team leaders to avoid repeating each other's work. We all have to work in concert with each other to produce structures that fit the environment and are pleasing to the American taxpayer. Outside the office, there are many critics. By the time a dam and lake is finished, the project is a success if critics admit, as a minimum, it looks nice."

Wayne continued to explain, "Design work for the dam and impoundment area will begin next week and finish in January 1969. At the same time we will be conducting soil testing and surveys, and taking stream flow data.

Wayne added his concerns, "I'm worried that the Trout River Dam and Lake will be a troubled project regardless of the best efforts of dedicated and talented Corps of Engineers personnel."

I've told my team, "Focus on your assignments. Don't become embroiled in the controversy."

# CHAPTER 5

On April 8, 1968, Wayne met with the survey team to develop a plan to map the four thousand two hundred sixty acres that would become the Trout River Dam and Lake. The survey team consisted of the lead surveyor Stephen Storey, and three other Ohio registered surveyors. Wayne told them, "By default, you will be the first government representatives to venture into the designated area."

On May 8, 1968, Storey and one surveyor were just getting into their assignment to determine property limits and establish ground contours. Another crew was working on the opposite side of the future lake area.

Unknown to Storey and the other surveyor an angry old woman stood hidden behind a dense growth of blackberry bushes, shotgun in hand. She was intently watching the two men approach her family property where she was born and had lived her whole life.

Storey and his assistant could see a dilapidated four-room shack, similar to those found in Appalachia. There were two front facing windows looking out onto a raw wood porch with a sagging, rotted surface. They could see an outdoor privy and a tin wash tub. Storey noted to his assistant, "Look at that! Their electricity comes from a two wire electric service stolen from a connection near the home of a neighbor. Behind the shack the land drops seventy feet in a steep slope, ending at the Trout River."

The two men, under Olga's keen observation from her hiding place, were oblivious to the unstable and dangerous woman who waited in ambush just in front of them.

When the two unsuspecting men approached within sixty feet of the woman she surprised them when she sprang from the bushes and shouted, "Git yer sorry government asses offa my property!" Before they could respond, she fired one barrel of buckshot at their heads. Fortunately for the surveyors, at a distance of sixty feet, the buckshot did nothing more than scatter, causing her to miss her targets.

When her son heard the commotion, he ran from the house and grabbed the gun from the woman. "Ma, what the hell are ya doin? He shouted, "You could've killed those fellers!"

She tried to wrestle the gun back from her son while yelling,

"That's what I'm a tryin' to do, you idiot! They're trespassers! They're here to take my land!" Fortunately for the two surveyors, her son had the gun and Olga was not able to fire the other barrel.

While Olga was distracted, the surveyors made a run for their lives. After about a hundred yards Stephen Storey, gasped to his partner, "Holy shit, what the hell was that? That old woman could've killed us! Come on let's get the hell out of here. I'm only sixty-one, and I want to live to see retirement!"

The angry woman was Olga McCoy. She was a property owner who would be forced to give up her property and relocate to make way for the four-thousand two-hundred sixty acres Trout River Dam and Lake. Olga vowed she would not go without a fight.

# CHAPTER 6

When surveyor Storey and his partner reached the Corps field office, they called the resident engineer, Wayne Henderson, at the Corps of Engineers building in Louisville, Kentucky. Wayne was in his upgraded office in the archaic and soon to be replaced Corps of Engineers district office in the 830 West Broadway Building in Louisville, Kentucky. Wayne answered, "Hello Steve, it's good to hear from you." Then he inquired, "What's going on?"

Storey related the incident to Wayne, "About an hour ago my partner and I were just starting to establish the boundaries of the Olga McCoy property when this pissed off old woman stepped from behind a bush and fired her shotgun at us. We got the hell out of there and returned to the field office. Then I called you."

Storey explained, "We need some local law enforcement to provide protection."

Wayne acknowledged the request, "Talk to the county sheriff but try to keep the incident from the media. We're already getting a lot of opposition, negative editorials, and protests on all five projects. The Trout River opponents are the most vocal and determined. No matter how angry you are, don't file a complaint. We don't need some anti-dam journalist twisting the story to sound like the government is picking on an old lady."

Storey responded, "Okay, I'll contact Jesse Spearman, the Clearfield County Sheriff, and do as you say. But before I call the sheriff we need to consider the magnitude of the crime committed. She shot at us and would have fired again if her son hadn't grabbed the gun."

Wayne agreed, "You no doubt had a close call that put you and your partner in jeopardy. No one was injured, and we don't know if she was just trying to scare you. Nevertheless, I'm outraged by the incident. We don't want anyone to be in peril while doing their job. However, the timing favors the opponents, and we don't want to give them a chance at a cheap shot. Excuse the pun."

Storey had to chuckle at the unintended pun. He acknowledged Wayne's counsel, "Thanks for the advice. I'll let the sheriff know we don't want publicity on this. By the way, get out of the office and come see us some time."

Wayne, with another call waiting, said, "I will. Keep up the good Work."

Storey immediately contacted the Clearfield County sheriff's office and asked to speak to Sheriff Jesse Spearman. "Good morning sheriff, this is Stephen Storey a Corps of Engineers surveyor working at the site of the new Trout River Dam and Lake. We are surveying the area that will be occupied by the dam and impoundment. A few residents have their shorts in a wad and won't let our surveyors near their property. Other than putting in a few stakes and benchmarks we are not disturbing anyone's property." Storey continued, "About an hour ago, one of the owners,

Olga McCoy, out at 1232 Lawn Lane, fired a shotgun at us. She missed but scared the shit out of us. Obviously shooting at somebody is a dangerous situation. However, the government does not want any publicity about the incident. We need to be discreet and avoid a media circus."

Sheriff Spearman agreed, "Mr. Story, when you need us, you just have your boys call the county dispatcher. We'll have a deputy or two respond right quick. By the way, Olga McCoy and her son are well known to us. We'll have a talk with them and accompany your crew when you survey her property. However, if y'all don't want publicity you'll not be able to file any charges." Storey agreed, "We just want to finish our work. But we need protection from that old woman. I'll call your office tomorrow to set up a time to go back out there."

Sheriff Spearman said, "If you have few minutes let me fill you in about Olga McCoy and her son Kenny."

Storey replied, "Yeah that would be interesting."

The sheriff began his story, "Olga's only 54, but her primitive lifestyle has taken its toll on her. She's diminutive but strong. She has mental and anger issues that started with the birth of her first son, Kenneth, 31 years ago. Kenneth, as had Olga, was born without assistance in their four-room shack. Kenny was born in 1937 when Olga was 23; the same year she met Kenneth's father, Oliver Thornton."

"Only one year later, in 1938, their second son, Michael was born. From the time he was cognizant Michael resented the family's poverty and complacency. In 1958, at age 20, he simply disappeared to seek his fortune. In the years hence the family hasn't seen or heard from him."

The sheriff continued, "The shack contains necessities

only, a wood burning cooking stove and parlor heater, a few chairs, a table, Olga's bed in one room, and two small beds in another room."

"They have no public water or sewer service. Maybe you noticed the McCoy's are stealing electricity from a neighbor. Everyone knows this, including the neighbor, and they ignore the problem. This stolen electricity provides lighting for the shack and power for the well water pump, a small electric water heater, and the television."

"Their luxuries consist of a twenty-one-inch black and white TV with a rabbit ear antenna and the ten-gallon electric water heater. The TV receives just two Cincinnati stations. There is no carpet or curtains, nor are there any other creature comforts that most people take for granted."

"Here's where the story begins. Oliver, Olga's partner and the father of both boys; everyone called him Ollie, sometimes worked beside Olga farming their ten hilly acres. It was back breaking work. In season they earned a meager living selling their homegrown vegetables from a stand supported on two barrels beside the lane in front of the shack. Remember, this was the late 30's, the great depression era. You probably noticed the shack is barely visible, set back three-hundred feet from the lane."

"Ollie's real income came from the sale of illegal whiskey that he made in a still located in the most substantial building on the property. The still was made to look like a chicken coop complete with a few dozen chickens pecking about, a little fake ramp to a closed chicken-sized entrance, and a false dilapidated appearance. It is still there but well hidden in the woods behind the shack."

"Here is the sad part of the story," the sheriff said. "Just two years after Kenneth was born and the same year Michael was born, 1939, Ollie was killed in a violent shootout with federal agents during a government sting operation in a derelict area of Covington, Kentucky. Involved were more than a dozen federal agents with their Thompson machine guns against three moonshiners. Along with Ollie, the feds also killed the other two moonshiners. Ironically, the three moonshiners were not working together. At the time of the raid, they were having an intense argument about marketing territories. They probably would have killed each other had the feds not intervened."

"When Olga received the news of the death of her partner, Ollie, the realization of being alone to care for and raise two babies nearly broke her already fragile psyche. The incident ingrained in her a deep rooted hatred for anything having to do with the federal government and its agents."

"I don't want to justify Olga's actions," the sheriff began, "But I want you to know what you're up against."

Storey said, "Thanks for the history lesson sheriff. It pays to know the background when there is a problem."

As planned, along with two sheriff deputies, the next day Storey and his partner completed the McCoy survey.

In August 1968, using partially completed boundary maps and property descriptions provided by the surveyors, the government began acquiring land needed to build the Trout River Project.

Concurrent with property acquisitions, the government completed survey work to map the entire forty-two hundred acres in November 1968.

# CHAPTER 7

On August 12, 1968, Wayne met with the team charged with acquiring the necessary land. He told them, "The survey to established property boundaries is almost finished. We know that one-hundred-eighty-five parcels of land, structures, farms, and dwellings need to be acquired to allow construction of the dam, impoundment, and surrounding recreation areas."

"We must start buying properties right now. The highest priority will be to obtain dwellings and structures within the footprint of the outlet works and the embankment for the dam. A second acquisition priority will be the area of the emergency overflow spillway; that's where we will obtain the earth and rock for the embankment. Construction is scheduled to start by February 1970."

On October 15, 1968, George Daniels, an acquisition specialist employed in the Corps real estate division, closed on the first property purchased for the dam. He called Wayne and told him, "Hey, I think we just bought you a house. It's right on Carney Road about a mile from the field office."

Wayne replied, "We'll check it out this weekend."

Daniels said, "I'll leave the keys in my middle desk drawer."

Four days later on Saturday afternoon Wayne, Melissa, and JD stood together in the driveway and assessed their new home. JD was first to comment, "It sure looks nice. There is a picnic table on the patio between the house and garage."

Melissa corrected JD, "That's called a breezeway. It's a roofed over space between the house and garage."

Wayne noted, "Yeah, there is a nice two-car garage. The home is all brick and on a big lot. Let's go inside."

They entered through a mud room. Melissa exclaimed, "There's a half bath off the mud room and hook up for a washer and dryer." When she entered the kitchen, she said, "I'm surprised, this home has recent updates and a modern kitchen with new appliances. Everything is spotless." She examined the dining room and living room, "Wow, lots of windows and natural light. The front door goes out to a screened-in porch. Everything looks beautiful."

Wayne said, "Let's check out the upstairs. This house is almost too good to be true."

JD led the upstairs tour. He called Melissa, "This is my room. I can see dad's office from here."

Melissa told Wayne, "There is a nice full bath off the hallway and a master bedroom with another full bathroom. There are lots of closets, too. I think you lucked out; this is way better than I expected." Giving Wayne a hug, she said, "This will be our home for the next eight years."

JD, an active 10-year-old, having lived in an urban setting, was excited about the openness of the land surrounding the home. He observed, however, "There are no kids around here. I hope I can find some when I get into the new school."

Melissa was concerned about access to shopping. "Where

are the stores and supermarkets? I didn't see any grocery stores or retail areas."

Wayne explained, "We'll probably have to make an occasional trip to the shopping malls near Cincinnati. Otherwise, we will frequent the smaller markets and local businesses."

Melissa rolled her eyes and agreed, "At least we'll probably be on a first name basis with the merchants at local stores. Back home you're lucky if they say, 'thankyou.'"

After looking around outside JD exclaimed, "Wow, there are miles of roads and paths where I can ride my bike." He became serious when he grabbed Melissa's hand and asked, "Where's the river where dad and I can catch fish?"

Wayne quickly answered for Melissa, "You can't see it from here but it is so close that we could walk there. We'll see part of it on our way home."

During the ride home, Melissa put her hand on Wayne's shoulder and with a smile told him, "I think you lucked out. The house is a lot better than I expected. For now, you are off the hook, but you still have to pamper me."

Wayne smiled back and said, "Yeah, we're both lucky."

Their home in Kentucky sold in December 1968, and they moved into their new home on January 18, 1969. JD, a fifth grader, enrolled and started attending the Stanton grade school.

\*\*\*

Wayne noted in a January 1969 report to Lipper, "Property acquisitions required for the more than four thousand acres needed for the project is progressing as planned. We are concentrating on properties in and around the footprint of the dam and in the area of the emergency spillway. My family and I have moved to the new house. The Corps field office and testing lab building are located at the end of Carney Road, about a half-mile past our new home."

\*\*\*

Cincinnati newspapers readily ran headlines leading to, usually biased, stories describing acquisition disagreements. Somehow a Cincinnati Daily News reporter, Roger Wilkins, obtained Wayne's identity and the location of his office. Wilkins, who was the source of most of the critical editorials and articles about the project, was eager to get a statement from Wayne. When he approached Wayne asking for an interview Wayne refused. He told Wilkins, "I've seen your work. You'll twist anything I say to fit your biased opinion. Take your requests to the Corps of Engineers public information office in Louisville." This brush off infuriated Wilkins and made a dangerous enemy for Wayne and the project.

In September 1968 the Corps acquisition team began in earnest to acquire the land required for the project. To assure local participation they contracted with three local real estate agents. One of whom, Harvey Barnes; unknown to anyone, had conspired with two other realtors and a county official to buy properties in the lake area expecting to profit when government acquisitions began.

On October 18, 1968, the Corps of Engineers Real Estate Division acquired the second property after the property purchased for Wayne Henderson and his family. Lonny and Jill Watkins told George Daniels, "We're happy to be out of our delinquent mortgage and end up with a little cash."

In October 1968, George Daniels, the official in charge of acquisitions, was transferred from the Louisville office to the Corps field office in Clearfield County. He believed his proximity to the area made purchases more convenient for all concerned.

After one particularly hectic day, Daniels told Wayne, "Some of the negotiations are stressful and adversarial. Federal law protects the sellers, provides relocation assistance, and a guarantee of fair market value to landowners who give up their property for government use. We have to abide by the law."

Daniels explained to Wayne, "There are one hundred-eighty-five properties needed to build the dam. We'll give the highest priority to properties within the footprint of the dam and emergency spillway. Those properties include six-hundred acres of public hunting land owned by the state of Ohio. Fortunately, the location of the hunting land was a significant portion of the area under the dam. Other properties within the footprint of the dam include Christ the King United Methodist Church, a small farm, and six dwellings. We're giving those properties the highest priority for acquisition."

"After the critical acquisitions, we have to relocate a cemetery and a historic one-room schoolhouse. Future purchases include a defunct seventy-acre gold mine, seven dormant farms, seven working farms, seven vacant dwellings, and one hundred fifty-two occupied dwellings."

Daniels looked at Wayne, "Your buddy the reporter Wilkins has a good time reporting about the impact the acquisitions are having on the lives of property owners within the area being acquired." He told Wayne, "It's sad but necessary that the adverse impact on the lives of those whose property we take is inevitable. Neighborhoods where people have known each other and who have shared celebration and grief are torn apart. Some of the occupants, after relocation, might never see lifelong friends again. Wilkins exaggerates all this and more. His objective is more about selling newspapers than reporting facts."

Wayne said, "I cringe while reading his exaggerated and biased stories that unfairly depicted the Corps' land acquisition efforts."

Toward the end of 1968, Wayne and George Daniels were again discussing the procurement process. Daniels noted, "Some owners are happy to have the chance to get out of their old house or farm. Before the Corps began acquisitions, some owners could only dream of a better life away from the Trout River and the floods. These types of homes are easy to acquire. Homes not affected by flooding and occupied by solvent owners present the most problems."

*** 

One day in February 1969 Wayne was in the Corps field office tending to matters related to acquiring needed land. A tall, gaunt looking man entered the office and identified himself as Fred Hatch, a writer for the Clearfield County Sentinel, the local newspaper. He asked to speak with Wayne Henderson.

Wayne overheard the man mention his name and stepped from his office and said, "I'm Wayne, what can I do for you?"

The man answered, "I'm Fred Hatch, a writer for the local newspaper. I'm planning to write an article about the dam."

Wayne immediately became defensive and rudely exclaimed, "All information about the project comes from the public information office at the district office in Louisville. You'll have to contact them."

Fred sensed the anger in Wayne's response and said, "I'm not here to do an expose. I want to tell the residents of Clearfield County what this dam will look like and what it will do for our people. I plan to write a positive and informative article."

Wayne was still skeptical but he agreed, "I'll give you an hour of my time on the condition you will honestly write about the positive aspects of the dam and lake."

Fred said, "Okay I agree, let's get started. Tell me what the dam and lake will do when completed."

"The most important benefit is flood control." Wayne explained, "The dam will protect properties located downstream from the dam. For them the annual floods that destroy property and, on rare occasions take lives, will be eliminated. Flood water will be stored in the impoundment behind the dam and slowly released after the storm."

Fred asked, "I've heard the term 'outlet works'. What is that?"

That is an easy question for me, Wayne answered, "Outlet works is an all encompassing name for three components that control the flow of water through the dam from the impoundment. The first element is the control tower. It is a two hundred twenty feet tall concrete structure containing slide and sluice gates that control the amount of water being released from the lake back to the river downstream from the dam. The second part is an eleven hundred foot long giant conduit that connects to the control tower and passes under and through the earth and rock dam. The conduit finally connects to the third component, the stilling basin, where the water is returned to the natural river."

Wayne then told Fred about the dam. "The last part of the flood control dam is the earthen dam embankment. The embankment is a two hundred foot high, one thousand seven hundred foot long earth, rock, and clay structure that spans across the valley. The earthen dam will be built two years from now when we divert the Trout River through the outlet works. The embankment requires eight million five hundred thousand cubic yards of earth, rock, and clay. All the material for the embankment will come from an emergency overflow spillway that will go around the outlet works." Wayne then gave Fred an artist's concept drawing that showed the finished lake.

Wayne had a few other tidbits to give to Fred, "Other parts of the project include a beach, boat launch ramps, paved roads throughout the park, playgrounds, campsites, and park offices. Sportspersons will enjoy hunting areas, fishing, kayaking, boating, and hiking. It will be beautiful."

Fred thanked Wayne and his staff and prepared to leave. "Thank you for all the information. I know my article will enlighten a lot of doubters around the county."

\*\*\*

A few day later Wayne buoyed by Fred's article but distressed by the continual negative drivel coming from other sources called his field office staff together to vent some of his concerns. "The reason I called this meeting," Wayne told the group, "Is that we will be facing many pitfalls and obstacles yet to be initiated by ardent and fanatical opponents. They are not just opposed to the Trout River Project, they are opposed to the concept of flood control and the damming of rivers and waterways in general. They know no bounds in their efforts to prevent us from fulfilling our Congressional mandated objective. Be aware, our opponents don't play by any rules."

Wayne warned the group, "We all have to be diligent as we go about our work. Watch for strangers and out of place vehicles. This property is a public place, but with construction scheduled to start in a year, activity will be increasing. We want to prevent anything bad from happening."

# CHAPTER 8

Wayne's job became more complicated as events beyond his control were demanding his attention. He was being forced to react to situations outside of his control instead of working with the Trout River team. His main responsibility was managing the planned construction of the dam. But in January 1969 he had to respond to new obligations requiring him to work with the legal teams defending the dam against its fiery opponents.

On January 20, 1969, Wayne was at his job site office when Richard Albert, General Counsel for the US Army Corps of Engineers, Louisville District entered, surprising Wayne. Wayne stood, shook hands, and told Albert, "This is a pleasant surprise. What brings you to the boondocks?"

Albert replied, "Wayne, I need your help with a situation concerning the Trout River Dam.

Wayne answered, "Of course, have a seat."

For a few minutes, they talked about work and families. Finally, Albert said, "Here's what's happening. Last Friday a citizen or citizens filed two actions in the Clearfield County Court of Common Pleas intended to kill the dam. These actions, if successful, will have a severe impact on the future of not only Trout River, but the other four dams as well. The first action brought by two opponents to the dam demand that the court order an immediate injunction to stop all activities while the court hears their main lawsuit. The U.S. Government is the defendant."

"Their main thrust and the second part of their action demand that the government stop all activities concerning the dam. They want to wipe the slate clean, no dam, no lake."

Wayne said, "I heard about opposition to the project, but so far it has been just talk and newspaper editorials. I'm directing my efforts to more technical matters." He asked Attorney Albert, "How does this involve me?"

Albert responded, "You are on the list of government employees the plaintiffs want to depose. I will be with you at every deposition. Beyond that, I would like for you to become the government spokesman during this trial."

Wayne expressed his concern, "I don't have a legal background. How will I know what to say? I don't want to be misunderstood."

Albert assured Wayne, "You have the most knowledge about this project. But to answer your questions, just tell the truth and don't volunteer information to the plaintiff's lawyer. If we go to trial and you have to take the stand to give testimony, give yes or no answers. If you don't know, say 'I don't know.' You'll do fine. Be assertive. Avoid speculative answers such as 'I think this or that' and 'maybe this or that happened.' Be positive and speak only about what you know."

Clearfield County Court accepted the case and assigned it to the Honorable Judge Hershel Obrien, a classic old school adjudicator. Albert described Judge Obrien to Wayne, "He is sixty-nine, retired from Hamilton County court when he was sixty-five, bought a lovely retirement home in Clearfield County, and went back to work as a common pleas judge."

Albert informed Wayne, "The judge has set a hearing for next Thursday, January 23. The purpose of the hearing is to hear motions from both sides and set up ground rules for the trial. Usually, no judgments are handed down."

Wayne asked, "Do I have to be there?"

Albert answered, "No, but it is best if you are. We need to start your legal education. I'm kidding about the 'legal education,' but it is a good idea for you to see the courtroom, the judge, and our opponents."

Wayne responded, "I'll be there. Why don't you come here and we'll ride together?"

Albert answered, "Sure, I'll drive."

The next day Albert called Wayne, "One tidbit of information. The plaintiffs didn't like Judge Obrien's action to schedule a hearing on their request for an injunction so quickly. They immediately filed a motion asking for more time. Judge Obrien denied their application. Apparently, their goal is to drag this out and delay the project."

On January 23, Attorney Albert and Wayne attended the injunction hearing.

Wayne told Albert, "I've never been in court, not even for a traffic ticket." Wayne looked around. The courtroom was old and antiquated. The room was wider than it was deep. The judge's bench was slightly elevated and looked out over eight rows of seats, sixteen seats in a row, equally separated by an aisle in the middle. There was a railing the width of the room that separated the seating area from the defense and plaintiff tables. The witness stand and a podium were off center to the right. The empty jury box took up unused space to the left. A big row of windows was behind the jury box. The entire room was polished wood. Wainscots, well-worn hardwood floors, cherry wall paneling, and a judge's bench highlighted the room.

When the hearing started the action was fast and beyond Wayne's understanding. He whispered to Albert, "What the hell is going on. I'm not following any of this."

Albert merely nudged Wayne and whispered, "I'll explain later." Albert slyly added, "I have a little surprise for the court. Be prepared for some verbal fireworks."

Wayne quietly said, "Oh boy."

The plaintiffs, Fuller, Harding, and a national environmental organization, et al., were represented by a hastily hired local attorney, Jeff Longworth. Albert whispered to Wayne, "Longworth has a good reputation. He is one of the area's most well-known and respected litigators. The other attorneys present were retained by the environmental organization and didn't have the credentials to practice in Ohio. It was agreed between the parties to waive a trial by jury and let Judge Obrien decide the case."

The judge was in no mood for dalliance, "I'm allowing each side a half hour to present their arguments."

After the plaintiff's half hour Albert got right to the point, "Your Honor, the plaintiffs have filed this action in the wrong venue. The Trout River Project has Congressional approval, involves a federal agency and, has performed the required environmental impact studies. Furthermore, the dam and lake will be on federal government owned land. Therefore the government's defense belongs in a federal district court. This county court does not have jurisdiction. You have before you a motion for dismissal based on the plaintiffs having filed their action in the wrong venue."

Longworth, lawyer for the plaintiffs, immediately jumped to up and shouted, "Your honor, I object! The defense should have notified us of this motion days ago. They had to know this was their only defense."

Judge Obrien looked at attorney Albert and then attorney Longworth. For several minutes he just sat mulling over the options. Finally, he leaned forward and said, "I am ruling for the government and grant the motion for dismissal. Court adjourned."

When they left the courthouse, Wayne asked Albert, "That's it? I was awed by how fast the action between the attorneys and the judge occurred. Before I could catch up to the motions and denials, the judge issued his decision. You wasted a three-hour drive for that?"

Albert observed, "The plaintiffs and their lawyers know it will be futile to pursue their cause by appeal in county court. I expect we'll soon see the plaintiffs in federal court."

Several weeks later Albert called Wayne to bring him up to date. "As I expected the plaintiff's zeal is intense. On March 13, 1969, they re-filed their lawsuit and request for an injunction in the U. S. District Court for the Southern District of Ohio in Cincinnati. Requests for injunctions usually get quick hearings. The court scheduled this hearing for March 27, 1969."

U.S. Attorney Albert was no stranger to legal issues concerning flood control projects. Although they were spending time together coordinating various issues and attending court dates, Wayne knew little about him.

On the way to attend the pretrial hearing for the Fuller and Harding trial, Wayne asked Albert about his education and experiences.

Albert replied, "First I'll brag a little. I graduated Cum Laude from Duke University and later was a distinguished graduate from the University of Michigan law school. I am admitted to the bar in Ohio, Kentucky, and Indiana. Many think I could do better financially in private practice. But I like the challenge of defending the government in cases ranging from criminal to civil. My wife and I enjoy the laid back life in our home state of Kentucky; we have no regrets. By the way, I almost forgot to tell you, the Clearfield County District Attorney, Rebecca Regan, will be part of our team."

On the date of the hearing for an injunction the presiding Federal Judge, the Honorable David Silverstein, listened intently as both sides argued back and forth for more than an hour. Judge Silverstein, 52, was a successful trial lawyer in Hamilton County, Ohio when at age 48 he was appointed to the federal court by President Lyndon Johnson.

The plaintiffs' recently hired attorney, John Lowenstein, presented their arguments. He made what would become the opponent's often repeated mantra. He told the court, "Your Honor, this project is unnecessary, environmentally unsound, and expensive for the taxpayers. We also assert that the environmental impact study performed by the government in May 1965 is flawed and out of date."

In rebuttal, Attorney Albert, standing at the podium with Wayne sitting at the defendant's table behind him, addressed the judge. "Your Honor, you have in your hand our motion for summary judgment and dismissal of the plaintiff's demand for an injunction. Our demand relies on the fact that the 1965 environmental impact study is current and abides by federal environmental guidelines. A new study will be superfluous and expensive for the taxpayers. Furthermore, the plaintiff's arguments that the project is unnecessary, environmentally unsound, and expensive for the taxpayers are not consistent with the 1966 mandate signed into law by Congress. Your Honor, the Trout River project, is a duly authorized federal project. We ask for summary judgment dismissing the plaintiff's demands."

Attorney Lowenstein flew out of his chair, knocking several documents and pencils to the floor, "Your Honor, I am outraged by this unprecedented action. The defendants did not give notice nor have we had a chance to examine the contents of the motion. I demand that you deny the motion and allow the trial to go forward."

At the end of the hearing, Judge Silverstein asked for final comments, afterward promising, "I will give my decision within a week."

Wayne noted that reporter Roger Wilkins was an attendee of the trial.

During a discussion with attorney Albert, Wayne said, "I see the Cincinnati newspaper had their star environmental reporter watching the proceedings. When I read his, so called, accounts about the happenings at the dam, I can't believe his bias and venom. His biased articles are so much for the opponents that they consist of more opinion and editorializing than fact."

Attorney Albert expected an immediate decision from the bench and said to Wayne, "I'm dismayed that the court won't issue a decision for a week. I'm worried that the federal court is giving this case more consideration than necessary."

Fortunately for the defendants his concern was unfounded. On Thursday, April 3, all parties were gathered in the federal courtroom to hear Judge Silverstein's decision on the injunction. He directed his decision to the plaintiffs, "I have concerns about the timeliness of plaintiff's action. The plaintiff and the public have had access to the 1966 environmental impact study for over three years. All the pertinent documents have always been available to the public. During the proceedings, you did not cite even one specific flaw in the environmental impact statement."

Judge Silverstein speaking directly to attorney Lowenstein said, "Your client had possession of many government documents during the past three years. Those documents prove the government has performed planning, surveys, design, disseminated information to the public, and has complied with the requirements of the Congressional mandate authorizing this project. The filing of this action at such a late time is unfair to the government and the taxpayers. My ruling is for the government. I deny your request for an injunction to stop work on the Trout River Dam. I also deny the environmental issue and the demand to stop all work. Case closed."

Afterward, Wayne thought, *"Finally I can focus on building the dam."* He couldn't know how wrong he was or how fleeting would be his feeling of relief.

\*\*\*

Starting in July 1968 environmentalist's opposition to some of the Corps civil projects, especially impoundments, grew and became more organized. Wayne speaking by phone with attorney Albert said, "We hear from some of the people living in the future lake area that actions taken by activists include sit-ins, camp-ins, public protests, newspaper editorials, and environmental organization meetings to rally opposition."

"They say that activists also include, but on a more subtle basis, a few local, state and national politicians and public officials. The most vocal of all opponents is Roger Wilkins, a reporter for the Cincinnati Daily News. He is personally opposed to the project and any other like it. He also has the newspaper through which he can vent the basis for his beliefs, whether true or not."

These activities adversely impacted the Corps acquisition program by giving residents false hope that they would not have to relocate, thereby stiffening their resolve to fight. Wayne told his staff, "Despite the protests, the dam and impoundment projects are destined to proceed and fulfill their mandate for flood control and recreation."

Because of the court appearances at trials and exposure to the public Wayne was no longer an obscure person whose job it was to see to the building of the Trout River Dam. The newspapers published his picture and included quotes attributed to him in numerous articles. Wayne was not a celebrity, but he could no longer retain his anonymity.

# CHAPTER 9

In 1966 two Clearfield County residents, Jack Fellows and Adrian McCarthy, purchased an abandoned gold mine known as the Jasmine Holdings. The old mine, established in the 1870s, was situated on seventy acres located within the future impoundment for the Trout River Dam and Lake. Through the course of its storied history, it was the source of many get-rich legends.

Jack and Adrian, had dreams of finding the mother lode. From 1966 until 1968, when the proposed dam and lake became public knowledge, they worked the old mine diligently but had nothing to show for their efforts. In 1968 they knew the government would eventually have to purchase their property.

Adrian explained to Jack, "I have a plan that I hope will greatly enhance the value of our property. We're going to salt the nine with real gold to create the impression that we have indeed hit pay dirt. Today gold is worth about $250 per ounce. I know of an off-shore source where we can purchase fifty ounces of low-grade gold bullion for $11,000. We will alter the gold bullion. We'll melt, chop, and grind it to powder, shave, and otherwise mutilate it."

"We'll heat some with sandstone to make it look like it was naturally present. Some of the gold dust we'll mix with mine dust, and we'll place chips in crevices and other out of the way and hidden niches. All of which we'll make to look as natural as possible."

In December 1968 Jack and Adrian put their scheme into action. While they were working to create the appearance of a producing gold mine on their seventy acres Adrian explained to Jack, "We have to sell a few ounces of the altered gold and make it look like we are doing it secretly. Of course, what we want is for rumors to begin about there being gold in the Jasmine mine."

Wayne was still at the district office while the gold scheme was developing. He asked George Daniels, "Have you heard rumors about the Jasmine Mine gold discovery?"

George answered, "In 1968 before we began acquisitions, there were rumors. I've never paid much attention to them. When I get up there, I'll look into the situation."

Jack and Adrian met with several gold buyers, including one local buyer. Jack showed the Stanton pawnshop owner, a small amount of gold telling him, "We have been very lucky. This gold came from our mine out by the Trout River. There is more in our mine. Are you interested in buying the three ounces we have so far?"

The pawnshop owner made some routine tests and stated, "The best I can do is the wholesale value of about $175.00 an ounce, say $500.00 for all."

Jack looked at Adrian and then at the pawnshop owner and exclaimed, "Are you crazy! It's worth twice that."

"Take it or leave it," said the pawnshop guy.

Adrian and Jack stepped aside; Jack whispered to Adrian, "I know we're getting screwed, but we need to get some of the stuff moving and create publicity about the mine. Just take the offer and let's get out of here."

Just two days later rumors of a Jasmine Mine gold discovery became newsworthy when the local newspaper in its weekly edition issued a bulletin, *"Is there gold in the Jasmine mine? Owners secretly sell three ounces from the mine."*

Adrian saw the item and a day later, frantically waving the daily edition of the Cincinnati Daily News excitedly told Jack, "Look we're drawing the attention of a major Ohio newspaper."

Jack replied, "You know, because of the publicity and to add to the rumors; we should hire a guard. That will enhance the appearance that something of value is present. On the downside, the expense of hiring a guard will add to our already substantial expenses."

A week later Jack told Adrian, "I'm getting concerned that the media is focusing too much attention on this farce. The mine has become a local attraction. Every day there is people trying to get in."

Adrian, responding to Jack's comment said, "I'm concerned as to why we haven't had inquiries from the government's acquisition team. They're buying up properties all around us." Wayne continued to communicate with Daniels about the mine, "I don't know what I'm looking for," he said, "But I'm tracking the activities of that pair. Their seventy acres as unused rural land is worth approximately $500 per acre, about $35,000. As a small working gold mine the value would be much greater, perhaps $300,000."

Wayne asked Daniels, "Did you know that another incident that involved a firearm occurred when the surveyors attempted to survey the supposedly worked out gold mine?

The three-man survey crew was denied access to the property by an armed and threatening security guard." The guard told them, "This is private property that contains valuable minerals. No one is allowed in here without the mine owner's consent."

Wayne related the incident to Daniels, "Survey crew chief Storey decided to avoid a confrontation and advised sheriff Spearman of the situation. Spearman contacted one of the owners, Jack Fellows, who granted access but stipulated, "No one is permitted to go into the mine or approach the portal."

Daniels commented to Wayne, "It is a surprise to me that there is anything valuable in that mine. I'm told the opposite; there might be contamination on that property that is a liability to the owner."

Wayne added, "Let's continue to wait. I believed if there is gold there the two might eventually work the mine out, making it worthless as an ongoing entity."

In August 1969 Jack and Adrian were arguing, Adrian said, "I know the government is avoiding us. I'm getting nervous because the government is continuing to make offers and conducting negotiations on other properties but there is no activity on our property."

After he had become a county resident in January 1969, Wayne made numerous attempts to visit the mine to investigate. He told Daniels, "Security has thwarted every attempt I've made to go in the mine. I'm becoming even more suspicious about the lack of mining activity. There is a security fence and a locked gate across the mine entrance."

Daniels replied, "We're taking a wait and see approach. The mine is not in the way of constructing the outlet works or the dam. We don't need that property yet."

During one visit, on September 16, 1969, Wayne was threatened at gunpoint by Julius Conte, a rent-a-cop. He immediately reported the incident to Clearfield County Sheriff Spearman, "Sheriff, earlier today I tried to take a look at the old Jasmine mine property, but a so-called security guard stopped me at gunpoint."

Sheriff Spearman agreed to investigate personally. The next day Spearman and a deputy went to the mine. The sheriff was surprised to see Conte, a small time local criminal and a convicted felon, guarding the mine. The sheriff alerted the deputy and cautiously approached Conte, "Mr. Conte tell me what you're doing out here?"

Conte, somewhat belligerent, replied, "Mr. McCarthy hired me to keep trespassers off his property."

Sheriff Spearman signaled his deputy to disarm and handcuff Conte. Conte attempted to resist, but the sheriff's threatening demeanor stopped further resistance. While the deputy put handcuffs on Conti, the sheriff informed him, "Mr. Conte, as a convicted felon you cannot own or handle a firearm. You are under arrest for violating the terms of your parole. You face ninety days in county jail.

Wayne attended Conti's arraignment on September 19. Conti had spent two nights in Spearman's jail. Conti pled guilty to the firearms charge.

The court scheduled Conti's sentencing appearance in County Court on September 24. Before sentencing Conti, the Clearfield County district attorney, Rebecca Regan, convinced him to tell her what he observed at the mine. He cooperated telling her and Wayne, "The owners occasionally go to the mine and quickly leave with a little gold. I have not seen any other workers. Mr. McCarthy told us to patrol the perimeter only. We are not allowed near the mine." For his cooperation, Conti received a shortened sentence of thirty days in jail.

On September 29 Wayne met with George Daniels, the Corps procurement specialist. He told him, "This mine business has taken on a new personality. Based on Mr. Conti's remarks I'd like to investigate the inside of that mine."

Daniels suggested, "Let's call in a mine appraiser. Then, if necessary, we'll continue to investigate before meeting with the mine owners."

Wayne agreed, "You make the arrangements and get back to me."

Three days later, with a court order in hand, Wayne, Daniels, a sheriff deputy, and Carl Daskovich, a certified assayer and mine inspector, went into the mine. After twenty minutes Daskovich declared, "This property has been seeded using a small amount of real gold. Except for minute amounts of unrecoverable gold, there are no remaining naturally occurring minerals here."

Wayne and Daniels made an appointment to meet with Fellows and McCarty on the following day, Friday, October 5, 1969.

In addition to the two 'gold miners', present at the meeting were Wayne, Daniels, Daskovich the appraiser, and the Clearfield County assistant district attorney.

The assistant district attorney bluntly told the two mine owners, "My office conducted a conclusive investigation into your mine with help from a professional mine inspector. It is our determination that your mine is bogus." The assistant DA informed them, "If you continue the scam and attempt to bilk the U.S. Government you will face criminal charges. So far no one has been taken except yourselves."

One day in November 1969 Daniels told Wayne, "Yesterday the government acquired the seventy acre Jasmine Mine property for its actual value of $42,500. The two 'miners' were allowed to keep any remaining gold and given thirty days to remove personal property left in the mine."

# CHAPTER 10

While the Jasmine Mine incident was going on other things needed Wayne's attention.

The location of Christ the King Methodist Church was in the area of the soon to be built outlet works. In May 1969 Wayne realized that his priority was to acquire and relocate the church. Wayne and George Daniels discussed the touchy situation associated with relocating the church and congregation. George said, "Wayne, I need your help on this. We have to acquire the land occupied by the church no later than December of this year.

That gives us just six months to purchase the property and get the congregation moved to a new location."

Wayne responded, "I don't know how I can help, other than to give you moral support. Why are you so late getting into this particular purchase?"

George answered, "Well, I guess I have been putting it off hoping for an easy solution. Also, I have been attempting to find an alternate location that I can propose to the congregation that will appeal to them. I've been contacting realtors in the area, and I came up with just one option."

"What do you propose?" Wayne asked.

George somewhat chagrined answered, "There is an unoccupied building, originally built as a church that is for sale just outside the village limits on South Main Street. The problem is, by the time we buy the old church, pay for the new building, and get them moved in we'll be way over the value the appraisers have put on the property. I don't think the church has any money. They are barely meeting their day to day obligations."

Wayne, being more concerned about getting his dam off to a timely start, chided George, "What the hell, don't worry about the appraisers. I'll back you up. Let's get a proposal together and get the leaders of the church together and start talking. Tomorrow's too late!"

George, taken aback by Wayne's strong response, said, "I'll set it up."

The church trustees, consisting of a committee of six church members, along with the Reverend Thomas Prichard, agreed to meet with George and Wayne the following Saturday, May 17, 1969. The six trustees were charged by the congregation and the West Ohio Conference of the United Methodist Church with the responsibility to work with the real estate procurement team to assure a fair price for their property.

George presented an outline of the proposal Wayne and he prepared for the meeting. George admitted to the trustees, "I am going beyond the value the government appraisers have recommended for your church. However, Mr. Henderson and I agree this is an unusual situation. Anyhow, here's our proposal. Under the terms of the proposal the government will pay $60,000 for your existing church building and land. Your congregation retains ownership of any components in and of the church."

After looking for a response and getting none, George continued, "There is a vacant church, that with some upgrades and renovations, will give you a larger facility with more open space and parking than you now have."

George explained, "The property is not far from here, is closer to Stanton, and faces South Main Street. Based on proposals from local contractors the government will pay up to $51,000 to remodel and upgrade the vacant church. The proposed building has been on the market for more than a year at the asking price of $40,000. We believe, considering the building's limited usage, the price is very negotiable. You will have a great church and money left over. Christ the King Church and your conference will have to purchase the new location."

Pastor Prichard, a tall, thin man, said, "We hear you and understand your proposal. I don't believe the burden for a decision should be on the trustees alone." The body language of two of the trustees suggested they agreed with the preacher. Wayne thought the other four seemed offended. Pastor Prichard added, "I believe the entire congregation and the United Methodist Church Conference should make this decision."

George didn't want to cause a confrontation, but reminded everyone, "This isn't about relocating your church or not. We are here to agree about how the government will acquire your church and how to make the relocation as beneficial as possible."

Reluctantly the pastor agreed, "I know we have to sell. But we will be a divided house unless a vast majority of the congregation agrees as to how the government goes about the process. Some of our people might simply go to another church."

The six trustees seemed to be in agreement with their leader's latest statement. One of them spoke up, "We will discuss your proposal at a charge conference that includes all church members and the conference superintendent. We'll do that as soon as possible and get back to you."

A charge conference meeting of the congregation on Sunday afternoon, May 24, 1969, was attended by almost all of the one hundred thirty-four church members. Usually, any meeting at the church, other than Sunday services, attracted twenty or fewer attendees.

Wayne and George attended this and all subsequent meetings concerning the church. Wayne told the gathering, "I realize the government is asking you to give up more than a building. Your church is seventy-two years old. You, your parents, and their parents have worshiped God and have been baptized on this hallowed ground." He added, "The church is people, the building belongs to God and provides a shelter where you worship." From the murmur and low voices he could tell the congregation, their leaders and minister were uneasy about his remarks.

Wayne noted, "You are a small congregation and your church building needs a lot of repairs. You do not have room to grow and your church is located in a remote area of the county subject to flooding."

Corps of Engineers real estate representative, George Daniels, was the next to speak. "Our proposal provides the ability to purchase a newer well maintained, but vacant, church with plenty of parking and the funds to make it one of the nicest churches in the county."

At this point, a church member, Paul Hastings, jumped to his feet and shouted for all to hear, "We're not giving up our church for any amount of money. You two and the government will go to hell before we leave this church." You could hear many amen's throughout the gathering.

The pastor, Reverend Thomas Pritchard, rose and asked for quiet, "Please everyone don't let this meeting become a shouting affair. Keep God in your hearts as we learn from our guests about the government's plans for our church. Remember nothing happens that is not in God's plan. Man cannot undo what He ordains."

George stood and addressed the congregation, "We want to see this church benefit from having to be relocated. Most transactions to acquire land for the dam are merely for the fair value of the property; they get what the appraisers recommend. We want to do whatever is necessary to relocate your church to a better place and, more importantly, assure this congregation stays together and prospers spiritually."

Wayne and George could feel the unrest within the meeting room. One church member asked, "What happens if we don't sell and stay here?"

Wayne answered, "That will cause a difficult situation. The government has to buy your church to make room for the dam and lake. Refusal to sell will cause a nasty court action that the government wants to avoid. Please understand, Mr. Daniels and I are only doing what Congress has mandated. We know that you think we are the bad guys. We regret that your congregation must be relocated to make way for the dam and lake. I know you have all prayed for guidance, so have we. The generous offer, a copy of which you all have, will make the relocation painless and rewarding."

George continued, "Our goal is to make the new location for Christ the King Methodist Church better than before. Only you, the people of this church, can make the new building a church."

Wayne and George answered a few more questions then left to allow the congregation time to discuss their options privately.

The following day the Monday morning edition of the Daily News contained a second-page news article, with a Roger Wilkins byline, about the church meeting and the Corps attempts to acquire the church. The newspaper quoted Wayne as saying, "The church is only a building and a shelter." And, "If you don't sell, we'll sue you." Wayne was upset. He was not about to be used in a political/environmental wrestling match. But, after cooling down, he decided to ignore the writer's acidic comments.

About a week later an angry Christ the King trustee contacted Daniels. "This damn dam is doing what Satan can't; it's pitting our congregation member against member. We have no agreement, our minister is noncommittal and discouraged because he can't bring us all back to Christ to be as one."

George responded, "We can't avoid buying your church. We want an amicable solution. Can we have another congregational meeting at the new location suggested in the offer?" The trustee reluctantly agreed to organize the meeting.

During the same week that the Wilkins article appeared Pastor Prichard called George to tell him, "A small group within the church has an unchristian opinion about the presence of you and Wayne. They have turned to reporter Wilkins for help."

The resulting story, as Wilkins told it in the next edition of the Daily News, was one of government harassment of church members and threats to burn down the church if they didn't sell at a very low price. Wayne and the entire Corps of Engineers organization were shocked at the brazen lie. No retraction was forthcoming, but the office of a Congressman from Ohio let the Cincinnati Daily News editor-in-chief know that other more honest newspapers would have priority access when there was breaking news from Washington. Meanwhile, the Corps of Engineers public information office did what they could to undo the public relations damage.

Wayne lamented to George, "We're running out of time. The outlet works portion of the dam is scheduled to bid in February 1970. A Court action to acquire the church could take six months resulting in the acquisition of the badly needed land as late as December 1969. We have to have another meeting."

Finally, the president of the trustee committee and the minister came to George's office. "There's a lot of opposition to meeting at the proposed new location. But we set a date for this Sunday afternoon. We'll see how many show up." There were more church members than expected at the second meeting. Before the meeting started the minister said a prayer asking God for guidance, understanding, and a clear vision about the move, and for any decision to glorify God.

Wayne was dismayed to see Roger Wilkins in the room, invited by church members opposed to selling the church just to build a dam. Also in attendance were a few non-members whose only interest was to prevent the building of the dam.

Wayne explained, trying not to threaten, "If we have to take court action you will only get what the court determines is a fair value. We have given you a proposal that goes far beyond a court-ordered settlement."

Wayne advised the fifty or so attendees, "If we have to adhere to a court decree that we don't receive until later this year; you will receive fair value for your church, but you will have nowhere to hold your services."

The remodeling contractor, hired by the Corps to prepare construction plans showing how the new location for the church would look after renovation, gave a presentation. He explained, "We will use as many components of the old church as possible; pews, altar, stained glass, even entrance doors. We have tried to make the new church as familiar as possible."

To Wayne and George, it appeared there was real interest. They gave the plans and sketches to the trustee. They stayed to answer questions but wished they had not.

The first person to ask a question was, of course, Roger Wilkins. "How does the Corps of Engineers justify confiscating private land, displacing families and embarking on a venture as useless as this dam?"

Wayne and George along with some of the congregation were shocked and unprepared for the confrontation poised by a non-member of the church.

Wayne wanted the group to know the identity of the troublemaker. He asked, "Sir, may we have your name, it appears no one here knows you?"

Wilkins responded, "I am Roger Wilkins, a reporter for the Cincinnati Daily News."

It took all of Wayne's self-control not to ask Wilkins to leave. However, within a few seconds he composed himself and responded to the query, "Mr. Wilkins, I know that you are not here out of concern for these good church members. You are looking for a story about the project in which you can twist the truth to suit your anti-dam agenda. You have shown in the past that your reporting is untruthful and biased against the dam and its benefits."

Wilkins tried to protest Wayne's non-response, but Wayne continued. "Mr. Wilkins you consider the Corps your enemy. You have made me your enemy. You have misquoted me and attributed statements I did not commit." Wayne was determined to leave no doubt about Wilkins intentions as he continued, "I am an employee of the Corps of Engineers, a duly authorized agency of the U.S. Government. The Corps has been mandated by the U.S. Congress to build a flood control and recreational dam and lake right here in Clearfield County. My job as an employee is to get it done. And I will get it done! When you write your biased story, please quote me accurately and choose if you are reporting facts or editorializing. Now we need to get back to the reason for this meeting and address the legitimate concerns of the Christ the King congregation."

A few questions from church members were asked and answered. The meeting ended with everyone going home with a lot to consider.

Surprisingly, Wilkins briefly reported that there was a meeting and the congregation made no decision.

Two weeks later, on June 23, the trustee, the minister and several other members of the church appeared in George's office. Pastor Thomas, as he was known, was the spokesperson. He said, "The congregation, at a meeting called a Charge Conference, and attended by the superintendent of the West Ohio Conference of the United Methodist Church, agreed to the proposal presented on May 24. Everyone agreed time is of the essence if our congregation is to be in our new church before year end. We look forward to celebrating the birth of Christ in our new church."

*\*\*\**

The Monday following the Christ the King agreement George told Wayne, "I plan to follow to the end the relocation of those fine people's church. Even so, I have a lot to do. My team is concentrating on buying other parcels in and near the outlet works."

"In addition to the church, the Ohio hunting land, two dwellings, and the gold mine; that we have already acquired, the government has to purchase one hundred fifty-eight dwellings, seven dormant farms, and five working farms. There are six dwellings and two working farms that are refusing all attempts to acquire them. We also have a historic schoolhouse and a cemetery to relocate."

Following the agreement to relocate the church, George told Wayne, "Now I know I have someone I can count on to assist with touchy situations. I'll be contacting you about the cemetery and the historic schoolhouse." George abruptly left before Wayne could respond.

# CHAPTER 11

By the end of 1969 the pace of government acquisitions of property necessary to build the dam and lake were at a peak. During this time the twenty-one illicit properties purchased by Halgren and his associates were acquired by the government. One by one the titles for the twenty-one properties were transferred to the government. At their real estate closings, the three insider realtors signed the documents for their respective properties and received payment from the government. The government lawyers performed transfer and filing of deeds and titles.

By December 12, 1969, ownership of the last of the twenty-one properties transferred to the government. Halgren's three co-conspirators owned, but didn't use, the properties for two years.

On a damp cold morning, December 21, 1969, the conspirators met in an unheated outbuilding on Halgren's mini-farm to divvy up the profits. Vincent Osgood, a respected local realtor, asked the other participants in the scheme, "Are we sure this was a legal transaction? I don't feel comfortable with what we have done. I deem our actions questionable. In fact what we have done and how we did it might be unethical."

Bert Walgren was quick to respond, "Vince, it is way too late to get cold feet. What we did, and the ensuing transactions are the result of typical real estate investments. Quit worrying; let's get on with wrapping up this deal."

Osgood reported, "On my six residences and two non-working farms I made a profit of $98,000. Splitting sixty-forty, Bert you get $39,200, and I keep $58,800. Not a bad days work."

Cooper asserted, "I cashed in a profit of $107,000. Bert, your share is $42,800 and my share is $64,200."

Bert looked at Barnes and, in a patronizing voice, said, "Okay Barnes how did we do?"

Barnes contritely answered, "We made only $40,000. After the math is done you get $16,000 and I get $24,000."

Osgood said, "Bert you received forty percent of all the profit giving you $98,000. That's good, considering you didn't do anything except come up with the plan."

Bert merely gave Osgood a withering look and turned to Barnes. "Barnes," he said, "You no good deadbeat, you're not entitled to a full sixty percent. I had to put up all the money so you could be part of the plan."

Financially Barnes's back was against the proverbial wall. He asked Bert, "What do you have in mind?"

Bert responded, "The best I will do is forty percent, and that is a gift netting you $16,000. You will get that only if you keep your mouth shut."

Barnes meekly mumbled, "Whatever you say, Bert. That puts another $8,000 in your pocket."

# CHAPTER 12

Wayne had just arrived at his office when the phone rang. He answered, "Good morning Corps of Engineers, Trout River."

A familiar voice responded, "Good morning to you Wayne. This is Richard Albert."

Wayne made a friendly groan and said, "Getting a call from a lawyer is not a good way to start a beautiful fall morning. What can I do for you?"

"The good news is I don't need anything right now," Albert answered. "The bad news is that yesterday, October 21, 1969; a second lawsuit was filed in Clearfield County Court. The lawsuit, filed by John Morrison whose home is in the impoundment area, is asking for an order to cease any activity relating to the construction of the Trout River Dam and Lake. Like the previous action, he is demanding an immediate injunction to stop further activities. Support for Mr. Morrison comes from the Ohio Public Interest Action Group and other public watchdog organizations." Albert explained, "Like the first lawsuit filed by Fuller and Harding this one also belongs in federal court. Tomorrow I'm filing a motion to dismiss based on the ruling from the previous case. I'm just letting you know what is transpiring. You don't need to do anything yet. However, for your information, I'm sending you a copy of the complaint."

When Wayne received his copy of the complaint, he said to Melissa, "The argument at the center of this lawsuit is to restore the area of the dam and lake to 'unspoiled land.' There is a fallacy in that argument. The contested land contains more than one hundred-eighty dwellings and farms. It is not unspoiled land. There are many septic tanks and lots of uncontrolled farm waste. It'll be interesting to see how the court handles this one."

A week later Wayne received another call from attorney Albert, "Wayne, I just want to let you know that Judge Hershel Obrien will be our judge for the Morrison case. Fortunately, he is the same judge who ruled that the Fuller and Harding action was governed by federal law and sent it to a federal court. For the same reason as before, he kicked this case to the District Court in Cincinnati."

Wayne received another call from attorney Albert, "As we expected, on November 10, 1969, Morrison's lawyers re-filed their action in the U. S. District Court, Southern District of Ohio. Judge Harvey Varner will decide this case. The pretrial hearing is December 22. I'll handle this myself because it is exactly like the previous lawsuit. I think we can get this thrown out just like the other one."

The day after the Morrison pre-trial hearing, Albert called Wayne to tell him, "As we hoped Judge Varner agreed with me that the arguments, in this case, were the same as previously heard by Judge Silverstein in the Fuller and Harding lawsuit. Judge Varner followed the precedent set in Judge Silverstein's court and dismissed Morrison's lawsuit. We dodged another bullet."

Afterward, Wayne told Melissa and JD about what happened. "Attorney Albert got the lawsuit thrown out, but the weird thing is Morrison owns Morrison Outdoor Sports Supply, a local sporting goods store that caters to hikers, boaters, and active outdoor sports participants. He is publicity conscious and sponsors several activities designed to get the store name recognized and create more business."

"Morrison has been quoted as saying, 'This project and all like it are detrimental to outdoor sports. They flood thousands of acres of unspoiled land. The cost is outrageous and unjustified. The environment will never recover from the adverse impact of this project.' The truth is Morrison's business can only benefit from activities at the lake and recreational areas." Wayne was becoming more involved in court appearances and assisting the Government lawyers and their staff. The entire time Roger Wilkins was like Wayne's shadow. Wayne steadfastly refused to speak to Roger and insisted all communication be in writing, directed to the public information office in Louisville.

# CHAPTER 13

In January 1970 Wayne and George Daniels were discussing property acquisitions. Daniels noted, "We have acquired every property that lies within the footprint of the outlet works, the embankment, and the overflow spillway. The acquisition of several dwellings, two farms, relocating a cemetery, and moving an old schoolhouse will have to occur while we construct the outlet works and dam. These acquisitions, although late, will not impede construction."

Wayne replied, "Good because we are just days from advertising for contractor bids for the entire project." Wayne explained the Corps of Engineers bidding process, "The invitation to bid is posted in various venues; major and local newspapers, construction industry publications, and the Federal Register. The advertisement fulfills the public notice requirement that bidding for taxpayer funded projects is made available to all qualified bidders."

Wayne told Daniels, "The invitation to bid officially kicks off construction of the Trout River Dam. It notifies interested parties that the Corps of Engineers will accept bids from qualified contractors on Tuesday, March 17, 1970, at four o'clock p.m. at the Louisville District Office. As you know, the Trout River Dam and Lake is the last of five flood control projects the Louisville District is having built. Construction of the other four dams is already underway or nearing completion."

\*\*\*

Eleven contractors from the Midwest, twelve subcontractors, and eight suppliers asked for and received the bid package.

Gary Allen, vice president and chief estimator for Arthur Aldridge Construction Company, and Herbert Flaherty, the president of Aldridge's Heavy Construction Division, were perusing the contents of the bidding documents for the Trout River Dam. Flaherty said, "Gary, as you no doubt remember, Aldridge bid and lost two previous Corps of Engineer dam and lake projects. I hope the knowledge gained from those experiences will help us be the successful bidder on Trout River."

Gary summarized his observation about the project, "Like the others, Trout River consists of two distinct parts, the outlet works, and the earth dam embankment. The two parts of the project are very different. The outlet works consists of a 220-foot high concrete control tower, an 1100 foot long outlet conduit, and a stilling basin. The outlet works will require about 28,000 cubic yards of concrete."

Gary continued explaining, "The second phase, the dam embankment, consists of a seventeen hundred feet long by two hundred feet high earth, clay, and rock embankment requiring about eight million six hundred thousand cubic yards of material. At its base, the dam is six hundred feet wide. Work on the dam embankment will not start for at least two years after the outlet works is complete. Then the river is diverted through the new water control structure. The 1970 Corps of Engineers construction cost estimate for the project is thirty-six million dollars."

The first order of business for Herbert and his vice president; chief estimator, Gary Allen, was to review the personnel, equipment, financial resources, and bonding Aldridge had available for this project. Herbert stated his opinion, "The project is well within company capabilities and resources. It's about three-hundred-fifty miles away. We have adequate bonding capacity, insurance, personnel, and equipment."

After a short discussion, they decided to submit a bid for the project. Gary hurried to put together an experienced estimating team capable of comprehending the nuances and magnitude of this project.

Gary knew that estimating the cost of a risky project, like the Trout River Dam, required comprehensive and accurate knowledge of cost and quantities. Guesswork was not an option. The estimating teams would have to work this project in with other ongoing projects that they were managing or estimating. 'I don't have time for that' was not an acceptable excuse. Those assigned to this project would work as many hours as necessary to diligently see to their responsibilities and meet deadlines.

Gary selected the best possible estimating teams from available people on his staff. Everyone selected already had other projects and duties with which they were involved. Gary noted to one of his team, "The life of a construction estimator/project manager is like trying to stop a waterfall; the projects, problems, and opportunities just keep coming."

By the end of the day on February 5, Gary made bid assignments for both teams, generally based on expertise for the scope of work assigned. Aldridge usually had five to eight projects in various stages of estimating.

Gary, 51, has been married for twenty-eight years to Frances. They have four children; three boys aged 16, 22, and 24, and one daughter, 18. Gary and Frances lived their lives modestly because they had one child just starting college and one preparing for college. The two older boys were out of college, but the Allen's have substantial debts from past college expenses and would have at least six more years of college costs.

Gary's role in the takeoff and pricing process included coordinating the efforts of the bid team. He also set up the bid form with pricing and other information. He was responsible for analyzing and pricing project overhead and, with input from Herbert, profit. Profit is not guaranteed.

The bid documents to be submitted with the bid exceeded twenty pages. Amazingly, stating the bid amount required only two pages of the twenty-page bid documents. The remaining eighteen pages required the bidder to provide information about the company, minority hiring practices, safety record, subcontractors, bid bond, a certification that there were no debarments from federal agencies, an agreement to buy American, non-collusion affidavit, and others to satisfy a public owner. Three of the bid documents required the seal of a Notary. Gary spent two days preparing the bid documents.

Gary knew that preparing an estimate was like putting together a complicated jigsaw puzzle. He had to assure all the pieces fit with no gaps or omissions. One of his functions as a member of the estimating effort was to determine the cost for project overhead; field costs not directly associated with the physical components of the project.

The estimating team knew that to accurately determine the cost for the project they had to establish the exact quantities of labor, equipment, and material. They would analyze historical costs, difficulty, and productivity associated with performing the work. These factors, when applied to the labor costs, determine total labor costs.

Gary told Herb, "The estimators for the Trout River Project will analyze over a thousand activities involving costs for labor, equipment, material, and subcontractors. The company commitment, with no guarantee that we will be the low bidder, will require more than a thousand employee hours and other expenses, totaling about forty thousand dollars."

Early in the time Aldridge had to prepare their price they sent out numerous invitations to material suppliers and subcontractors asking for their bid on the portion of work on which they were interested. The responses would vary widely as to scope and magnitude. The subcontractor and supplier quotes usually arrived un-priced. The estimators analyzed all subcontractor and supplier quotes for completeness, competitiveness, and the proposer's ability to do the work. Subcontractors and suppliers don't like to reveal final pricing until about two days before the bid is due.

Wayne held a pre-bid meeting on Monday, March 1 allowing all bidders to view the location of the dam. At that time the bidders could discuss problems, concerns, and ask questions. The pre-bid meeting also gave the bidders a chance to meet the Corps engineers and procurement specialists.

On the day of the pre-bid meeting, Aldridge sent a team of estimators and field management to the location of the project. After the meeting, they looked at the terrain to determine the need for access roads, clearing, and tree removal. They also had to determine the method and cost to control ground and surface water, flooding risk, overhead and underground obstructions. During their visit to the site of the work, the team investigated the availability of local workers and the quality and capability of suppliers and subcontractors. They also took numerous photographs.

As the day bids were due neared, Wayne was keeping abreast of bidding activity. Wayne, as the Corps resident engineer, was the person to whom all the bidders directed their requests to enter the area. The bidders asked numerous questions about site conditions. They also requested clarifications of ambiguities and inconsistencies concerning the bid documents. Wayne had to log the questions and answer them in writing. Before the bid due date a document or documents, known as an addendum to the contract was issued to all plan holders. This document provided answers to all bid-related issues and questions.

For six weeks the Aldridge estimators poured their hearts into preparing the bid to build the Trout River Dam and Lake. On the eve of the bid due date, there were still many pieces of the puzzle in question.

The day of the bid and the few hours leading up to the bidding deadline, four o'clock p.m., were tumultuous. All the information; prices, labor costs, quotes, schedules, field overhead costs, and equipment utilization had to be poured into a theoretical funnel to come out with a firm bid for all the work to construct the Trout River Dam.

Most of the material supplier and subcontractor final prices were verbal, received by telephone. The estimating teams also coordinated among themselves to assure there were no omissions or overlaps.

After adding a percentage for office overhead and profit, Aldridge's bid of thirty-six million, three hundred seventy thousand dollars for the entire package was submitted by an employee courier at two minutes before four o'clock p.m. at the Louisville District Office.

At exactly four o'clock p.m. an authorized representative for the Corps of Engineers closed bidding and publicly opened the six timely bids submitted. The representative who opened the bid then publicly read the amount of each responsive bidder. Aldridge's bid of $36,370,000 was the lowest of the six bids submitted. The other bids ranged from $36,800,000 to $39,320,000. The Aldridge bid was about one percent lower than the second bid.

At the St. Louis office everyone was happily congratulating each other. After a short celebration, everyone returned to work, and the office atmosphere returned to normal.

\*\*\*

On March 24, 1970, the Corps of Engineers procurement department approved awarding the thirty-six million three hundred seventy thousand dollar contract for construction of the Trout River Dam to Arthur Aldridge Construction Co. of St. Louis, Missouri.

As requested in the Notice of Award letter from the Corps of Engineers, dated March 27, 1970, Gary signed the contract and sent it back via overnight express delivery to the Corps of

Engineers District Office in Louisville. With the contract, Gary sent proof of liability and builders risk insurance, Ohio workers compensation insurance, and the performance and payment bonds. The bonds alone cost three-hundred thousand dollars.

On April 7, 1970, Aldridge received the executed contract and a Notice to Proceed, clearing the way for them to begin work.

# CHAPTER 14

Wayne, when he saw the name of the low bidder, was curious about the Aldridge Company. He decided to call the district office to find someone who knew anything about Aldridge. He decided to start with his boss, Jordan Lipper.

Jordan told him, "I had some experience with Aldridge back in the late forties. Arthur Aldridge Construction Company was a struggling builder making a name for themselves on small highway projects. I was a young engineer with the Missouri Highway Department. They've come a long way since then. I doubt that Arthur is still with us."

Lipper after a moment said, "You know there was an article about Aldridge in the *Engineering News Record* several months ago. I'll have somebody dig that up and send a copy to you."

Wayne said, "Thanks, I'll watch for it. Get out of that office and visit us some time. Get some fresh air. Again, thanks for the information."

Two days later Wayne received a big envelope with the promised story about Aldridge Construction Company. He began reading it immediately.

DAVID GRINSTEAD

## *ALDRIDGE CONSTRUCTION RACKING UP BIG NUMBERS*

*Although the Aldridge family ownership ended about ten years ago, the company continues to thrive. Arthur Aldridge died in 1962 at the age of seventy-two. Before Arthur's death, ownership of the company passed via stock bonuses and buyouts elevating eleven employees to shareholders. Of the eleven shareholders three own seventeen percent each giving them a controlling interest of fifty-one percent of the company. The other eight shareholders each own from three to twelve percent of the company. This arrangement is typical and was dictated, including the interests of Arthur Aldridge's heirs, by a succession plan and his will.*

*The Aldridge business philosophy is for management to be involved in every aspect of the company's business. The three men who own controlling interest in Aldridge have each been with the company for more than twenty years. Before being employed by Arthur Aldridge Co, they held responsible positions with other construction companies.*

*When Arthur died, the three were already in control of the company and were active owners. As part of the succession plan, they agreed that when a stockholder vote is required all three will vote with any two of the other votes. Thus, combined, the three majority shareholders have a controlling interest of fifty-one percent.*

*The three principal owners have their individual areas of responsibility.*

*Herbert Flaherty, 61, is president of the Heavy and Highway Construction Division. This division builds roads, bridges, water and wastewater facilities, and other heavy construction projects.*

*Victor Shearer, 58, is president of the Building Construction Division. His part of the company concentrates on building hospitals, university buildings, public buildings, and monuments.*

*Robert Warden, 62, is president of the Industrial Construction Division. His part of the company concentrates on factories (especially steel and auto related) and industrial construction.*

*Arthur Aldridge started the construction company in 1920 doing excavating work. Back then they used horses and mules to pull skids upon which they would heap and move earth. Eventually, Arthur went all out financially and bought a six-year-old steam excavator. He trained himself to operate the complicated and contrary piece of 'modern' construction equipment. At that time he was president, owner, equipment operator, project superintendent, and bookkeeper. There were four employees.*

*Diligence through the roaring twenties enabled the company to flourish and by 1929 they had converted from horses and mules to mechanized earth moving equipment. The conversion resulted in some debt and the following market and banking crash almost caused Arthur's company to fail. At the end of the building boom in 1929, he had twelve employees, three pieces of equipment, four-thousand dollars of debt and thirty-two-thousand dollars of work under contract.*

*In the early 1930's one of his projects, for the State of Missouri, was a small section of highway just north of what is now Center City in St. Louis. Eventually, as work on the project neared completion, about 1931, the State realized there were no funds to pay Aldridge for the completed project.*

*On May 4, 1931, the State agreed to give Aldridge one-hundred-sixty acres of state-owned land in the Grand Prairie area of St. Louis. The land was in exchange for the amount owed Aldridge for unpaid highway construction contracts. In 1931 the land was worth about fifty dollars per acre, eight-thousand dollars total. Aldridge became land rich and cash poor.*

*The company barely survived from 1931 through 1938, the great depression years. In 1939 the U.S. government realized it needed to equip itself for an impending war in Europe.*

# BEHIND THE DAM

Arthur was fifty-one when the US became involved in World War II, too old for the draft. In 1939 Aldridge Construction was given a contract to build an arsenal to manufacture 105 MM mortar shells in an outlying area near Danville, Missouri, eighty miles west of St. Louis. They had six months to have the facility in production. Arthur and a team of women and older male construction workers got the job done in five and a half months. In addition to a nice profit, Aldridge received an early completion bonus. The new Arthur Aldridge Construction Company was off and running.

After the war there was another building boom and the land earned in the State Highway payment became more valuable. Grand Prairie land was selling for three-hundred to five-hundred dollars per acre. Arthur sold the whole one-hundred-sixty acres for four-hundred-thirty dollars an acre, almost seventy-thousand dollars.

Every penny from the land sale went back into the construction company. When Eisenhower convinced Congress to fund the building of an interstate highway system, Arthur Aldridge was ready and willing to become a highway builder. From 1956 to the present Aldridge has built miles of interstate highways. During the fifties and sixties, Arthur diversified and developed the skills of the three men who succeeded him.

*Arthur, before he died, once said during a speech he gave at a Construction Association management seminar, "In our industry, we rely on our backhoes and bulldozers. We brag about our equipment fleet and keep it productive and profitable. We brag about how much money a piece of equipment will earn during its productive life. Wake up! Our attention should be on our people, especially the young ones. A good estimator, superintendent, foreman, or project manager with the right support and incentive can make your company a hundred times what a good piece of iron earns during its lifetime. Our people are our best investments. Value and reward them."*

*Aldridge Construction is a well-recognized name throughout Missouri and the Midwest. The company has a net worth of approximately fifteen million dollars, including over nine million dollars invested in construction equipment and facilities. In 1968 their annual sales were approximately one hundred sixty-five million dollars. Their work covers a broad range of public, private, and industrial projects; including roads, bridges, water and wastewater facilities, massive concrete, earthwork, industrial plants, hospitals, and government buildings.*

*An important part of any construction company is its equipment yard and the people who maintain, repair, and transport the company owned equipment. The Aldridge yard inventories an extensive assortment of lumber, concrete forms, tarps, pumps and hoses, air compressors, concrete curing products, pipe, and many other items including items returned from projects that may have a future use. At Aldridge, there are six full-time yard employees. Plans include bringing younger workers into more responsible management positions, moderate growth, and more community involvement.*

Engineering News Record, August 11, 1969

# CHAPTER 15

The day after Aldridge received their Notice to Proceed, Herbert told his vice president and senior project engineer, Dean Richardson, "Dean, I'd like you to go up to Ohio to be the project manager for the Trout River Dam. We're asking you to make a three-year commitment to build the outlet works. Somebody else will take over for the earth and rock embankment. I know you'll have to make sacrifices, as will your family. You'll be expected to be full-time at the dam. The company will pay your travel, lodging, per diem, and other expenses."

Dean was thirty-six, married for twelve years to Diana, two years his junior. They had two girls, Michele, 10, and Heather, 8. They lived southwest of St. Louis in the suburb of Clayton. Dean was a dedicated family man who looked forward to going home from work to his family. Dean and Diana had the usual parental problems and concerns with the kids. In general, though, there was a strong bond, and they enjoyed family vacations and lots of family outings. Dean knew the three hundred fifty mile commute to the Trout River Project and the long hours would necessitate being away from home and his family during the week.

Dean asked Herbert, "This seems like a demotion. Is there something wrong?"

Herbert reminded Dean, "Do you remember telling me that you believe there is a gap in your career because most of your work experience is from behind a desk in the office? You seemed to be concerned that you have no experience managing a project from the field. This opportunity, let's call it a challenge; it is in no way a demotion. You've earned the opportunity."

Dean told Herbert, "I know we have talked about an opportunity where I can get some field experience. I didn't anticipate a long term opportunity like this. Give me a couple of days to talk with my family."

Dean went back to his office and sat looking at the pile of drawings, specifications, and documents that accumulated on his desk. He knew this would be trying for his family. He thought, *"I might as well go home, tell Diana and the girls, and see how they react. I'm not looking forward to being away; I can't imagine how they will feel about me being away."*

Dean went home to talk to Diana. He started by saying, "You know we have a contract to build a dam in Ohio."

Diana said, "Yeah, You were real happy when you told me you guys were the low bidder."

Dean nervously said, "Mr. Flaherty wants me to go up there and manage that project. The problem is he wants me to be on site during the work week. I'll have to be away all week. It's a three-year commitment."

Diana sat silently trying to absorb the implications. She was visibly upset by the news. After a moment she asked, "You're saying you will be gone all week? How can you even consider this? What about the girls and me?"

Dean answered, "For the first time in our marriage we will be apart. We are going to have to make a big decision. We'll have to talk it out for the next day or two."

They spent dinner time talking to the girls about daddy working away from home. Later that evening the entire family discussed the change in Dean's responsibilities.

Both girls were upset. Heather was confused. She asked, "Will you be away without us?"

Dean answered, "Yes, I'll be in Ohio from Monday morning until Friday evening.

Then there were tears. Dean tried to appease the girls by promising them, "If I accept the position, we'll spend family vacations and time off from school together." In his mind, he questioned how a summer away from friends and near a construction site could be called a vacation. He lamely promised them, "We'll have access to a great place to explore when you're not in school."

Through all the worry and sadness shown by the girls, Diana sat stoically mulling over her thoughts and concerns.

When the girls were in bed, Dean and Diana faced the reality that Dean had to accept his new responsibilities. Dean hugged Diana and said, "This will be a challenge for all of us." In his mind, he was thinking, *"How can an absentee husband and father remain the role model I am expected to be? There are so many things that can go wrong."*

The next morning after the girls went to school Dean called Herbert and asked for the morning off. "Diana and I need more time to talk about the transfer. I'll be in after lunch."

Herbert agreed, "Take as much time as you need. You have to make a big decision. This assignment will require sacrifices of you and your family. We'll talk later."

Dean and Diana analyzed their decision from all sides. It was apparent the negatives far outweighed the positives. Diana said, "By going off like this you are shifting all the household responsibilities to me. I'll be responsible for the upkeep on our house, see to mowing, snow removal, keeping the cars running, pay bills, have sole responsibility for the girls, plus do all the stuff I do now. If you take this assignment, I'll support your decision, but we have a ton of other things to address first."

Diana became more upset and continued, "You have always focused on your job. People use you. Herbert uses you and your talent. You always take the path of least resistance. I pray to God that this time you make the company pay you for the job and the sacrifices. We should expect rewards if we're going to jump in the deep end of life where we have to sink or swim."

Dean was surprised at Diana's outpouring of concerns. He agreed with her, "You're right; there must be rewards. Other than the good feeling one gets for a job well done and a thank you, what are the rewards? The decision is on me. I agree we have not been challenged like this before. Maybe it's time we make our life more complicated. In any case, the rewards must be worth the risk. Let' make a list of the pluses we need for us to sacrifice several years of our lives. I need ammunition to use when I talk to Herb tomorrow."

When Dean arrived at work, he went straight to Herbert's office to talk to him about the decision. He got right to the point, "Herb, accepting the position of project manager for a thirty-six million dollar Corps of Engineers project carries a tremendous responsibility. Diana and I are upset and worried but, provided there are some rewards associated with the sacrifices; we have decided to accept the risk that goes with an assignment away from home."

Herb acknowledged Dean's concerns by telling him, "You are the perfect person for this job. I'll allow you leeway when you have pressing family matters. On any project of that size, there will be crisis situations. There will be times when the job has to take precedence over concerns for your family."

Dean answered, "I have immediate financial concerns for my family and me. Our expenses, because I won't be there to do many things I do myself, will increase significantly. Diana will need help with the girls. I need to know what the company policies are when we yank people from their home to work at a remote job site."

Dean's bluntness annoyed Herbert. Dean thought about an apology to ease the situation. Before he could say anything Herb said, more calmly than expected, "Dean you're right. Because of the burden we are placing on you, the company must be cognizant of you and your family's financial needs. If you are away for what will be an extended length of time you and I both need to be confident that your family is safe and secure. Let's talk about this tomorrow. I need time to put together a plan that suits you and is within company policy."

The next morning Herb told Dean, "The other two owners and I have put together a salary and benefits package for you and others who are asked to travel away from home for extended lengths of time. We've put it in writing, look it over and, later today, tell me if you think it's fair."

Dean studied 'the plan' and determined it to be more than

fair. Before he talked to Herb, he decided to call Diana. "Diana, Herb has given us a good deal that provides for a generous raise and expenses while I'm away. We're still going to have a tough time adapting to a new way of life. But I'm satisfied our financial needs are being met. It's our emotional needs about which I'm still worried. I hope we both have the strength and the will to do this."

That same day Dean told Herb, "If you still want me I'll go to Trout River."

Herb was elated. To avoid any misunderstanding Herb explained, "You are presently responsible for three active projects and one that is nearly finished. You need to reassign all of your ongoing projects. I can take over some of your vice president duties, but you are still a company vice president."

Before continuing, Herb took a moment to outline Dean's new responsibilities, "You will be the key person on this project. In addition to coordinating all aspects of the job you will be responsible for costs, schedule, and monthly requests for payment. All Aldridge employees involved in the project, including the project superintendent, will report to you. As a team, you'll work together to maintain the challenging schedule and meet aggressive costs."

Herb went into more detail, "Your team is responsible for procuring materials and supplies that meet strict Corps of Engineer specifications. Dean, you must make sure everything that goes into that job has prior Corps of Engineer approval and be available when needed. Subcontracts must be issued and executed. All contracts with material suppliers and subcontractors must stipulate compliance with the contract documents."

Herb piled it on "Dean, you will be the liaison between Aldridge and the Corps field staff. That Corps team will no doubt consist of a resident engineer, an inspection team, and a field engineer or two. The Corps of Engineers puts strict and unforgiving inspectors on their projects."

Herb added, "An important part of your responsibilities will be to coordinate the work being done here in the St. Louis office with the Corps office in Louisville. A large part of your job will be calculating the quantities of work in place each day and preparing monthly requests for progress payments. Do you have any questions?"

Dean simply replied, "No."

As Dean left Herb's office, he thought, *"For many reasons, including the effect on my family, this decision to leave my position in the office and move to the Trout River field office in Clearfield County, Ohio is a necessary, but potentially trouble packed decision."*

\*\*\*

At the St. Louis office Dean's team consisted of Matt Wilson, a forty-two-year-old civil engineer, Troy Anderson, thirty-two, a scheduler and knowledgeable construction engineer, and several younger project engineers of varying levels of experience.

At the project, he would rely on Tom Wilkerson, 23, a recent civil engineering graduate from the University of Cincinnati. Tom was Aldridge's quality control engineer. In addition to Tom, Dean's management team at the job consisted of a project superintendent, various foremen, and essential workers.

\*\*\*

On April 20, 1970, Aldridge began moving workers and equipment onto the project site. The initial schedule included building an access road, removing trees, and clearing the work area. Also on April 20 Dean supervised moving in and setting up a three bedroom, one and a half bath, twelve foot by sixty foot modular home. This building would be his home away from home for the next three years. The 'abode,' as it came to be known, would also be a temporary home for a few other Aldridge employees who had work assignments on the project.

On his first day on the job, Dean visited the Corps of Engineers field office to meet the people with whom he and his team would be working. He spent nearly an hour talking to Wayne Henderson, the resident engineer. They talked about family and generalities concerning the project. They had a chuckle about being Carney Road neighbors. They noted the similarities of their situations; being transposed from a home office job to a project in a rural part of Ohio.

Wayne introduced Dean to others in his office. First Dean met chief inspector, Brian Towelson, two other inspectors, and a project engineer. Dean's only concern was the attitude of Towelson, the chief inspector. He couldn't get over the man's cold demeanor that bordered on hatred. *"Oh well,"* he thought, *"time will tell."*

Dean came away with a good impression about Wayne.

Wayne thought, *"Dean seems to be a serious and practical project manager."*

Work was barely underway when the first of many delays and problems began.

# CHAPTER 16

On the first Earth Day, April 22, 1970, a camp-in to protest the building of the Trout River Dam occurred at the entrance to the construction site, the intersection of State Route 223 and Carney Road. Carney Road was the only access to the site.

Wayne explained to Dean, "We believe the goal of the protesters is three-fold. Try to make a statement to the Corps of Engineers that the project is unwanted and unneeded. Second, attempt to hamper the contractor's startup efforts. And, finally, bring public attention to the project and the impact it will supposedly have on residents of Clearfield County." Dean replied, "Yeah, the beginning of the camp-in coincides with our startup efforts. This marks the first day on the project for three of my key employees."

"The outlet works superintendent and my second in command is George Knowles. He is 51 and a hard-nosed, no nonsense individual. George has been with Aldridge more than twenty years and has completed many projects within budget and on time. George and I worked together on two other projects. George has a temper, is hard as nails and, at times, he is grouchy. Aside from his gruff personality, George knows how to organize efficient work crews and maintain progress as scheduled. George and his wife have rented a nearby home. Having Knowles supervising the work allows me to concentrate on management responsibilities."

Dean introduced the second team member, "The lead labor foreman, David Trumbull has been with Aldridge for sixteen years. He is about 50, African American, smart, hard-working, and dedicated. He is one of my favorite people on and off the job. Dave is married to Ella, his equal in every way. They have a son, Sam, recently returned from Viet Nam. Unfortunately, Sam came back an addict. With family support and the VA, he is trying to recover. Dave and his wife have been married for 32 years. She says, 'David robbed the cradle.' They moved into an apartment near Cincinnati. I believe they choose the urban location because of concerns about prejudice in rural Clearfield County. After returning from two years in the Army, where he served in Korea, David attended Wayne State College for two years."

"The other key employee, Duane Richards, is an equipment operator and jack of all trades. He can fix anything. Duane is a native Ohioan from the Dayton area. Duane has worked with the company for ten years. He can operate, maintain and repair bulldozers, backhoes, and cranes. He's married with two children. Otherwise, I know little about him other than he is knowledgeable about construction equipment and dependable. Duane will commute from his home twenty-six miles away. Danny Barr is Duane's helper and an equipment oiler. He goes where Duane goes."

Wayne said, "Thanks for sharing the background on your key team members. Now let me share with you what I know about the camp-in and the participants."

He Told Dean, "The camp-in is organized but not controlled.

All the people out there come from communities outside Clearfield County. They include residents of Mount Adams in Cincinnati, Yellow Springs and Waynesville, Ohio. Included are professional protesters hired by environmental organizations dedicated to conserving wildlife and wilderness. Ironically no known Clearfield County residents are participating in the camp-in. They state they are peaceful but other Corps projects have seen violent outbursts. We need to keep a close eye on them. Whatever happens, have your employees stay away from the protesters."

While the protesters were erecting their tents, George Knowles had workers clearing trees and making the site ready to begin construction.

Because of the volatility of the situation and the potential for a violent confrontation; Dean and Wayne requested and received, compliments of Jesse Spearman, the county sheriff, the presence of two sheriff deputies. The Louisville District Office made arraignments to add two Army MPs from the Clearfield County Ohio National Guard.

Dean kept one eye on the protesters and the other on newly hired workers and their assigned tasks. Some of the people involved in the protest were members of a national environmental and conservation organization. Dean, Wayne, and others were confused by the glaring inconsistency in the group's objective. After all, the project would utilize over four thousand two hundred acres, removing habitation and creating a place where nature reigns.

A near riot occurred on the second day when the protesters armed with well-made signs attempted to prevent everyone, including the construction workers, from entering the project. They attacked cars and trucks, smashed a few windows, and dented some fenders and doors. About ten of the zealots placed themselves on the road as a human roadblock. The deputies quickly removed the human roadblock, unceremoniously dragging them to the side of the road. Access to the work area was unimpeded for the rest of the day.

Three of the most obvious vandals were arrested and taken to the Clearfield County Jail where they were charged with the willful destruction of private property and malicious mischief. On Friday, April 24, the three were arraigned in county court where they pleaded guilty and received a sentence of three days in jail. They were also ordered to make restitution. After their release they left the county, restitution be damned.

Wayne noted that the professionally made signs that read: "STOP THE TROUT RIVER DAM" and "THE CORPS DOESN'T CARE" appeared out of nowhere. Somebody spent a lot of money on signs.

The workers whose vehicles sustained damage at the hands of individual protesters wanted to retaliate; they wanted satisfaction. Dean begged the newly hired workers "Keep moving through the protester's blockades, but stop before injuring anyone."

Eventually, without using force, the National Guard and deputies contained the protesters. After the workers had made it through the crowd, the ex-hippies turned environmentalists, dispersed to the so-called camp area. Harassment of workers, Corps employees, and visitors continued for three days. Wayne observed that most of the protesters were products of the hippie culture of the sixties, who going into the seventies, adopted saving the environment as their mantra.

By the morning of Friday, April 24 Wayne had seen enough potentially violent behavior to request legal action. He called his boss, Jordan Lipper, and told him, "There are about forty protesters who have caused damage and pose a threat to the public. We need to get them out of here!"

Lipper, the Corps Louisville district chief engineer, with a cooler head explained, "We have dealt with these situations before. I will get our lawyers on it, but the best we can hope for is a restraining order and a restriction limiting them to a designated area."

On the same day at three o'clock p.m. in Clearfield County Court, with the Honorable Judge Koppel presiding, an attorney representing the U.S. Government sought and received an injunction and restraining order restricting the protests to the area within the boundaries of their camp-in and lying north of the entrance on Carney Road. Based on Wayne's testimony and description of the access road the judge's order also prohibited the protesters from entering the work area, interfering with the work, and preventing or impairing the public use of Carney Road.

The injunction did not deter the protesters. They continued ranting and milling about through the night of April 24. Leaders of the protest used bullhorns to shout the message to 'shut down all work.' The protesters, in violation of the judge's order, continued forays into the work site creating more damage and attempting to set fires. Deputies and MPs, working in shifts, did the best they could to keep protesters out of the work area. At daylight on the 25th, the protesters moved back to the designated entrance area. There were no arrests.

On Monday, April 27, after a quiet weekend, David Trumbull reported to Dean, "A confrontation occurred between six of my workers and about a dozen protesters. The protesters slipped through the project perimeter and attempted to disable a dozer and forcibly take the worker's chainsaws and tools. My guys were clearing trees to extend the access road."

David articulated, "Their commitment to the cause exemplified their zeal and bad judgment. My much stronger workers prevailed, sending two protesters to the Clearfield County Hospital ER with cuts and abrasions. Luckily, sheriff deputies quickly quelled the disturbance herding the remaining protesters back to the camp."

During the next week, Dean noted that protester night raids into the work area continued, lessening as the days went on. Minor damage occurred and, thanks to some contractor employed security, trespassing protesters, when caught, were turned over to the county sheriff, given a lecture, and a court summons. When and if they appeared in court, they received a small fine and were released. The court issued arrest warrants for non-appearances. The situation remained explosive. Wayne noted in his daily report, "All hell broke loose today, May 4, 1970, when word of the shootings at Kent State University reached the protesters. The camp-in participants had dwindled to about fifteen, and it appeared they were running out of enthusiasm. As word about the incident at Kent State spread, many protesters returned with renewed vigor. They tried to burn construction equipment, upset two workers cars and blocked Carney Road. On the night of May 4, the National Guard, with reinforcements and local law enforcement quelled the violence. The rest of the night and the next day were unsettled."

On Saturday, May 9, once again, the protesters began leaving.

There were many summonses issued but only two more arrests. By this time neither Wayne nor Dean was keeping track of who the lawbreakers were. They just wanted the protests to stop and the unruly crowd gone.

Dean stayed over Friday night. On Saturday morning, the Aldridge modular home being only a quarter mile away, he walked to the protesters camp. Things were relatively quiet with about twenty people still there.

One man acknowledged him and asked, "What do you want?"

Dean identified himself and answered, "It appears to be quiet today, and I'm not working. I'd like to meet your leader and some of your associates. I have no agenda; just call this a social visit."

The protester seemed to relax and replied, "We don't have a leader, but I've been with this movement from the start. I live in the Mount Adams area of Cincinnati. I'm a part-time student at the University, and I'm presently unemployed. I'm not married, have a girlfriend, no children. My name is Lawrence Poole, call me Larry."

Dean responded, "I don't support what your group is doing, but I respect your right to protest peacefully." He continued, "Sometime under different conditions maybe you can enlighten me about your agenda and the environmental movement in general. You're welcome to visit our project field office. Just tell whoever is there you are Larry and you want to see Dean. I'll be glad to show you what we're doing. Late afternoon is best."

Larry answered, "I'll see you soon."

By Monday, May 11, the protesters were all gone except for the dregs of their stay. Cleaning up the mess left by the protesters fell to county workers.

\*\*\*

After the protest was over Dean and Wayne met in the Corps field office. Wayne complimented Dean, "Your employees showed admirable restraint. I would be furious and look to punish anyone who deliberately damaged my car or my property."

Dean agreed, "We have some very pissed off employees. The sad thing is our society, and judicial systems appear to be lax in the punishment given to lawbreakers who are demonstrating for a cause. There were arrests made, court appearances, and penalties issued. But the guilty parties just scoffed and more or less thumbed their noses at the court. A couple of people spent a night or two in jail, but the court released them without bail. People who were fined and ordered to make restitution merely went home, scot free."

Wayne said, "I acknowledge the lack of justice for, let's call them as they are, criminals who violate other people's property. Others in the Corps tell me that real punishment is seldom doled out to protesters."

Dean said, "The Company and our insurers are attempting to assess the damage and will probably start settling claims next week. It's a shame that others will bear the responsibility to pay for damage caused by the protesters."

# CHAPTER 17

After the protesters had left, Wayne sat down with Melissa and JD to talk about safety and concerns about the relatively isolated location of the government furnished home.

Their government provided home, located on Carney Road, was about 300 yards from where the protesters staged their camp-in. The Trout River protests had ended, but protest intensity ebbed and flowed centering about the Corps of Engineers five Congressional mandated flood control projects. Wayne's concern for his wife and son, now 12 years old, increased every day that the threat of protests continued.

Wayne's son, in the sixth grade at Stanton Elementary school, had developed several friendships among his school buddies. The Henderson's government owned home was situated on a half acre in what was part of more than four thousand two hundred acres that would become the Trout River Dam, Lake, and Recreation area. Their nearest neighbor lived a quarter mile away. JD's friends were not nearby. However, being located on lots of open, wooded, and interesting land, JD's home and the land around it became a favorite hangout for the kids.

Wayne explained to his family some of the dangers of rural living in a secluded setting. He told them, "Be aware of unexpected visitors, people looking for work, hunters, fishermen, poachers, people opposed to the dam, looters, and just curious lookers. Eventually, there will be a lot of construction workers and traffic." He warned them, "Watch where you walk. Wildlife, especially snakes, are dangerous when surprised."

As a serious hunter, mostly small game, Wayne owned several firearms. Melissa and JD had an awareness of the guns and the danger they imply. Melissa was from a family that owned guns, and she was proficient in their use. Wayne taught JD about gun safety and had been doing some target shooting with him. Wayne, if there was a threat to his family, wanted them to be safe and not defenseless.

Although they were gone, he didn't anticipate an organized group of protesters camped three hundred yards from his home. During the protest, to assure the safety of his family, Wayne convinced Melissa to return to her parents' home in Louisville. JD stayed at the home of a school friend until the protest ended.

*** 

The employee parking lot and the Aldridge modular home was Dean's job site home. The home located on Carney Road was about four hundred yards past Wayne's house. Dean and those staying in the modular home got little sleep during the protest camp-in. Despite the protest, there were numerous job-related activities to be accomplished by the project team. By the time the protest ended they were all tired from lack of sleep and increased diligence resulting from the actions of the protesters.

***

Concurrent with the protest camp-in, Aldridge needed to build up Carney Road to withstand the heavy construction traffic and start clearing the work area. Also needed were upgraded electric and telephone service to the Aldridge field office, the modular home, the quality control building, and the Corps of Engineers office.

Before beginning work on the outlet works they had to clear the field office areas, place gravel in the parking areas, extend the access road into the construction site, and build a levee to divert the Trout River around the outlet works construction site.

Cisterns for water, septic tanks, and the services to maintain same were also required.

\*\*\*

Carney Road was a straight and level unpaved country road. It began at State Route 223, passed Wayne's house on the left, continued past the employee parking lot and the modular home, and ended at the Corps of Engineers field office.

Trout River and the work area for the outlet works were located in a picturesque valley at the bottom of a steep hill two hundred feet below Carney Road. David, Duane, and their crews had to build fifteen hundred feet of winding dirt and gravel road for access to the work area. The road was steep with turns and switchbacks, winding in and out of the hillside. Dean told the road building crews, "This road has to last for the duration of the project. It has to sustain over five thousand loads of ready mix concrete and hundreds of loads of construction equipment, rebar, gravel, and construction materials. Our goal is to provide a road to get from Carney Road to the river bottom, two hundred feet below, while keeping the grade such that heavily loaded trucks can descend safely and be able to climb back out unassisted."

The road failed in many ways. Every rain floated mud from below the gravel surface to the top. It was necessary to re-grade and apply new gravel after every rain storm. Even so George Knowles, the project superintendent, ordered that a midsized bulldozer be available for the duration of the project to assist vehicles up, and occasionally down, the access road.

The access road, an absolute necessity, was like an unhappy and demanding spouse. It required constant maintenance and was a source of contention and dissatisfaction. Truck drivers, Corps of Engineers personnel, visitors, workers, anyone using the road did so with trepidation.

Trees, when they fell, did not fall into the woods; they fell across the road. Rocks that came loose did not roll down the hill; they rolled onto the road. Only on rare and dry occasions could a passenger car or two wheel drive truck make it up and down without help.

Duane and a couple of his crew dug out and surfaced with gravel, an employee and visitor parking lot off Carney Road adjacent to the modular home. A four-wheel drive pickup truck, equipped with wood benches in the bed, transported employees and visitors in and out of the work area. The primitive conditions required the employment of a full-time truck driver for the four wheel drive pickup to provide transportation in and around the site. George hired Elmer Haney to drive the truck. The access road was primitive but ready to use by May 12, 1970.

# CHAPTER 18

Actual construction of the first phase of the Trout River dam and lake started May 12, 1970.

Dean held a meeting with Knowles, David, and Duane to examine the construction plans and explain what they were building. He began by telling them, "The project will be built in two phases that are dependent on each other. The first phase, the outlet works consists of three components; a two hundred twenty foot high formed concrete water intake structure, known as the control tower. Connected to the outlet side of the control tower is an eleven hundred foot long by fourteen-foot high conduit that ends at the stilling basin where the velocity of the flow through the conduit is slowed to allow the water to gently reenter the natural confines of the Trout River."

"The second phase of construction is the dam embankment. The embankment is a massive earth, rock, and clay barrier that stretches seventeen hundred feet across the valley. The dam is six hundred feet wide at the bottom and rises two hundred feet high. Before the dam can be built, diversion of the Trout River through the outlet works is necessary. After diversion takes place, the massive earth structure will take three years to place and compact using eight million six hundred thousand cubic yards of material. Impoundment for the lake will begin when the dam is finished.

Dean continued, "The outlet works will be constructed parallel to and about 100 feet west of the northwest flowing Trout River. Before construction can begin, we have to remove trees, brush, and debris in an area beside the river about three hundred feet wide by two thousand feet long. We'll start doing that right now." There were no comments or questions and the meeting ended.

Clearing the work area of trees, bushes, and undergrowth generated so much debris they couldn't find places suitable for disposal. Finally, Dean received approval from the county fire chief allowing them to burn all the waste. While burning the waste, smoke was observed from several miles away.

Getting in and out of the work area was time consuming. Moving within the work area, by foot or by vehicle, was difficult.

Clearing the work area to make it ready to begin construction was made difficult and dangerous by the presence of numerous snakes including water moccasins, black snakes, copperheads, and one four foot long rattlesnake. Most of the reptiles left on their own, but the workers eliminated some of them.

One of the laborers, outspoken Abe Silverman, working to clear the area complained, "I don't mind hard work, I just don't like snakes watchin' me do it." The workers performing this work let it be known that they were very uneasy until the area was clear enough that they could see the ground and the surrounding area.

The cleared area contained many walnut trees and other hardwoods that had value when sold to local sawmills. On Friday, May 15, before the workers left the job, Knowles had five loads of logs stacked and ready to be loaded and shipped to a local sawmill. Upon returning Monday morning every stick of valuable lumber, worth twenty thousand dollars, was gone.

Dean attempted to learn where the trees went. He questioned workers, searched sawmills, and had the sheriff investigate. They never located the missing lumber. How the thieves loaded the logs, transported them up the steep access road, and off the project leaving no evidence remained a mystery. To further mystify the situation the transporters for the stolen trees had to enter and leave by way of Carney Road, right in front of Wayne's house. During the weekend of the theft, no one saw or heard any trucks entering or leaving the area.

Working conditions were usually atrocious. Depending on the season, the weather was hot and humid or cold and damp. When it rained the entire site became a quagmire, workers feet sank six inches in the mud and equipment got stuck. Abe Silverman, the self-appointed spokesman for all employees, said, "Pulling your feet from the mire is like freeing yourself from the tentacles of an octopus. Sometimes he keeps your boots."

Excavation for the outlet works control tower started on May 20.

Laborers local union 339 started trouble on May 25 by trying to force employment of a local general laborer foreman to replace David. A minor union official and three goons from the laborers union came to the project threatening to shut the project down if Aldridge did not comply with their demand. The leader told Knowles, "You have to get rid of the foreman you brought in from Missouri. We have an excellent man available to replace him."

Knowles, near his boiling point, with clenched teeth told them, "We are abiding by our contract with the Ohio laborers. That agreement explicitly allows us to appoint the first laborer. David Trumbull is that man. We have already employed a foreman and four laborers from your local. Now get the hell out of here!" Later, Knowles described the leader, "As having the appearance of one who had never put in a day of hard work."

To defuse the situation, Dean made a call to the president of the St. Louis Laborers local. He asked him, "Will you call the president of the Cincinnati area laborers and vouch for Aldridge's union commitment?" Apparently, this worked because about an hour later another official from the Cincinnati local arrived and spoke with the four visitors. They all left soon after.

While the four union visitors were present, everyone ignored them and attended to their work. After they left Knowles told Dean, "Aside from their crude innuendos what they wanted was to open the door for Aldridge to hire a bunch of their relatives and buddies from the union who are faithful to the regime, but are not good workers. This threatening gesture was an example of union politics and chest pounding."

Knowles warned, "Later, as the project progresses, construction union disputes over work assignments might cause disrupting and dangerous situations."

\*\*\*

Excavation for the control tower that started on May 20 was scheduled to take about three weeks. Duane explained to Dean, "As we discussed, all the excavated material is being placed between the work area and the river to form a levee. The levee will protect the work area from the river during flood conditions. I plan to apply gravel on top of the levee to create a long extension to the access road. The levee road will extend about two thousand feet from the control tower to the stilling basin."

It required many tons of gravel to keep the worksite roads serviceable. Regardless of constant maintenance of the roads they frequently became rutted. One joker put a crude sign at the bottom of the hill reading, "BE CAREFUL WHICH RUT YOU TAKE – YOU MIGHT END UP WHERE YOU DON'T WANT TO GO."

The weather improved to typical early summer conditions. The control tower excavation crew worked together with everyone doing their part and helping anyone who became overloaded. After a few days working together, assignments became clear, and the crew worked together as one.

The weather was typical for the season; cool in the morning, warming through the day and sometimes rainy. The soil in the area to be excavated was considered moisture sensitive. A little water caused the soil to become just plain mud. After only a light rain the mud made walking difficult.

Duane Richards supervised the excavation crew. His crew of seven, and a surveyor as needed, would require about three weeks to excavate for the control tower foundation.

The survey team was responsible for checking elevation and alignment. Data generated by the surveyors was also needed to calculate the amount of earth and rock removed each day.

Wayne's inspection team diligently monitored Aldridge's methods and progress. They kept notes, took photos and compiled them in daily reports.

Dean was also responsible for keeping a daily report. In addition to hours worked, the number of employees, and their activities; he reported equipment usage, weather, visitors, and completed work. The contractor's daily report also included a narrative about problems, progress, deliveries, and any incidents affecting the work. Every week Dean's daily reports, including progress photos, were sent to Aldridge's St. Louis office with copies to the Corps resident engineer.

On June 3, 1970, control tower excavation was into bedrock when Duane showed Dean some excavated sandstone rock containing fossils.

Dean asked Wayne to look at the fossils. After examining the rocks, Wayne exclaimed, "Shit, we have to notify our geologist before you go any further. Stop work in this area immediately." Within thirty minutes he confirmed the 'stop work order' in writing.

George Knowles instructed Duane, "To mitigate the delay, move the entire excavating crew into the conduit area and continue excavating."

Two government geologists arrived a day later, Thursday, June 4. They dug and poked around in the excavated area for about three hours. One female geologist finally exclaimed, "The fossils are probably from the Ordovician period. They are about five hundred million years old."

Dean immediately asked, "How will this affect us and the work we are doing?"

The geologist answered, "We will take samples during the remainder of the day. When we're finished work can resume as usual."

After the geologists had left, talkative Abe Silverman told David Trumbull, "We're sorry to see them go. That girl is a lot better to look at than anyone on this godforsaken project. She made this crappy place look good." Apparently, the Aldridge work crews didn't see many women on their projects. There being a woman on the site was a real treat compared to looking at dirty and disheveled fellow male workers.

The control tower excavation incurred a two-day delay to stop and start while allowing the geologists to examine the fossil find. The contract required Dean to keep a record of the delay and notify Wayne. When he delivered the notice of delay to the Corps field office Dean told Wayne, "This is for information only but, as stated in the notice, we reserve the right to pursue time and expenses later if necessary."

Wayne thought Dean's notice of a delay was a cheap shot and told Dean how he felt, "Dean this is a chicken shit way to put us on notice that Aldridge might ask for time and money for the fossil investigation."

Dean realized that Wayne was on his first assignment as a Corps field representative and told him, "The contract clearly states that the contractor waives his rights for future consideration for failure to give timely notice of anything that affects the project. This document is a notice for your files. It will only become a serious issue if this kind of delay occurs frequently. You're going to see a lot of stuff like this. Some notices will potentially have a big impact; other notices will be, like this one, a notice to preserve future rights. Get used to it. There is no need to create a conflict."

Much later Dean learned chief inspector Towelson advised Wayne on many pressing matters. Dean believed Towelson was using Wayne's inexperience concerning field operations to cause havoc and distrust within the project.

# CHAPTER 19

While work continued at the project site, work in Aldridge's St. Louis office was at a frantic pace. Matt Wilson and Troy Anderson were busy procuring a long list of supplies, materials, and subcontractors. Their motto was, 'first things first.'

From suppliers they needed diesel fuel, a long list of concrete accessories, gravel, sources for equipment maintenance, and parts. Material suppliers included ready mix concrete (about 28,000 cubic yards), water control gates, bridge girders, and fabricated metals. To supplement the work performed by Aldridge's workers they needed competent subcontractors to supply and install reinforcing steel, painting, mechanical work, electrical work, and the gate control hydraulic system. There were dozens of unexpected miscellaneous items that would be needed.

A major item on the list of needed items was the four primary six feet wide by fourteen feet high hydraulic operated fabricated steel water control gates.

Dean was in his office at the job on June 8, 1970, when he received a call from Troy Anderson. "Dean, I'm having a problem with a potential supplier of the big water control gates. Their representative wants to deal directly with you, the project manager. He's going to contact you to meet with him up there. The guy represents a Canadian fabricator, and I'm not comfortable with going across the border to buy anything."

Dean, surprised by this request, told Troy, "I'm busy; he'll have to come here if he wants to meet face to face. Why can't he just call me?"

Troy explained, "I don't know. We have two quotes for the gates. The other one is from a fabricator in Tennessee. The Tennessee quote is the highest at $290,000; the Canadians are at $279,000. Both are sticking to their original prices."

Dean replied, "Let's wait a day or so and see what happens." The next morning, June 9 before nine o'clock, Dean received a call, the caller identified himself as Armand Glaisyer.

Dean asked, "What can I do for you Mr. Glaisyer?"

Glaisyer responded, "I represent the Canadian National Steel Fabricating Company. We're more commonly known as CNSF. We gave your company a quote to fabricate and deliver the four main water control gates. I'm in Ohio, and I would like to meet with you to discuss our proposal"

Dean replied, "I'm pretty busy. You'll have to come to the job." After giving Glaisyer directions, Dean said, "I'll see you at eleven."

Promptly at the agreed time, Mr. Haney, who drove the four wheel drive truck, brought Glaisyer down the access road to the field office. After introducing each other and making some small talk, the two got down to business.

Glaisyer observed with a slight French accent, "We don't know your company and you don't know ours. We have supplied the control gates on a similar project in Indiana. We want to provide these gates too."

Dean informed him, "Troy Anderson is responsible for purchasing the gates. I believe you know that."

Glaisyer sounding troubled said, "I'm not getting any information from Troy."

Dean was annoyed by the intrusion, and knowing about Troy's reluctance to buy from a Canadian company, bluntly said, "If by not giving you information about other quotes, you're right. You won't get information from Troy. Let's put that aside and get right to it. What's the bottom line, what's your best price?"

Glaisyer, after a moment's pause, answered, "If you agree to purchase the gates from CNSF I will personally give you $10,000."

Dean blurted, "Are you offering me a bribe!"

Glaisyer, taken aback by Dean's strong response, tried to defend his action by explaining, "It's not a bribe. I'm merely willing to share my commission." It became apparent to Dean why the meeting had to be in person.

Dean was thinking fast. Commission sharing or not he wanted nothing to do with Glaisyer's offer. Unless there was a significant benefit to Aldridge, he did not want to do business with this sleaze-ball. He had no intention of accepting Glaisyer's bribery offer. But, regardless of his personal feelings, he knew the gates were an important part of the project. He also knew CNSF already had the low price.

Dean had no intention of accepting $10,000 for placing the order. In fact, Dean wouldn't take a dollar unless it benefited Aldridge. After thinking about the situation for a few minutes, he decided to turn the situation so that Aldridge would benefit. He made a counter offer to Glaisyer, "Tell you what. I'll forget about your attempt to buy me if you will sell the gates and operating cylinders, delivered on time, per contract requirements, and in compliance with international import/export laws; for the total price of $250,000. Oh yeah, including all import taxes and duties."

Glaisyer was surprised by Dean's offer. In his business, he was comfortable with business deals requiring an exchange of money for business. Dean's counter offer surprised him, but he had put himself in an untenable position. "Okay," he said, "We have a deal, 250,000 US dollars."

Dean added, "This agreement is subject to favorable credit and banking references." Glaisyer nodded his head in agreement, and they shook hands.

As soon as Glaisyer left Dean called Troy to tell him he agreed to purchase the gates for the reduced price of $250,000. Troy exclaimed, "You just made the company $40,000! We had the other bidders' price of $290,000 in our bid!"

Dean never told anyone of the attempted 'bribe' or how Canadian National Steel Fabricators got the coveted order. Glaisyer had left a bad impression; Dean hoped he would never see the man again.

As procurement progressed suppliers and subcontractors had to submit, for the Corps engineer's approval, drawings, samples, and manufacturers data in sufficient detail to assure the products going into the project met the rigid requirements of the contract documents. Nothing was released for delivery until it was proven to meet contract requirements and had the Corps stamp of approval affixed.

To get the necessary supplies bought, approved, and delivered to the job as needed required several months of diligent work by Matt and Troy.

After Matt and Troy's efforts, Dean had to maintain files of all the approved documents at the project. He also had to assure the approved information was being provided to and was used by everyone performing the work.

\*\*\*

Part of Dean's responsibility was to prepare a monthly request for payment. The progress payment request, as it was known, itemized over two hundred lines of work items, quantities, and values. Each month for the duration of the project Dean calculated quantities of completed work, the value of the items, prepared the monthly pay request and took it to the resident office for approval.

The Corps' resident engineer office staff scrutinized the pay request from top to bottom and item by item. Only after they verified each item and corrected it, did a draft copy go back to Dean to be resubmitted. After making the corrections, the pay request went back to Wayne's office where they approved the corrected copy and forwarded it to Louisville for payment. Aldridge could expect payment, less five percent retainer, in about three weeks. When Aldridge finished the project, six years from now, the government would hold about one-million-nine-hundred-thousand dollars of retained monies to assure satisfactory completion of the work.

After approval, Dean personally assured the pay request went to the proper authority at the district office. When payment was issued, usually in about three weeks, Dean would notify the St. Louis office, and someone would go to the Corps district office and personally pick up the check. When it came to large checks, Herbert didn't trust the U. S. Postal Service.

# CHAPTER 20

Before Aldridge's arrival at the project, the Corps of Engineers established a field office and quality control building. The primary purpose of the quality control building was to provide a facility where the technicians performed testing of concrete materials. Later, as the embankment progressed, the testing lab would be used for soil testing. The testing lab was the domain of the Corps of Engineer's inspection team. They shared it with Aldridge's quality control engineer, Tom Wilkerson. Contractor provided, and Corps approved, concrete mix designs provided the basis for the proportions of cement, sand, aggregate, water, and specified additives to achieve structural concrete with a twenty-eight day compressive strength of four thousand five hundred psi.

The Aldridge quality control engineer, Tom Wilkerson, was a recent civil engineering graduate from The University of Cincinnati. He was single and lived with his parents about twenty miles from the job. He had a clean-cut demeanor, and seemed unflappable. He confided to Dean that the stress of his job and interference by Brian Towelson, the Corps chief inspector, caused his stomach to tighten and his mind to reel. Tom also admitted that Towelson belittled his lack of experience.

Tom was wrapping up his daily tests on the sand and gravel that went into the concrete. Towelson entered the lab in his usual manner. He emitted a commanding presence. He was probably about 45. He was a large bear-like man with a full beard and neck length hair. He was overbearing and had a know-it-all attitude. He never smiled; he always had a hard look about him. When he entered the lab building, his bulk and attitude seemed to suck the air from the building. Tom didn't fear him, but he didn't like to be near him either.

Without saying 'good morning' or 'how ya doin' he stated, "The aggregate samples failed again. At this rate, you idiots will never get this job done."

As he did every day, Tom had been at the concrete plant at five o'clock a.m. with his sampling tools. Every day before concrete could be batched for the day's concrete needs, sand and gravel samples had to be taken and returned to the lab. At the lab, as required by the contract documents, Tom performed exacting gradation and moisture tests. If the samples met the specifications he told the concrete plant to begin preparing daily concrete requirements. He also logged all samples and reported test results on forms provided by the Corps of Engineers.

On June 2, excavation for a portion of the control tower foundation was deep enough to require David Trumbull's team to place the concrete fill. The afternoon before the fill placement, labor foreman David Trumbull ordered twenty-six cubic yards of concrete for delivery in four trucks thirty minutes apart. He asked for the first truck to arrive at eight o'clock the next morning.

All was ready the next morning on June 3 to make the first official concrete fill placement. The first ready-mix concrete truck did not arrive. Neither did the second truck. At eight thirty David called the supplier, "Hey, where's my concrete?"

The dispatcher replied, "Inspector Towelson cancelled that delivery. You'll have to ask him why he canceled."

David immediately called Tom about the cancellation. He said, "I have a whole crew standing by waiting for that concrete."

Tom told him, "I just found out myself, Towelson cancelled the concrete for today. You better find Dean and let him know what happened."

Dean upon being notified told David, "Find other work for this morning. I'll get back to you."

In the lab building Tom was trying to stand up to Towelson. Dean interrupted the argument. He told Towelson, "In your position as the Corps of Engineers senior inspector you perform the same quality control tests as Tom. Today, the first of many concrete placements, you belatedly notified us that the aggregate gradation tests prepared by you failed. I know Tom carefully sampled the same pile, supposedly in the manner, as you and his samples passed. What the hell is going on?"

Towelson responded, "I don't care about the results of your samples. Because my samples failed, I cancelled the concrete delivery."

Dean asked Tom, "Are you sure you sampled and tested the aggregates according to the contract specifications?"

Tom confidently replied, "I am positive I performed the tests according to the specs. Towelson takes his entire sample from one place on the aggregate pile. The specs require that we obtain the aggregate samples from three different locations. Tom, by now irate, accused Towelson, "You're not following the requirements of you own specifications!"

Towelson merely scoffed and walked out.

Dean, when he became aware of the disagreement about the procedures, went to the resident engineer's office. "Wayne, you know Towelson is very strong willed and opinionated. But my quality control engineer is following the sampling requirements to the letter. We're frustrated that your inspector refuses to follow the contract specs regarding the correct way to sample the aggregate piles. Today, for no apparent reason, he canceled our concrete delivery."

Dean had become agitated, "Common courtesy and protocol require that Towelson notify us of situations like this. We learned of the cancellation from the dispatcher at the concrete plant. We expect timely notification about anything affecting the project and our progress. This incident today goes way beyond common courtesy. It smacks of sabotage."

Wayne responded to Dean's outburst by defending his chief inspector. "Look, Towelson is just doing his job. I suggest you get your quality control guy some expert help. He is as green as the grass."

Later Dean told Knowles, "In the short time we've been at our respective positions, Wayne and I have not developed a trusting relationship. Wayne had been in charge of design and preliminary activities on the project for four years, it is his baby. But, like me, he has been involved in the construction phase for less than two months. I guess both of us are like young lions in our respective fields. However, until now, Wayne was a designer, never a constructor."

Knowles observed, "Wayne is academic and you are nuts and bolts. You're both good in your chosen fields."

Towelson's tests, which Tom suspected he rigged to fail, were delaying concrete placements. Numerous times a daily concrete placement had to be canceled.

After the third unexpected cancellation of a concrete delivery David, about as mad as the mild-mannered foreman could be, told Dean, "Placing of the concrete fill has to occur the same day the rock is exposed to air and water or the rock surface deteriorates. When deterioration happens, it is necessary to over-excavate to sound rock and place additional concrete fill at our expense. In many areas, solid rock occurs more than a foot below the structure bottom requiring additional excavation and concrete."

David continued, "We can't keep going like this. Towelson is delaying us; it is like he has taken control of our schedule. We need to act fast."

Dean knew the quality control situation was causing devastating scheduling problems and delaying the entire project. It cost Aldridge thousands of dollars. No concrete placement exacerbated the rock deterioration problem.

On June 8, Dean, exasperated at the stop and go concrete deliveries, went into to the lab and angrily confronted Towelson with copies of the conflicting aggregate sample reports.

Towelson angrily responded, "Don't blame me. Blame your inexperienced technician and your concrete supplier. My decisions stand."

Dean had already talked to Hamilton Ready Mix Concrete Co. about the situation. The batch plant foreman told him,

"Brian's sampling procedures are a joke. He deliberately samples the aggregate piles in an unorthodox manner that assures failed test results. Technicians from the Ohio Highway Department are in our plant every day, and we might have one in a hundred failed samples. We've sent thousands of loads of OHD approved concrete to the I-275 interstate project near Cincinnati."

When Dean told Towelson about the Ohio Highway Department positive test results, Towelson stated, "Their criteria are not as strict as ours."

Tom cut in, "The Ohio guys run the same tests as we do." Towelson walked out of the lab saying, "Get your act together and we'll not have a problem."

After Towelson had left, Tom said, "Dean, there is no way we will satisfy that asshole. He's out to punish us. I don't know why he is like that."

Dean decided to talk to Wayne again about the aggregate testing situation. Wayne, trying to avoid the problem, told Dean, "I stand behind my inspector; we blame your concrete supplier and the inexperience of your technician."

Dean disagreed, saying, "I don't know how two people can sample the same aggregate source and get such divergent results. I have personally monitored Tom's work and testing procedures, and they are in strict conformance with the contract requirements. He's meticulously following the contract documents. It's not complicated testing."

Wayne sarcastically suggested, "Dean, why don't you contact the Corps of Engineers experimental station at Vicksburg, Mississippi for advice." With a smirk, he added, "Maybe they can send an expert to evaluate your procedures."

Unknown to Wayne, Dean thought that was good advice. His contact at Vicksburg was no help other than to suggest that Dean contact a retired Corps of Engineers concrete expert living in Louisiana, Mr. Loren Hauser.

On June 12, after a week of failed aggregate tests; Dean, following the advice of the person at Vicksburg, contacted Mr. Hauser.

Houser told Dean, "I recognize your problem and I can help you. I don't know when I can get there, but I will be there as soon as I can." Houser arrived the following week at exactly eight o'clock on a hot and muggy June morning. For lack of seasonal air movement, the mugginess was always worse in the valley by the river.

Loren drove from Louisiana to Ohio in his ten-year-old Jeep station wagon accompanied by his dog, an old but beautiful golden lab. Dean liked this old fart from the moment he climbed from the Jeep. Loren was gregarious, direct speaking, wore a cowboy hat, and looked like he had just returned from a hunting trip.

After introductions, Loren went right to the problem. He said, "Get me a copy of the concrete specs and show me the testing lab. I want to meet your quality control engineer and the Corps technician doing the testing."

This day was indicative of what happened numerous times before; Tom and Brian's aggregate tests did not agree. Loren and Dean walked into a heated argument where, typical of other arguments, Brian was prevailing solely because of his position of authority and domineering personality.

Loren after observing the bitter exchange introduced himself and suggested, "We can achieve a more conclusive outcome by going to the concrete plant, examine sampling procedures, and obtain meaningful samples. We can then return to the testing lab and run the required procedures, all according to the specifications." Loren spoke directly to Tom, ignoring Brian who had moved a safe distance away.

As they were preparing to leave for the plant, Loren turned to Brian and asked, "Are you going to obtain new samples?"

Brian replied, "I've already done my testing for the day." After Loren and Brian had gone aside to talk, Brian agreed to redo his tests; he said, "I'll meet you at the plant."

When they arrived at the aggregate piles, about an hour later, Brian was already there and had all his samples bagged and ready to return to the lab.

Loren bluntly told Brian, "I want to observe your sampling method, please discard those and get new samples."

Brian refused, but Tom interrupted, "He only samples from one place on the pile."

Loren asked Brian to confirm Tom's observation but, without comment, Brian threw his sample bags and contents in his Corps truck and left crunching sand and gravel in his wake.

Under Loren's supervision, Tom obtained the required samples, in accordance with contract specifications, from three places on the stockpile.

Loren asked, "Is that the way you always do it?" Tom replied, "Yeah."

When they arrived back at the project and the lab, Tom, with Loren supervising, proceeded to do the required gradation tests. Dean went back down to his field office in the work area. About thirty minutes later he was asked by Tom to come back up to the Corps office trailer.

Dean arrived five minutes later. Present in the office were Wayne, Towelson, Tom, and Loren. Loren took control of the meeting by stating that Tom took his samples correctly, and the test results were within limits outlined in the contract documents.

Brian immediately announced, "Those samples are not acceptable." Brian tried to defend his indefensible position by giving a brief resume intended to establish him as a concrete expert, thus making the results obtained by anyone else questionable.

Loren listened to Brian's outburst, but speaking to Wayne, he said, "Before I retired I worked for the Corps of Engineers for over thirty years. Ten of those years were in the Vicksburg Experimental Station doing research on concrete and ways to improve it. Many of the improvements resulting from my team's work are in use. I also worked for four years in Washington, D.C. in the Corps of Engineers specification library. Among other duties, I rewrote and improved the concrete specifications." Then looking directly into Brian's eyes he said, "So you see Mr. Towelson, I wrote the specifications that you ignore and disrespect."

Wayne asked all to leave except Loren. After an hour long discussion with Wayne, Loren went back to Aldridge's field office. He told Dean, "You won't have any more problems resulting from aggregate testing inconsistencies. Wayne will discuss the information I gave him with Towelson and instruct him to sample according to the specifications." Within fifteen minutes he and his dog were on their way back to Louisiana.

\*\*\*

Occasional problems concerning concrete still occurred but Aldridge was getting deliveries as scheduled. Dean predicted, "Towelson will be an obstacle from now on. His overzealous approach to all situations is controlling the progress of the job."

A carpenter from the Dayton area, Brian's hometown, gave Dean a possible explanation for Brian's behavior. He told Dean, "Towelson's father is a union organizer for the UAW. He is known for his temper and violence. Brian Towelson has a reputation for hating contractors, undermining project budgets and schedules by overzealous interpretation of contract requirements."

Brian's hostile behavior was perplexing to Dean because Arthur Aldridge Construction was a one-hundred percent union contractor with a reputation for treating its employees fairly. Dean decided Brian was simply a person known as a 'contractor buster.'

Dean told Knowles and David, "I don't know why the Corps employs a disruptive individual like Towelson. I guess some people, for no reason at all; make their life miserable by making life miserable for others. Those types of people thrive by making problems where there are no problems. The unavoidable truth is they enjoy being troublesome. Maybe someday I'll understand the reasons behind Towelson's behavior."

Dean was not ready to close the matter of a Corps technician deliberately sabotaging project expenses and progress. Using information from the laboratory reports he prepared a detailed account of the time and date of each incident where Towelson relied on his corrupt reports to hinder progress. He then compiled a claim for reimbursement for Aldridge's added expenses caused by delays and lost productivity resulting from the incidents. The scheduled completion date for control tower excavation was June 12. Because of the deliberate interference by Towelson the excavation and fill concrete was not finished until June 22, a delay of 9 calendar days.

Two days after the impact of Towelson's fraudulent testing methods was known Dean sent Wayne a documented demand for payment for added expenses. Dean told Knowles, "Our demand for added money is strengthened by the fact that every day Ohio Highway Inspectors sampling the aggregates for use on interstate highway projects approved the same aggregates that Brian rejected. The total amount of our claim is $57,650 and 12 calendar days delay. I've sent the letter and documentation to Wayne at the Corps project office."

The Monday following receipt of Dean's claim letter Wayne called Dean and angrily told him, "Why didn't you let me know this was coming? You blindsided me!"

Dean explained, "I'm following contract requirements to promptly notify your office in writing of any disputes or claims for added time and compensation. As you know, the contractor can lose its rights to recover expenses and time by failing to adhere to the timely notice requirements."

Dean chided Wayne, "You guys see to it that we comply with every contract requirement right down to minuscule details. But when the requirement is spelled out to protect the contractor you interpret our actions as being devious and wrong. We're only doing what we are supposed to."

Wayne replied, "Okay, we'll take a look at the stuff you sent with your claim."

Dean decided this was a good time to vent his feelings about Towelson. He said, "Wayne we have to trust each other. What Brian is doing is disruptive not only to the project but to yours and my responsibilities. I have to tell you that Brian's malicious behavior scares the hell out of me. If that behavior continues, you are going to see a lot more letters like the one you received today. I am going to monitor and record every subversive and detrimental action that he initiates. If he wants to be adversarial; well, we'll play that game."

Despite this and other disagreements, Wayne and Dean begrudgingly respected each other. They were not friends and did not socialize. But they maintained a tense but cooperative working relationship. They dealt with the numerous problems and conflicts in a businesslike and acutely direct manner.

# CHAPTER 21

Dean was reviewing recent project activity with the superintendent, George Knowles. Dean lamented, "I'm pissed off about Towelson's undermining our effort to maintain a tight schedule. The crew started the control tower excavation and concrete fill on May 25 and didn't finish until June 22; at least nine days later than scheduled."

Dean continued his one sided discussion with George, "I'm happy we're storing all the excavated rock and soil between the work area and the river to form the continuance of a levee. I notice we have already started to use the top of the levee as an access road."

Knowles said, "Yeah, that road provides good access to the control tower."

After a short pause, Knowles tackled another issue, "Qualified local labor is difficult to find. Workers are assigned by the unions and, in general, are lazy friends and relatives of union officials. We're also in an out of the way location; nobody wants to come way out here. We need, but we're not getting, productive and reliable people."

Knowles, feeling a little guilty, said, "I didn't tell you about this, but earlier this month a guy came to the field office and asked about a carpenter foreman job. His name is Don

Peterson. He said he is a union carpenter and knows some other guys who he can get. In fact, he claimed he has a whole crew he could bring with him. I admit I blew him off because I didn't believe him. I'll ask him to come back when we can both talk to him."

Dean told George, "Yeah, get him back."

Before they met with Don, Dean called the Carpenter Union Hall to verify Don's information. The union official he spoke with had nothing good to say about Don Peterson. "He doesn't follow union rules; he's hard on his men, won't come to meetings and pushes the work too hard."

Dean thought, *"It's strange, that union official didn't criticize Don's honesty, work, or habits, nor did he have anything bad to say about Don personally. From an employer's viewpoint, this is a positive recommendation."*

The next day Knowles called Don, "I'm George Knowles, project superintendent for Aldridge Construction at the Trout River Dam. I spoke with you a week or so ago. We'd like to talk to you again. Would you be able to come out here this afternoon?"

Don answered, "Sure, is two o'clock okay?"

George replied, "We'll see you then."

Don showed up at exactly two o'clock. They shook hands and Dean started the interview. "I see that you live in Northern Kentucky. Won't you have to commute through Cincinnati rush hour traffic?"

Don replied, "I don't have a problem with the commute." Adding, "No matter where the work is it takes one to two hours to get there. Commuting to Trout River is no problem."

Knowles inquired, "Do you have a following? Can you bring some qualified people with you?"

Don answered, "That's a definite reason for hiring me. I have a good bunch of guys; carpenters and laborers, who go where I go. I promise to put together a crew of carpenters and laborers using people I know and trust."

Before the interview ended, Don said, "You should be aware, there is a big uranium enrichment plant being built in Portsmouth, Ohio that is employing a lot of carpenters and laborers. The thing is they are working weekends and long hours. A lot of the guys I know who are working there are fed up with the long hours; they want a regular five day, forty hour job. We can get good carpenters and laborers right now."

George spoke with Dean, and they agreed to hire Don.

Dean told Knowles, "I have a good feeling about him. It'll be one of our best decisions."

* * *

Don reported for work Wednesday morning June 29, 1970. After he was through the hiring paperwork, he told Knowles, "I'd like to look at the project and then look at the plans and the schedule."

Knowles said, "When you're ready we can talk about how you see your work going and what you'll need to get it done."

About an hour later Don returned to the office trailer ready to talk. Knowles discovered that Don was more action than words. Their first discussion began with Don. He said, "We need a lot of wood and steel concrete forms for the control tower. I don't see anything on the job. I'll have a list by the end of the day."

Don described his plan to Knowles and Dean, "The base of the control tower is very complicated, thick walls, lots of openings and cutouts, and odd slopes and angles. That part will require custom made formwork. The rest of the two hundred foot high tower is straight walls. We'll build that in sections, each ten feet high. The system I recommend utilizes prebuilt plywood and steel panels that will be used over and over for each of the ten-foot-high wall sections."

Don continued to explain the plan. "The outside wall form is similar to the inside form with the exception that outside the wall we will include a work platform and handrail. We also need wood framing for a stairway the full height of the control tower."

Dean promised, "I'll check your design and get a list of the materials needed to Matt in the office. We should have everything we need within two weeks."

Don reminded Dean, "We need the same system for the big walls in the stilling basin."

"Thanks for reminding me," Dean said, "I'll get everything we need."

# CHAPTER 22

Wayne stopped by Aldridge's field office to talk to Dean. They spoke of the schedule and unresolved issues. As he was leaving Wayne said, "Oh, by the way, I'll be gone for a few days. There's been another annoying lawsuit filed in the federal district court. I'll have to go to Cincinnati every day until it's over. This lawsuit is the third action to stop the project. On June 16, 1970, a group headed by a national environmental organization filed this lawsuit. These are the same people who helped to stage the camp-in just two months ago. They are affiliated with the watchdog Nader organization. This group calls themselves "The Friends of Clearfield County against the Trout River Dam Project. I suspect none of the 'friends' live in Clearfield County."

After he had returned to his office, Wayne received a call from Richard Albert general counsel for the Corps. Albert said, "I want to bring you up to date about the pending lawsuit. The complaint was filed June 16 and has been scheduled for a hearing before Judge Hench on July 10, 1970. The Honorable Judge Leroy Hench has been a sitting federal judge for fourteen years. He is a fair but no-nonsense judge."

Albert continued, "We're dismayed that Judge Hench, despite the failure of similar actions, allowed this trial to proceed. However, he did knock down the plaintiff's motion for an injunction. The lack of an injunction allows construction of the outlet works to continue throughout the trial."

"This action is not a feeble attempt to stop the project. The plaintiffs are well funded and organized. They have retained Shelley, Spencer, and Thornton, one of the largest and best law firms in Cincinnati. They also asked for and got a jury trial."

Wayne asked, "How much will this affect me."

Albert answered, "A lot. You are the named government representative. They'll want you to give one or more depositions. You'll have to be at all the hearings, and you'll have to be in court every day of the trial. In addition to that, the plaintiff will bombard you with demands for documents and answers to questions. My office will help you."

\*\*\*

As expected, Wayne gave two depositions. Both times the testimony took about three hours. The questions were repetitive and inane. When he could, Wayne followed Albert's advice and gave yes or no answers. He concentrated on being as vague as possible.

On July 10 the courtroom was crowded. The first spectator Wayne saw was his nemesis, reporter Roger Wilkins. They made brief eye contact, the kind of look duelists make before they pace off ten steps.

Wayne looked about the room. He noted the dissimilarity between the small multi-use courts in Clearfield County and this large two stories high marble and granite edifice. The judge's bench, constructed from polished walnut, was elevated four feet above the floor. Even the jury box was walnut with well spaced cushioned chairs. The courtroom, located on the eighth floor, had space to seat two hundred spectators. A reserved section on the left served the press. Wayne, Albert, and two assistants sat at the defendant's table on the left. Attorney Lloyd Spenser and his two assistants were at the plaintiff's table on the right.

Wayne whispered to Albert, "This room is nearly empty. Why don't they put us in a smaller room?"

Before Albert could answer, the judge entered, the bailiff called the court to order, and announced the name and number of the case. The judge asked if there were any matters that the lawyers needed to bring before the court. He nodded at Spenser. "Do the plaintiffs have anything?"

Spencer immediately rose and said, 'The plaintiffs are filing a motion asking for a directed verdict to stop the project and cut off funding. It is common knowledge that the project serves no useful function, is a waste of taxpayer money, and is causing irreparable harm to the environment."

The judge looked at Albert, "Before I rule do the defendants have anything to say?

Albert responded, "I'll answer the plaintiff's statements in the same order as presented. The useful function of the project is flood control. The project will prevent millions in property damage and possibly save lives. Second, for the same reasons I've already stated the project benefits the taxpayers. Third, the project when finished will revert to a pristine lake and a recreational area free of human habitation."

Albert looked at the judge and said, "The court ruled for the government in two previous trials that relied on the same unsound arguments. He argued, "The plaintiffs have not presented anything new in this frivolous action. Your Honor, the government, demands a directed verdict dismissing all claims by the plaintiffs."

First Judge Hench denied the plaintiffs motion for a directed verdict to cut off funding, ruling, "The plaintiffs have failed to provide factual evidence to support their allegations."

Then Judge Hench ruled, "I also deny the government's motion for a directed verdict on similar grounds. If there is no more business to come before the court, we'll set a trial date. If there are no objections, the trial will begin on August 4, 1970. I've allowed two days for jury selection."

Spenser looked like he was going to object but merely let out a long breath.

***

On August 6 the jury was seated, and the plaintiffs began presenting arguments. Wayne, Albert, and two other government attorneys had been through similar proceedings before. Albert believed they were well prepared to defend and justify the need for building the Trout River Project.

The trial continued throughout the week of August 10. At one point Albert whispered to Wayne, "I have the feeling these people are desperate to stop the project. We need to be alert for surprises and trickery."

On August 13, unknown to anyone, a juror, Amy Ann Vincent, contacted Lloyd Spencer one of the plaintiff's lawyers and a partner in his law firm. She asked him, "How can I help you win this lawsuit and put a stop to this awful dam?"

Spencer exclaimed, "Miss, are you crazy? You can't talk to me. We could both be in trouble with the court. I am shocked and surprised that you would risk charges of jury tampering and perjury to help your agenda."

Amy Ann, a twenty-five-year-old divorced mother of a three-year-old daughter, admitted to Spenser she lied during juror screening. She said, "I lied when I affirmed, 'I have no preconceived feelings nor do I intend to influence the outcome. In fact, I am personally committed to stopping all work on the dam and restoring the work area to an undisturbed condition."

As he reprimanded her Spenser thought, *"We are going to lose this lawsuit. Our case is weak, and the courts have dismissed two other similar actions."*

When Spencer was over his initial surprise at the audacity of the juror, he asked, "What is your Name?"

She answered, "Amy. I won't give you my full name."

Instead of reporting her to the Bailiff and disqualifying her, Attorney Spencer responded, "Don't talk about this to anyone. How can I contact you?" Amy promptly provided Lloyd with her contact information.

Over the weekend at a clandestine meeting in a downtown public park, Attorney Spencer told Amy, "I have a plan whereby you will try to sway the jury to decide against the government, or failing that, attempt to create a hung jury." He quickly explained the plan to her and left.

The trial began its second week on August 17. During breaks in the trial proceedings Amy talked with several other jurors about her opinion. She was hoping to sway the other jurors or, at least, get a feel for the mood within the jury. She planned to inform Lloyd about what the jury might decide.

Unfortunately for Amy, her fervor against the project

was her undoing. Another juror, Martha Goodling, believed that Amy was out of line by questioning other jurors and stating her opinion before the jury had heard all the arguments. Martha asked the bailiff to let the judge know about her suspicions.

Judge Hench was furious that a juror was so blatantly irresponsible. The next morning, before the trial resumed, he ordered Amy and both attorneys to his chambers. In the presence of the attorneys for both sides, the judge questioned Amy about the allegations.

She wouldn't admit to any wrongdoing but was obviously opinionated when she told the judge, "I have made up my mind. It's a free country, and I'm entitled to my opinion." Then she blurted out, "I told Mr. Spencer about my feelings, and he didn't say it was wrong."

The judge, when he regained his composure, asked everyone to leave except attorney Spencer. "Mr. Spencer, have you anything to say that will prevent me from removing you from my courtroom and reporting this incident to the bar association?"

Lloyd Spencer merely acknowledged the judge's imminent action.

Judge Hench had more to say to the attorney. "You must know that when the bar association hears about this ethical violation, you will face suspension, possibly disbarment! Even worse you could be guilty of jury tampering, a federal offense. Get out of this courthouse."

The judge immediately brought all the other attorneys into chambers. He informed them, "There is a tainted juror who has been removed and replaced by one of the alternates.

Mr. Spencer is also unable to continue. The judge very forcibly stated, "This court will not tolerate any further misconduct."

Several weeks later, Spenser resigned from the law firm, pled guilty to jury tampering, was disbarred for five years, received two years probation, and was ordered by Judge Hench to serve five hundred hours of public service. Amy pled guilty and received a year of probation.

Roger Wilkins's second-page article about the incident played at the extreme of biased reporting by casting Amy Ann as a martyr.

The trial continued for three more days. After closing arguments on August 25, the jury began deliberations. They returned one and a half hours later with their verdict. "Your honor the jury finds for the government. Building the Trout River Dam and Lake will continue."

## CHAPTER 23

The third trial was over, and Wayne was trying to get caught up on what transpired while he was gone. He made another visit to Dean's office on the levee above the river.

First Wayne told Dean about the trial. "You should have seen that courtroom. It was two stories high, marble and polished wood everywhere. The room would hold at least two hundred people. The good news is that the government won. We can keep building. The bad news is that the courtroom activity was so boring I could barely stay awake."

Dean said, "It hasn't been boring here. We've been erecting concrete forms and placing rebar for the control tower foundation. I heard Don tell the surveyors that the base of the tower is a complex structural component and how location is critical. We want to make sure all the openings are as they are supposed to be."

Dean decided to tell Wayne about the lack of good workers. "Knowles has probably told you that we've been getting the dregs of the earth from the unions. A month or so ago we hired a carpenter foreman who has helped get qualified and willing workers. His name is Don Petersen. He brought us nine people; seven carpenters, and two laborers. They have made a difference. Don splits his time between the control tower, the outlet conduit, and the stilling basin. We plan to have work going on in all three places. I'd like to keep David Trumbull at the conduit. With him, I'll put another carpenter foreman, five more carpenters and three laborers. The smaller crane and crew will stay with the conduit. They'll need to be working on three conduit sections at a time."

Then, with a friendly smirk, Dean told Wayne, "Knowles is still in charge. But his job is made easier with Don's help. Knowles is directing the excavation crew. They need to wrap up the excavation and concrete fill."

Wayne said, "Thanks, Dean, I need that information for my daily report."

Dean added, "With the excavation crew at full strength we have over forty employees."

\*\*\*

Occasionally Dean made a tour encompassing all the work areas. One day after such a visit he noted to Knowles, "The typical construction crew does not work quietly. Apparently maintaining a good tempo requires a lot of verbal communication. Some of the communication is by two-way radio. They are constantly on the two-way or shouting orders to one or another."

Dean continued with his observation, "The work area is not quiet. In the background there is the roar of the diesel crane and air compressor engines, the hiss from the water blaster, shouted instructions, and the clamor from nearby work areas. I don't know how they can hear well enough to understand the spoken information."

Don entered the office and caught the end of Dean's observations. He volunteered, "The casual observer doesn't hear the conversation among the guys. The stigma that construction workers lack education, and work as they do because of ignorance is false. Some of them have a year or two of college. They work smart and earn a healthy living. The hourly pay and benefits for construction workers are better than most other industries. The primary limit on their income is the seasonal nature of their opportunities."

Other than serious business or planning, Don's praise of fellow workers was the most that the usually reticent general carpenter foreman had ever spoken. Don kept going, "Guys like Duane become indispensable because, in addition to being a good equipment operator, he is a skilled mechanic. Other workers have similar qualities. A few people coordinate all the activity; the rest just seem to know what to do."

Knowles, getting into the conversation added, "During the work day there is lots of job-related information communicated between the workers. There is also talk about news from home, sports, politics, weather, cars, girlfriends, social plans, and problems. Construction workers do have a life away from work, and they talk about it. There are also friendly, but personal jabs such as, "Man where you been? You look like you was rollin in the mud like a pig." Or, "Come on, we've been waitin' a half hour for those clamps. Sometimes they brag about their favorite team, 'hey did you see the Reds crush the Cubs last night'."

Don was really into the personality of the construction workplace as he said, "Important information is passed along about the bar with the prettiest women and cheapest drinks, "Hey, you have to check out Manny's Bar on Route 52. Four to seven o'clock they have twenty-five cent beer and the women are oldies but goodies."

Dean said, "An example of the free spirit of one of our workers that the guys talk about is 'The Legend of Charlie Easley.' Charlie is a thirty-something journeyman carpenter. He is brash, strong, handsome, witty, and a hard worker. His late night escapades at local bars and quick recovery are making the man a legend among our Trout River workers. No matter how late he is out carousing, he is always at work the next morning and puts in a second full day of hard work. In fact, I have personally seen Charlie enter the employee parking lot at three or four a.m., sleep in his car for a few hours until the men get on the job truck and, wearing the same clothes he wore the day before, get on the truck and go to work. His escapades occur once or twice a month."

Dean added, "The sad part of the legend is that on the mornings following a Charlie escapade I always receive a call from Charlie's wife." She'll meekly ask, "Is Charlie there?"

I say, "Yes ma'am."

She asks, "Is he okay?"

I assure her, "Yes he is."

Mrs. Charlie responds, "Thank you."

"No crying or recriminations, she only wants to know if he is at work and is okay. I admit, after a few such calls, I'm curious about the woman. Is she the stay at home type? Does she also stray from their marriage? Are they happy? What about their two kids? Then I think, 'Oh well, I have more pressing concerns.'"

*\*\**

Abe Silverman, the notorious talkative laborer, stuck his head in the office trailer and said to Dean, "Man you know that pump we use with the water blaster to clean concrete surfaces? You know we put that pump in clear water holes in the River. The problem is we are always movin' it to a new place in the river. Every time the pump has to be moved we have to get a crane to leave its work area and lift that ole pump to its new location."

Dean, curious about where this conversation was going said, "Yeah I know about that pump."

"Well," said Abe, "Today when we moved the pump, Jim Washington tole us, 'don't bother with the crane, I can move that pump.'"

Abe, thinking he had a captive audience, elaborated, "Jim is the big guy who brags that he was on the Bengals football team. Well, I'm here to tell you today he made believers out of us. As big as you please he walked down that steep levee embankment and lifted the two hundred pound pump from the river; mud, hoses, and all, and carried it on his back up to the top of the levee where he dumped it at our feet. Now we call him 'Big Jim.'"

\*\*\*

That morning the field office was a busy place. Just as Abe left and went back to work, Tom, Aldridge's quality control engineer, entered the office. He told Dean, "I've been observing the time and intervals that the concrete trucks leave the batch plant. When they load the trucks at the specified intervals, they stamp the batch ticket with the departure time. The project specifications limit the time to deliver and unload each load of concrete to one hour and thirty minutes. If they exceed the time restriction Towelson or another Corps technician will reject the truck and any unloaded concrete."

Dean wondered where this was going but continued to listen. Tom disclosed, "A potential crisis was averted when, acting on a tip, I discovered some of the concrete delivery truck drivers were leaving the batch plant without getting the time recorded on their batch ticket. Then they circumvent the time limit by inserting a fictitious time; falsely giving them added time to deliver the concrete. They usually used the added time to stop for coffee or lunch. Other reports alluded to stops for more clandestine reasons. With help from the plant owner I received assurance that they will record the departure time on all of the delivery tickets."

Dean asked, "How are other testing activities going?"

Tom answered, "The quality control team also checks the slump of the concrete to get an indication of moisture content. Then they prepare numerous six-inch diameter x twelve-inch long concrete test cylinders. Twenty-eight days after the concrete placement the test cylinders are crushed to assure that the concrete has reached the required strength of four thousand five hundred psi, minimum. Inspector Towelson is always present giving his degrading opinion about procedures and test results. We are usually within the specified limits. We always make extra test cylinders to test at thirty-five days if necessary."

Tom said, "While I have your ear you should know about one more concrete issue. An idiosyncrasy with concrete deliveries concerns the load capacity of the streets and roads that the concrete carrying trucks travel to get to the project. Because of load limits on one inescapable road, the nine cubic yard capacity trucks can haul only seven cubic yards. We are placing thirty to more than three hundred cubic yards of concrete almost every day."

Dean said, "Tom we all support you and know how difficult it must be dealing with Towelson every day. All of the stringent activities, procedures, and specifications make for a fertile field from which he can create havoc, hamper progress, and waste Aldridge's money. The man takes all of my patience and diplomatic skills. Attempting to curb the adverse effect this man is having on our hard work and planning is a never- ending battle. Towelson's devious nature has a significant impact on the work we are doing. He is personally adversely affecting our profit on this project. I'm keeping records of the extra cost his over inspection is costing us."

***

Don had a pep talk with the crew working on the control tower foundation. He told them, "On August 12 we'll be making the first structural concrete placement for the control tower foundation. As you know, this will be the first of hundreds of other concrete placements. This structure requires a lot of custom made formwork. The base that forms the bottom of the tower contains large openings through which the operators can manage the flow of water from the lake into the outlet conduit and, eventually, through the stilling basin back into the Trout River."

Don continued to explain the custom work for the tower base, "When we complete the tower, water will flow through the tower base and through two openings six feet wide by fourteen feet high. As the water passes through each opening, it will be controlled by like sized hydraulically controlled gates. In parallel with the front openings, there are two identical secondary openings for backup in the unlikely event that the front gates fail. These openings have to be perfectly formed and finished. Don't guess, check and double check your measurements."

Don, as usual, cautioned the surveyors, "Proper placement of the frames for the water control gates is critical. Make damn sure they are plumb and properly aligned."

\*\*\*

David joined the discussion with Dean, George, and Don. George Knowles emphasized, "To keep all areas of the work proceeding simultaneously three crews are needed, one for each location; control tower, outlet conduit, and stilling basin. Though the crews are dedicated to working in their assigned area, the assignments are flexible. Workers can and should be moved from one area to another as needed."

Don cautioned, "All the work is hard and dangerous. The stilling basin walls are twenty to thirty feet high, and the concrete forms are large and cumbersome. A crane is utilized to handle them."

Don added to his concern, "The higher the tower gets, the more dangerous it will become. Removing the large preassembled wood and steel form panels is difficult and hazardous. When the crane begins to gently lift the form a worker has to lean over the wall and pry the panel free from the concrete wall. You guys have to stand clear as the form panel swings free. I don't want anyone riding the form panel. To do so is a free ride to the unemployment line. As the tower reaches heights of forty, fifty, sixty feet, and on up to the two hundred-twenty feet level, climbing and utilizing proper safety gear requires skills and a monkey-like ability to climb. We'll support every suggestion that makes us safer."

***

Nobody noticed David Trumbull who had joined the group. He said, "May I add my two cents?"

Dean was pleased that David was there. "Of course, jump right in."

David told the group, "The procedure for the eleven hundred foot long outlet conduit is the same as for all the work. Excavate to at least one foot below the bottom of the foundation or to solid rock, whichever is greater, and place concrete fill to the lower elevation of the foundation. In one area, to achieve solid rock, we had to excavate to thirteen feet below the foundation. Despite Towelson's efforts to hinder everything that we do, we are making real progress."

Suddenly From outside the office, there was a loud whoosh and thump. David's two-way radio crackled and a voice yelled, "Massa David git down here now!"

# CHAPTER 24

David ran from the office talking into the radio, "Where are you? What happened?"

A breathless voice answered, "Middle of the conduit excavation. A tree fell and hit Bernie. He's hurt!"

Two minutes later David could see that a tree that had been standing on the steep hillside above the excavation for the conduit had slid, still standing, into the outlet conduit work area.

The laborer who narrowly missed injury told David, "The tree and its root system smashed into Bernie. It spun Bernie around, knocked him down and the tree trunk fell on top of him."

David kneeling beside Bernie could tell that the man was severely injured and unconscious. David, using his two-way radio, called Dean in the field office and shouted, "Call the Clearfield County emergency team. Hurry, we have a worker down in the conduit area!" He ordered another worker, "Go to the equipment shed and get the chainsaw."

The whole time David was observing Bernie and getting a sense of the extent of his injuries. Finally, he saw a slight movement of Bernie's legs and some eye flutter. David warned Bernie, "Don't move; we have help on the way. But first, we are going to get this tree off of you."

When they had Bernie comfortable, one of the nearby workers yelled, "Look out, here comes another tree!" David glanced over his shoulder and saw that another tree, standing erect, was sliding down the hill toward the conduit trench. The tree hit the top lip of the trench and toppled harmlessly into the excavated area.

David turned to the others and said, "Everyone who is not needed, get out of this area, now!" Pointing to one of the men he ordered, "You, stand watch until we can all get out of here."

After he could see that the second tree was not a danger, David returned his attention to Bernie. He was glad to see him regain conscious and become responsive. David again told Bernie, "Lie still; we're going to remove the tree that is lying across your body."

David yelled to a nearby worker, "Tell that crane operator to move his crane up here, near the injured worker." The crane operator responded quickly and moved to the designated position on the levee above the accident area. The operator saw David hand signal to lower the hook near where the tree rested on McBride. He did so, and they wrapped a web sling around the tree trunk. The crane operator carefully lifted the tree from Bernie's torso.

David muttered to himself, "This will be the first test of the emergency response protocol." He told a worker who was standing nearby, "Go to the top of the hill and wait for the ambulance. Stop them. Don't let them come down the hill. We'll bring Bernie up. And tell that truck driver to get his ass right back down here." The worker jumped in the truck and was taken up the access road to the top of the hill.

After Bernie was free of the tree, the truck driver and rescue team arrived. The rescue leader told David, "The rest of the rescue team with the ambulance stayed on top. This man has serious injuries. We'll carefully lift and place him in a rescue basket. When we have him secured, using that crane, we'll lift him out of the excavation and lower him into the bed of the pickup truck." The rescuer anxiously added, "Then he'll be transported up to the ambulance and taken to the Clearfield County Medical Center."

The three laborers working with Bernie had narrowly missed getting hit.

The same day Bernie was injured, August 4, 1970, Dean, Wayne, and others examined the fallen trees and their root system.

George Knowles observed, "A lot of rain fell this week saturating the ground above the work area. Look at the lack of a root system on the two trees. If these trees do not have adequate roots, neither do any of the others standing above the conduit area. The hillside is so rocky trees can't establish root systems sufficient to hold them in place. We're going to see a lot more trees slide down that hill."

Dean added, "We'll keep everybody out of the work area pending an investigation as to what is causing the trees to break free." He looked at David and said, "Get barricades and warning tape around the entire slide area. We don't want anyone in there."

Dean and Wayne met to discuss the situation. Before the discussion ended, Wayne told Dean, "This is a contractor safety issue. You should make the slide area safe and have a plan to correct the problem before anyone can reenter."

Dean curtly pointed out to Wayne, "The contract stipulates that the trees on the hillside are to remain. In fact, there are specific notes on the contract drawings that forbid us from removing any of those trees. Don't play with safety concerns to avoid having to admit to a flaw in the contract documents. Tell us what the government wants us to do."

Dean believed he and Wayne had a detached but good working relationship. His concern was that this fallen tree incident would strain the already fragile relationship.

The next morning, as soon as Wayne arrived; Dean, after fretting about the tree situation all night, confronted him. "We had a worker survive a near fatal injury caused by a tree unexpectedly crashing into the conduit work area. According to the contract documents, we are not permitted to remove any of those trees."

Dean became more annoyed, "You have control of this site Your engineers and geologists should have known what will happen when we cut the bottom of that hill away to excavate for the outlet conduit. We need directions on how to proceed. There has to be a change in the contract to allow us to remove more trees."

Wayne interrupted Dean's outburst, "Calm down Dean, let's talk about this."

No one had ever seen Dean lose his temper. Until now, he had been thought to be easy going and calm. Dean's outrage was a result of the dangerous situation and the Corp's attempt to shift responsibility to Aldridge. Wayne's staff that, upon hearing the disturbance, had emerged from their cubicles began to recede as the tension eased.

Dean and Wayne argued back and forth for thirty minutes. Finally, Dean said, "I see you're not accepting responsibility for what happened. I can't proceed without instructions telling us how to stabilize the area. We'll proceed with all other work, but we won't work in the slide area until it is safe."

Dean told Wayne, "I'll have a letter to you by noon tomorrow documenting what happened and the fact that the area is unsafe for workers to enter. In the letter, I will ask for directions telling us how the government wants to correct the problem."

The next day Dean went to Wayne's Office and said, "I took photographs of the slide area and documented the events leading up to the incident. As promised, here is a factual narrative about the situation, including our evaluation that the incident resulted from an 'Unknown Condition', as described in the contract documents."

Dean continued his explanation, "To do any work to correct the problem we require written instructions from the Corps. We followed the contract requirements and notified you in writing that the incident resulted from an unknown condition. When they can be determined, Aldridge expects to be paid for expenses and lost time. The contract requires the government to pay the contractor for added work and delay." The next day Dean reminded Wayne, "We still need instructions as to how the Corps wants to proceed."

Knowles told Dean and Don, "The past two days should be called the invasion of the zombie trees. Approximately thirty more mature trees have broken free and slid down the hill, standing upright, before crashing into the conduit work area." Don noted, "Thankfully all work has stopped in the conduit until instructed by the Corps of Engineers how they want us to proceed. There is a big mess to clean up."

Dean needed to get out of his office. He went to the testing lab building where Tom was working on some recent test reports. Dean said, "I don't get up here very often. I hope you don't think I am avoiding you. Has our recent clash with Towelson changed anything?"

Tom replied, "No he's still the commensurate asshole, complaining about every little thing. At least he was forced to back down on the aggregate sampling."

Dean said, "I need to talk to a fresh mind about the sliding tree problem. The Corps continues to deny responsibility claiming this is simply a risk that the contractor must resolve. The recent additional tree movement added credence to our assertion that an unknown condition caused the tree slide. Wayne disagrees that the tree invasion is extra work."

Dean pressed on, "From my point of view, the contract documents make it clear that we are not to remove the trees in the area of the slide. But, hey, thanks for listening. Let me know if you have anything to add to the argument."

There were two more days of ongoing arguments. On Monday, August 10, Wayne instructed Dean, "To mitigate additional delays, Aldridge workers are permitted to remove trees from the affected slide area. You may clear the hillside of remaining trees that pose a threat, and you can remove and dispose of felled trees. I'll confirm this in writing by the end of the day."

Dean bluntly asked, "Wayne are you giving us verbal authorization to perform additional work? As you know, this incident has already caused the loss of five work days." Wayne answered, "In no way am I authorizing payment for added work and time. The government is merely giving you what you asked for; permission to remove enough trees to make a safe work area."

Dean, although furious at this deemed slap in the face, allowed his diplomatic skills to take over. "Alright, we'll do as instructed. But we are notifying you that we will expect payment and an extension of the contract time commensurate with expenses and actual days of delay."

Wayne responded, "You can do that, and we'll consider it. There is no guarantee we'll approve your claim."

Dean laughed and said, "So it's now a claim! I promise I'll pursue this to hell and back."

Actual tree removal started August 11 and finished August 13, 1970. Work in the conduit area resumed on August 14.

Dean, planning to get Tom more involved, discussed the mechanics of filing a claim against the government with him. He explained to Tom, "Before submitting a claim the Contract, in the General Conditions section, states that we must meet specific requirements before the government will consider a claim for added money and time. First and foremost is timeliness. Then you need documentation of the conditions before, after, and during the situation that caused the claim."

Dean said, closing out the explanation, "We have finished the tree removal and clean up of felled trees. Yesterday I gave the resident engineer documentation and photos along with detailed expenses, backed by time sheets and invoices, for fifty-seven thousand dollars and nine days extension of the contract time."

Dean added, "My guess is it will take six months of on and off negotiations, audits of the claim, job site meetings, and discussions before the district office will finally agree to discuss, as they put it, the claim.

As Dean predicted, six months later, on February 10, 1971, negotiation on the tree claim finally occurred at a meeting in the Louisville district office. Dean, alone, carrying all the pertinent documents, entered a thirty-foot long oak-paneled conference room. He noted the room contained a rectangular dark wood table, fourteen leather arm chairs; one chair at each end and six on each side. There were people in seven of the chairs. One chair at the far end of the table immediately caught Dean's attention. Below a large painting of an unknown general sat Lieutenant Colonel Chad Ramsey, deputy director, of the US Army Corps of Engineers, Louisville District. He was in full uniform with all the area of operation bars prominently displayed near his left shoulder.

Awed by the presence of the deputy director Dean managed to say, "Good morning."

Dean sat where indicated and everyone introduced themselves. Dean was aware engineers and procurement representatives were present. Adding to Dean's apprehension was the presence of a U.S. attorney. Dean thought, *"If intimidation is their goal, they succeeded."*

The meeting started, as scheduled, at nine o'clock. Dean had traveled three hours and had been up since five o'clock a.m. He felt exhausted before the meeting even started.

Dean planned to present his case, get it approved, and be on the way back to Ohio by ten O'clock. To his dismay the discussion covered every minute detail; time frames, alternatives, and contract compliance. Dean was overwhelmed. Finally, at ten o'clock they took a break.

Dean was standing outside the room and a person who was attending the meeting but who, Dean noted, did not participate in the discussion came up to Dean and bluntly informed him, "You are talking to the wrong person in there."

It took a moment for Dean to acknowledge the man before he replied, "I don't know what you mean."

"I mean," said the man, "You are directing your comments to the deputy director, you should be talking to the guy on my right. He will make the decision and, believe it or not, he agrees with you. With a little give and take your claim will be approved."

Sure enough, only a half hour later, the Corps legal representative agreed to a slightly reduced amount and everyone went their separate way.

The next day Dean told Wayne about the experience including the name of the decision maker. Wayne chuckled and told Dean, "The guy you negotiated the settlement with, Richard Albert, is a government Attorney; he is head of the district's legal department."

Sometime later Dean complained to Tom, "As I predicted the tree slide took at least six months to finalize. We just received the necessary paperwork and change-order so we can get paid."

Months later, Wayne asked Dean, "Whatever happened to the guy who got hit by the tree?"

Dean answered, "He made a full recovery. His healing and rehab took four months. He eventually returned to work, but with another company."

## CHAPTER 25

Before work started on August 13, 1970, Knowles stopped to talk to David and told him, "We've lost nine days because of the damned tree thing. Now that the area is safe we need to expedite the excavation and concrete fill. I know we can't make up the lost time, but we need to think about the weather. If we can get the entire eleven hundred feet length of the conduit excavated and place the concrete fill before winter, it will expedite building the outlet conduit."

David replied, "Okay boss we'll hit it hard."

After talking with David, Knowles cornered Don, "We've got to plan how we're going to form and place the concrete for the conduit."

While Knowles and Don were talking, a helicopter landed on the access road/levee behind the field office. To everyone's surprise, Herbert Flaherty, Dean's boss and head of the division, emerged from the noisy machine and approached the field office. He heard Knowles talking with Don and said, "Good morning, I don't want to interrupt your conversation. When you're done talking, I have some information that is pertinent to your discussion about the conduit."

Everyone welcomed Herb. He said, "This is my first visit to this project, but I came across some information that concerns the conduit formwork. I think it's worth our time to go over pictures from a similar project that an acquaintance of mine built two years ago. Herb explained, "Their outlet conduit is different in size, but the design appears to be the same."

After making sure he had everyone's attention, Herb continued, "The concrete form system shown in the pictures consists of steel inside surfaces that, after seven days, you can collapse enough to remove by rolling it on integral wheels to the next section of conduit."

Don asked, "What about the outside forms?"

Herb answered, "The outside, fabricated from steel, uses the same method as the inside. It looks like an upside down 'U.' After the concrete has cured the crane will lift and move it to the next location."

Herb ended by showing some pictures, "The beauty of this is that my friend will give us the design and drawings of his system. All we need to do is change the dimensions by marking up the shop drawings, send them to some fabricators for prices and, if we get a good price, order the number of sets we need."

After a short discussion, they all agreed the system described by Herb was the way to go.

Don told the group, "To meet the schedule we'll need to purchase three sets of the reusable steel forms for the outlet conduit. Forty-four individual concrete placements will be required to build the eleven hundred foot long outlet conduit. We'll use each set of conduit forms about fifteen times."

Dean estimated, "It will take eighteen months starting now through February 1972 to build the outlet conduit."

Don cautioned Dave, "Even though the conduit forms are fabricated steel you still have to be careful and not place the concrete so fast that you snap the steel ties holding everything together.

Dave's sarcastic retort, "You guys are always bitchin' about us not getting done fast enough, and labor costs are too high. But then you tell us to slow down. I don't get it!"

By mid-October 1970 work was about fifteen percent complete, and they were making progress. Work on the project was taking on a productive rhythm.

\*\*\*

Herb stayed and listened to the discussions. Before he left and the others had gone from the field office, he told Dean, "I have a sensitive subject to go over with you. Is there a Corps inspector named Towelson on this project?"

Dean answered, "There sure is. He's a real pain in the ass. He has cost us a lot of money. He deliberately slows the work by forcing us to do unnecessary work. He interprets the specifications and contract requirements in the most outlandish ways. We caught him falsifying concrete material test reports. He should have been fired for that alone. For some misguided reason, the Corps keeps him here and allows him to control the pace of the work."

Herb said, "I think I know the reason for his behavior. My friend, Herman McGraw; the guy who gave us the conduit formwork design, warned me about a person named Towelson. Towleson was the chief inspector on a project in Indiana that McGraw's company is just now finishing. McGraw described him the same as you did."

Herb continued, "Some time ago they dug into his past and found he had worked for a large Ohio contractor. For some unknown reason, they fired him. After the company had fired him, Towelson tried to get a job with his former employer's main competitor. Here's where the story gets worse."

"They didn't hire him. Instead, the competitor who was angry at McGraw for winning the contract to build the dam made a deal with Towelson." He asked Towelson to, however he could; get a job with McGraw at the dam.

"McGraw didn't hire Towelson. But Towelson did the next best thing; he got hired by the Corps. Lo, and behold he ended up as an inspector On McGraw's Ohio dam project. Through a mutual friend, McGraw found out that the losing contractor, after he learned that Towelson was an inspector on McGraw's job, contacted Towelson and asked him to harass my friend's company and make them sorry they got the project. Towelson agreed but wanted paid to do the surreptitious work. The other contractor is still paying him!"

Dean said, "I'll admit the guy does have good qualifications. He graduated from the University of Dayton with high grades and a degree in civil engineering. I'm shocked. I can't believe Towelson would do what your friend is accusing him of doing. How should we deal with the situation?"

Herb replied, "I've given this a lot of thought. I think we should keep this to ourselves. It could become our word against his word sort of thing. But we should stay vigilant. Even if you have to hire another engineer you've got to keep track of his every move and the cost in money and time."

Dean promised, "Now that I know I will be even more aware of what the bastard is doing to us." As an afterthought, Dean said, "No matter what, I agree this should remain confidential between you and me. We're just beginning to make real progress."

But as Dean later admitted, good times were not to be.

# CHAPTER 26

During the sit-in at the start of the project in April 1970, Dean met Larry Poole, one of the protesters. Late one Friday afternoon on a bright, hot and humid day in August 1970 Larry entered the field office unannounced. He had walked in from Carney Road.

Dean didn't immediately recognize him and assumed he was somebody looking for a job. Dean asked him, "Can I help you?"

Larry Replied, "We talked back in May, you invited me to visit you. Here I am."

Dean recognized him and remembered the conversation. "Yeah, now I remember. Come in and have a seat."

Dean explained, "Because it is Friday and the end of the work day the foremen are coming into the office to record hours worked for every employee in their crew. They also have to assign the hours worked to the correct labor cost account. Give me fifteen minutes to get this out of the way."

Finally, he told Larry, "Sorry to keep you waiting but Fridays are hectic. I have to get everything done before I catch my flight to go home for the weekend."

Larry replied, "Maybe this is not the right time for my visit."

BEHIND THE DAM

Dean said, "Oh, don't worry, I've got time. Yeah, I remember you were involved in the April camp-in. We probably have differing political philosophies."

Larry responded, "I'm not a radical on any issue. I am non-violent. I don't believe some of the drivel spewed by the hardcore protesters. I do believe in the environment and the fact that we need to protect it."

Dean formed a favorable opinion of Larry. He said, "In spite of potentially diverse political thinking it sounds like we agree on the environment,"

Larry observed, "I notice the piles of work on your desk, yet you have to take time doing what should be done by a timekeeper or assistant." They talked some more about the administrative and time keeping situation.

Dean said, "Yeah, I have a situation that is driving me crazy. We have twenty-four employees, and we're hiring more almost every day. I remember you told me you're not working. Have you found a job?"

Larry answered, "No. I've done some work at the university, and I've been doing a little work as an intern at the newspaper. But I can type, and I'm a good organizer."

Dean said, "Larry I don't know why I asked, but your interest in easing my burden is the reason I inquired about your work status. I'll be direct, are you interested in coming to work out here? It's a seven in the morning to three-thirty in the afternoon position with a half-hour for lunch. You will have some fringe benefits, terrible working conditions, and a relatively long drive from Mt. Adams. You will also be the project gofer." He added, "The job pays $4.25 per hour. The minimum hourly wage is $1.60 per hour. $4.25 is a good starting pay."

"The offer is attractive," Larry said, but asked, "May I have until Monday to talk to my girlfriend and think it over?"

Dean said, "Okay, I look forward to hearing from you."

On Monday Larry called Dean, "I accept your offer. I'll be there at seven o'clock tomorrow morning."

Several weeks later Knowles observed to Dean, "You and Larry are a good team. The foremen like Larry and rely on him to help them get their time sheets done correctly."

Dean added, "And he answers the phone, keeps the office clean, assists visitors, gets supplies, types, and files correspondence."

George noted, "Because we're out here in the middle of nowhere there are no nearby hardware stores or other dependable sources of supplies. We have to rely on Larry and the job truck driver when anyone needs a hard to find part or building material. Those guys are becoming indispensable."

George told Dean, "Do you know that the truck driver, Elmer Haney, is over sixty years old? In spite of his age, Elmer bobs around like a man half his age. As a local man, he knows every nook and cranny of Clearfield County. In addition to his duties to get people in and out of the work area, Elmer takes on many other self-assigned jobs. He can find hard to get items, new or used. Haney turns away unwanted visitors, does odd jobs, keeps watch at Wayne's house and family, and sells vegetables and other items from the back of his truck. We're lucky to have him. One of his best attributes is that he knows people outside the project who can provide services. We affectionately call him Mr. Haney, the character from the 1960 TV series, Greenacres."

One day in late September Dean told Larry, "Sometimes after work, when the weather is nice, a few of us gather by the river to cook hot dogs over an open fire and drink a beer or two. You're welcome to join us."

A week later on a beautiful fall afternoon, Larry carrying a gallon jug of amber colored liquid asked, "May I join you?"

Duane answered, "Of course, what's in the bottle?"

Larry rather smugly replied, "This is some of the finest nectar know to man. I've brought some Boone's Farm Apple Wine. It should be a part of every cookout. And at about two bucks a gallon, it's affordable."

## CHAPTER 27

After work on Wednesday evening, October 21, 1970, Dean told the guys living in the modular home, "I know it's cold and raining, but this is hump night, the middle of the week. Tonight we're going to break out of this place and enjoy some good food and drink."

Everyone agreed, including Duane who decided to stay overnight instead of going home. He said, "Let's go to Hixon's Restaurant, they always welcome us and, according to Charley Easley, the Hixon's have three daughters who are good pool players."

After eating, drinking, and playing a little pool with the girls, Dean gathered the group and said, "It's ten o'clock, time to head home."

The other three members of the party, Roy Brothers, Danny Barr, and Ted Dominic all complained but wrapped up their game of pool and left with Dean and Duane.

On the way back from dinner Dean exclaimed, "Wow, look at all the water on the road and in the low areas! There must have been a helluva rain storm while we were in the restaurant."

About that same time a news bulletin came on the radio. A news announcer sounding full of himself said, "Three inches of rain fell on Hamilton and surrounding counties in just two hours. Flood warnings are out for everyone living in low-lying areas."

It was after ten o'clock when they returned to the modular home. Duane asked Dean, "Do you think we should go down to make sure the job is okay?"

Dean replied, "I sure do!"

Everyone put on work clothes and went to the parking area to get the four wheel drive job truck. As they left the abode, Dean said, "Shit, Elmer the truck driver took the pickup home."

Ted, who had the most to drink, saved the day when he exclaimed, or rather slurred, "My truck has four-wheel-drive. We can use it."

Duane warned him, "Ted you didn't work today and you've been drinking. You had a few more at dinner. You're in no condition to navigate the hill."

Ted, also in no condition to argue said, "What the hell. Duane, you drive, and the rest of us will just pile in, two in the cab and three in the truck bed."

Duane was the first to notice the aftermath of the storm. He told Dean who was seated on the passenger side, "The access road is in bad condition. A lot of it is gone, washed away. We're going to be very careful. I'll go as far as I can."

Then Dean noticed, "There are several downed trees that are blocking the road. We need a chainsaw."

Ted, who was barely cognizant and whose slurred speech was apparent, once again saved the day, "I have a chainsaw in my tool box."

When they reached the bottom of the hill and entered the work site, Dean observed to the other three (Ted was asleep),

"It took us an hour to reach the work area. Look around; there is water everywhere. The river has breached the levee and is flowing fifteen to twenty feet deep through the entire area excavated for building the control tower, the conduit, and the stilling basin. Anything that floats is being carried away."

Duane said, "Anything that doesn't float is submerged. I'm going to start the crane. Danny and I will try to salvage any partially submerged equipment or supplies. Danny can ride the ball above the lifting hook. I'll swing him out over the water to where he can latch the hook onto and recover salvageable equipment."

Once, to make sure Danny was paying attention, Duane jokingly yelled, "Danny, do what I tell you or I'll dunk your ass!"

Dean said to Roy Brothers, "You and I need to grab anything that floats and pull it from the water; plywood, lumber, boxes, and tarps."

Later after an exhausting four hours, Dean told the team, "You guys worked your asses off. Thanks to you we recovered everything possible. It's about three a.m.; we're worn out. Let's go back to the abode. We still have a full day ahead of us. I noticed Ted slept in his truck during the entire recovery operation."

The next morning Dean reported to Wayne, "The River has receded leaving a lake on the work side of the levee. What was meant to keep the river out is now keeping the water in, it's created a basin-like containment. All the work completed to date is submerged. It'll take days to pump the water out, dig out mud and sediment, and repair damage to the levee. It will take another two weeks to restore the work area. We estimate activities can resume in all the work areas by the second week in November. After this, we aren't looking forward to the coming winter. Our primary concern right now is rebuilding the access road."

# CHAPTER 28

Ordinary winters in Southern Ohio were slightly milder than winters in Northern Ohio. The winter of '70 – '71 was an exception. It began early and lasted late. The Trout River Dam project required placing massive amounts of concrete. The Corps' specifications and good concrete practice required the temperature of newly placed concrete to be kept above forty degrees Fahrenheit and protected from ice and snow for at least twenty-eight days.

Dean told Knowles, Don, and David, "It's October and time to prepare for winter. We'll order everything we need from the yard, get it here, and be ready. Winters here are about like what we have in St. Louis. There should be no surprises."

Knowles said, "We need tarps, plastic sheeting, insulated plastic blankets, propane heaters, thermometers, and lumber for building enclosures. That stuff is available through the yard. I've already ordered a one thousand gallon propane storage tank. It will be delivered tomorrow, set in place, and filled."

Dean told Knowles and Don, "You guys work together and get the order into the yard today. They'll be bombarded with calls from other jobs asking for the same stuff we need."

Don, speaking to Knowles, said, "Safety is a concern for all areas but particularly in the control tower. Work areas become treacherous when ice and snow build up on the stair and work platform surfaces. The higher the tower gets, the higher each worker has to climb to get to the work. During winter, the high work areas are buffeted by bitter winds. We'll just have to work smart."

David added, "We'll work through the winter on the conduit and stilling basin. Don and I are both aware how tough the winter is for our employees. Productivity will suffer as they contend with cold, rain, ice, and mud. We expect the worsening weather situation to be used by Towelson in his gleeful and merciless condemnation of our effort to follow the contract requirements. He takes on a godlike attitude, 'I can do no wrong – you can't get anything right.'"

\*\*\*

One late fall day when Dean and George Knowles were in the field office, Dean asked, "George, do you ever wonder what a typical day is like for someone employed at this project?"

George answered, "Yes I have, and they put in a long day just to earn eight hours pay. For most of our employees, their day begins at five a.m. Then there is a hectic one to two-hour drive through commuter traffic in Cincinnati. They arrive at the job by six forty-five am. They have to be in the work area, not the parking lot, at the starting time of seven a.m."

Continuing George said, "They climb aboard the open job truck, clean snow, frost or rainwater from the wooden seats, and get jostled down the access road to the work area. Then they trudge through mud, ice, or dust to their assigned work area. They work all day in all kinds of weather and spend one or two hours in rush hour traffic going home. I bet when they finally get home, usually after five o'clock, they're ready for dinner and bed."

"Like most employers, sometimes we fail to acknowledge a job well done," Dean said. "I'll try to be more visible and talk with everybody. They need to know we care."

Dean had an afterthought, "George you know what? When we finish this project, and there's a beautiful dam and lake for the public to enjoy, the people who will enjoy this place will not give a thought to the sacrifices made by the people who are here today."

"It's good that you appreciate the people who work here," George agreed, "But they know they are leaving behind something to be proud of even if the powers that be take all the credit."

David Trumbull added to the conversation, "Even the necessities make you uncomfortable. You haven't lived until you have to use the porta-potty when the temperature is twenty degrees." He added, "It's even worse at ninety degrees."

\*\*\*

David observed to George, "As expected, inspector Towelson is interpreting the specifications for winter concrete in a most strict and demanding way. He uses weather related working conditions and difficulties to increase the intensity of his harassment."

"We follow the contract requirements to protect the concrete and keep it above forty degrees. Complying with this specification requires a source of heat and enclosures to keep the heat from escaping. Whether the temperature is sixty or twenty degrees Towelson demands that we protect all concrete placed between now and spring with insulated blankets, enclosures, and a heat source."

David continued his complaint, "Our workers regard the winter protection procedures as normal and expected. What they do not expect is the intensity and meddling coming from the inspection team, especially Towelson."

\*\*\*

One winter evening as the modular home residents were relaxing, Danny Carr reminded Dean, "Tonight it's your turn to check the heat on the conduit segments."

Dean responded, "You don't need to remind me. I'll be going down there about one o'clock."

The next morning as the group was eating breakfast Dean told them, "Last night when I flipped the insulating blanket back on one of the conduit segments to check the propane heater a black wooly creature jumped from the closure. You know there are rumors of black bears being in the area. So when this creature sprang from the enclosure black bear was the first thing that came to my mind. I fell on my ass fearing for my life. What jumped from the enclosure was that friendly black dog that has adopted the work site as his home. The guys have named the dog S.O.B."

Danny asked why S.O.B.?

Dean answered, "The dog is always following and annoying George. He has been heard to yell at the dog, "Get out of my way you S.O.B.!"

The other four guys laughed and chided Dean for his near death experience.

Dean, somewhat chagrined, said, "It appears I've made a mistake by telling my story. I suppose when things get dull I'll be reminded of the dog/bear story and my reaction to the imaginary bear. You don't need to remind me that real bears hibernate in the winter."

\*\*\*

Dean wrote in the daily report for December 21, 1970, "Today a heavy winter rain occurred resulting in two inches in two hours. This time the crews were better prepared than when the heavy rainfall occurred in October. The river still prevailed and rose enough that some water breached the levee causing a small flood in the work area. The crews worked all night and through today to pump the water out and clean debris from the work area. There are photos filed with this report."

In his report on December 23, Dean recorded, "Because the adverse weather is predicted to continue I shut the job down for the holiday season. Work will resume on January 4, 1971. The last work day in December was Wednesday the 22nd. I invited everyone to come to the modular home on Thursday morning after 10:00 a.m. to pick up their paychecks. The midmorning time allowed time for UPS to deliver the paychecks from St. Louis. I also decided to provide refreshments for everyone."

Thursday morning after everyone but Don had left. Dean told him, "Everybody was interested in examining the inside of the home. One guy, Big Jim Washington, after examining every room asked me, "Do any women live here?"

I answered, "No."

Big Jim replied, "Do you want some?"

Of course, I told him, "No, but thanks for asking. Apparently, Big Jim doesn't envision life without women even when you have one you love back home."

\*\*\*

As the season edged toward spring 1971, Dean and Wayne were having a rare non-confrontational weather related conversation. Wayne noted, "The end of winter and onset of spring brings a combination of many different types of weather. Some days the temperature is sixty degrees, other days it is ten degrees. I bet that drives you crazy."

Dean replied, "Working conditions vary from solid frozen ground to wet soggy mud. There are times when it rains one day, snows the next day, and the sun shines the following day. Everybody has learned to tolerate the weather extremes. Surprisingly there is very little absenteeism despite the weather."

Dean added, "We are progressing despite the season and all the variations of weather. This winter we built nine complete twenty-five foot long conduit segments. By April a total of seventeen of the required forty-four segments will be complete."

## CHAPTER 29

In the spring of 1971, the pace of work on the outlet works was picking up. So was the intensity of property acquisitions.

Wayne received a call from Richard Albert, "I want to let you know that we are filing eminent domain actions to take the last eight properties. On May 11 a notice will be served on each of the holdouts giving them thirty days to sell before the government invokes the right of eminent domain to acquire their properties."

The move didn't surprise Wayne. But he had a personal concern about one of the un-acquired working farms belonging to Willard and Annette Norton. The Norton's grandson, Wesley, and Wayne's son JD had become close friends. To further complicate matters the Norton's son Raymond and his wife were friends of Wayne and Melissa.

Wayne told Albert, "I feel sorry for those people. Melissa and I personally know one of the affected families, Raymond and Carole Norton. Ray's father owns the farm but he is in poor health and Raymond runs the business. They are good hard working people. They'll be devastated."

Wayne added, "Their two-hundred-forty-acre farm is a thriving family business, one of the best family-owned farms in Ohio. Willard and Raymond Norton are respected and admired by the farming community throughout Ohio and Indiana."

Albert replied, "The government had been trying to acquire the Norton farm since May of 1969 when government procurement agents made the first offer. I understand why the Norton family does not want to give up their farm and start over. But we don't have a choice; we have to acquire the land. As far as I know, they have refused every attempt to buy them out."

After the call from attorney Albert, Wayne called Raymond Norton. "Hi Ray this is Wayne Henderson, JD's dad."

Raymond answered, "Hey Wayne, good to hear from you. What's up?"

Wayne explained about his call from Albert, "I received a call from one of the government attorneys who told me they are starting condemnation or eminent domain action against your dad and seven other holdouts. We're sorry they have to do that. I know your families have worked your whole lives to build the farm into a thriving business."

Ray replied, "Wow, I thought there was still a lot of time to work things out. I'm shocked. I believe they have only talked to us twice. The first visit was in May 1969. That time a guy named Harvey Barnes; an independent, so-called, expert appraiser spent about two hours appraising the land and buildings. He came up with $200,000, an amount that didn't include the value of outbuildings, fencing, other improvements, and crops. His low-ball appraisal reflected the property only as a home and land, not a thriving business. His offer was half the replacement value of our business. The second appraisal, four months later by another government employed appraiser, valued the home and land the same as Barnes. Both appraisals ignore the fact that the farm is a thriving ongoing business. Then a short time after the second appraiser's visit, in November 1969, my dad and I were contacted by the real estate agent who did the initial appraisal, Harvey Barnes. He gave us false hope when he informed us that he believed the original appraisal was low. Barnes dashed my hope for an equitable offer when he told us he made the government increase their offer to $210,000 plus $10,000 for expenses. Of course, we didn't accept the government's woefully inadequate offer. Barnes appeared to be half drunk. I told him to get the hell off my property."

Wayne said, "Give me some information and history of your farm. I'll talk to Albert. Maybe I can convince him to get the government appraisers to take another look."

Raymond was proud of their farm. He gave Wayne all the information about the Norton farm.

The next day Wayne called attorney Albert. "I need to take some of your time, and I hope you don't think I'm out of line. I have some information about the Norton farm. I want to ask you to have an appraiser take another look at their property." Albert said, "Coming from the resident engineer, that is an unusual request. Give me the information; I'll pass it down to the real estate people. I'll have to leave it to them if they reappraise or not."

Wayne said, "Thanks. The Norton's story is long, but here goes."

"The Norton's farm consists of two hundred forty acres, a well-kept home, barn, and many outbuildings. The farm, known as 'Blissful Acres,' also has a four-acre lake. Annette and Willard are second generation farmers. Willard inherited the farm twenty-one years ago from his father, who had farmed it for forty years. Their eldest son Raymond, his wife, and three children live with his parents in the homestead. The home is large and comfortable, with modern amenities."

Wayne continued, "Raymond told me he has researched available farms within a hundred mile radius and obtained comparable pricing for similar properties. The nearest match he could find is seventy-five miles away and priced at $385,000. That property is in need of a lot of costly work. Moving costs for household goods, farm equipment, and livestock will be an additional $25,000. The least amount they need for their farm and business that would, in due time, put them in an equal position is $410,000. Raymond believes the present appraisals value only the house and land and don't include any value for the business or other buildings."

Albert promised, "I'll pass this on to the real estate department. There's no guarantee they'll do anything."

\*\*\*

The Norton family farm business continued unaffected until May 11, 1971. At that time they received the certified letter from the County Court that gave the Norton's thirty days to sell before the government took action to acquire the property by eminent domain.

At the time the eminent domain threat was given, work on the outlet works for the dam was well underway. From some locations on their farm, the Norton's could see the massive concrete control tower rising above the ground. They knew their time was limited.

The pending forced acquisition and relocation process caused Willard, Raymond, and the entire family to feel embittered toward the Corps, the government, and the agencies they represented. During a two-week period in May 1971, Raymond had several unsuccessful and acrimonious confrontations with realtor Harvey Barnes.

When Willard's health worsened, Raymond assumed full responsibility for dealing with the frustrating negotiations with the government. Raymond argued with Barnes, "We can't relocate and replace half of our farm for the amount offered by the government. Can't you do something to help us?"

Barnes merely shook his head and said, "We're being as fair as we can."

Raymond was angry, all six feet and two hundred ten pounds of him. Thanks to hard farm work, he was strong and in good condition. He was intelligent and kind but had a reputation for being a person you do not want to challenge. After one of the confrontations with Barnes, Raymond assured his father, "We're going to fight this every way we can. We can't allow unknowing and uncaring government bureaucrats to destroy our lives."

After the futile conversations with Barnes and the pending eminent domain action, Raymond decided to get assistance from County Commissioner Walgren whom his family had supported during his past election campaigns. Raymond had no way to know that Walgren was the mastermind behind the insider purchase of twenty-one properties before the public knew of the dam's proposed location.

Prior to this Raymond had not met Walgren face to face.

As a public official, Walgren was well known throughout the county. Raymond followed procedures and through the Commissioner's office scheduled a meeting with Walgren; now serving his fourth term. The meeting was scheduled for Thursday, May 20, 1971, at eight-thirty am.

After the commissioner kept Raymond waiting for thirty minutes, he finally admitted him to his office. They exchanged pleasantries for five minutes, and then Raymond was direct with Walgren, "The government is cheating us out of two generations of hard work building a farm business. Our family has worked for sixty-one years to establish one of the finest family owned farms in Ohio. The government appraisers and realtors value only the land and home, but not the business. The loss of our home and business will ruin us. To make matters worse a week ago the government initiated an eminent domain action to force us to sell."

Walgren listened and then lied, "I don't know anything about the government's appraisal or acquisition process."

In fact, Barnes had confided with Halgren just two days earlier telling him, "I am sticking to the low ball offer for the Norton place. When they become desperate, we can slip in there and pluck that property for $300,000 and they'll think they got a good deal. When we get our hands on it, all we have to do is wait about a year. I know I can convince the government to buy the place for $400,000. You and I will split the profits."

During the remaining fifteen minutes of the meeting, Walgren was very evasive and only responded when Raymond asked a direct question.

Raymond sensed Walgren was lying, but he didn't know

why. He left the meeting angry at Walgren for not offering support or offering advice about the family's alternatives. Barnes and Walgren had seriously underestimated Raymond Norton's resolve and determination.

Raymond decided to shake things up and headed for the family attorney, Fred Hubble. Hubble, 60, was a respected local attorney known for his tact in court and patience with his clients. Fred always wore a suit, white shirt, and necktie. Locals joked that he probably wore a tie in the shower.

Hubble advised Raymond, "You should take this situation to Louisville and meet with the head of the real estate procurement department."

Raymond, after considering the advice said, "That's just what I'll do." After a moment Raymond asked, "What can we do about the eminent domain situation?"

Hubble answered, "We'll keep fighting for an honest appraisal. You should be aware that I'm prepared to file an answer to the eminent domain action should the government initiate it. What we will say in our response is that the government is relying on faulty appraisals. We'll ask for the court to address the situation. Let me know what you find out in Louisville."

## CHAPTER 30

Dean, Larry, and George share the field office that is located on the temporary levee about one hundred fifty yards away from the emerging control tower. The field office is accessible by way of the steep access road from Carney Road and the levee road. After traversing the hill and the levee, the field office is accessible to everyone in the work area.

Dean and Larry were engrossed in their daily responsibilities. Dean interrupted Larry and said, "Before you started to work here, this office was disorganized. Contract drawings, specifications, schedules, shop drawings and reports laid about helter-skelter. Everyone thought they knew where to locate the item they need, so we made no attempt at organization."

"Now that you have worked your organizational skills on the place, once again we know where everything is." The compliment continued, "Even though we used to be able to find what we needed now we find the same things in a lot less time."

Dean added "Because the office is more or less inaccessible to outsiders, there is no need to impress anyone. But you have impressed everyone."

\*\*\*

Early Monday morning, April 19, 1971, shortly after work began, a carpenter, Sid Grimm, was assisted to the office complaining of an ankle injury sustained when he climbed the stairs to the control tower work area. He insisted he was able to drive himself to the medical center.

Don radioed Elmer Haney, "There is an injured man at the control tower. He's refusing ambulance service and just wants to go to his car. Come and transport him up to the employee parking lot. From there he'll go to the hospital in his vehicle."

Dean, when he heard what had occurred told Don, "Every accident gets the full attention of project management and the home office. I have to document the occurrence by getting eyewitness reports and photographing the area where the accident is reported to have happened. I also have to file a report with the resident engineer."

As Dean was finishing his report on this accident, David Trumbull entered the office and inquired about what occurred. Dean told him about the accident. David scoffed, "That man's ankle was already injured when he arrived at work this morning. I heard him tell another carpenter he was injured in a neighborhood football game yesterday."

David Continued, "He wants Workers Comp Insurance to pay for treatment of the injury. That way he gets his medical bills paid and he will get paid while he is unable to work!" During the day Dean verified the fake injury story with other workers.

Dean reported the attempt to deceive to the home office. He was told, "Fake injuries are a common occurrence."

Dean said, "I'll leave it in the hands of the personnel department to resolve. But that guy won't be coming back here to work."

***

On June 14, 1971, the second protest camp-in started. Larry did not become involved; in fact, he ignored the protest and the participants. Other than to acknowledge it existed, Larry did not say anything for or against the protest. He told Dean, "They are not the same participants who were in the camp-in back in April 1970."

Dean responded with a friendly dig at Larry, "No, unlike the disruptive 1970 camp-in there is no violence, attempts to stop work or damage equipment."

The only problem the protesters caused was publicity that attracted the media. On several occasions, reporters and newspaper photographers attempted to enter the work areas. Roger Wilkins was reporting activity for the Cincinnati Daily News. Wilkins was a reporter who had been, with his biased and fiery anti-dam reporting, fueling the opposition efforts for four years. Wayne was very familiar with Wilkins and his one-sided reporting.

On June 16 Wayne met with a group of the protesters in front of the Corps field office. Wayne, without explaining the condition of the access road said, "You are free to enter the work site. You cannot drive on the access road; it is accessible only by specially equipped vehicles. The only way you can get to the work area is to walk. You should understand no attempt will be made to help you get down, and you'll receive no help getting back up. You're on your own. It's been raining, and today the project is very muddy, almost impassable."

With his statement made, Wayne left them to their decision. The reporters and others in the group decided not to attempt entry into the project. They wisely realized they were not properly equipped to traverse the steep and treacherous access road. They did not want to get their feet muddy.

To assure peaceful behavior by protesters and media, the Corps of Engineers placed two security guards at the entrance to the project. The camp-in lasted almost three weeks. By June 25 they had left, leaving their mess behind. The county had another cleanup job.

\*\*\*

Dean was able to spend more time planning and scheduling as work on the outlet works was becoming more repetitive He spent several days early in the summer of 1971 talking to foremen and key workers to get their input about the job and how to improve the way they were building the outlet works.

On one such foray into the work areas, Wayne accompanied Dean. As they were standing near the stilling basin, a laborer approached them and said, "I'm Joe Hazelton, the guys call me Hazey." He told them, "We appreciate the safety concerns and the fact that you don't just talk safety, but you are concerned and make us work safely. All of the people working here are making sacrifices. We could be working in town building a cushy shopping center and earning the same wages. The people that are working here like the fact that we're building something worthwhile. Every day brings new challenges and new opportunities to learn. To cap it off, look around, even on a bad day this is a beautiful place!"

Afterward, Wayne told Dean, "Talking with the people working here give me more than insight and opinions. Most of these people have a good attitude and understand their job."

Dean decided this was a good time to remind Wayne of the problems, lost time, and added expenses caused by Towelson's artifice. He bluntly confronted Wayne, "Have you been able to get Brian to back off and just require compliance with the contract?"

Wayne answered, "I've told you before, I try not to tell my inspectors how to do their job, especially Towelson."

Dean replied, "I've talked to him numerous times. I've tried to explain to him that he makes us do way more than required by the specifications. Recently he made us leave the forms on a section of the conduit for almost three weeks because, according to him, the concrete wasn't up to strength. The actual concrete strength tests were well within the specifications in seven days. Many times he has made us over excavate before placing fill concrete, we dig out sound rock and replace it with concrete; at our expense. He pulls shit like this all the time. He's on a mission to bankrupt us!"

Wayne replied, "As I said, I won't tell my inspectors how to do their job."

Dean, by now, very agitated angrily told Wayne, "We're keeping records and documenting every instance of malfeasance by your inspection team, especially Towelson. Nearly a year ago we gave you written notice about the blatant attempts by your team to hamper progress and add to our expenses. They aren't just doing the job they are paid to do; they are making the rules as they go."

Wayne threw his hands in the air. As he left, he said, "I've got a cemetery to relocate. I don't have time for this BS."

Before tackling the cemetery relocation, Wayne called his

boss, Jordan Lipper, to discuss Towelson and his inspection practices. After answering a few questions about the project, Wayne said, "I might have a problem with chief inspector Towelson. I get a lot of complaints that he purposely delays the project, causes expensive rework, and is overzealous in his inspection techniques. Aldridge's project manager has sent numerous notice letters claiming extra work and delays. They're claiming considerable added costs."

Lipper responded, "Come on Wayne. Contractors are always bitching about too much inspection. Those guys are a bunch of cry babies. You can't tell Towelson to back off without it looking like you are in bed with the contractor. Just let him do his job."

Wayne somewhat chagrined, said, "Okay, but I believe that sometimes he goes too far. I'll let you know if anything unusual happens. Thanks for listening."

# CHAPTER 31

As the government lawyers had promised, on Thursday, June 17, 1971, they filed eight separate condemnation proceedings in Clearfield County Court. The action asked the court to evict the Norton and Connor families from their farms and six other dwelling owners, including Olga McCoy.

The eminent domain action by the government upset Barnes and Walgren's plan to scam the Norton family out of their farm. Walgren tried unsuccessfully to have the Norton property removed from the eminent domain action so that he and Barnes could buy the property from under the government. George Daniels, the Corps real estate specialist, noticed this unusual activity. He told Wayne, "A county commissioner attempted to remove the Norton farm from the eminent domain proceedings. That seems odd. I'd sure like to know what is behind that."

Wayne replied, "I know the Norton's, and I know Raymond was in to see one of the commissioners about their situation. Raymond's son Wesley told my son his dad was mad because the commissioner wouldn't help him."

As required by law, the government provided notice and deposited with the court an amount equal to the alleged fair value appraisals.

The government still needed to relocate the recently acquired historic schoolhouse and cemetery. There was no activity concerning these two properties because the Corps real estate office believed there were unique situations and subject to ongoing activities. Neither property was in the construction area.

Raymond believed, in the Norton case, the government erroneously placed an unacceptable value of $220,000 on their property. This low-ball valuation was, coincidentally, the same amount of the fictitious appraisal and the amount that realtor Barnes had offered them.

Raymond Norton told his father, "I'm losing faith in the judicial system and the way in which the federal government uses it. It disgusts me to know that they can take away the results of decades of hard work without our consent. If the government prevails, we will lose tens of thousands of dollars of our assets. We will be unable to restore our livelihood to what it was before the dam. We are facing a desperate situation."

***

The eight defendants named in the eminent domain actions knew they were going to have to give up their property. However they all had legal representation and were determined to fight.

Raymond told attorney Hubble, "We all believe the government offers are just not enough. Except for Olga McCoy, we're not greedy. We only want to receive an amount equal to what we need to purchase and relocate to a similar dwelling or farm. Olga doesn't want to sell at all. Like us, the other six defendants and have at least one independent appraisal that proves the government appraisals are too low." Hubble said, "We will rely on the Fifth Amendment to the U.S. Constitution that requires the government to provide fair value for property taken for the government's use."

Fred Hubble and the other lawyers responded quickly. On Monday, June 21, 1971, they filed a class action answer in County Court, Judge Joseph Givens presiding. Fred Hubble was the spokesman for the group. He stood at the podium to present the defendant's answer. "Your Honor, speaking for the eight condemned properties we respectfully inform the court that the appraisals relied on by the government are faulty. Our clients demand an independent appraisal of their properties by impartial appraisers hired by the court. Furthermore, we demand payment to the defendants, in accordance with federal regulations, for the fair value for each of the eight condemned properties."

Later attorney Hubble told Raymond, "It will be tough to beat the government in this type of case. However, we have a good defense and a very sound appraisal that includes all the property assets. We will show by testimony and physical evidence that the government erred when they unfairly determined the value of your farm and business. My job is to convince the judge of the facts."

During his turn to testify, Raymond Norton told the court, "Our property and business is worth a fair value of $400,000. With our answer to the government's lawsuit, we have provided county records and real estate transactions showing comparable property sales. These documents prove the government appraisers are unfairly undervaluing our property and business. As asked by attorney Hubble, we beg the court to employ disinterested appraisers to independently reappraise our properties."

As recommended by Attorney Hubble, Raymond asked for and received an appointment with The Corps of Engineers, Louisville District, Deputy Commander Lieutenant Colonel Chad Ramsey and the civilian head of the Real Estate Division, Edward Soliare. Ramsey was a dedicated US Army lifer having a twenty-five-year commitment that included deployment to most major areas where U.S. military action had occurred. He was a strict leader who expected every employee, military and civilian, to always give their best. There was no mollycoddling at this district office.

Soliare had been with the Corps for three years. Before that, he was a successful Louisville realtor for twenty-two years. Raymond's appointment was for Tuesday, June 22, 1971, at two o'clock p.m. Of course, Ramsey and Soliare knew of the eminent domain proceedings and the defendant's answer. Soliare asked attorney Albert to attend the meeting.

Raymond entered the meeting confident he could make a difference. He was a successful businessman whose business was farming. As a businessman, Raymond wore a conservative well tailored dark gray suit, white shirt, an appropriate tie, and well shined expensive shoes. He would look good in any boardroom.

Lieutenant Colonel Ramsey, who expected a 'hayseed' farmer, was impressed by Raymond's appearance. He welcomed Raymond and, took a direct approach; he asked him, "What do you expect from this meeting?"

Raymond explained, "The government's haphazard appraisals and low-ball offers do not place a fair value on our

BEHIND THE DAM

farm business. Unknown people and agencies are victimizing us."

Attorney Albert interrupted him stating, "We can't discuss anything related to the ongoing condemnation proceedings."

Raymond acknowledged the restriction placed on their discussion but continued, "We believe the appraisals do not fairly value our farm because, to date, none of them take into account the farms many structures and features and the fact that we are an ongoing family owned business. The cost to relocate and reestablish our business in a new and unfamiliar area will take at least two years. During that time our farm income will suffer. All we want is fair compensation for our farm and business. The real problem is no one will listen to us!"

Raymond had a thought, *"They don't want me to talk about anything related to the eminent domain action. I'll tell them about our family and our farm."*

Raymond said, "Let me tell you about my family and the farm. I have a brother, Howard. He, his wife, and two children live in Cincinnati. He is a doctor with a successful medical practice. My sister, Elizabeth, is married with two children. They live about thirty miles away from the farm in the small town of Sabrina, Ohio."

Raymond kept going, "My dad, Willard, is nearly seventy-one years of age. He suffers from heart and lung problems. My wife and I with our three children live on the farm and are already doing most of the work. Except for the building of the dam we would have eventually become the third generation to farm the property."

Raymond spoke to Albert, "Mr. Albert, I know you received

a call from Mr. Henderson, the Corps' resident engineer. I didn't mean to step out of line or do anything underhanded.

We know Wayne and his family through our son, 13-year-old Wesley. Through that friendship we allow Wayne and his family to fish and hunt on our property. We seldom speak about the pending sale of the farm. However, Wayne is aware of our growing animosity toward the government and the appraisers."

"My mom Annette enhances the property with flower gardens that are the envy of Clearfield County. In season she also cultivates a large vegetable garden where she grows sweet corn, tomatoes, green beans, and many other vegetables that she and my children sell from a stand at the front of the property."

"The home and land are owned free and clear, but there is a $30,000 open-ended note owed to Stanton Bank and Trust, secured by farm equipment purchased during the last five years. We've never missed a payment."

Raymond looked around the room. Not seeing any disinterest he kept going. "The situation that faces our family is typical of that facing the other farm business. Relocating and reestablishing our business at another location requires a matrix of demanding activities and actions. First, we have to find acreage of quality and size sufficient to re-establish our farm. When we find a suitable property, we'll have to adapt the new location to our needs. We have to transport our animals to the new location. Crop production will take at least one full growing season to till, plant, and harvest. It will be two years before we can establish cash flow as well as we had before we were forced to move."

"Finally, there is the cost to move to a new home and the complications associated with packing and transporting belongings, unpacking and setting up at the new home. As my father and I are trying to prove to the bureaucrats, there is considerable value and expense over and above the value of the real estate. The owners of the other farm, the Connors, are facing the same difficulties."

Raymond said, "One final comment. This tidbit is strictly rumor. There is talk around the community that some realtors have bought and sold several properties within the lake area and have made a nice profit because they knew about the dam before anyone else. I hope the same guys aren't mucking about our farm."

After hearing Raymond's explanation, Ramsey said, "All we can do from here is to ask the government attorneys to carefully examine the documents you have presented to the court."

Soliare agreed but cautioned, "When these things reach the point where lawyers are involved it's difficult to turn them around."

After hearing Raymond's enlightening speech, Albert sensed, but kept it to himself, that there is something wrong with the remaining acquisitions. He asked Soliare, "Do you have an objection if I talk to Judge Givens and let him know we will be reappraising the eight properties?"

Soliare looked at Ramsey who nodded his head indicating he agreed. Soliare said, "That's okay. Please tell the court what we're doing. I'll get going on the reappraisals."

A short discussion followed. Lieutenant Colonel Ramsey looked at Raymond and promised, "We'll look into the matter."

After Raymond had left the district office, Soliare made a phone call to realtor Barnes, but Barnes failed to answer. He then called Commissioner Walgren. Walgren stonewalled him and lied, "Don't bother talking to Harvey Barnes he doesn't have anything to do with the appraisals."

After that meaningless conversation, Soliare decided it was necessary to look further into the matter. His first contact on Wednesday, June 23 was with George Daniels, the Corps real estate procurement specialist.

George, 48, a civilian, had been with the Corps for five years and came to this position after sixteen years as a very successful realtor. Soliare asked, "George, what the hell is going on in Clearfield County with the last of the Trout River land acquisitions?"

George answered, "Boss, things stink up here. I know of at least twenty-one property owners that sold out in 1968 for amounts less than our estimated values and guess what! The people who bought those properties back then are three prominent local realtors who purchased the properties from the original owners. All twenty-one of the properties remained vacant until we acquired them in 1969."

Daniels continued, "A strange thing happened right after the filing of the eminent domain action. Unknown to the Norton's; realtor Barnes and Commissioner Walgren, using Walgren's political connections, tried to get the Norton farm removed from the proceedings." He added, "I plan to examine all twenty-one of the transactions attributed to the three realtors. I'll get back to you soon."

Soliare said, "I look forward to our next conversation. Keep up the good work."

# CHAPTER 32

Before Raymond returned from his meeting in Louisville, his father, Willard, suffered chest pains and was rushed to the Clearfield County Medical Center. The stress and anxiety caused by the knowledge that he was going to lose the family farm taxed his already weak cardiovascular system. By the time the ambulance got him to the hospital, he was in critical condition, and some of his organs were shutting down. At about seven o'clock p.m. on June 22, 1971, Willard, now seventy-two, died. Raymond got home from Louisville at eight fifteen p.m., too late to see his father alive.

Willard's funeral was on Friday, June 25. The day was unseasonably cool, the kind of day Willard loved. The family was grief stricken. Willard was a big part of the farm. His going left a hole in the heart of every family member. Calling hours were Thursday and were very tiring for the family, especially his widow, Annette.

Willard was known and respected throughout the farming community. Scores of families from the county and surrounding area attended calling hours and the funeral. Everyone wanted to console Annette. She just wanted to be surrounded by her family and share their grief. On Saturday the family welcomed time alone.

Annette was the sole heir, but Raymond was now the family patriarch. Annette confirmed what Raymond already knew, telling him, "You are stepping into a big pair of shoes. You are responsible for continuing the family farm business and dealing with the potential disaster concerning the forced selling of the farm."

Ray hugged his mom and promised her, "I won't let them kick us into the ditch."

*** 

On the afternoon of June 22, when Raymond was meeting with Ramsey and Soliare in Louisville and the day Willard died, Barnes and Walgren were meeting in the commissioner's office having a heated discussion about George Daniels. Barnes told Bert, "The asshole's in the courthouse looking at all twenty-one of our sales to the government. He is certain to make a connection to the other guys and me."

Walgren thought, *"I don't have to worry, there is no paper trail to me. My cut has been all cash sent to an offshore account."* He said, "Harvey I suggest you and the guys figure out what to do about Daniels before he goes to the Louisville district with his findings. You need to act now, or you'll be too late."

Later, on the day of his discussion with Walgren, Barnes met with the other two realtors involved with him in the twenty-one insider transactions. Barnes' involvement was limited to four of the transactions; realtor Osgood had done eight and realtor Cooper had handled nine.

Barnes gathered the other two conspirators together, and they met in the back room of Barnes's brother's tavern, The Goose Call; a popular hangout known for its greasy burgers, but otherwise a drinking spot.

Osgood started the conversation, "Our biggest problem concerns how to deal with our situation if we are exposed. There is also the fact that none of us have a legal background. If we go to a lawyer, we might be admitting we are guilty of something. I don't know if what we did was unlawful or not. I'm concerned that the deals were, as a minimum, unethical. If exposed we could lose our licenses.

Barnes related, "Commissioner Walgren implied that drastic action was needed immediately." After a heated discussion that lasted until about four o'clock p.m., the three men decided to confront Daniels when he left the courthouse.

Osgood summarized their goal, "We must convince Daniels the properties we bought were merely ordinary real estate transactions acquired for investment purposes."

Barnes, because he had no defense to object to the smarter and more convincing co-conspirators, was chosen to lead the confrontation.

About five o'clock p.m. on August 17 they spotted Daniels as he left the courthouse and motioned for him to join them in a nearby secluded alley.

Daniels knew something was wrong but decided to see what they wanted. When he joined them, they questioned him about his business in the courthouse. He replied, truthfully, "I am looking into some of the property transactions for the Trout River Dam acquisitions. After examining the county records, I'm certain some of the government's purchases are suspicious."

Barnes asked, "Be more specific, do you think there are irregularities?"

Daniels replied, "I know something is going on." But dodging the truth, he said, "I don't know what, but it could concern the improper use of inside information."

The three conspirators knew they were going to be exposed. At some time during the discussion Daniels stepped away from the curb to avoid a passing car in the adjacent narrow alley and inadvertently bumped into John Cooper. Cooper's bad temper kicked in, and he pushed Daniels who fell backward into the path of another car driven by a newly licensed teen driver. The driver panicked dragging Daniels twenty feet before stopping.

Osgood screamed at Cooper, "What the hell have you done, that man might be dead!" Cooper, a coward, ran to his nearby car and fled to his home on the outskirts of the Village.

The Village police arrived at the courthouse accident scene within two minutes of the accident. A county ambulance arrived five minutes later. Apparently, Daniels was severely injured but responsive. They rushed him to nearby Clearfield County Medical Center where he received treatment for his injuries and a thorough examination.

The ER doctor, Timothy Burke, determined Daniels had a broken collar bone and a broken ankle plus numerous cuts and abrasions. The medical center admitted Daniels to the ICU at nine o'clock p.m.

At the same time the investigation was going on at the accident scene, other Village police arrived at John Cooper's home where they arrested him for assault and fleeing the scene where bodily injury occurred. He spent Tuesday and Wednesday nights in jail until Thursday morning when a county judge released him on his own recognizance. Judge

Augustus Leon set the time for Cooper's hearing for two weeks later on Tuesday, July 6, 1971. The court didn't charge the teen driver.

After admitting Daniels, the hospital notified Daniel's wife, Emily, about his injuries. Emily at their home in Louisville received the news poorly but had the sense to alert their twenty-year-old daughter, Susan. Susan lived with her boyfriend, Kris, in a cross-town apartment.

Susan and Kris immediately rushed to Emily and the three of them sped up I-71 and I-75 to Stanton, arriving after midnight. By the time they got there Emily was extremely distraught to the extent Susan and Kris had to use a wheelchair to help her into the hospital. They were allowed to visit George, but only for five minutes.

The painkillers and sedatives given to George made him unresponsive. Dr. Burke accompanied them and assured Emily and Susan, "George will make a full recovery, but right now he needs rest." He also provided Emily with an anxiety medication to calm her down.

Emily, Susan, and Kris got George's room key for his per diem lodging in the old but well kept Starlight Motel. That night they slept fitfully. Before seven o'clock a.m. on Wednesday, June 23, they left the motel to visit George. The hospital representative told them they couldn't see him until eight o'clock a.m. While waiting, they ate, or more correctly, picked at breakfast in the nearby Sunnyside Café. As soon as they could they went to the hospital where they found George awake, but groggy, sore, and in pain.

On Friday, June 25 George Daniels was able to be transported to his hometown where he entered the

University of Louisville Hospital. He was able to go home the following Tuesday, June 29, 1971. The combination of the collar bone and ankle injury caused him to be wheelchair bound for another three weeks. Now that he was home George was under the care of their aged but capable family doctor, Charles Rayen.

On the date of John Cooper's 'assault and leaving the scene' hearing on July 6, with Emily driving, George was able to painfully travel by car, with his wheelchair, to the Clearfield County Courthouse.

During the hearing Cooper confessed to pushing George into the path of an oncoming car and leaving the scene. His fine was $500, and the judge waived sentencing. John was free to go. Before Cooper left Judge Leon warned him, "This matter is not over. Civil proceedings for damages are likely to be filed by the injured party. Don't get too comfortable."

Scrunched in the wheelchair, George told Emily, "I'm undecided about pursuing action against Cooper on the chance the incident was accidental. My concern, though, is that it was intentional, at least careless. But, thanks to paid sick leave and insurance we have few expenses. I like to think I'm a forgiving man but I've developed a serious dislike for John Cooper."

# CHAPTER 33

George was determined to disclose his findings of insider activities to the proper authorities at the Louisville District Office. Because of Daniels injuries and police involvement Barnes, Walgren, and the others were helpless about pursuing their attempt to warn Daniels not to disclose his findings. Now their only defense would have to be that what they did would be deemed routine real estate transactions.

On Wednesday, July 14, 1971, George, by now on crutches, had a meeting at the Corps of Engineers Louisville office with Deputy Commander Ramsey and Real Estate Division head Soliare to show them his findings concerning Barnes, Osgood, and Cooper. At that time he did not know about Commissioner Halgren's involvement. Wayne Henderson, resident engineer, was also at the meeting.

Included in the meeting, invited by the Corps, was the Clearfield County District Attorney, Rebecca Regan, and the Corps' general counsel, Richard Albert. Regan and Albert knew and respected each other from their mutual involvement in various issues and legal actions that occurred earlier in the project. They were 'on the record', so they cautioned Daniels not to discuss anything related to the eminent domain suit in County Court.

Daniels was first to speak, "I have documented my findings from two weeks of work were I analyzed thirty questionable transactions that occurred during the Trout River acquisitions. I've summarized my findings on accounting spreadsheets. Three licensed realtors initiated twenty-one of the suspicious transactions at the same time in late 1967."

Daniels continued his report, "At that time a guy named Vincent Osgood bought six residences and two farms. During the prior fifteen years Osgood never personally purchased any form of real estate. He never rented, occupied or used the eight properties in any way. The government bought the properties in 1969 for considerably more than Osgood paid for them."

"There is more to the report; I did the same analysis on properties purchased by a man named John Cooper. He bought seven residences and two farms. In 1969 those nine properties, when sold to the government, netted him a nice profit." Daniels noted, "During the prior fifteen years Cooper bought and kept one rental property that is not in the area of the lake. With a wry look, Daniels added, "Cooper is the guy who pushed me and caused my injuries. I think there is more to this than what is apparent."

Daniels continued to describe the tainted government acquisitions. "Harvey Barnes. Now there's a piece of work! His purchases are the ones that got my attention. Barnes is living on the edge of bankruptcy; unpaid bills, unpaid rent, and a poor credit rating."

Daniels continued, "All of Barnes purchases, like the others, were for cash. He bought three residences and one farm. Like his buddies, in 1969 he sold the four properties to the government for a profit. But, here's the thing, according to county records, Barnes doesn't have any assets and did not borrow from any local source. Someone had to provide him with money, and that person is probably behind this whole scheme."

After Daniels had finished giving his report, the discussion turned to the legality of the actions taken by the three realtors. Clearfield County District Attorney Regan said, "I don't see any apparent criminal activity." She added, "However, if we can trace the source of Barnes money it might lead to the identification of a conspiracy that made the government pay more than necessary for twenty-one properties."

Government lawyer Albert agreed, "Any group that conspires to an action that costs the American public more than it would if not for the conspiracy, has committed a federal crime against the U. S. Government. The actions of these three people appear to be part of a conspiracy. This is a Federal Government issue. We need to get the U. S. Attorney's Office involved."

Albert said, "We'll also notify the FBI to look for wrongdoing. They'll probably ask the IRS to investigate. They'll want to determine if the realtors paid income tax on their profits. If the feds didn't get paid the State of Ohio is also due taxes."

The meeting ended with Regan and Albert agreeing to begin a coordinated investigation with the U.S. Attorney's Office that would include getting statements from all three realtors.

By Monday, July 19, Attorney Albert had collected and sent

all the incriminating documents concerning the purchases along with Daniels report to The U. S. Attorney's Office asking for an opinion regarding any wrongdoing. To be sure he informed everyone, he sent copies to the Cincinnati FBI office, the IRS, and the Ohio Attorneys General. Along with all the documents, Albert sent copies of Osgood, Cooper, and Barnes's personal information.

Federal government actions against the three realtors, who were now officially classified as 'the conspirators,' sprang to life on Wednesday, August 4, 1971. On that day a U. S. Marshall served subpoenas to the three realtors charging them with defrauding the federal government by conspiring to purchase property, using inside information that allowed them to unjustly benefit financially. The subpoenas required them to appear before a federal magistrate on August 18 in the United States District Court for the Southern District of Ohio in Cincinnati. Albert noted, "The federal district court is a seemingly busy place thanks to the Trout River Dam."

Two days later the three conspirators received certified letters from the IRS notifying them of unpaid taxes for the year 1969. The IRS gave them fourteen days to respond. All three notices reminded them that state taxes might also be owed.

The three appeared, as ordered, On August 18 before a Federal Magistrate, the Honorable Samuel Parkinson. Attorney Michael Brubaugh represented all three as a group. Brubaugh is a Cincinnatian admitted to the federal bar.

Because the government already owned the land about which the conspiracy proceedings were concerned, there was no need for Wayne to become involved. He stayed out of what had become a criminal proceeding. He Told Albert, "I'm here if you need me. I believe the federal prosecutors and the Corps acquisition team can best perform their job without me."

The government prosecutors charged Osgood with illegal gains of $98,000, Cooper with illegal gains of $107,000, and Barnes with $40,000 of illicit income. At meetings with attorney Brubaugh during the preceding two weeks the three confided that their personal gain was only sixty percent of the amount claimed by the government.

Brubaugh told the three, "I am shocked to learn there is a fourth person involved who masterminded the scheme and remained anonymous reaping forty percent from Osgood and Cooper and sixty percent from Barnes. The presence of this person brings the matter closer to a conspiracy. You will now have a tough time proving to the court that what you did was merely an investment."

On advice of counsel the three admitted to actions that resulted in illegal financial gains, but not to the extent claimed by the government.

Attorney Brubaugh asked to approach the bench. "Your Honor," he said, "There is another person who until this time has remained anonymous. That person is the mastermind of this scheme. We ask for a continuance until this person can be charged and tried along with my clients. I will provide the court with all available information concerning this individual."

After a long, off the record, conversation in chambers between the Magistrate, Attorney Brubaugh, Osgood, Cooper, Barnes, and the federal prosecutor; the Magistrate allowed a continuance until Friday, September 3 so they could charge Bert Halgren along with the other three. The magistrate ordered, "I'll see all of you back here next week."

Bert's fury was off the chart when, only two days later, his involvement was disclosed. At the county commissioner's office, a U. S. Marshall served Walgren with a subpoena ordering him to appear before the federal magistrate on Friday, September 3 in the United States District Court for the Southern District of Ohio in Cincinnati. Bert knew his part in the scheme could only be exposed if his three partners had disclosed his involvement. The entire county office building reverberated with Bert's booming voice and violent outburst damning all the ignorant people with whom he had to deal.

To prepare for the hearing Bert had to obtain legal counsel. Like his three cohorts, he chose a highly regarded Cincinnati lawyer, Christopher Langton. Osgood, Cooper, and Barnes appearances were scheduled for the same day and time. Magistrate Parkinson wanted to see all four of the men together and face to face.

Parkinson, 61, had served the Federal Court for twelve years. He was a smallish man with a big ego and a legendary temper. Stories about his courtroom explosions and reckless penalties were the talk of the Cincinnati legal world. Both attorneys knew to tread lightly and show respect in his court.

On the day of the hearing, Bert made the mistake of upsetting Parkinson's court by, as soon as he entered the courtroom, verbally attacking the other three and loudly accusing them of, "Being ungrateful, breaching their promise of secrecy, betraying his trust, and lying."

The magistrate ordered Bert restrained and separated from the others. He told Bert, "Any more outbursts and you will be arrested, jailed, and fined for contempt of court."

The three realtors admitted, under oath, they had indeed profited as charged. But, because forty percent went to Bert they did not profit to the extent charged.

Their accountant and CPA, Charles Goodly, testified, "I examined their records from the time of the incidents and determined the so-called illegal profit for each defendant was: Osgood $58,800, Cooper $64,200, and Barnes, $16,000.

The accountant testified, "I am not privy to Mr. Walgren's records, but from the others records I can accurately determine Bert's profits." This disclosure brought an immediate objection from Bert's attorney. The Magistrate took the objection under advisement but allowed Goodly to proceed.

Bert Halgren's lawyer had to restrain him to keep him from an outburst that would have put him in jail.

CPA Goodly stated, "Based on my clients' records; Bert made $39,200 from Osgood, $42,800 from Cooper and at 60 percent he earned $24,000 from Barnes." He testified, "Bert made a total profit of $106,000."

The Magistrate accepted the CPA's testimony and, after issuing a bench decision, sentenced Osgood, Cooper, and Barnes. "The three of you must make full restitution through this court to the U.S. Government within seven days. I will waive prison time for you provided you comply with this order. If any or all of you do not comply, all three of you will serve six months in the federal prison at Ashland, Kentucky."

Magistrate Parkinson added, "Compliance with this order

does not end your punishment. I am placing the three of you on probation with the U.S. Marshall's Cincinnati office for one year. You are also ordered to forfeit your real estate licenses for five years." The court continued Bert's case to an unnamed future date.

Several days later Bert's attorney advised him, "You have no legitimate defense; you will end up wasting a lot of money on a federal court trial that you will inevitably lose."

Burt made one last show of defiance but eventually he acquiesced to his attorney's advice. One week later in front of Magistrate Parkinson Bert plead guilty.

Like the others, he was ordered to make restitution in seven days and given probation for one year. Unlike the others, the magistrate sentenced him to thirty days in a federal minimum security prison in Kentucky. As a convicted felon, by Ohio law, Bert couldn't hold public office. He forfeited his job as county commissioner, becoming just another resident of Clearfield County.

***

The three realtors still had to address their tax problems. By the time federal and state tax agencies were through with them, all four were financially devastated, especially Barnes who lost his home and in January 1972 filed for bankruptcy under chapter seven of the code.

# CHAPTER 34

Before Osgood, Cooper, and Barnes had their day in federal court; in Clearfield County Court the eminent domain court case was beginning before County Judge the Honorable Joseph Givens. The parties agreed to waive a jury trial and have the case decided by the judge. The Corps was anxious to clear the way for the construction of the dam and lake when the preliminary hearing began on Thursday, July 22.

Ordinarily, a preliminary hearing's sole purpose was to establish ground rules for the trial. After hearing Daniels report and knowing that the government would bring criminal action against the three realtors, the Corps sent Attorney Albert, Daniels, and the appraisers responsible for the low valuations to the trial. Also present were Attorney Hubble and several other attorneys representing holdout owners.

Corps Attorney Albert surprised the court when he asked Judge Givens, "With the court's permission our appraisers have requested to meet individually with the eight eminent domain property owners and their counsel." Albert said, "Based on the information given to us by a team of independent appraisers we determined there are errors in our appraisals, and we request the opportunity to restate our position with each of the affected property owners."

After consulting with all the attorneys and owners, Judge Givens ruled, "I'll allow until Monday, July 26 at five o'clock p.m. for the government to restate their position on individual owners who are willing to meet. I am adjourning the court until Tuesday, July 27, at nine o'clock a.m."

During the next several days all eight owners appeared at their assigned time to hear the government's latest offer. Most were pleased with the revised value the government placed on their property and settled on the spot. A few haggled and received a few dollars more when they realized the futility of continuing to hold out.

By the end of the day on Monday, July 26, 1971, all but two owners agreed to the new, more realistic, offers and signed the sale documents. The Norton's were among the six who agreed to allow the government to acquire their property. Despite the anguish and anxiety caused by the imminent relocation they went away happy it was over; but sad and concerned about having to relocate. The final agreed price of $415,000 would allow them to make a fresh start.

The properties owned by the two holdouts were located in the impoundment area and did not affect the construction of any part of the outlet works and dam embankment. The owner of the dwelling was the infamous and mentally unstable Olga McCoy who shot at the survey team and sued to stop the project. The Connors family owned the working farm. Because both properties were well away from the dam, the Corps decided to delay eviction, even though the county court had ordered the holdouts removed.

## BEHIND THE DAM

\*\*\*

The Norton's, without Willard, were among the last to settle. They were allowed to harvest any crops in their fields and salvage buildings and other improvements. They had ninety days to leave the dwelling, but harvesting would be ongoing.

After Raymond had executed the agreement to sell, Attorney Albert told him, "If not for you and George Daniels bringing to our attention the secret deals and misconduct by certain local realtors, this thing would have become very ugly as it wound its way through the court system. Further," he explained, "Under eminent domain, the government has the right to evict holdouts from their dwellings as soon as they deposit the amount of the government's appraised value with the court! We are glad we never had to resort to eviction."

On Tuesday after leaving the courthouse, Raymond decided to call the family together at the homestead to inform everyone about the agreement and have a good old-fashioned barbecue. The stress of the sale and the death of their father and husband had taken its toll on all of them.

Despite the hot and muggy day, on Wednesday, July 28 at six o'clock pm, the families gathered together. The get-together included Howard his wife and two children, Elizabeth her husband and two children, Raymond, his wife and three children, and mom. They were fourteen close-knit and loving family members.

Before anything got started, Annette announced, "I am turning the whole damned thing over to Raymond. Then I am going to settle down in a small retirement community just north of town." She continued, "I'll still be close to all of you so don't make it a big deal."

Raymond had his eye on three hundred acres of vacant land that had the potential for establishing the new Blissful Acres farm. After dinner, he discussed his plan with the family. He said, "There is a beautiful piece of land about twenty miles away in the eastern part of the county. It's relatively level and suitable for farming. It even has a small steam flowing across one corner. The asking price is $300.00 per acre. I'm going to offer them $200.00 an acre, cash. They've had the property for sale for a long time, more than two years, they should welcome our offer."

Raymond continued, "We will have to start from scratch; build a house, barn, milk house, grain storage silos, chicken coop, and mirror everything we have here. We will also need fencing, county water, and sewer, upgraded electric and telephone service, garages, and driveways."

"I've talked to mom, and she is in total agreement. We should also consider adding space to the house so she can have her suite instead of going into the retirement community."

On August 19, 1971, Raymond, as executor for the family, closed on the three hundred acres for $60,000. With assistance from a local architect, they prepared plans for a new home. The new place was not as spacious as the homestead, but modern and roomy. The plans for the new home included a suite for mom, who decided not to go to the retirement community.

As Work progressed, Raymond added two farm hands for seasonal work. The family commented that it took two new farm hands to replace their dad. Both of the new employees had worked on farms taken by the government for the dam and lake.

Within a year several crops were planted and growing on the new farm, ripening for harvest time. By September 1972 the new Norton farm was well along the way to being productive. In the interim, the Government allowed them to remain on the old farm while building the new house and barn.

# CHAPTER 35

By the end of summer of 1971, the Federal Government owned almost all of the four thousand two hundred sixty acres needed to build the dam, lake, and surrounding recreational area. The state of Ohio had to relocate state routes 24 and 156 out of the impoundment area. The road relocations were done with state funds and completed before 1972. Each utility company performed the relocations and abandonment of gas, water, sewer, electric, and telephone services.

Aldridge Construction's work building the outlet works was fifty percent complete. Placing the earth and rock embankment dam would not begin for another year.

Property acquisitions, however, were not completed. The government still needed the Connor farm and the Olga McCoy lands. They still need to relocate the schoolhouse and cemetery.

***

Local newspapers and media, led by biased reporter Roger Wilkins, were quick to report negative items about the Trout River project.

Troubling news about the dam worried Wayne's wife, Melissa. She believed Wayne, the Corps, and the project, in general, were being unfairly depicted by the media and in news reports.

Melissa, when she read about the anti-dam lawsuits, confronted Wayne. She asked him, "Are you in danger, can these people hurt you or your family?"

Wayne answered Melissa, "I'm acutely aware of the opposition and, when asked, I take an active role in some of the legal matters. However, I prefer to leave legal matters in the capable hands of the real estate and legal people representing the government. The media frequently quotes me, and my picture has appeared with news stories about the dam. Despite these distractions overseeing construction of the Trout River Dam is my primary responsibility."

Wayne added, "I'm not in danger. The worst that can happen is a confrontation with someone connected to an incident or a disgruntled homeowner. My obligation, should anything concerning legal actions or acquisitions occur, is to refer the matter to the proper authority. I try to be diplomatic and tactful, don't worry."

Melissa did not appear to be appeased, but gave Wayne a hug and said, "Just be careful, I love you."

Wayne did have a concern. He cautioned Mellissa and JD, "There are reports of looting. The looters usually work at night, concentrating on vacated or soon to be abandoned homes. In some instances, looting occurs in occupied homes." Wayne said, "We live in a very visible location. We need to be alert and cognizant of what is going on around our home."

\*\*\*

Wayne was concerned about a lack of activity to wrap up the acquisition of the four remaining properties needed for the dam and lake. George Daniels, the real estate acquisition specialist, moved back to Louisville in August 1971. Several months before Daniels returned to his office in Louisville he asked Wayne, "Will you handle the cemetery and schoolhouse relocations? One of the districts' real estate personnel will finalize the acquisition of the Connor farm and the McCoy property."

At the time he was asked to help with acquisitions Wayne's commitment was to oversee the activities of Aldridge Construction Co. Wayne replied to George, "Construction schedules and issues with the contractor are my first priority. For you, I'll do what I can to get those two things done. Don't expect miracles, though."

# CHAPTER 36

While Aldridge was fighting floods, enduring punishing inspection tactics, and building the control tower, conduit, and stilling basin; Wayne had his own problem, relocating a cemetery.

Before Wayne left for work on Monday, June 17, 1971, Melissa noticed he was quiet and restless. She asked, "What's the matter, honey? Do you have the Monday blues? Is something wrong at work?"

Wayne still in a funk answered, "Today I have a meeting with George Daniels and Jarrett Ashbaker. Ashbaker is the Corps expert on relocating cemeteries. I have the task of overseeing the relocation of the Riverside Cemetery. The location of the cemetery is on Long Road between the river and the old gold mine. I am very uneasy about disturbing the resting place of the dead. I believe it to be abhorrent. Even more repugnant to me is moving graves and headstones so that the living can have a place to enjoy and have fun. This assignment is the most significant and heart-rending of anything I've tackled on this project."

To begin their meeting George Daniels, the Corps acquisition specialist, explained to Dean and Jarrett, "The Riverside Cemetery is on a small rise near the Trout River.

Its location won't interfere with the outlet works or the dam. Although when we fill the lake, it will be submerged. The government has agreed to provide space for five hundred forty spaces in a new location selected by the cemetery association."

Daniels continued, "The cemetery contains three acres and two hundred thirty-one occupied graves. There are about three hundred unused spaces. The Riverside Cemetery Association owns the land. A board of directors and Ohio law governs the use of the property." With those remarks, Daniels said as he left, "I'll leave you two to your task."

Jarrett and Wayne spent the entire day planning how to relocate two hundred thirty-one graves. Jarrett had done his homework and explained the Corps guidelines, "Two years ago, as required by state law, we gave notice to the Riverside Cemetery Association that we need to acquire their land."

Jarrett said, "The Corps made an offer of $40,000 for the land and payment of all relocation expenses. The cemetery board of directors accepted the offer. The cemetery board then purchased a three-acre site away from the river. They have cleared zoning and all other regulatory requirements regarding the new cemetery. We are ready to go."

Jarrett continued his explanation, "In the interim, the cemetery board prepared a site plan for the new cemetery. It's complete with the layout of drives, walkways, water lines, drains, fencing, gates, combination maintenance and office building, and a chapel. They have a well-engineered plan. A big plus is that the plan includes a layout of all the graves numbered to correspond with the old cemetery. We expect to complete all of the preliminary work by the end of the month. Their surveyors are marking the location of the new grave sites as we speak."

That afternoon Wayne and Jarrett continued to make plans to move the cemetery. Jarrett told Wayne, "The cemetery association's board of directors notified every friend, family member, and next of kin of the deceased about the move and the new location for the interment of the remains." Jarrett noted, "The deceased's survivors have been given the option to handle the removal themselves and be reimbursed by the government. Or, if survivors can't be located or are unwilling to see to the relocation, we will be responsible. A preliminary count indicates there are about ninety graves that we'll relocate. Of course, before we fill the lake, we have to be sure we have moved all graves for which we are responsible."

Jarrett continued his discourse, "Other things we must do; keep meticulous records, involve the county coroner, follow legal requirements, meet with families at the new landscaped and fenced internment site, and open all existing graves by hand. We must involve a licensed funeral home to move the remains the same day. The remains must be placed in the same order as they were at the original cemetery." He added, "The relocation cemetery is required to have the same number of spaces for graves as the old cemetery. Graves and spaces for graves have to be in the same order as in the original cemetery."

Wayne was impressed by all the work Jarrett had done before their meeting.

Before finishing, Jarrett said, "I've employed a licensed funeral director who has knowledge of internment procedures. We'll be working with C. W. Amesly, located in Cincinnati and licensed in Ohio. They are recognized experts for the relocation of cemeteries. Tremont Funeral Home in

Stanton will handle moving the remains."

Wayne said, "I see we received responses from over four hundred living relatives and concerned friends. Many of the deceased's families plan to follow the moves carefully. Some of the deceased have no one following their move to the new cemetery. For those who know and care about the disruption of their loved ones resting place it will probably bring back the pain and grief they thought they had overcome."

Wayne followed Jarrett's advice and turned the complicated disinterment and interment process over to the experts. One family, however, tested Wayne's compassion and diplomacy. He was beginning to see the effect on the living; some cannot let go."

Early in July 1971 a grieving family of five, mother and four children, accosted Wayne in his job site office. The mother tearfully told him, "You can't just rip my husband up." Pointing to the children the mother said, "You can't take their father from his resting place and put him somewhere else."

Wayne and the others in the office did not know how to react in a way that would soothe the woman's renewed grief. The oldest child looked to be about sixteen and the youngest about six. The family appeared to be struggling financially. They all had a haggard look that alerted Wayne to the possibility that the father's death was recent.

Wayne explained to the grieving wife and mother, "The cemetery relocation is unavoidable. The disruption caused by relocating the graves saddens me." Wayne asked, "Do you have a minister or priest who can help you?"

The widow and mother, Mrs. Johnston, replied, "Yes, our

pastor performed the funeral service just two months ago."

Wayne was very concerned about the Johnson family's mental state. He suggested, "May I call your pastor and explain the situation to him? Maybe we can meet with him and get consolation that I can't provide. If you wish, I'll be happy to go with you."

Mrs. Johnson agreed, "Please, let's call him. He is at the Stanton Baptist Church; here is the phone number."

Wayne called and explained his concerns. The minister, Reverend Mitchell, agreed to meet with the family and Wayne within the hour. Wayne was concerned about becoming involved. The situation could become unmanageable if the family and the Reverend join in condemning moving the deceased. Wayne was relieved when Reverend Mitchell consoled the family telling them, "I will bless the move and spend time with all of you when the move occurs."

Mr. Johnson's interment would be the following day. There were ten people, including five family members and Reverend Mitchell, present throughout the day as they relocated the remains and headstone to the burial site at the new cemetery. The Reverend gave an appropriate and touching graveside message.

Wayne was relieved when Mr. Johnson was in his new resting place. Mrs. Johnson gave Wayne a kiss on the cheek and thanked him for being there for her and her family. Wayne was gratified and surprised at the change of heart.

There were other instances of family belligerence about moving their loved ones. Wayne and Jarrett personally addressed each situation. Subsequently, except for stirring up sad memories among the families, all went well. The cemetery relocation took about eight weeks. The Corps completed the entire cemetery relocation before the end of September 1971.

The overall grave moving process left Wayne emotionally drained. Melissa understood the reason for his mental state and, fortunately for Wayne; he didn't have to grieve for the survivors alone.

# CHAPTER 37

Safety was foremost for the entire project. The safety of those working on the control tower was an even bigger concern. A safety net was installed to protect those working on the control tower and to protect those working on the ground below. The net fully encircled the tower and was installed in a manner that allowed it to move up with the formwork so that it was always just below the work area.

As was typical of his no-nonsense management style, Don told the men working on the tower, "Any crazy bastard who purposely jumps into the safety net will be left there for the crows to eat. But not before I fire him."

Dean noted in a March 1971 conversation with George, "It's going to take until June 1972, over a year from now, to complete concrete work for the control tower."

George acknowledged what Dean said, "Now that spring is here we're increasing the pace of the work and, correspondingly, the size of the workforce has to increase. Most of the workers we laid off during the winter are being called back. By early June excavation for the stilling basin will be complete. By mid-July, we will finish all the excavation and concrete fill work."

Don entered the office, and George Knowles asked him to join the informal planning discussion.

George continued, "After we finish the control tower foundation and associated work, we'll begin work on the two hundred- twenty foot high tower. After that, we will build the two hundred foot long steel and concrete access bridge. When we finish the bridge, we will have access to the control tower from Carney Road. The center of the bridge is supported by a large concrete one-hundred foot tall pier."

Don added, "The control tower and access bridge have the longest schedule duration, two years. This part of the job also requires the most workers. We're installing a plywood walkway and railing near the top of the outside form encircling the tower. That will give us a platform from which to place the concrete."

Don pointed out, "There is a problem. We have to provide a better means to get to the tower work areas. By the time we finish the tower, the workers will have to climb the equivalent of a twenty-two story building to get to the highest work level." Don looked at Dean, "Do you think we should consider a temporary elevator?

Dean answered, "That was in our original plan. After we got here and were set up on the job we found out there is not enough electric power to run an elevator. We'd have to bring additional power from Route 53; that's about five miles away. The cost is over fifty thousand dollars. Way more than it's worth."

Don replied, "I see what you mean. I'm going to plan B. To make access to the high work areas easier we'll make a personnel box that, using the crane, we can lift and deposit at any height, four workers at a time. We'll still have other access using the wooden outside stairway. The workers will have to take all their gear and lunches up to work with them."

"Each ten-foot high wall lift takes about three weeks." Don

was sharing plans that he had been keeping in his head, "To do twenty-two lifts, if all goes well, just the tower concrete will require sixty-six weeks. Factoring in lost time for weather, unanticipated delays, and the fact that we lose productivity the higher the structure rises; the total time required is seventy-eight weeks."

Dean said to George, "That's what we thought." Then he added, "Thanks, Don."

\*\*\*

Preparations for the stilling basin concrete began on June 16, 1971. The first concrete placement for a large section of the stilling basin base slab, about three hundred cubic yards, was scheduled for July 13. On the day they were to place the concrete, Dean observed two laborers on their bellies, crawling around between layers of rebar, cleaning up small patches of water on the surface of the concrete fill.

Brian Towelson was directing the unnecessary and time consuming cleanup effort. Two ready mix concrete trucks were waiting, and the placing crew was ready.

Dean confronted Brian, "If you were responsible for placing this concrete, would you do what you have ordered those men to do?"

Brian replied, "No I wouldn't."

Dean angrily told him, "They shouldn't either! You have no business directing our workers, especially having them doing something as unnecessary as what those guys are doing."

Having said that, Dean called to the two workers, "Come out of there. Let's get this going." He turned his back on Brian and ordered the concrete placement to begin. The Placement of the stilling basin foundation proceeded without further incident.

# CHAPTER 38

While Wayne was trying to assist the real estate specialists, Aldridge continued their work building the outlet works.

Don emerged from the area of the control tower and entered the field office. He sat beside Knowles's desk and asked, "Do you have time to discuss the crane situation at the control tower?"

George answered, "Of course I do. I've been thinking about that."

Don, as was his nature, went right to the issue, "The eighty-ton crane will only get us eighty, maybe a hundred feet high. To safely handle concrete forms and place concrete for the increasingly higher concrete placements we need to replace the eighty-ton crane with a much larger one."

George reached into the catalog and reference information he had accumulated and withdrew a crane load capacity chart. George and Don studied the load chart and considered various options.

Finally, after reviewing the crane load and reach charts for various crane lifting configurations Don decided, "To reach the top of the tower we need a crane with at least two hundred forty feet of combined boom and jib. To safely handle that much boom and jib we need a one hundred fifty-ton capacity truck crane. Let's get Dean going on this."

Dean checked local sources for crane rentals and found a crane meeting the requirements available for rent in the Dayton area.

A rental agreement, starting on July 1, 1971, was negotiated that included a crane operator and oiler. Dean was shocked by the rental firm's quoted moving costs of two thousand dollars in and the same amount to move the crane out. The crane owner explained that the crane had to be partially disassembled to meet highway load and permit restrictions.

Dean had no choice but to agree to pay the outrageous moving costs. When Dean and the workers arrived on the job Monday morning, they were surprised to find the crane and eight truck-loads of crane and boom sitting on the site. Don told Dean, "Apparently the crane owner illegally moved the crane during the weekend and at night without obtaining the overweight and oversize permits. They charged us two thousand dollars for a legal move and saved considerable money by illegally moving the crane and boom during the weekend and at night."

Dean noted, "I believed the two thousand dollar charge was for a one hundred fifty-ton crane assembled and ready to work. I contacted the crane owner, and he adamantly stated the cost is for moving only. We have to put the damn thing together."

Knowles utilized a crew of ironworkers who were installing rebar to assemble the crane. It was necessary to make use of the eighty-ton crane and crew to assist in the assembly that took seven days. A delay in the assembly and another unpleasant surprise occurred when they realized that the crane owner neglected to ship the two-inch diameter pins that held the boom sections together.

When the assembly was finally complete, another surprise occurred when Dean found out the crane was incapable of lifting its own two hundred forty feet of boom and jib without assistance from the smaller eighty-ton capacity crane.

Finally, after almost two excruciating weeks, the big crane was ready to go to work. At least that was what Dean thought.

With the crane assembled and the boom upright and ready to work the crane operator called George over to the machine, "Mr. Knowles I notice there are frayed sections on the hoisting cable. For safety reasons, until you replace the hoist cables, I can't make a lift."

Dean immediately notified the crane owner about the frayed cables. The owner matter-of-factly said, "Look at the rental agreement. You are responsible for ordinary maintenance, including the hoist cables."

Dean complained to Don, "I'm pissed that the crane owner knowingly sent us a crane needing the hoist cables replaced. At the same time I'm embarrassed about the way I've been deceived and led into an unfortunate situation. I'll find a way to get back at them."

Herbert Flaherty, Dean's boss, was also unhappy. He curtly told Dean, "This fiasco is costing a lot of money and delaying work on the control tower. Another three working days have been wasted lowering the boom and jib, unspooling one thousand feet of wire cable, installing the same amount of new, and hoisting the boom and jib up to its working position. After almost three weeks of hassles, expenses, and lost time with this fiasco, are we finally going back to work?"

Dean answered, "Yes we are."

Dean promised himself that this outrageous treatment by a duplicitous crane rental firm would not go unanswered. First, though, he needed to utilize the crane for the intended purpose.

Billy Ray Collier, who owned a Clearfield County farm, operated the big crane. Collier was a good operator. His conversations about the crane and how he expected people to respect the size and height of the crane were more like a business executive talking to his board of directors; very professional.

Collier discussed ground rules with Don, "When moving the inside forms the crane hook is out of my sight. I have to rely on hand signals from my oiler and two-way radio communication with the carpenter foreman to know when to lift and swing the load. No one else should direct what I do."

Don explained, "One by one the wall forms will be repositioned up to the next level, aligned, and secured. This procedure is repeated until we've reset all the formwork and the surveyors have determined that the next level of the tower is plumb."

Collier pointed out, "The form lifting process is dangerous because the forms, when they are free and suspended from the crane, act like a big stiff sail and move with the wind. A sudden gust can blow the form sideways and, in extreme conditions, put a lateral force on the crane boom resulting in failure and collapse. During windy conditions I expect you and Knowles to stop all work requiring crane assistance."

As they re-positioned the forms, joined, and secured

them the iron workers installed the tons of reinforcing steel that went into the walls. After all the reinforcing steel was placed and inspected, the outside forms, which had been lowered to the ground, were lifted and secured in place.

The placing of structural concrete occurred after final approval by the Corps' inspection team. The cycle repeated for each lift about every three weeks.

## CHAPTER 39

Wayne and Dean were discussing project progress. Dean said, "As of right now, February 1972, the outlet works is about seventy percent complete. Everyone is aware that the outlet works is at least a year from completion. We're planning to divert the river through the outlet works in March 1973."

Wayne told Dean, "Considering your current rate of progress, building the embankment should start about May 1972. That will allow you to take advantage of the 1972 summer building season. You'll be able to prepare the site for placing and compacting of the massive amounts of earth, rock, and clay required to build the embankment."

Dean knew that the schedule had slipped, he noted, "We're going to push the stilling basin work. We worked in that area throughout the winter. Despite cold weather, spring floods and constant harassment from your inspectors, the stilling basin will be finished in April 1972."

Dean updated Wayne about the Conduit, "Utilizing three sets of steel forms we worked through the winter of 1970 and 1971. By taking advantage of every possible work day, we'll finish the outlet works conduit by the end of May 1972. Except for installing handrail at the stilling basin, cleaning, and concrete surface finishing, the outlet conduit, and stilling basin should be finished by August 1972.

Wayne ended the meeting when he said, "I've got to go make plans to move the old schoolhouse that sits on that little lane off River Road."

# CHAPTER 40

Wayne reluctantly agreed to meet with George Daniels to plan to move the historic schoolhouse. He told Daniels, "There is a lot of activity at the dam. I know I promised to help out, but this needs to get done so I can concentrate on my real job; building the dam."

Wayne noted, "The cemetery relocation required tact and caring. Moving the schoolhouse will require muscle."

Daniels warned Wayne, "It will take more than muscle. You'll still need a lot of tact and diplomacy."

Wayne asked, "What's the story behind moving the school?"

Daniels answered, "The schoolhouse dates from 1894. But burned and was rebuilt on the same site in 1921. It is of sturdy wood frame construction on a masonry foundation. We won't reuse the old foundation. A new masonry and concrete foundation the exact size as the old one has been prebuilt at the new location."

"The school is owned by the Trout River Heritage Society. Mrs. Pomeroy, the society president, took charge of coordinating the sale of the land the school sits on to the government." Daniels said, "You'll soon meet her. As he left, Daniels said, "I've got to go, remember tact and diplomacy."

During his first trip to look at the school, Wayne met Mrs. Pomeroy. In a distinctively well educated voice she told Wayne, "Mr. Henderson, I want to cooperate but the society insists that the school is relocated, not razed. We also demand that it be relocated to property we own. The location of that property is about two and a half miles away."

Wayne assumed Mrs. Pomeroy was accustomed to having her way. Her family was, by Clearfield County standards, very wealthy. She had an, 'I'm a Pomeroy and you're not attitude'. Wayne was uncomfortable around her.

Wayne Told Mrs. Pomeroy, "There is an agreement and the government will comply with the society's demands. If I can take some of your time, I'll tell you about the move."

Wayne explained, "The work preparing and moving the school will be performed by Pappas Brothers, a house moving contractor located in Cincinnati."

Wayne continued to describe how the school will be moved, "The route to the new location is mostly rural but has numerous obstacles including low headroom electric and telephone wires. In April I contacted both utilities and warned them about the move and its destination. They are cooperative, and we will pay them for their work. The plan requires service employees to precede the movers and either shore up or remove and reinstall interfering wires."

Mrs. Pomeroy was losing interest but Wayne continued, "Another concern is the weight of the school traveling over buried utility lines. Everyone involved believes there will be no damage to buried pipe and therefore no protective measures are being taken. We will repair damage to street surfaces."

Wrapping up his dissertation Wayne concluded, "There are seventeen trees whose branches interfere with the move. I've had these trimmed before starting the move. Although the trees are on the lawn strip that is part of the public right of way, property owners consider that the trees are their property. I had to use my best diplomacy skills to avert outright violence. I had the tree trimming professionally done a week ago."

Wayne added, "There is one other complication. Bad publicity stirred by a Cincinnati Post reporter, Roger Wilkins, has exacerbated the problems caused by distraught tree protectors and is bringing unneeded attention to our school moving efforts. His articles report all the bad comments and ignores public praise about your society's efforts to preserve the old schoolhouse."

"As I said, the Corps has contracted with a Cincinnati demolition and house moving firm, Pappas Bros., to perform the move. Pappas Bros. owner, Kris Pappas, is aware of the school's historic value and has provided assurance of a safe move. Pappas Bros., per their contract, provided the required insurance protection."

Moving the school began on May 5, 1972. Wayne was appalled at the appearance of the mover's crew. They looked like, and probably were, maverick bikers. To a man, they were extensively tattooed and muscular. They wore tattered black tee shirts emblazoned with sayings like, "HELL HATH NO FURY LIKE A MAN WITH NO BEER," and worse.

Wayne's dismay at the moving crew's appearance was insignificant compared to Mrs. Pomeroy's blatant outrage.

The school, located in a pastoral setting, was on a seventy-foot long lane off of River Road.

Kris Pappas explained to Wayne, "The first activity will be to expose the foundation by excavating around the school. Then holes, two at each end, will be cut lengthwise through the foundation. Through these holes we will insert long steel beams, called needles, extending the length of the building. The beams are then wedged against the underside of the building and securely braced to serve as the lifting platform and to prevent flexing during the move. We will then cut away the old foundation freeing the school from its original supports."

Despite the worker's appearance, Wayne was impressed by their strength, professionalism, and knowledge about how to carefully move the school. Mrs. Pomeroy was not impressed by anything.

The building was secured to the platform and supported on hardwood cribbing at each end. Then the workers jacked the building up enough to place multi wheel assemblies at the corners. Hardwood placed under the wheels provided a smooth runway. A bulldozer gently pulled the building forward onto the access lane. After being pulled well onto the lane, the building, supports, wheels, and pulling tongue were carefully inspected to assure the assembly would hold together for two and a half miles. The school was secured and left on its wheels ready to start moving on Monday.

On Monday a powerful semi tractor was connected to the tongue, and the move began. A tricky move was immediately required at the ninety degree turn onto River Road. There was an uneven transition from lane to road that caused Wayne and the moving crew apprehension when the building swayed as it traversed over the bumps. The old girl held up with no damage, and everyone was relieved as the move progressed along River Road.

Wayne told Kris Pappas, "Mrs. Pomeroy has followed every move, but she barely notices the tense moments."

The move took two days and encountered many glitches; all were handled and solved by the Pappas Bros. crew with help from the utilities, proving Wayne made the right choice for the moving contractor.

At the new location, Pappas expertly slid and settled the building onto the previously built foundation. The contractor who was hired to build the new foundation, rebuild the chimney, and do whatever else was required to establish the schoolhouse at its new location, then took over the work. Included in the relocation plan were a new asphalt drive, parking area, and landscaping. The move and all related work were complete by May 23.

Wayne walked with the moving crew the entire length of the move. Along the way, he spoke with many bystanders. Later he told the people in his office, "I was pleased to learn that most county residents support the dam and lake. They're glad for the flood control and are looking forward to enjoying the recreational features. The feeling I got is that supporters far outnumber opponents. The opponents, however, have media support and they are more vocal about their agenda. I cannot remember the media editorializing anything other than an anti-dam viewpoint."

Inspections performed after the move revealed some roadway damage that they quickly repaired. Two days after the move sewage water seeping up from below appeared at one intersection. Excavation to uncover the leak revealed a broken fifty year old twelve-inch sewer. They quickly repaired the damage.

Wayne had been up for nearly sixty hours, catching an occasional cat nap in his Corps pickup. When he got home his wife and son were excited to hear his stories about the move, although they probably knew more than he did from watching the coverage on television. All Wayne wanted was sleep.

A few weeks after the move Wayne was surprised to receive a note from Mrs. Pomeroy praising the work done by the Corps of Engineers and Pappas Bros.

# CHAPTER 41

While Wayne was having the schoolhouse moved in May 1972, Herbert Flaherty was finalizing assignments to supervise construction of the embankment phase for the Trout River Dam and Lake.

Herbert told Dean, "I'm transferring Harold Schneider to the project as the embankment superintendent. You've worked with Harold before. He's 58 and a lifelong operating engineer. George Knowles will continue to supervise the completion of the outlet works."

Harold arrived at the job on June 12, 1972. He elected to take up residence in a nearby well kept one story motel, the kind where you park at your door. His wife, Elaine, stayed at their home in St. Louis. After thirty-two years of marriage she accepted Harold being away and kept busy attending to her gardens.

Harold's work was his life. When he had time he liked to golf and hunt. He could operate and repair almost any type and make of construction equipment.

Included in his relocation package, Aldridge paid Harold a per diem allowance plus his moving and living expenses. The company also provided Harold with a pickup truck.

At the home office in St. Louis, Matt Wilson and Troy

Anderson, who've assisted Dean for three years, would continue performing purchasing, expediting, and engineering. A newly hired project engineer, Darrel Hightower, would help Dean with scheduling, approvals, and determining daily earthwork quantities placed in the embankment.

To assure everyone was aware of scheduling, equipment, and material needs Aldridge's Trout River team including Dean, Harold, and the project engineers met on July 11, 1972. Harold started the meeting. "Our first order of business is to remove fences, building remains, brush, and trees on one hundred seventy acres in the area of the overflow spillway."

Harold kept going. "Next we will strip about 50,000 cubic yards of topsoil and store it in a nearby location to be used three years from now on the downstream slope of the finished dam. That will take us into this August when we will start work on as much of the diversion dam foundation as is available pending completion of the outlet works."

Dean said, "Working with the estimating team we analyzed the productivity calculations made for the original estimate. From this data, we've developed a realistic schedule. The schedule does not allow for court-ordered work stoppages. It shows work for the diversion dam beginning in April 1973 and ending in June 1974. The entire embankment is scheduled to finish in March 1976. Filling of the impoundment is scheduled to start in April 1976. Factored into the schedule are weather, equipment downtime, and seasonal productivity variations."

Newly hired Darrel Hightower said, "Excavation in the emergency overflow spillway area is not intended to be precise. The sole purpose of the overflow spillway excavation is to obtain material for the embankment. The team has mapped out, using subsurface information provided by the Corps, the various strata and thickness of the material within the overflow spillway. Our overall conclusion is that we can obtain the required quantities of embankment material in the top five to ten feet of the excavation."

Darrel continued, "The downside is that the required materials are not in the right order. We will have to excavate some materials and stockpile them to get to the needed materials. The estimators included this cost in our original estimate."

Harold said, "Through the spring of 1972 into the summer of 1973 the equipment fleet will grow as we add large dozers with rock ripping teeth, loaders, compactors, off-road trucks, conveyors, and a rock crushing machine. As rock is ripped out by the dozers, we'll load it into the off-road trucks. Then we'll carry it down by the spillway to a hopper and conveyor that lifts and dumps the rock into the crusher. There we'll process the rock into the specified size. The dam foundation consists of three feet of crushed rock with appropriate drains to bleed off seepage."

Trout River was still in its original location. Large stockpiles of suitable materials from the overflow spillway would be stocked near the river bank. When the rock foundation for the diversion dam was complete, rock and earth would be rapidly bulldozed into the river permanently blocking its path and diverting it through the newly constructed outlet works.

# CHAPTER 42

Harold Schneider and Don Peterson were getting to know each other. It was June 1972, and they were talking about all the equipment coming from the Aldridge equipment yard to the job. Harold told Don, "The Aldridge equipment yard contains more than twelve acres of row after row of well cared for construction equipment. Desmond White is the yard manager. He is unforgiving to anyone who abuses a piece of equipment that is under his care. No equipment is bought, rented, sold, repaired, maintained, moved, or otherwise used without his knowledge and approval. He manages the yard like a totalitarian dictator. When a request is made to move anything from the yard to a job, Desmond has to know where, what the terrain is like, how long it is needed, and why before it is loaded and moved."

Harold warned Don, "Project superintendents rue the day they do not return unneeded equipment."

He added, "Desmond is small but mighty, about five feet six inches and one hundred fifty pounds. He's a dynamo of a man. Nobody knows about his life outside the workplace. He is always in the yard when needed; he seems to appear from nowhere. Desmond rules his domain by his strict set of rules.

He looks like an elf when his thick head of charcoal and white hair creates a halo effect when it protrudes from around his hard hat. Don't let his looks deceive you."

***

Early in the summer of 1972 the project engineers, along with Harold and Dean continued to work and rework their game plan to move eight million six hundred thousand cubic yards of earth and rock. Harold explained, "The objective is to move the material as fast as possible, travel the shortest distance, and place it as close to its final resting place as possible using a minimum number of load and unloads. Stockpiles, when needed, will be placed as near as practical to their final location."

In June 1972 Harold and Desmond agreed on an equipment utilization plan. Desmond told Harold, "You'll get your equipment as it is needed. But you need to let me know in advance. To move equipment to the job, we are required to obtain state permits for oversize and overweight loads. A load of earth moving equipment going from our yard here in St. Louis, Missouri to the Trout River Dam in Ohio will require separate permits for Missouri, Illinois, Indiana, and Ohio. There are two people employed in the yard office to handle permits, licenses, insurance, preventive maintenance, tools, and parts inventory."

***

As equipment arrived at the Trout River Project it was carefully unloaded, inspected and, if required, assembled to make it ready for use. As more and more equipment arrived the site began to look like a used construction equipment sales facility.

As a company in a high-risk industry, Aldridge got a lot of scrutiny from banks, bonding, and insurance companies. Debt to asset ratio was of paramount importance. Aldridge's equipment fleet was a large part of their assets. No company with construction equipment needs as large as Aldridge paid cash for equipment purchases. Aldridge, even with careful asset and debt management, owed their bank about six million dollars on a revolving line of credit. Aldridge pledged some of their equipment as collateral.

# CHAPTER 43

Harold was organizing his team and beginning to strip and store topsoil. He was amassing an army of bulldozers and scrapers, setting up fueling facilities, equipment maintenance sheds, and field offices. He told Dean, "We'll have some good Ohio weather from now until late October. I plan to take advantage of every day."

No sooner were the words out of Harold's mouth when Wayne appeared at the office door. "I hate to do this, but we have a court issued stop work order. It appears it only affects the work on the embankment. Work on the outlet works can continue."

Harold, who knew legal issues plagued the building of the dam, said, "Is this a result of the anti-dam bullshit I have heard about?"

Dean answered, "Yeah, I think this is the fourth one."

Wayne followed up, "This is the fourth and, what we hope final, attempt to stop the project. The plaintiffs filed a lawsuit in the United States District Court, Southern District of Ohio in Cincinnati yesterday, June 30, 1972. The Ohio Public Interest Action Group sued on behalf of the infamous Olga McCoy. McCoy owns a rundown shack on ten acres just outside the impoundment area of the lake."

"There's a history behind this," Wayne explained. "In 1968 Olga attempted to force two government surveyors from her property by firing a shotgun at them. The Ohio Public Interest Action Group was also a plaintiff in the second lawsuit with homeowner John Morrison. The government's acquisition team made numerous failed attempts to buy Olga's property. Through eminent domain, the government already owns her property, but she won't take the money, and she won't leave."

\*\*\*

Two days later U.S. Attorney Richard Albert met Wayne in the Corps field office. He told Wayne, "In addition to all the previous arguments opposing the dam the plaintiffs added a new and desperate approach in this action. Organized opponents led by Olga spent months surreptitiously searching the Trout River banks and surrounding areas looking for endangered plants or species."

Albert continued, "A week before the trial was scheduled to start, a representative acting for the plaintiffs brought a plant to the attention of their attorneys. The representative; Olga's oldest son Kenneth, claimed they discovered a few plants of an endangered species known as the Northern Monkshood, growing in the area of the proposed impoundment."

Albert said, "The introduction of the endangered plant changes the focus of the plaintiff's effort to stop construction of the dam. Instead of the usual 'the dam is unnecessary and wasteful' arguments, the focus shifts to the Corps Environmental Impact Statement."

Albert had more to say, "An amended filing was presented to the court claiming the Corps failed to adequately prepare or update the 1964 environmental impact statement by omitting the presence of an endangered plant. They are now relying on the newly enacted National Environmental Policy Act of 1969, signed into law by President Nixon on January 1, 1970."

Attorney Albert told Wayne, "I've talked to the person whose team did that report back in 1964 and she says it is impossible for that plant to exist in Clearfield County."

Wayne asked, "What the hell can we do at this late date?"

Albert answered, "Can you and a couple of your people go to the area in question and carefully scour the area and try to find another plant? Take photos of your efforts."

Wayne thought, *"What else can go wrong?"* But he said, "Sure we'll go over there Wednesday, the day after the 4th of July holiday."

On Wednesday July 5, Wayne and two others, on their hands and knees, searched the designated area. About two hours into the search one of the searchers yelled, "Wayne, come see this!"

There it was, one lonely half dead Northern Monkshood nestled in a rock outcropping. The plant, about eighteen inches long with blue hood-shaped flowers, matched the photo Wayne obtained from the court. Wayne and the others carefully photographed the plant and surrounding area and then removed the plant and surrounding soil and placed it all in a plastic container.

While they were removing the plant, Olga McCoy with her ever present 12 Gauge strolled up to Wayne and the two others. "I see ya found another of those rare plants. Jus' what do you plan to do with it?"

Wayne answered, "We're going to compare it with the ones your lawyer gave to the court." Olga seemed happy with his answer and without a word she turned away and went back to her shack.

One of the men working with Wayne, Elmer Arnold, watched Olga as she left. He said, "Wow, I thought she meant to use that cannon she's carrying."

Wayne smiled, "She has been known to let it go."

Elmer asked, "Are we going to turn this over to the court?"

"No, not yet." Wayne replied, "You are going to carefully take the plant and dirt to the Ohio Department of Natural Resources in Columbus. I notice there are two colors and textures of dirt present in the root system. We need to find out if that plant came from somewhere else. Be careful; don't disturb the dirt or any part of the plant."

When they arrived back at the office, and the endangered plant was on its way to ODNR, Wayne called attorney Albert, "I think we are on to something. We found a half dead plant that appears to be a Northern Monkshood wedged in some rocks. We dug it out along with some natural dirt, and I sent it up to the ODNR in Columbus. I asked them to have the species confirmed and to analyze the soil to determine its origin. We should have an official report on Friday."

Albert was pleased, "Good work, let me know as soon as you hear from ODNR."

Wayne said, "Before you go, let me update you on the status of the project. When McCoy and the Action Group filed their lawsuit to kill the Trout River Project; the first phase of the project, the outlet works, was approximately seventy-five percent complete. The contractor, Aldridge Construction Co. was preparing to begin second phase work, building the earth and rock embankment. That has now stopped."

Albert agreed, "The purpose of the McCoy action is to stop work on the second and last phase of the project, the earthwork for the dam embankment. Without the dam, there will be no lake thus avoiding the flooding of more than two thousand acres and leaving the river in its natural location. The plaintiffs are trusting that a favorable decision will be won based on what I suspect is a falsely attested to presence of an endangered flower."

Albert updated the status of the trial, "The plaintiffs, through their attorney, Frederick Hartshorne, were unable to get Federal Judge, Oscar Briscoe, to grant an injunction to stop work on the entire project. However, Judge Briscoe did grant an amended motion for a temporary injunction stopping all work on the earth embankment only. As you know, work on the phase one outlet works will continue. The temporary injunction is to be effective until the court decides certain legal matters."

Wayne Told Albert, "The Aldridge Construction project manager, Dean Richardson, told me they have parked all earth moving equipment amassed at the project site and sent home the workers hired to operate the equipment. Work is continuing on the seventy-five percent complete outlet works."

***

On July 14, 1972, Albert and Wayne attended the pretrial hearing. Albert whispered to Wayne, "The parties have agreed for the Honorable Judge Briscoe to decide the outcome, no jury. At the pretrial hearing, both sides will present witness lists, documents, photos, and items to be relied on during the trial. All the evidentiary materials are assigned exhibit numbers." The trial began on August 10, 1972. The courtroom was partially full, including several members of the press. Seated among them was the project's nemesis,

Roger Wilkins, representing the Cincinnati Daily News. Wayne noted Roger's presence and thought, *"He has probably already written his story. I haven't seen the truth in any of his articles."*

Both lawyers made brief opening statements.

The plaintiff's lawyer, Frederick Hartshorne; a partner in the large firm of Smyth, Leonard, and Hartshorne, had just two statements. He said, starting his opening statement, "First, the old environmental impact statement is not valid today. Evidence of the heretofore undisclosed presence of an endangered plant within the lake area justifies the need for a new statement. Flooding the impoundment area will forever destroy this rare and valuable asset."

"Second," he continued, "The need for a flood control dam is not financially justified or wanted by the people of Clearfield County. Thank you."

Albert also made two points. "First, he said, "In three previous trials the government prevailed, proving the project is necessary, beneficial, and authorized by Congressional mandate. Second the environmental impact statement performed in 1964 was the valid guideline when Congress, in 1966, authorized the project."

Attorney Hartshorne presented his client's case that relied on the lack of an up to date environmental impact statement and the alleged presence of an endangered floral species. The plaintiffs rested their case after three days of testimony that consisted mostly of witnesses telling how meticulous they were in their diligence to find the endangered plant.

In rebuttal, U.S. Attorney Albert decided to go right for the jugular vein of the plaintiffs. His first witness was Wayne. After Wayne was sworn in as a witness, Albert asked him,

"Describe to the court the purpose of the Trout River Dam."

Wayne kept his answer short, "The primary purpose of the dam and lake is flood control. During the more than one hundred year lifetime of the dam, it will save untold millions of dollars in property damage and possibly prevent loss of life. An added benefit is a two thousand two hundred acre lake and another two thousand acres of mostly wooded recreation area containing camp sites, boat launching ramps, a beach, and hunting areas. Other benefits are opportunities for fishing, hiking, and all kinds of water sports."

Albert was anxious to get to the crux of the issue, "Wayne, describe an investigation you conducted about a month ago."

Wayne also wanted to get it over with, "On July 5, along with two other Corps of Engineers employees, I went to a location designated by the plaintiffs as being the natural habitat of an endangered flower, the Northern Monkshood. We searched the site on our hands and knees for more than two hours. Eventually one of the guys helping to look for the plant, found a specimen matching the description of the endangered plant. Ms. McCoy was also there and observed us looking for the plant. She saw us find one of the plants in question."

Albert asked, "Then what happened?"

Wayne Answered, "I told everyone to back away so as not to disturb the area. We were hoping that we would find more plants. We could only see one plant wedged in a rock outcropping. We very carefully removed the plant, its root system, and the surrounding earth. It was all placed in a plastic container we brought with us."

"Then what happened?" Albert asked.

Wayne continued his testimony, "We went back to the project office and secured the container and the plant, undisturbed. Our primary goal was to keep the plant alive. The same day it was transported by the guy who found it to the Ohio Department of Natural Resources office and laboratory in Columbus. They accepted and signed for the delivery. We asked them to identify the plant species, where it originated, and provide a written report. Our delivery person returned to the project office and resumed his normal duties."

Albert said, "Thank you, Wayne." With consent from the judge and a nod from attorney Hartshorne, they added the ODNR report to the exhibits.

Attorney Hartshorne elected to cross-examine. He asked Wayne, "Please identify the person who found the flower."

Wayne responded, "Elmer Arnold."

Hartshorne pressed on, "And what are his qualifications." Wayne responded, "He is a civil engineer in training."

"Not a botanist?" asked Hartshorne. Wayne answered, "No."

Hartshorne sat and stated, "I have no more questions for this witness; I reserve the right to recall."

Albert then called his only other witness, ODNR botanist, Dr. Sheryl Hopkins. After swearing in and the usual preliminary introductions and establishing credibility, Albert asked, "Dr. Hopkins, On July 5 did you receive a plastic container holding a plant and dirt, hand carried to you by Mr. Arnold, an employee of the US Army Corps of Engineers?"

Hopkins replied, "Yes I did."

Albert pursued his line of questioning, "And what did you do with it?"

Hopkins answered, "As instructed I determined the species and origin of the plant. I was elated to see it is a very rare and endangered Aconitum noveboracense, commonly known as Northern Monkshood. I notice it is identical to the other example here in the courtroom."

Albert noted that this was not Hopkins first time as a witness. "Alright, Dr. Hopkins, what else can you tell us about this particular plant and its origin?"

"This plant," said Hopkins, looked directly at Olga, "Does not grow, in the area where the plaintiff claimed it originated. In fact, it is not indigenous to any place in Clearfield County. The only known location in Ohio where a few plants survive is a small and specific place in Hocking County, about a hundred miles away." Hopkins added, "The botanist responsible for Hocking County reported to the ODNR office more than a month ago that a robbery occurred at the site and plants taken from the protected area. I believe at least one of those stolen plants is in this courtroom."

Before anyone could react to the doctor's testimony, Olga McCoy was on her feet and, showing surprising agility for a sixty-something woman, jumped over the plaintiff's table and headed straight for Dr. Hopkins screaming, "You lyin bitch, I'm gonna show you who knows about plants and flowers. If I had my piece, you'd be dead."

Two bailiffs quickly grabbed Olga and, with great effort, subdued her. The judge ordered her restrained and removed to a holding area outside the courtroom.

Dr. Hopkins did not appear to be upset by the violent

outburst. She sat as an observer with her arms folded over her chest.

Judge Briscoe slammed his gavel down and declared, "Court is in recess until tomorrow at ten o'clock. I want to see both attorneys in my chambers, now!"

Attorneys Albert and Hartshorne meekly followed an angry Judge Briscoe into chambers. The judge sat in his oversized chair, but made no indication for the two lawyers to do likewise. They both felt like school boys in the principal's office.

The judge started on Hartshorne. The judge's granite gray piercing eyes discouraging any attempt at confidence, "What the hell is going on out there? Have your clients brought perjured evidence into my court?"

Hartshorne stammered and stuttered to find words. Finally, he meekly answered, "Your Honor, I have no idea what has transpired. Back in June, my clients brought me a flower that they claimed will clinch their case. They seemed very sure that the existence of an endangered plant in the lake area would force the government to stop building the dam. After hearing Dr. Hopkins testimony, I request some time to sort this out. Two days are all we need."

Judge Briscoe sat in silence for a moment. "Based on the overwhelming evidence that perjury has occurred I'm excluding the plaintiff's evidence and ruling for the defendants. I'm lifting the injunction and all work on the dam can proceed immediately. The judge continued, "Furthermore, I am notifying the Hocking County Prosecutor that a crime, namely the theft and disturbance of an endangered plant species, has occurred in their county. This court believes one or all of the plaintiffs committed the robbery. I'll reconvene court long enough for me to issue my decision."

The McCoy lawsuit to stop work spanned one month and ten days of on and off legal maneuvering by the plaintiffs and counter maneuvers by the government. Other than occasional public protests, editorials, and outcries by environmental groups, legal wrangling was over.

In September 1972 the Hocking County Prosecutor charged Olga and son Kenny with theft of state property. They pled guilty. Olga, because of her mental state and age was sentenced to thirty days in the county jail with the jail time suspended and given a year of probation. Kenny, who was the actual thief, was sentenced to thirty days in jail.

In Clearfield County, local opposition continued. However, the negative publicity generated by the lawsuits had a reverse effect that brought out supporters of the project. By the end of 1972 supporters far outnumbered opponents.

\*\*\*

After the conclusion of the fourth lawsuit; the first but not the last McCoy action, Wayne told Melissa, "The ironic aspect of all the legal measures taken to stop the dam is that not one of them addressed the human element. How it affects the displaced people who are making sacrifices and the impact on their lives. All four lawsuits were about environmental and economic issues."

Wayne continued to observe, "The opponents appear to be more about seeking publicity for their agendas than acknowledging this project will return more than four thousand acres of private habited land to pristine public wilds and within that area create a two thousand two hundred acre lake. All of the lake and amenities will be for public use and enjoyment."

# CHAPTER 44

Knowles and Don were having one of their frequent schedule coordination meetings. Don said, "It's finally spring of 1972 and work on the control tower is far from complete. To wrap up all the control tower concrete, we need to complete the last thirty feet of control tower walls and the control tower access floor."

George wasn't satisfied with Don's summary of uncompleted work. He told Don, "You're only looking at the tower. We need to get going on the center support pier for the access bridge and the access bridge abutment on Carney Road."

Knowles listed other work, "Concerning the tower, we have to install four main water control gates, ten Intermediate water control gates, hydraulic piping and operating console for the control gates, and finish the electrical work. Other than the area of the tower, after we finish the pier and abutments, we need to erect the access bridge support girders, place the concrete access bridge deck and curbs. We've got a lot left to do."

Six weeks later Don was talking with Knowles and Dean. "We just finished topping out the last thirty feet of the control tower. Man, it was scary. The crane and workers had to work at their maximum capabilities. They had all they could handle.

But the control tower concrete, except for removing a little formwork and concrete cleaning, is all done."

Dean said, "This Friday, let's see that's June 6, we'll have a topping out party in the lab building. Tell everyone. I'll invite the people from the Corps office."

Then Dean got serious. He ordered Knowles and Don, "Plan to expedite all remaining work requiring the use of the damned one hundred fifty-ton crane and crew. We need to get rid of that bitch as soon as we can."

The week after the topping out party Don and Knowles were discussing how to complete the remaining work inside the tower most expeditiously. Don explained, "When we finish the work for the operating level floor, we need to get the mechanical sub in to do the hydraulic piping and hook up the fourteen water control gates."

Knowles reminded Don, "To have easy access to the control tower we'll need the access bridge. To erect the bridge we need to build the center pier and abutment. Let's continue to make them our priority."

\*\*\*

On June 12, 1972, after topping out the control tower, the big crane was moved halfway up the hill to the center bridge support pier. Don told Duane, "Rough out a road to the center pier and then have the dozer help the crane move up to that location. Before doing that, we're going to remove forty feet of boom and the entire jib from the crane. That will give us one hundred sixty feet of main boom for finishing the center pier." Don addressed the center pier crew, "You will be working up to a hundred feet above the ground. Make sure you follow all safety precautions and watch Billy Ray; he has the best view of the work area. He'll let you know if he sees a potential problem."

While work on the center pier was going on, the bridge abutment beside Carney Road was being built. The small crew assigned to this work felt lucky. They told each other, "This is the only part of this job where we don't have to ride that damn truck down to work. For once we can drive right up to and park beside where we'll be working."

On August 14 the small crew started to build the Bridge abutment. They finished it on August 29. About the same time, on August 28, the center pier was topped out and ready to receive the bridge girders.

# CHAPTER 45

During the summer of 1972, almost a year before the river could be diverted through the outlet works, Harold was mobilizing earthmoving and compacting equipment and was beginning to remove and store topsoil from the borrow area. The embankment work was getting back to speed after Olga McCoy' frivolous lawsuit and, Aldridge's earth moving crews were gaining momentum. The company had a huge commitment of equipment and manpower.

The court ordered injunction stopped work on the embankment from July 1 to August 10. The resulting work stoppage had a devastating effect on the project schedule that lasted beyond the forty days of lost time. All the Aldridge employees committed to the embankment had to be laid off. They lost the momentum that was happening in June. Work scheduled for the summer of 1972 would occur in less favorable conditions in the fall and winter.

When work resumed in August Aldridge had to rehire equipment operators and laborers. Only a few of the first group of workers returned. Most had found other employment. Harold had to start over. It took two weeks to bring the pace of the work back to pre-lawsuit conditions.

Dean, as required by the contract, put the Corps on notice that Aldridge had lost substantial time due to Olga's lawsuit. He stated in the notice letter that due to lost momentum, lost productivity caused by seasonal differences, rehiring and reorienting workers, the delay totaled sixty-five calendar days. Aldridge's average overhead and idle equipment expenses were $302 per hour, a total of $113,500.

Wayne, as usual, was peeved by Dean's blunt request for time and money.

***

Roger Wilkins, Wayne's nemesis during the past five years, was elated when he heard about the order to stop work. As in the past, he was right in Wayne's face, obnoxious as ever, demanding a statement. Wayne refused to be baited and told Wilkins, "As I've said many times; I have nothing to say. For information, you may contact the public information office in the Louisville District Office. Now get out of here."

Another happy person, although as a government employee he couldn't show or express his feelings, was the chief technician and inspector, Brian Towleson. His elation occurred because of the hardship the stop order placed on the contractor, causing lost time and money. Over the past three years, Dean's been aware of Towelson's unabashed glee whenever bad luck or setbacks of any kind hampered the contractor's progress.

There had been several court-ordered work stoppages. Dean, following Wayne's advice, kept accurate records of time and expenses incurred during the court-ordered shutdowns. Every day that elapsed during a court-ordered shutdown Dean prepared a complete summary of the idled equipment, the date, the weather, worker inefficiencies, and a narrative describing the impact on the project, complete with photos.

Injunctions and stop work actions were filed on and off over the next three years. Aldridge workers and equipment danced to the tune but, once given the go ahead, made good progress building the dam embankment.

Wayne and Dean had one of their rare discussions arising from the stop work orders. Dean said, "Wayne you measure real progress by the amount of work in place compared to the project schedule."

Wayne replied, "You measures real progress as the amount and cost of the work for the same period compared to the anticipated cost." Wayne switched gears asking, "Will you be able to work during the winter?"

Dean answered, "Yeah. The good thing is that a lot of the excavated material we are placing in the embankment we can place in cold weather. Wise use of the weather will allow limited work placing embankment fill to continue during winter months."

## CHAPTER 46

A lot of work remained to complete the control tower. All of that work would be made easier after erecting the two-hundred foot long access bridge from Carney Road to the control tower. Dean told George Knowles, "Berger Iron Co. in Dayton has the contract to fabricate and deliver the six-foot deep steel girders. He added, "I've subcontracted the erection of the bridge to Santoni Steel Erecting and Crane Service. They are from Cincinnati but, other than that, I don't know much about them."

The access bridge consisted of a two-hundred foot long span using two parallel six foot deep girders supported at the center by the recently completed concrete pier. To span the two hundred feet, between Carney Road and the tower, the two girders were each made from three massive sixty-foot lengths and one twenty foot long filler section. Each sixty-foot girder section weighed about eleven tons. The two girders were separated ten feet apart, and connected by heavy cross bracing spaced every twelve feet the full length of the bridge. There was also a maintenance walkway and handrail located below the bridge deck.

The Santoni crew arrived with five ironworkers and a foreman on Tuesday, September 5, 1972. Berger Iron made two over-length girder deliveries on the same day. Two more deliveries of sixty-foot girders came on Wednesday and Thursday. Delivery of the final two lengths of the twenty-foot fillers occurred on Friday, September 7.

On September 6 Dean and George meet with Charley Dooley, Santoni's foreman, to discuss erecting the girders. Dooley explained, "We will start with one sixty foot section resting on the abutment. Beginning with the left side of the bridge, using two cranes, we will slowly lift and scoot the girder until it is about halfway out. Then we will connect the next sixty-foot section to the first one. We will continue lifting and scooting until the assembled girder is within reach of your one-hundred-fifty-ton crane near the center pier."

Dooley's explanation continued, "Using your crane at the pier and our crane at the abutment we will place the forward end on the pier and set the aft end on the abutment. We'll repeat that procedure for the other girder."

George asked, "Can you handle that length without temporary stiffeners or cross bracing to prevent lateral bending?"

Dooley became defensive saying, "We know what we're doing, just let us do our job."

George, becoming agitated, pushed the issue, "You need lateral bracing. There's no way to set those girders out there without temporary stiffeners. When you get those things in the air, it will be like trying to move a piece of spaghetti."

Dooley stood up, ending the meeting and having the final word, "Just let us do our job. We don't want your interference!"

By the end of the day on September 8 the Santoni crew had all the bridge girders sorted out. The first sixty-foot long girder was aligned with the bridge and sitting on the Carney Road abutment, projecting about twenty feet toward the center pier. It was Friday, so the ironworkers made it secure and left for the weekend.

The following Monday, September 11, using two cranes the Santoni crew began easing the girder a foot or two at a time toward the pier. When the first sixty-foot long section had progressed far enough, they aligned the next sixty-foot section and bolted it to the forward section.

Billy Ray in the one-hundred-fifty-ton capacity crane remained at the center pier to receive its share of the load as soon as the girder was close enough. By early afternoon the one-hundred-twenty foot long girder was scooted to within fifty feet of the center pier. An ironworker crawled to the end of the girder and mated the hook from the one-hundred-fifty-ton capacity crane to a lifting lug near the end of the girders. He then retreated off the girders to solid ground.

George Knowles was observing this from his field office. About two o'clock he stormed from his office and went to the Carney Road scene where ironworkers continued the dangerous process of lift and scoot progressing toward the center pier. "Dooley," he shouted, "Stop before you kill somebody! That hunk of iron must be braced before it collapses and takes cranes and all with it. Bring it back in!"

Dooley and Knowles were face to face shouting at each other. Finally, Dooley had the last word, "Listen, old man, I'm in charge of how this will get done. Go back to your office and let us do our work!"

Knowles shook his head, "I've tried to warn you." He then went back to his office.

Progress lifting and scooting increased when the big crane had hold of the forward end at the pier and the eighty-ton capacity crane had the aft end over the abutment. The forward end of the assembled two sixty foot long girder sections finally reached and was barely resting on the center pier. A hundred feet of the girders spanned from the abutment to the center pier. There was twenty feet remaining to be scooted forward before the aft end could be seated into the abutment and the girder properly bearing on the pier.

Dean was working on his reports when he heard Knowles shout, "There it goes!" When Dean looked up, the girders were still suspended from the cranes but no longer straight and true. The entire one-hundred-foot length between the abutment and the pier was bowed and sagged to the right. It was on the brink of folding up and collapsing.

Everything stopped. For about ten minutes everyone just stared at the damaged and sagging girder. When Knowles and Dean arrived back at the abutment Dooley was ordering Billy Ray in the big crane at the pier, "Hold steady but ease the load onto the pier. Don't let go, keep tension on the hoist cable, but make contact with the pier." Then he gave the same instructions to the crane operator at the abutment.

Knowles keyed his two-way radio and found Duane who was just about ready to leave for the day. He told him, "Duane, find at least two-hundred feet of good wire rope cable and bring it with the dozer up to the Carney Road bridge abutment. Hurry!"

Dooley, somewhat contrite at this point, asked, "What are you planning?"

Dean observed that Knowles and Dooley knew they had to use both of their skills to avert a catastrophic accident. Billy Ray, the crane operator in the one hundred fifty-ton crane, was in extreme peril. He couldn't leave the crane when there was a load on it. To his dismay, he knew if the girder collapsed it would take the crane boom with it and probably tip the big crane over. His life was in jeopardy.

Towelson and several others from the Corps office had gathered nearby. Most were silently watching the tense scene. Dean could hear Towelson as he gloated, "Look at those stupid contractors; they can't even erect a simple girder without botching it."

Dean heard the cocky words and shot Towelson an angry glance. Towelson averted Dean's eyes and looked away.

Knowles had to deal with more important issues. He asked Dooley, "Do you have someone who can go out on the girders and attach a cable at the midpoint of the bowed section? We'll then connect the cable to the dozer and put some strain on the girders in the opposite direction of the damage. We can lessen the chance of a complete collapse."

Dooley looked at his crew. "You heard him, will one of you volunteer to do that?" The youngest of all, a 21-year-old apprentice ironworker immediately stepped forward, "I'll do it." In a quiet voice, he muttered, "Maybe I'll get some respect from these guys, and they'll quit raggin' on me about learnin' the trade."

Using a rope, the young ironworker made a makeshift safety harness. Crawling on his hands and knees, he made the perilous foot by foot journey across the damaged girders. The wooded hillside was a hundred feet below. The courageous young man faced serious injury or death if the damaged girder suddenly buckled. If the damaged girder fully buckled, it would also topple both cranes with their operators. The young ironworker continued crawling across the unstable girder until he reached the damaged area near mid-point. The other crane hoisted the cable out to him, and he securely attached it to the center of the severely damaged hundred foot long section of the girder. Duane attached the other end of the cable to the bulldozer. As soon as the connections were secure, the young man scurried off the girder. The dozer then pulled until the cable was taut securing the girder from further bending. The girder was safe, at least for now.

It was dark by the time the cable was secure and the crane loads adjusted to have the right amount of lift. The girders were equally supported by the pier and abutment, and by the cranes. Because both cranes had a load on their hook, the operators were not permitted to leave the cranes. The crane crews agreed they would stay on duty all night and receive pay according to their union contract.

During the night and early morning, Dean or someone from the modular home tended to the needs of the crane crews making sure they had food and water.

***

The following morning, Tuesday, September 12, Dooley and his ironworker crew returned with a supervisor. Everything was the same as when they left Monday night.

The new supervisor quickly took charge but not before Knowles told him to explain their plan. Knowles asked, "How are you going to bring the girders back to land?"

The supervisor, none other than company vice president Vincent Santoni, answered, "We are going to ease them back very carefully in the same manner we got them out there. We believe if we can get them back just twenty to twenty-five feet it will significantly reduce the danger. We can then bring them all the way back, separate the two sixty foot sections, and set them on blocking in the road. We need your dozer to continue keeping tension on them until they are at least halfway back."

Billy Ray, the operator of the one-hundred-fifty-ton capacity crane, agreed to the plan. His skill at gently handling the load was the key to successfully recovering the girders.

At one point in the recovery operation, Wayne came from his office and called Dean over to him. "I know you have a crisis on your hands, but I have a problem related to your problem. This project is receiving adverse publicity, especially by the press and a reporter named Roger Wilkins."

"Please," Wayne pleaded, "avoid making this incident newsworthy. Wilkins will have a reporter's field day. We will have photographers, TV cameras, and protesters all over the place. Nothing good will come of creating a media circus."

All Dean could promise was a weak, "We'll do what we can."

Slowly, inch by inch, the girder was backed off the pier toward Carney Road. By noon they were about twenty feet closer. Work continued through lunch. No one wanted to let up in the effort to save the girder. "But more important," as Knowles observed, "We want to prevent the impending disaster should the girder completely collapse."

By mid-afternoon, the girder was more than halfway back, and two smaller cranes on Carney Road were able to handle the weight. The ironworkers unhooked the crane from the girder, and Billy Ray heaved a huge sigh of relief. He quickly retreated to a safe place.

By five o'clock the badly bent girder was separated into its two sixty foot sections and placed lengthwise on Carney Road. The crisis was over. Corps inspectors were all over the girder sections claiming they were damaged goods and not suitable for use on this project. Brian Towlson was the most vocal.

On Tuesday afternoon Dean called the fabricator, Berger Iron Company to advise them of the situation. They agreed to have their shop superintendent inspect the damaged girders Wednesday morning.

\*\*\*

At nine o'clock am Wednesday morning, September 13, Harold Greene, Berger's shop superintendent, and two others arrived at the job. Inspector Towelson was first to approach them, "You are wasting your time. The girders have been deemed unsuitable for use on this project." Neither Wayne nor Dean was present during the exchange nor, as Wayne explained later, did Towelson have the authority to make such a decision.

Greene politely responded to Towelson, "I supervised the shop fabrication of the girders. I'll verify that the Corps of Engineers had inspectors in our shop and after initial fabrication, due to heat generated during welding; the girders looked worse than they do now. We can straighten them with no harm to the steel or the load carrying capacity. Now, who are you?" Dean and Wayne arrived as the conversation between Greene and Towelson was becoming confrontational. Wayne stepped in and told Towelson, "Let's not make a rash decision here. A metallurgist from the research center in Vicksburg will be here this afternoon. We need that input before we take any action."

Greene said, talking to Dean and Wayne, "While we wait for the metallurgist my foreman, Johann Wingerter, and I would like to spend some time inspecting the damage and taking some measurements." Everyone agreed to back off while the two Berger people went about their inspection.

Towelson stayed close by annoying the two as they tried to make a judgment about the condition of the girders, and a plan for repairs. He was determined to see the two girder sections removed from the job. Dean thought Towelson's determination to condemn the girders centered on his desire to punish the contractor rather than the actual condition of the girders.

As promised that afternoon the metallurgist arrived. He took some microscopic samples from the welds and bent areas of the top flanges. "I'll get these to our lab by tomorrow morning and, hopefully, we'll have a report on Friday."

While standing beside the girders, the metallurgist had a long conversation with Harold Greene. Harold told him, "If there is no tearing or damage to the steel, and we don't see any, we can straighten it right here using the same methods employed in the shop. After fabrication, any girder of this size requires a lot of straightening."

During the next two days, several engineers from the district office poked around the massive, but damaged girder sections.

On Monday, September 18, a meeting was held in Wayne's

office to discuss the fate of the damaged girders. Present were Wayne, Dean, Towelson, Greene, Johann, Santoni, the Vicksburg metallurgist, and an engineer from the district office.

Wayne asked Harold Greene, "What happens if the girders can't be straightened?"

Greene responded, "We will have to schedule shop time and fabricate new ones. To obtain the steel and make room in the shop we estimate it will take at least eight to ten weeks." He continued, "We can straighten them here on the site according to the requirements of the American Steel Institute and all other steel fabricating codes in about a week. We can't rush the straightening procedures. We have to take as much time as needed."

The metallurgist agreed, "It is possible, using strict guidelines, to straighten them here. There is some risk, especially if it rains or it is windy. The heat required to straighten them must dissipate slowly on its own."

Greene agreed, "If the Corps approves the option to straighten the girders, Berger and the contractor will assume all risk for a straight and true outcome."

Towelson objected and said, "That piece of iron sitting out there is no better than scrap. If we allow these guys to do what they want and the girder fails sometime down the road where does that leave us?"

Wayne started to say something, but Dean interrupted, "Right now that's our problem. We've heard the experts, and it appears, with the Corps approval, we have the option to repair and straighten."

Wayne agreed, "If you opt to straighten, Aldridge will

have to assume full responsibility for like-new girders. Before erecting the girders, we will need a final inspection and approval from the District Office."

Dean said, "We'll straighten it. Just give us the go ahead." It took three days, until Thursday, September 21, for the Corps to approve the plan. Wayne informed Dean, "The District Engineer agreed to allow straightening of the girders; but Aldridge and Berger must submit the repair plan in writing and assume full responsibility."

The next day Dean gave Wayne the required letter describing the straightening procedure.

\*\*\*

On Monday, September 26, Greene and two shop workers arrived with tanks of oxygen and acetylene, large rosebud heating torches, and their safety gear. Before their arrival, a crew from Santoni Steel Erectors separated and positioned the two damaged sixty-foot girders as directed by Greene.

The straightening work performed by the Berger employees was amazing. They heated specific areas of the bent girder to a reddish orange glow. Then they stopped for fifteen to eighteen hours to allow the heated areas to cool naturally, no water or fans. As the metal cooled, one could actually see the Girders move. Little by little, day by day the two sixty foot girders miraculously became as straight as before the accident. After six days the engineers, using measuring and alignment checking devices, proclaimed them straight and acceptable for use in the bridge.

On October 2 Charley Dooley and the Santoni ironworker crew returned to resume erecting the bridge. A somewhat contrite Dooley met with Dean and Knowles. He explained how they planned to reassemble and safely erect the girders. "Before work resumes, we are installing a safety net from the tower to the pier and from the pier to the abutment."

Charley continued, "We will set two of the sixty footers side by side and install the cross bracing between them. By installing the cross bracing, we will create a box girder effect with much greater stiffness than one girder alone. We will then proceed the same way we did before, slowly lift and move the girder assembly until we align it with the bridge centerline."

"We will then lift and scoot it until it is about twenty feet toward the pier. Then we will assemble the next pair of sixty footers with cross bracing and bolt them to the forward assembly."

Dooley continued his explanation, "Using the one-hundred-fifty-ton capacity crane at the pier and the eighty-ton capacity crane at the abutment, we will move the entire assembly forward until it is setting on the abutment and pier bearing surfaces. We will leave about twenty feet cantilevered off the pier toward the tower."

Charley, with Vincent Santoni listening, further explained, "Then the one hundred fifty-ton crane will be repositioned between the pier and the tower. The last two of the eighty-foot girders will be moved down the hill to a position below the space between the installed girders and the tower and assembled with the cross bracing. The big crane will be reconfigured to handle thirty tons, the weight of the last eighty-foot long girder assembly. We will hoist it into place as a one piece unit, completing the span from the abutment to the tower."

Knowles asked, "When will you install the maintenance walkway that is between the girders?"

Dooley answered, "We have already started, working from the abutment to the tower. We want to be out of here in three weeks." As promised they were. By October 25, 1972, the Santoni crew and their equipment were gone.

Santoni, when confronted about delays and expenses incurred by Aldridge, agreed to consider a back charge. Dean and George decided they were delayed at least 18 working days at $1275 per day, and incurred direct expenses, including charges from Berger, of $22,000. Dean sent Santoni an invoice totaling $44,950. Santoni, after negotiations, agreed to pay Aldridge $40,000.

## CHAPTER 47

On October 23 Don Peterson, carpenter foreman, and his remaining crew, began formwork for the reinforced concrete access bridge deck to the control tower. The bridge deck was twelve feet wide with a one-foot high integral curb on each side. The crew formed and placed the concrete and removed the formwork in five weeks.

Next, they installed a three-foot-six-inch high aluminum railing on each side of the bridge roadway. Finally, on November 21, 1972, access to the control tower became much easier via the control tower access bridge.

***

Wayne and Dean, regardless of differing motives and goals, have addressed and solved the problems, challenges, and delays that have affected the construction of the dam. The solutions in some instances were ugly and not beneficial to Aldridge Construction Company or the Government. With the completion of most of the concrete work Dean anticipated clear sailing to wrap up the remaining work for the outlet works. Not so. Union disputes were about to create havoc on the Trout River Dam.

Most of the remaining work consisted of installing water control gates and their operating system in the control tower.

The water control system consisted of two, six feet wide by fourteen feet high, main control gates each topped with a large fourteen foot long hydraulic operating cylinder. Two equally sized backup control gates were placed behind and in line with the main gates. The remaining water control gates consisted of ten, 5-foot by 5-foot sluice gates mounted at various heights on the outside face of the control tower.

Electrically operated valves and a hydraulic oil pump assembled in a master control panel controlled the flow of hydraulic oil to individual gates. Stainless steel tubing supplied hydraulic fluid to open and close each gate.

George assigned installation of the gates to Aldridge employees from the millwright union. Dean subcontracted furnishing and installing the hydraulic piping system to a Cincinnati contractor, J & M Mechanical Co.

J & M pipefitters arrived on the job Monday, November 27 to set up and start laying out their work. The pipefitter foreman, Carl Spooner, met George with a barrage of demands about working conditions. George asked him, "Didn't you anticipate the challenging and confined working space inside the tower."

Carl curtly responded, "Hell no. We didn't know we'd be working in the air suspended from work baskets." Carl was surly and uncooperative throughout the time it took to complete their work. His crew had the same disruptive attitude. No matter what Dean and George said or did, even when they tried to help, Carl took it as criticism and was defensive.

When Carl started his work, George had a crew of millwrights installing the fourteen water control gates. The second day the pipefitters were on the job Carl stormed into the field office shouting, "Why are those fucking millwrights installing the sluice gates? That's pipefitter work!"

George Knowles answered, Carl, "I make the work assignments on this job. Get your ass back to work."

George was about to lose his famous temper but Carl left saying, "You haven't heard the last of this." Ten minutes later Carl was back with another demand, "We need a work platform every eight feet in the tower."

George responded through clenched teeth, "Look at your contract, your company is responsible for access to all work areas. As agreed, and stipulated in your subcontract, we have provided supports for scaffolds or suspended work baskets and safety lanyards. The rest is up to you."

Almost every day Carl or one of his crew complained about some problem preventing them from doing their work. George told Dean, "The J & M workers are awed and displeased by the magnitude and height of the area where it is necessary to do their work. The J & M crew probably believes their boss assigned them to a crappy job."

Dean responded, "It is possible they are unhappy and afraid of working in the high and dismal control tower where most of their work occurs."

On Wednesday, November 29 Herbert Flaherty, president of Aldridge Construction, received a call from the pipefitter business agent, Joseph Lech. Herb later described the call as the most unprofessional and threatening outburst he ever received. He related the conversation to George, "This asshole from the fitters union threatened to bring forty pipefitters to the job, break the place up, and throw those scab millwrights off the site. Keep your eyes open for troublemakers."

Herbert continued, "I diplomatically offered to meet with Lech to explain the assignment. I also informed Lech that Aldridge does not have a labor agreement with the pipefitters. We make work assignments according to our agreements with the respective labor organization. Then Lech abruptly ended the call. I never had the opportunity to schedule a meeting. I don't know what will happen. Keep alert; this could get ugly." About an hour after the phone confrontation between Herbert and Joseph, Dean noticed a newer four-door Buick with a driver and three occupants working its way down the access road. Dean was alone in the office. He was amazed to see a passenger car on the work site. It was very unusual for any vehicle without four-wheel drive to use the access road.

Not only did the shiny black car descend the hill, but it also kept going onto the levee road leading to the field office. The car was covered in mud by the time it reached the office.

The four men entered the field office. The one in the suit introduced himself as Joe Lech, pipefitter business agent. The other three, who could only be Lech's muscle or thugs remained nameless. Joe confronted Dean, "Where the fuck is Herbert Flaherty? I'm here to meet with him."

Dean responded, "I don't know for sure, but he is probably at our home office in St. Louis. Can I help you?"

Instantly, Lech grabbed Dean by the front of his shirt and slammed him against a filing cabinet yelling, "I don't want to talk to no peon son of a bitch, I want to talk to the man." Then he threw Dean across the office into the wall and desk.

Dean staggered to his feet ready for another attack. He

tried to push Lech's arms away, but he was no match for the big man. With Lech's arm against his throat, Dean could hardly talk. He tried to explain, "I'm sure Herb will meet with you, now let me go."

Before Lech could do more damage, one of the goons pulled Lech away and whispered, "That's enough boss." Lech backed off and there was no more violence. The three goons were more than enough to remind Dean of the danger if he fought back or retaliated.

Dean said, "I can try to get Mr. Flaherty on the phone, but first I want you to get out of my office."

Lech responded, "I want to talk to Carl, the fitter foreman. Where is he?"

Dean used the two-way radio to ask Don to have Carl come to the office. He also asked Don, "Send a couple of big carpenters. We have a situation down here and need to keep an eye on things,"

To Dean's satisfaction, Lech and his three 'helpers' left the office and waited outside. When Carl arrived, the five of them had a half hour discussion. The four union representatives prepared to leave. Dean, the two carpenters, and Larry stayed in the office watching the activity outside. Dean checked his body for injuries. His throat hurt where Lech grabbed him, and he had a bruised shoulder where he hit the filing cabinet. Dean was mad but thankful he did not escalate the incident. Lech was about six inches taller and at least seventy pounds heavier.

Don came to the office soon after the two carpenters arrived. When Don saw Dean and heard about what Lech did to him, Dean had had another problem. Don wanted to; as he put it, "Get an ounce of flesh and take my hammer to those assholes." Dean calmed him down and asked him not to escalate an already bad situation.

Don in his authoritative style confronted the four pipefitter representatives telling them, "What you did here today only shows you as cowards and bullies. You're not welcome here. You have five minutes to be up the hill and gone before the sheriff gets here."

The Buick was mired in mud. Lech got in the car, and the muscle attempted to free the car by pushing and rocking back and forth. They had to turn the car a hundred and eighty degrees to drive out. They finally got the Buick turned around, and the Buick was able to move on its own. Now, not just the car, but the passengers had mud caked on them. Several workers who stood by and observed the scene applauded as the entourage slowly made their way off the levee and up the hill.

Dean told one of the carpenters, "Good riddance. That asshole and his three goons, their suits, and the car need a good cleaning."

This incident was just the beginning of more union disagreements. On November 30, 1972, the fitters union filed a grievance with the Cincinnati Building Trades Council. On the same day the fitters filed their complaint the ironworkers filed their grievance claiming water control gate installation.

Herb discussed the situation with Dean, "We are installing the control gates per our collective bargaining agreement with the millwrights. The pipefitters, who are employees of J & M Mechanical, are only required to install the hydraulic system for the gates. We have to respond to the grievances filed by the pipefitters and the ironworkers."

Dean told Herb, "To compound the situation, George and David suspect that J & M's fitters are doing everything they can to sabotage the gate installation. Gate parts are missing, we've found deliberately disfigured anchor bolt threads, and even the safety hasps on our work baskets have been tampered with."

On a cold and damp Friday morning, December 1, armed and angry Ironworkers prevented workers from entering Carney Road and the work site. The iron workers were asserting that control gate installation was within the realm of work performed by them. At least two shotguns, two rifles, and several handguns were evident. By nine o'clock the sheriff and three deputies arrived, peacefully broke up and sent away the crowd of seventeen ironworkers. By ten o'clock everyone was back on the job.

After the situation was over Sheriff Spearman commented to Dean, "My deputies and I spend so much time out here we feel like we're part of your crew."

***

Aldridge was not a member of the Cincinnati Building Trades Council. But concern over the ironworker incident prompted Herb to notify the council of the ironworkers' dangerous action and sabotage that was occurring at the project. The council responded by scheduling a meeting between Aldridge, the pipefitters, and the ironworkers on Tuesday, December 5, 1972, at six p.m. in the council offices.

Dean and Herb were there promptly at six. The trades council meeting room was half full, occupied by about thirty people, equally divided between ironworkers and pipefitters.

Dean recognized Carl; two pipe fitters, and Joe Lech. The president of the Building Trades Council, William Bishop, called the meeting to order although there were still conversations causing a buzz in the room.

Joe Lech immediately jumped to his feet and shouted, "This is a bogus dispute. The contractor has illegally assigned our work to the millwrights."

Before Lech could say more, Bishop asked him, "Joe is it true that you physically assaulted an Aldridge employee and made threats to the president of the company."

Joe stammered a reply, "We had some disagreements."

Bishop warned him, "You're lucky you're not in jail. Assault and battery are serious offenses. Now sit down!"

While Joe was still standing, the head of the Ironworkers union, Carmen Marinara, jumped to his feet and began shouting, "The work is ours and we'll fight to protect it." President Bishop was pounding on the table trying to get order restored. Joe Lech and Carmen Marinara were face to face, their features contorted with rage, spittle flying between them. Others in the room were shouting to support their individual union.

Over the din, Marinara could be heard, "You want to settle this? We'll settle it the old way. Let's go outside."

Lech responded, "You're on!"

The two combatants went into the hall outside the meeting room and began to duke it out. Like a playground fight, the others merged into two groups cheering for their man. Then the two sides began pushing and shoving. The free-for-all became a full blown battle when spectators begin punching, pushing, and shoving. The battle lasted about five minutes until Bishop,

Dean, Herb, and a few calmer union members managed to stop the melee. There was some blood let but nothing serious.

For the pipefitters and ironworkers, it was all for naught. The Building Trades Council unanimously agreed with Aldridge based on their contract with the millwrights and an absence of contracts with the fitters and ironworkers. The meeting adjourned. Dean said to Herb, "Let's get the hell out of here while they are still arguing." They left quietly, Herb going to the airport and Dean returning to the modular home at the project.

*** 

Work aimed at finishing the outlet works portion of the project continued. The pipefitters were moodily installing the hydraulic system. Other J & M workers installed roof and bridge deck drains, HVAC systems, and other miscellaneous piping.

On December 8, 1972, when they finished the concrete and other miscellaneous work, Knowles had to lay off Don and the remaining carpenters. Before Don left, Knowles and Dean praised him for his outstanding leadership and dedication.

Dean gave Don a manly hug and exclaimed, "Don, you have been a blessing. Your knowledge of the work and organization benefitted the project. You brought more than building ability. You were a coach. You were the cheerleader, motivator, and team leader. You got things done, thank you!"

***

Five millwrights continued to slowly but surely install the water control gates. By December 21, 1972, the gates were installed.

Before the gate installation was complete, on December 12,

1972, two laborers, David Trumbull and Horace Whitestone were caulking and checking sluice gate seals on the upstream face of the control tower. The workers stood in a work basket suspended from the control tower parapet. The ground was about a hundred feet below. Their work was difficult, dangerous, and tiring.

Suddenly two rifle shots rang out. The bullets ricocheted off the face of the concrete tower wall near where the two were working on the gates.

The worker on top of the tower immediately began retracting the cable supporting the work basket to get the men out of sight on the roof of the tower. The lifting hoist reeled the men and work basket up, but the hoisting mechanism was slow exposing them for several crucial minutes. At last, they reached safety but were terrified during the time they were exposed.

David Trumbull was in the basket with Horace Whitestone. After they jumped from the work basket and hid behind the roof parapet, Horace exclaimed, "What the hell just happened?"

David, just as excited said, "Someone took a couple of potshots at us! Let's get off the roof and find out what's going on."

Wayne and several Corps employees heard the shots and rushed out of the office. Too late they saw a car roaring out of Carney Road onto the state highway. They were unable to identify the vehicle or the shooter. At the same time, Wayne looked toward his home and saw Melissa at the door. Wayne told one of his engineers, "Call the sheriff, tell them there have been shots fired and to get here as soon as possible." He then jumped in his truck and went to make sure Melissa was safe.

Melissa told him, "I heard the shots and ran to the door. I saw the car as it went past our house; it is a dark blue Chevy sedan, Ohio license number Q 553 Y."

Wayne was amazed, "You stood at the door and got all that information? You're lucky you weren't shot!" He hugged her and said, "I'm glad you're safe."

Sheriff Spearman and a deputy arrived in less than ten minutes. He immediately radioed the shooters vehicle information to his office where they sent out a bulletin to other agencies alerting them of the fleeing driver and the description of the car.

Fifteen minutes later the sheriff received a radio message from the Ohio Highway Patrol, "Hey Sheriff, we've got your guy and a 30-30 rifle, recently fired."

Sheriff Spearman responded, "Thanks for your help. That was quick work. Take him to the county jail. I'll be right there."

The shooter was Thomas White an out-of-work ironworker dismayed about the millwrights doing what he considered was his work. He was charged with attempted murder and held without bail awaiting arraignment.

Much later, in March 1973, during the shooter's trial he and his attorney claimed all he was guilty of was the misdemeanor discharging a firearm in a restricted area.

Despite the defendant's pleas the jury believed the prosecutor and found him guilty of attempted murder because he intentionally fired at living people. The jury didn't agree with his testimony that he intended to miss, that he only wanted to scare the men. The judge sentenced him to five years in the Marion Correctional Institution, possible parole in three years.

Dean reported the sentencing to Wayne telling him, "His and his family's lives needlessly ruined."

\*\*\*

After the millwrights had finished installing the water control gates, the pipefitters installed the hydraulic piping and finished their work on the hydraulic system. Operational testing of the system began. Knowles was anxious to be rid of the fitters, so on January 5, 1973, he gladly watched them leave for good. He decided the testing could go on without them.

During the lull between finishing the outlet works and diverting the river, Dean was splitting his time between the dam and work in the home office. He decided to take the last two weeks of December 1972 off and enjoy the Christmas season with his family. Diana and the girls were happy to have him home.

During December 1972, Herbert was pushing hard to speed the project into the embankment phase. The project was six months behind schedule and Herb wasn't happy with Knowles. Knowles, now going on 54, wanted to get back into the carpenters union so he could add to the pension he earned before going on salary. A mutual parting of the ways occurred December 29, 1972.

David Trumbull, the labor foreman, became responsible to oversee finishing the outlet works. In early November Trumbull's wife, Ella, moved back to their home in St. Louis. David continued to stay alone in their Cincinnati apartment during the week. Their son Sam was still living at home in St. Louis and fighting the drug monster within him.

***

Wrapping up all work on the outlet works continued through the winter at a snail's pace.

Testing of the water control gates and the hydraulic system began on January 10, 1973. The problems started with the testing of the first water control gate. The gates were opened and closed hydraulically from a console on the operating floor of the control tower. David Trumbull demonstrated the gate operation. "You activate a gate simply by flipping a switch to start a pump, which sends hydraulic fluid to the selected gate, which pushed a piston, which moves the gate disk up or down.

On the first test, a fitting that joined two sections of tubing carrying hydraulic oil to the gate failed causing the connection to separate spewing oil all over the inside walls of the tower. The gate was shut down, and testing of the next gate began. That gate tested satisfactorily, but the third gate failed just like the first one.

David was in charge of demonstrating the gate operation to Wayne and several engineers from the Louisville office. After two out of three failures he informed them, "I'm terminating all testing until we verify that all the tubing is installed correctly."

When Dean was notified of the problem, he told David, "Get your laborers to help you. Working on the same platforms as the fitters used, repair and recheck every coupling in the system. I don't trust the fitters. I'm not going to have them come back and correct their faulty work."

David knew he and his crew were being asked to perform what the trained fitters had failed to do. He promised Dean, "I have three good workers. There are at least four hundred fifty joints in that system. We'll check and retighten all of them."

The next day, January 11, David and his best worker, known only as Papa, began retightening the couplings on all the fittings and pipe. Papa noted as he was going about the retightening process, "Ya know der is no way in hell des tings was done right." David noticed that some of the joints were merely hand tightened.

In his report for the week, Dean noted, "It is evident the pipefitters have purposely left many joints un-tightened." He continued with his observation, "They lost the gate installation assignment, but they have their revenge. I'm going to back-charge them for every dime we spend to correct their work."

It took six days to check and retighten all hydraulic system tubing connections. It took another four days to high pressure wash the oil from the walls and mop up the dirty water and oil. On January 26, 1973 David, Wayne, the engineers and, this time, Dean, again began the control gate testing operation. Finally, all fourteen gates worked as designed. The entire system, gates, tubing, couplings, valves, pumps, and position indicators performed flawlessly.

After the gate testing ordeal was over, they resumed preparing to divert the Trout River through the outlet works.

Dean deducted four thousand dollars from J & M Mechanical's contract for the cost to fix their shoddy work. J & M's president was upset by the back charge but when Dean explained what happened he reluctantly agreed to the charges.

By February 1973 they were nearing completion of the outlet works phase of the plagued and troubled project. Dean noted in one of his reports, "It is amazing considering the problems, delays, floods, weather, anti-dam lawsuits, unexpected extra work, and unresolved claims that we are just six months beyond the outlet works' original scheduled completion."

David Trumbull and two of his best laborers were left with the task of moving Aldridge's unneeded property back to the St. Louis equipment yard. There were twelve items that need to be corrected or completed before the Corps would declare the outlet works ready to accept diversion of the Trout River. David and his crew diligently worked on all of the remaining items but didn't finish by Friday, the end of the work week. They had to return the following week.

For Dean personally, the worst was yet to happen. On Monday, February 5, 1973, he was in the St. Louis office pushing hard to wrap up work on the outlet works when he received a call from Papa, "Boss, I cain't find Massa David. His car is gone and der is nobody at his apartment."

Dean was trying to locate David's home phone number when Charlene, the office secretary, called Dean on the office intercom, and between emotional breakdowns and sobbing informed him, "It's on the news...; David's son, Sam, shot and killed his mother and then killed himself."

Dean had to shut the door to his office so that those elsewhere in the office could not hear his sobs. David and his family often joined Dean's family on holidays and special occasions. Dean knew David would not be back to the dam. Sam's suicide, his drug addiction resulting from eight months in Viet Nam, multiple failures at rehab, and in particular, becoming a fraction of the person he was; to Dean it seemed more like a mercy killing than suicide.

Herbert opined, "It is an embarrassment to our heritage that thousands of America's best come back from that war mentally and physically scarred. It is a war no matter how the cowardly politicians try to label it otherwise. Upon returning, our soldiers are greeted with jeers and obscenities."

Dean hypothetically asked Herb, "Do those, like me, who didn't have to go, have the right, even considering our constitutional right to free speech, to mock and belittle those who did?"

Dean's emotional pain didn't stop with the killing of Dave's wife and son. About three weeks after their funerals, on February 28, David ended his own life. At first, Dean thought the pressure to finish the project and David's extended stay away from home caused his death.

On closer examination, Dean told Herb, "I believe David took his own life, not because he was despondent; but he knew that life on this earth, for him, could not continue without his beloved Ella. His only recourse was to be with her."

On February 28, 1973, ironies occurring on this project continued. The same day of David's suicide; Aldridge received notice that the Trout River Outlet Works was satisfactorily complete and they could begin diverting the river through the control tower, conduit and stilling basin.

All that remained on the outlet works portion of the project was the demanding process of resolving outstanding claims, change orders, and time extensions. Dean immediately prepared all the required documents and submitted them to the Corps' resident engineer.

## CHAPTER 48

In December of 1972, as the outlet works neared completion, Wayne and Dean acknowledged to each other that they have different but mutual goals. Before the Christmas holiday they talked about different expectations.

Wayne noted, "I want perfection in the quality of the project and the paperwork. Dean, you are focused on time and money."

Dean replied, "Yeah, I am more concerned with schedule and costs, but we are always working toward good quality."

Wayne acknowledged, "During the past three years we have been through some bad experiences. Ordinarily what might be bad for you is good for me. Those situations will cause some people to clash and become enemies. But by working together we've been able to use each of our talents and, I believe, we've done a hell of a good job. We can both be proud."

Dean agreed, "I enjoy working with you. We have been friendly toward each other, but we have not become friends. I have no choice but to protect the interests of Aldridge. You have no choice but to protect the government's interests. We have to walk a fine line."

Wayne extended his hand and they shook hands confirming their efforts so far. Wayne said, "You're right about the friend thing. During all this time we have never had a moment when we are not working. No lunches, no after work socializing, just work, work, work. Maybe we can let go by taking our wives to dinner the next time Diana is up here."

Dean responded, "That is a good idea. You pick the restaurant, and I'll get Herb to pay."

\*\*\*

In December 1972 starting with the advent of winter, Dean began spending more time in the home office. Diana and the girls, now twelve and ten, were elated to have husband and father back home even if it was part-time

Harold Schneider, who had been the embankment superintendent since June 1972 was busy during the winter months planning crew sizes and preparing the large fleet of earth moving equipment that was beginning to arrive at the dam.

Early in February 1973, Herbert asked Dean to come to his office. After some office chit-chat Herb said, "Dean, on behalf of the whole company I want to thank you for your outstanding effort in getting the outlet works ready so that the river can be diverted."

Dean responded, "Thanks, Herb, I appreciate the compliment, but I had a lot of help."

Herb had more on his mind saying, "Obviously the outlet phase finished later than scheduled. Most of the reasons for the late finish were things that are beyond our control. We can still save this project by efficiently performing the work for the dam embankment."

Dean thought, *"Gee, the praise was canceled by the late finish lecture."* He asked Herb, "What are your plans to manage the embankment phase?"

Without hesitating Herb answered, "I'd like you to stay on as project manager. You know the job, the union idiosyncrasies, the Corps inspection team, and the resident engineer. There are also a lot of unresolved issues hanging out there,"

Dean's reaction took Herb by surprise, "I committed almost three years of my life up there. Even though I've learned a lot, my family and I have suffered. I miss my kids. They are growing into young women, and I'm not part of their lives. I've been looking forward to being back at my old job and back with my family. No! I can't do what you are asking. Find someone else to manage the rest of that project."

Herb was not used to employees refusing his assignments. Dean was not the first to balk at his authority, but he was the first vice president to adamantly refuse to obey a request. Herb recoiled and said, "Dean, what the hell are you saying. I had no idea that you'd turn down the opportunity to finish that job."

Dean, more calmly said, "Herb you have to understand. I promised my family I would be gone for no more than three years. I committed to building the outlet works phase only. Now it's almost finished, and I thought I'd be going home."

Herb, concerned that the best person to lead Trout River through the embankment phase was slipping away made a suggestion, "What if we move you and your family up to Clearfield County?"

Dean wasn't surprised at the offer. He knew Diana wouldn't like the idea. Dean replied, "All I can do is talk to my family about what you've asked of us. For now, I will only commit to working on the project through April." Herb agreed to discuss the matter at a later time.

When Dean was back in his office, he reflected on the time he was away from home. *"I went home every weekend. Every Friday I left the job about three o'clock in the afternoon, drove to the Cincinnati Airport, arrived in St. Louis about nine O'clock, where Diana and the kids picked me up. We arrived back home by about ten. This schedule worked most of the time. Sometimes Eastern Air had schedule problems causing me, Diana and the kids to get home much later than ten p.m."*

*"Being together every weekend, for Diana, caused more stress than enjoyment. Compounding the stress was my leaving and being taken to the St. Louis airport Monday morning at five o'clock. Diana has become more vocal about her displeasure with the situation."*

*"I called home nearly every day. During the summer and holidays our family got together at a nice motel near the job. Even these reunions became troublesome for Diana. She thinks they are more for me than the family."*

*"I know that responsibility for the children's schooling, discipline, and social activities fall squarely on Diana; she resents this shift of parental duties."*

*"The talk every weekend is centered on living separate and how to cope with it. There's no easy solution. The separate living has become a ticking matrimonial time bomb."*

Dean realized his thoughts had drifted away from his work. As he sat there he thought, *"I still have to go back up there and finish the part of the Trout River Project that I started. I know I can turn it over to someone else by April. I'm not going to tell Diana about Herb and the situation. I'll have to tell her soon, though."*

***

Dean's work to close out the first phase of the Trout River Project was going good, in fact, better than expected. At home in St. Louis the going was not so good. In mid-February, Dean related to Diana about his conversation with Herb. Dean bluntly told her, "Herb wants me to stay on the project."

Diana was immediately upset that Dean was even considering re-upping, as they say in the military. She reminded him, "The original plan was for you to be away about three years building the damn outlet works. Now you are considering staying there for three more years. You and the company have betrayed me."

They ended the conversation when Heather entered the kitchen and asked, "Are you guys fighting?"

Diana answered, "No we're just talking about daddy's job. He's having some problems. You won't understand."

Dean was scheduled to be on the job all of the following week. The usual flow of events occurred; airport drop off, work Monday through Friday, airport pick up, Diana upset, and Dean at a loss about how to cope.

On March 29, 1973, Dean decided to leave the job and go home early. He left the job on Thursday instead of Friday and caught an early flight that got him home about four in the afternoon. He called Diana to let her know when to meet him at the airport. At the airport, Diana was happy to see him, as were the girls; Michele, now thirteen, and Heather eleven. However, during the brief ride home Dean sensed that Diana was tired and tense.

When they returned home, Dean announced, "I am taking next week off. Since you girls are on spring break, how about some vacation ideas. I don't think we want to just sit around here." The kids had plenty of ideas but no certain plans.

That evening after dinner Diana told Dean, "We have to talk. I understood that you would be coming home to stay in three years. That your part of the project would be finished, and we could resume a normal life. Now, although you haven't committed to three more years, I can tell it's on your mind. You still haven't said no. If we have to move up there, the girls will be seventeen and fifteen by the time the dam is finished. We haven't been a real family for three years. We can't go on like this."

Tearfully Diana continued, "For all practical purposes I am a single mom. I see to the girls school work, I pay the bills, I maintain our home, and I'm the disciplinarian. I am the only one the girls can turn to when they are troubled, and I have no one to support me when I'm troubled. In my life you only exist on weekends, and then you are so wiped out and anxious about the damn job you are like a stranger in our home."

Dean could only put together a mild response, "I can't continue to let you down. I hear and understand all you've said. I've had my head in the sand. We have all week to work something out. I'll start by going to the office tomorrow to talk to Herb. I don't want to miss any more of the girls as they grow up, and I do miss you and our life together."

The following morning, before Herb became involved with other matters, Dean talked with him. He started by saying, "Diana and I are having a family crisis centered around our lack of a real life together. I don't want to disappoint you but, as I've said before, I believe I have fulfilled my commitment to Aldridge." But, he admitted, "Three things are important to me, my job, my wife, and my family. Herb, at this point in my life I have to put my wife and family first, and they don't want to move to Ohio."

Herb asked Dean, "Will you and Diana give me a few days to come up with something that might not solve the problem, but will ease you through the next three years?"

Dean realized Herb's answer did not address the problem but he didn't have any answers either. He told Herb, "Yeah, let's think about it. I'm taking a week off to enjoy a vacation away from here with my family. I'll be back to work a week from Monday."

On the drive home, Dean contemplated what Herb said. All he came up with was that Herb would put the job and company first. He and Diana need to make a plan that favors her and the girls.

When Dean got home he told Diana, "We need to really think about this. I don't believe Herb will make a plan that helps us. He'll probably try to solve it with money and, as a family; emotionally we won't be any better than we are now. I'll quit and find another job before I let our lives continue like this. Let's enjoy the week and trust that we can determine our fate."

They had a great vacation, went to the Ozarks in Arkansas and then to Gatlinburg, Tennessee. While traveling, a plan to save the family and his job began to form in Dean's mind. He gave his plan a couple of days to take shape.

He was sitting with Diana and the girls at the Peddler Steakhouse in Gatlinburg when he outlined the plan to Diana. "Before I went up to Trout River we discussed selling our present home and buying a larger one. If you and I agree to this plan, we will have the opportunity to sell our house and temporarily move to Clearfield County at company expense."

Diana exclaimed, a little too loud, "Oh no! We are not going to be uprooted and plopped down in some Ohio hick town!" Dean asked her, "Please hear me out. If I can convince Herb to pay all our expenses for three years, we will not have a mortgage, property taxes or utility expenses. We will be able to save more than we do now and apply it toward a new and better house in a better area when we move back. If you agree we can sell our old house now, move to a nice home near the job. I'll stipulate the company will pay all utilities, rent, and all sale and moving expenses."

Dean brought the two girls into the conversation, "What do you think of moving to the country?" Both girls were dismayed.

Michele was worried, "We'll lose our friends and maybe we won't be welcome over there. We don't know what the schools and teachers are like."

Heather said, "I'm just getting good at lacrosse and basketball. I'll have to start over."

Michele added, "I'll graduate from a foreign school. It might keep me from getting into a good college."

"Okay, okay," Dean said, "let's enjoy what's left of our vacation. We'll mull this situation over and keep trying to work something out."

When they returned home, and Dean was back to work, he didn't tell Herb about the plan. He decided it was best to wait until, and if, his family was satisfied. He would not do anything without the agreement of the whole family. Even if he had to change jobs, their happiness came first.

Dean spent Monday, April 9 in the office, but on Tuesday after their week together, Dean had to return to the project. Before he went to the airport Diana told him, "I've been thinking about the plan. Depending on our finding a nice home I honestly believe I can live with your plan. I'm concerned about how the move will affect the kids, their lives, and futures. This week the girls and I'll talk about moving. There will be more to talk about when you come home Friday."

Dean was surprised when everyone was at the airport upon his return on Friday, April 13. Dean could tell the girls were bursting to talk. Diana was first to speak, "The kids and I had lots to talk about this week. They want to see the homes, schools and athletic facilities in the area where you want us to move. We want to see where we will live if we move. Nobody has a closed mind."

The next week, after Diana and the girls told him of some interest in moving, Dean decided to let Wayne know about their interest in seeing the area to which they were being asked to relocate. "Wayne, do you remember our conversation about getting together with our wives for dinner?"

Wayne answered, "I sure do, is Herb ready to treat us?"

Dean replied, "Ready or not he will. We're coming here for the weekend. There is more to this than just dinner. We're bringing the girls so they can check out the schools and stuff. We're considering moving here, and we need a tour guide."

Wayne agreed, "Melissa and I will be glad to show you guys around."

Dean and Wayne's families had a great weekend. The girls thought Wayne's son, JD, was quite a hunk. Dean took a fatherly interest in their comments.

As they were about to leave the restaurant, Melissa said, "I just thought of something. A couple we met while Wayne was working to relocate the Methodist church are going to Liberia for five years to serve as missionaries. They have a beautiful home that they will lease while they're gone. It's about ten miles upstream from the dam. The location is awesome. The house sits on a bluff overlooking the Trout River and a valley."

Dean, looking at Diana, said, "We might be interested. Tell us how to contact them."

Melissa answered, "Jody and Steve Huff own the home. Here's how to contact them."

The next day the Richardson's looked at the house. An hour later they had an agreement to lease the house for three years. As Herb promised, the company paid all the expenses for the home.

Their new home was located in a beautiful setting high on a forty foot bluff overlooking the Trout River about ten miles upstream from the dam construction.

The Huffs are Methodist missionaries, who had taken a five-year assignment in Liberia. They were glad to have a reliable tenant.

At the back, the home overlooked the Trout River. The front faced Gold Rush Road. It had an attached two car garage, three bedrooms, two full bathrooms, a modern kitchen, and a rustic living area with a fireplace. The side facing the river had a full-length deck and porch overlooking the river and the wooded valley.

Herb readily agreed to Dean's plan. It took three weeks for the entire moving plan to emerge and satisfy the whole family. On May 12, 1973, Dean and Diana listed their St. Louis area house for sale. Before the school year ended the house was under contract to sell.

After school had ended for the year, in June 1973, the Richardson family became temporary residents of Clearfield County.

In September Michele would be a sophomore and attend Trout River High School. Heather would be in the eighth grade at Stanton Middle School. Thanks to Wayne's son, JD and local farmer Raymond Norton's son, Wesley, the girls met a few of their future classmates.

Dean discovered the decision to move had a secondary benefit because the Aldridge modular home sat in the area designated for the embankment borrow pit.

An equipment operator working on the project expressed an interest in buying the 'abode.' Dean quickly worked out a deal and within a week the modular home and all appurtenances were gone.

Wayne and Dean had many challenges to face and problems to solve, some old and some as yet unknown. Efforts to build the dam continued as Aldridge crews geared up to place the millions of cubic yards of earth and rock for the embankment.

## CHAPTER 49

By February 1973, work was finished on the control tower, outlet conduit, stilling basin, and bridge. Aldridge workers and the Corps of Engineers, were ready to divert the Trout River through the outlet works.

On March 8, 1973, Dean and Harold met in the St. Louis Office with Darrel Hightower, a project engineer assigned to the Trout River Project. Harold asked Darrel, "How many cubic yards of earth and rock do we need just for the diversion dam?"

Darrel answered, "About one point five million. The good news is that we can place the entire diversion embankment in an area that will become part of the permanent dam. More good news is that all of the million and a half cubic yards are in the top strata of the borrow area. You can start moving it right now."

The three men knew the diversion dam would, as its name implied, divert the flow of the Trout River into and through the completed outlet works and back into the river downstream from the dam. After diversion, the area of the dam embankment would be free of river flow and available for work to begin on the dam's rock base and foundation.

Darrel continued to share his knowledge of the soil and its characteristics. "Back in 1967 and 1968, the Corps authorized

## BEHIND THE DAM

a comprehensive subsurface investigation of the entire area where the dam will be built. They determined the quality and type of soil underlying the proposed location of the dam and lake."

"The subsurface study consisted of one hundred thirty-two soil borings at specified locations where we will build the dam and outlet works. They also drilled many test holes in the proposed borrow area. They drilled some holes to ninety feet below the surface of the ground. In the area of the emergency overflow spillway, where we will obtain all of the embankment materials, the holes were drilled only fifteen to twenty feet deep."

"All you guys have to do is take a small army of dozers, scrapers, off-road trucks, and compactors and move the dirt from the borrow pit to the diversion dam and, later, the main embankment dam."

Dean told Darrel, "You tell a good story, but we don't see a specific plan emerging. We want to hear or see a plan of attack. How many of each type of equipment do we need? What are the haul routes? Good progress is dependent on how well the soil compacts and the expertise of the compaction equipment operators. What kind of productivity can we expect?"

Darrel, a dedicated and talented civil engineer, responded, "Are you saying that I need to define what I meant by a small army? Okay here goes; to finish the diversion dam in fourteen months, you'll need twelve scrapers and eight dozers. Plus you'll need six compactors working the embankment."

"At the same time that we are placing the diversion embankment dam, we need to be preparing the foundation and clay core for the main dam. As we complete the diversion dam, we will shift all the equipment to the main dam. The main dam will require an additional seven million cubic of earth and rock."

Harold said, "Okay let's talk about the equipment fleet for the main dam."

Darrel was ready, "The scheduled completion date is March 31, 1976. We have from March 1974 until March 1976 to place the main dam; twenty-four months. Allowing for weather and other productivity factors, we'll need a fleet of fifteen scrappers, nine dozers, and eight compactors working two shifts."

On May 14, 1973, Aldridge began the long-awaited diversion of the Trout River through the newly completed outlet works.

# CHAPTER 50

The summer of 1973, Dean and Harold discussed placing and compacting the main dam's clay core. Harold commented, "Towelson's demanding soil compaction requirements are slowing our work and increasing our costs."

Harold continued, "I know and expect the Corps' technicians to perform constant, but necessary, soil and compaction testing. Compaction of the clay core area of the dam, at sixty feet wide and rising the full two hundred feet height of the embankment, is critical. We are obtaining good clay from the borrow pit, but Towelson is making it difficult. He is so strict that the only clay he approves is consistent with what a potter needs to throw a pottery vase. Our excavators will have to dig through almost two million cubic yards of clay to obtain nine hundred thousand cubic yards of material that is acceptable to Towelson. The subsurface investigation conducted by the Corps concluded that almost all of the clay material in the borrow area is suitable."

Dean interjected, "Inspector Towelson, at his despicable worst, interprets the earth compaction specification at the most stringent level. The measure of compaction effort required to assure compliance with contract requirements, empirical at best, is subject to interpretation. Towelson has made himself the god of acceptable earth compaction. To comply with Towelson's unreasonable demands, we are spending countless unnecessary hours running our compaction equipment back and forth over soil that cannot benefit from more effort."

Dean added, "Spending unnecessary time on compaction also slows the scrapers and dozers that are hauling and placing earth that we are removing from the borrow area. The additional wear and tear on our equipment is adding tens of thousands of dollars to our expenses. Towelson is single-handedly delaying the work and costing us thousands of dollars."

Harold noted, "This is where interpretation becomes a factor. The Corps technicians performing compaction testing, who are working along with the compaction equipment operators, know how many passes over the earth are needed to obtain the required density. Towelson constantly belies the density test results, ordering more and more effort thereby extending the time we have to work in a given area."

Dean thought, *"I don't know how long I can keep it a secret that Towelson is a paid trouble maker."* He told Harold, "Keep doing the best you can. I assure you Towelson will pay for his actions."

In July of 1973, the third year of tolerating Towelson's impossible to satisfy inspection methods, Dean told Harold, "I have decided to speak with Brian about a more trusting working relationship. My goal is to achieve an atmosphere of tolerance and working together instead of the constant bickering and condemnations uttered back and forth. I want to give him one more chance to be a real human."

Dean found Towelson as he was criticizing a compactor operator for, in his opinion, not making enough passes over a specific area of the embankment.

"Brian, do you have a minute?"

Towelson, having never liked Dean, looking annoyed said, "Yeah, what do you want?"

Dean thought, "*I'll be damned if I am going to let this guy intimidate me.*" He answered, "I want to talk about mutual trust, respect and working together. We have never given you a reason to mistrust us nor have we ever done any shoddy work. Our workers are ordered to comply with the contract requirements. Yet you wrongly believe that we need constant oversight and the broadest and most stringent, even to the point of excessive, application of the contract requirements."

Brian started to interrupt; Dean continued, "Let me finish. We have never given you, Wayne, or other members of the Corps staff reason to doubt our intention to comply with the project documents. We want to be proud of the work we do and we hope you are too. Why don't we work together to make this a project for which we can all be proud?"

Dean was shocked by Brian's response, "The only reason work on this project is of the highest quality is because I make it that way. If I don't keep on every one of your half-ass workers they will cheat, substitute inferior products, and cut corners at every opportunity."

Dean was trying to remain calm, all he could say was, "Brian, I feel sorry for you. A real person has to have a basis to mistrust another person. You mistrust everyone before you give them an opportunity to show their trustworthiness. I'm sorry you look upon us as cheaters, and no matter what we do to prove our mettle, you won't change. Thanks for your time."

Dean knew not to say anymore, so he walked away.

A few days later Dean spoke to Wayne about his conversation with Brian. Dean said, "I've been trying for three years to establish rapport with Brian. Other than the concrete testing incident we've never openly questioned his integrity or motives. Personally, I have gone the extra mile to appease him and comply with his demands. The bottom line is that he is costing us money, a lot of money. His overzealous inspection is causing morale problems among our employees. He is so critical, to the point of being insulting, that we are having a problem keeping good employees. We lost a good dozer operator today who, before he left, said the inspectors here are so harsh he'd rather work where he is appreciated."

Wayne said, "Don't you think you are just being the typical contractor, any inspection is too much inspection?"

Dean replied, "No. I've managed other projects where state inspectors are all over the place. I have never complained." He added, "Wayne, the hell of it is, Brian is very talented. He knows the contract documents inside and out. But he uses his superior knowledge to manipulate and pound us to the extent we are forced to exceed the specs on much of the work. Our costs, like most other contractors, are based on meeting, not exceeding the contract requirements. We're in a competitive business; we can't give more than required by the contract documents. I suspect that Mr. Brian Towelson has a secret agenda! I'm going to do whatever I can to expose him. I hope you remember that three years ago we put the government on notice that the inspection on this project is overzealous. We will prove that. We will expect payment for what amounts to nothing less than criminal activity concerning Mr. Towelson."

***

Work continued on the diversion dam until it reached a predetermined height and entirely spanned across the valley from hill to hill. Thick layers of rock were strategically placed to protect the upstream face of the diversion dam from scouring by the river.

The basis for the design of the diversion dam was simply to make way to build the embankment dam. Local hydrological data and usual rainfall statistics show a need for an eighty-foot high diversion dam. Aldridge's project team opted for a higher one-hundred-foot height, to build in more factor of safety. Later events would prove this was a good decision.

A one hundred foot high diversion dam with the same characteristics as the embankment dam, spanning the entire width of the valley, required about one million five hundred thousand cubic yards of earth and rock.

On August 16, 1973, the diversion dam, although not complete, was ready to be closed thereby diverting the Trout River through the control tower and the rest of the outlet works.

By May 1974 the diversion dam was almost complete, and foundation work for the embankment dam was progressing. At that time Wayne and the Corps management team, except Towelson, were pleased with the overall progress of the project and the diligence of Aldridge management and employees.

# CHAPTER 51

The project history since the beginning had been one of obstacles, delays, protests, misfortune, injunctions, and just plain bad luck.

On June 12, 1974, work was nearing completion on the hundred foot high diversion dam. The first shift was ending. The work crew operating seven scrappers, eight large dozers, and five compactors were hauling earth and rock from the borrow area and placing it in the diversion dam. The second shift was ready to start. Their shift would start at three o'clock p.m. and end, under floodlights, at eleven p.m.

The sky was dark with clouds and rain was predicted during the early evening. The bleak weather forecast was not a deterrent and work continued as scheduled. By nine o'clock in the evening there was some rain but the Aldridge second shift was able to complete their shift with only minor inconvenience. At eleven, the crew secured their machines and headed for home or their motel.

The late shift consisted of twenty-four workers; eight dozer operators, seven scraper operators, five compactors, two surveyors, one laborer who tended the floodlights, and the dirt foreman.

# BEHIND THE DAM

As usual, before turning in, some of the crew stopped at Dominic's combination grocery, restaurant, pizza shop, and bar for dinner and refreshments.

***

Wayne was jarred awake by a thunderous lightening strike and boom. Thunder rumbled across the area echoing and reechoing throughout the valley. It sounded like mortar and cannon fire during the Battle of the Bulge. A glance at the bedside clock showed the time was one-fifty-one a.m. The phone rang as he adjusted his pillow to go back to sleep. Wayne thought, *"What the hell? Who'd call at this hour?"* He answered with a groggy, "Hello."

The excited caller said, "Wayne, this is Jordan Lipper."

Wayne was trying to get his mind working. Lipper was his boss. "Mr. Lipper, what in the world prompts a call at this hour?"

Lipper responded, "Wayne, I was just alerted by our chief hydrologist that the anticipated Trout River impoundment resulting from the rain we are receiving will crest higher than the diversion dam."

Lipper continued, "As you know if the flood crests over the dam there will be a major disaster resulting in extensive downstream property damage, and possible loss of life. This flood will cause an emergency of the highest order."

Wayne, now fully awake, replied, "We need to get the contractor's crew out there to raise the top of the diversion dam at least two feet above the anticipated flood. I'll get them going!" In two minutes Wayne was fully dressed, and five minutes later he was pounding on Harold Schneider's motel room door. "Harold, Harold, wake up there's a flood!"

Wayne had to repeat the warning several times before Harold opened the door.

"Wayne! What the hell do you want?" Wayne, standing in the pouring rain, anxiously told him, "The Trout River is flooding. It will crest over the diversion dam. We need to get your crew out there and raise the top of the dam."

Harold didn't hesitate, "We're on our way."

By three a.m. Harold had four dozers working to push the sides of the dam higher, and by three thirty he'd added four more. Meanwhile, the rain continued. At one time it was recorded at more than five inches in two hours.

At Dean's rental house, ten miles upriver from the dam, his whole family woke to the noise created by the thunder, lightning, and the downpour. The river was climbing the bluff and flooding the area on the other side of the river. Dean's rental home was higher than most because of its location on top of the bluff. The flood water on the other side of the river, where there was no bluff, was rising and approaching several homes. By mid-morning, the river had risen to more than four feet in some of the low-lying homes.

Dean dressed and immediately went to the Aldridge field office. There was not much he could do. Harold was fully utilizing every worker and piece of equipment that would fit on the diversion dam. They were all engrossed pushing the earth and rock from lower sections of the dam to the top attempting to raise the crest to a height that will prevent overtopping by the flood waters.

To prevent the flood waters from cresting over the dam, the eight dozers and their operators continued working all night into the morning; pushing the lower embankment dirt to the top of the dam. The dozer operators were exhausted. The frantic pace in the rain and mud was taking its toll. By eleven o'clock a.m. it appeared the top of the dam was adequate to keep the waters behind the dam and continue diverting the flood through the wide open gates of the control tower. At noon the exhausted workers returned home or to their motel.

At two that afternoon, Wayne received another alert from Lipper, "Wayne, additional rain is falling upstream! We are predicting a flood crest higher than before. We need to get everyone back out there. The hydrologist told me we are getting an additional two inches of rain per hour."

After the second alert, Harold didn't waste any time. He already had a partial crew working in the borrow area. The continuous rain had caused him to tell some of the crew to remain at the motel or stay home.

By three in the afternoon, he had nine dozers back on the diversion embankment pushing dirt to raise the top of the dam even higher. The impoundment caused by the flood was noticeably rising. The Corps hydrologist, Dorothy Horner, was concerned that the level of the impoundment was increasing faster than the workers were able to raise the crest of the dam. Harold was using all the bulldozers he had. There was more water in the flooding Trout River than could squeeze through the gates in the control tower. She immediately passed the information to the district office.

Horner told Lipper, who was in his Louisville office, "I have concerns about the situation at Trout River. We need to start warning downstream residents about an impending disaster. Overtopping is a reality. We are facing a dire situation."

Lipper replied, "There are several high ranking Corps officials at the site. Give them your first-hand information about the flood. Make sure Wayne Henderson is in the loop. Get local law enforcement, firefighters, emergency rescue people, and volunteers organized and go house to house for at least two miles downstream. Tell everyone to evacuate. I'll alert the Clearfield County National Guard. Go!" Lipper took control of the situation and alerted the National Guard. He then sped to the project arriving about four hours later.

The county sheriff and other volunteers took their vehicles and went door to door warning downstream residents to evacuate. Overtopping, if it occurred, would be accompanied by exponential rupture of the dam. Combined with the maximum flow going through the outlet works it would cause a downstream flood surge more than a normal flood.

The dozer crews continued pushing dirt and mud to the top of the dam. The operator's arms, legs, and backs ached from the stress of the constant back and forth movement and manipulation of the equipment controls. Their fatigue was made worse due to straining against the seat belts caused by working back and forth in the mud and on the uneven slope.

Harold, anticipating failure despite the most extreme efforts, started six off-road trucks hauling rock from the stock- piles to the dam. He ordered the rock placed in an area he designated as a temporary spillway. He reasoned if the flood over crested the dam they could direct the flow through the rocks, prevent erosion, and keep downstream damage to that of a normal flood. By now he had seventeen workers and the same quantity of earth moving equipment committed to the effort.

The workers continued pushing rock and dirt to raise the crest of the diversion dam. They were keeping placement of rock to the designated area to force overtopping through a zone protected from erosion by the rock face.

The stress and speed at which they were working were taking its emotional and physical toll on the workers. The dozers, trucks and other equipment had a roof that is integral with rollover protection. This OSHA required safety roof was not intended to provide protection from the elements, in this case, torrents of rain. Made worse by thunder and lightning, the rain pelted the equipment operators, and added to the stress of their mission to quickly raise the top elevation of the diversion dam. The operators were exhausted.

At one a.m. on Friday the situation became dangerous for the dozer operators when the contained impoundment reached the top of the diversion dam and water began to trickle over the crest onto the downstream slope of the dam. The danger of being washed away by mud and water caused the workers, one by one, to give up their efforts and withdraw to a safe area.

Aldridge's crews worked an eight-hour shift ending at eleven o'clock p.m. on Wednesday. They were called back at three o'clock a.m. on Thursday morning and worked until eleven o'clock that morning. At three o'clock Thursday afternoon they went back to work until they began to give up at one o'clock a.m. Friday morning. The emergency crew worked twenty-six hours during a thirty-three hour period.

One dozer operator, twenty-one-year-old Jeremy Oldham, would not give up. He continued his effort until he and his twenty-ton dozer were almost washed off of the slope. When he reached safety, Harold was quick to let him know about his feelings, "You dumb ass! You could have been killed and for what? The water is already going over the top; there is no way to stop it." Then he gave Jeremy a slap on his back, "But I'm proud of you."

Wayne, Dean, and about fifty other onlookers were watching the activity from an observation area overlooking the dam. Wayne and Dean had been doing all in their power to assist in the emergency. Dean had been on the phone helping Harold roust workers from homes and motels. Wayne had been with the sheriff and National Guard evacuating downstream homeowners. Neither man had slept for forty-eight hours. They both felt helpless.

The observers could see that the level of water was even with the top of the dam. At several places along the length of the dam water was beginning to trickle over the top. They watched in silence as the workers gave up, fearing for their lives. Their expressions were grim. Some were praying.

About fifteen minutes after one a.m. the hydrologist, Dorothy Horner, shouted, "Look! The water has stabilized. It's not rising. I've been monitoring the level of the impoundment with nails in a tree. The level is slightly below my top nail!" A few minutes later she yelled to the crowd, "The water has receded a half inch. I think the worst is over!" By daylight, the water was about ten feet below the crest.

At eight o'clock that morning, Wayne told the water control gate operator, "Start closing some of the gates and let's slow the flow going downstream. We can start to let the water out of the impoundment slowly."

The crew's efforts and Harold's foresight placing the rock

to form a spillway did not prevent flooding of downstream residents, but it contained the impact of the flood. Without the diversion dam and the efforts to raise it; the Trout River left on its own, would have caused devastating damage to downstream riverfront life and property. Even in its partially completed condition, the Trout River Dam prevented a catastrophe. The concentrated efforts had also saved the diversion dam.

On Monday, June 17, 1974, building the Trout River Dam and Lake resumed.

The after effects of the flood were everywhere. Six-inch thick mud covered the work area; all the equipment needed mud removed from tracks and drives; haul roads were washed out, and everything needed maintenance and fuel. Desmond White, Aldridge's equipment manager, was personally supervising the activities. His diligence reinforced his reputation as being unforgiving regarding the care of the company's equipment.

Before work resumed on the embankment all of the earth that was pushed to raise the diversion dam has to be removed, stored in a place where it would dry, and then be replaced in its proper location and re-compacted to meet contract requirements.

Brian Towelson's zeal was undiminished. He cared little about the damage and Aldridge's efforts to put every cubic yard of material disturbed by the effort to stem the flood back in place. Instead, he glorified at the opportunity to cause havoc on Aldridge's efforts to restore the work area back to its pre-flood condition. He viewed restoration efforts as an opportunity to cost Aldridge as much unnecessary expense as possible. He was uncaring about the fact that Dean was keeping meticulous records and documenting the added expenses incurred by Aldridge's response to the government's orders to prevent or mitigate flood damage. Towelson had confided to a few like-minded individuals, "I just want to bust their balls."

\*\*\*

On Monday Wayne and Dean met to discuss the effect the flood had on the project. Although they were meeting by mutual agreement, their purposes were not mutual.

Wayne was concerned about the impact the flood had on progress and potential repercussions from flood victims. Dean was concerned about the impact on costs, schedule, and recouping the value of extra work performed by Aldridge.

Wayne asked Dean, "What can be done to recover the lost time caused by the flood?"

Dean answered, "There are several ways. We are already working two shifts, but we can put on a third shift and work around the clock, or we can work two ten hour shifts and pay for overtime. A third option is to bring in more equipment and hire more operators, but that will lower efficiency. The result of all three options is the same; we will have to accelerate the work if you want us to maintain the old schedule. Acceleration means additional cost. The alternative is to acknowledge the delay caused by the flood and grant additional contract time. Anything we do to make up lost time will result in added costs."

Wayne was fighting back his anger at how quickly Dean made added cost the solution to the problem. He asked, "Why can't you work out a solution that does not involve added costs? Every time we ask you contractors to do the least little thing you want change orders and more money."

Dean had been down this path before. He decided to explain from a contractor's position. "We have a very tight budget and a cost control system to monitor our budget. It's my job to meet the restraints imposed by our budget. Competitive bidding on public funded projects eliminates the luxury to include contingencies in our bids. Contingency money is in the owner's pocket. Therefore we can't do non-contract work without reimbursement. No matter what we do we will abide by the contract."

Thinking of his boss, Herbert Flaherty, Dean continued, "We both have to answer to someone at our home offices. I have to answer to an owner who doesn't want me giving away the company's money. You have your boss and government auditors who are in your face. Let's try to work out a solution based on the working relationship we have established during the past four years."

Dean suggested, "Face it; no matter what we do it will involve added costs. We should work together to come up with the most economical plan. I'm not going to gouge the government for drummed up added and phony expenses. All I want is to see my company treated fairly for agreed to added work and expenses for added time. To accomplish anything we have to work together."

"Okay," Wayne responded, "Let's come up with a plan."

During the next two hours Wayne and Dean, to their mutual surprise, agreed on a plan to partially recover the lost time and pay Aldridge for added work.

After the meeting Wayne told Dean, "Just so there is no misunderstanding, as agreed, the flood was an act of God.

Aldridge will perform cleanup and flood recovery activities for no additional cost to the government. The government will extend Aldridge's contract time commensurate with the time lost because of the Flood. Aldridge will be paid for their expenses to prevent over cresting of the dam and expenses for restoring the dam to pre-flood conditions. We agree that time is of the essence. Work will resume as planned.

Three weeks later, July 8, 1974, the project was back to normal.

# CHAPTER 52

On July 8, 1974, Aldridge workers, after cleaning up debris and damage from the flood, resumed work on the foundation for the dam.

Aldridge excavated a cutoff trench, sixty feet wide by twenty feet deep, for the entire seventeen hundred feet length of the dam. The cutoff trench was the start of the sixty feet wide by two hundred feet high clay core that rose to the full height of the dam and formed its impervious center.

The clay core and the random fill on each of the upstream and downstream sides were placed and compacted more or less at the same rate. Concurrently, as the embankment rose, a three-foot thick rock face was placed on the upstream face over the random fill. This layer of rock served as erosion protection.

When the embankment was finished topsoil would be placed, and grass planted on the entire downstream slope.

Aldridge obtained all of the millions of cubic yards of material placed in the embankment from the borrow area that would become the emergency overflow spillway. Over many years and many flood control dams the Corps of Engineers conservative design parameters have proven the emergency overflow spillways to be unnecessary. The real purpose for the overflow spillway was to obtain the materials needed to build the embankment.

Aldridge workers finished the diversion dam in August 1974. With the diversion dam performing its intended purpose the area under the massive dam was ready to receive the materials needed to build the dam. A lot of work, mainly in the cutoff trench and the dam foundation, was completed from March 1974 to August 1974. In August loading, hauling, placing, and compaction of the various components of the embankment dam began with a flurry of activity.

Aldridge put their best efforts, equipment, and manpower into building the embankment. To finish the embankment by April 1976, Aldridge would work two shifts, 7:00 a.m. to 3:30 p.m. and 3:30 p.m. to midnight. They needed a combination of fourteen off-road trucks and scrapers just to haul and place earth and rock. They utilized eight dozers to assist loading the scrapers and spreading the material as it arrived on the embankment. Four articulated loaders worked to load rock onto the trucks. Completing the small army of construction equipment were six compactors working back and forth over the embankment that would become the Trout River Dam.

Wayne and his inspection team, except Towelson, were impressed with the attention to quality by Harold, Dean, and their team. Dean had many discussions with Wayne about the adverse effect on Aldridge's cost caused by the flood, lawsuits, and Towelson's detrimental actions. Wayne let Dean know that he was watching the situation and for Dean to keep accurate documentation of all potential claims for added cost and time. They were both dedicated to paying attention to conditions as they became apparent.

Operation and maintenance of the equipment fleet for the first shift required equipment operators, surveyors, drivers, someone to direct traffic, laborers, and two survey crews for grade control. One other person, usually an equipment operator, would see to equipment fueling and scheduled maintenance. Including foremen and supervision there were thirty-seven Aldridge employees on the first shift. The second shift had slightly fewer workers and an added generator and flood light operator.

Until this time, six major events adversely impacted schedule and cost. There were four injunctions, for which Aldridge had to stop and restart all work, the devastating flood, and overzealous inspection by a corrupt technician. Other factors that hampered progress included two unusually severe winters and wetter than normal spring weather in 1974. The constant stopping and starting made it difficult to keep a stable work force.

Towelson's harassment and overzealous interpretation of the project specifications prompted Dean to take proactive counter measures.

Dean told Harold, "It is apparent Towelson's attitude and demeaning comments to Aldridge employees about the alleged unsatisfactory work they do is filtering back to the union halls. Potential employees are made aware of the strict, uncompromising aura at this particular project. Towelson has made the Trout River Dam an unfriendly place to work."

Harold observed, "Our crews and his fellow inspectors know Towelson is demanding more than required by the already strict requirements concerning compaction of the earth embankment.

Dean said, "I'm fed up with the Towelson situation. To get independent verification of Towelson's overzealous requirements; today, September 8, 1975, I'm hiring a soil testing technician from the largest and most respected testing laboratory in Southern Ohio, Columbus Testing and Inspection, Inc. Columbus Testing is sending us Brent Tally. Tally has worked as a soils technician for Columbus Testing for twelve years. Brent is one of their best soil density and moisture testing technicians. He'll have the best testing equipment available."

The next day, when Brent arrived, Dean instructed him, "We want you to randomly test areas as you would on any project. When it looks like an area is ready, make your test and note the time, location, and outcome of the test. Our objective is to determine if one of the government inspectors is causing us to spend needless effort and time performing over compaction of the embankment fills, especially in the clay core of the dam. You can't miss the inspector with whom we're concerned. He's the big burly guy with a full beard."

After three days Brent reported to Dean, "I made many satisfactory compaction tests most of which I was able to correlate with the same tests deemed unsatisfactory by inspector Towelson. What's with this guy? He is deliberately falsifying his test reports. He's making you guys do a lot of unnecessary work."

Dean said, "Thanks for your help. We're trying to correct that situation."

Later Dean told Harold, "I've compiled Brent's results against those that Brian made in the same areas. Brent's compaction test results prove that Towelson's inspection is overzealous. He is making us spend hours and hours over compacting the earth fill in areas where the compaction already met contract specifications."

Dean said, "I won't enjoy this, but I have to notify the resident engineer of the subterfuge going on within his organization. I'll also give him written notice that we will demand payment for added expenses and a corresponding extension of the contract completion time.

Upon receiving Dean's notice that they had proof of Towelson's illicit activities Wayne lost his composure, "What the hell is this piece of shit claim you have sent us?" Without waiting for an answer he ranted on, "I have never been more angry and frustrated with a contractor representative than I am with you."

Dean responded, "I'm also the first contractor representative you've had to work with."

More seriously Dean replied, "This particular inspector has an obvious agenda to bust our balls. Remember that we proved he falsified aggregate gradation tests at the start of the project. Yet the government took no action. We still have an unresolved claim for those expenses. Six months ago I verbally notified you about his unorthodox and overzealous compaction testing and no action has been taken. This written notice of a claim should come as no surprise. The ball is in your court."

Shortly after Wayne's tirade and Dean's response, Towelson stormed into Dean's office shouting, "What do you think you are going to accomplish by undermining my authority? The hiring of an outside technician to recheck my work is a waste of money. My record speaks for itself, there are no mistakes."

Dean calmly replied, "You're right Brian, your record does speak for itself. It shows you are a fraud. It shows you are a very talented and knowledgeable technician who prefers to bankrupt contractors instead of using your talents in a way that benefits your career and the construction industry. You are a disgrace to the Corps of Engineers. Get out of my sight." Dean decided he would not let this incident fester. He waited several days before he called Wayne to ask for a meeting with him and Towelson.

Wayne tersely responded, "You'll get our response in writing."

It was over a month before Dean received the government's written response to the compaction claim. It stated there are no grounds for a claim. Dean simply replied to the denial that Aldridge would continue to pursue time and money.

Once again Dean and Harold were discussing the Towelson situation. Harold observed, "The double testing and proof of Towelson's extraordinary compaction requirements did help. I can see a marked increase in productivity. One thing I have observed is that the other inspectors are doing more testing and less is being done by Towelson."

***

Harold told Dean, "Another problem we're having concerns the size of work force we need. Among our employees there is a broad range of experience, ability, and dependability. A few of our operating engineers own farms. In the spring, when we need them the most, farmers need to be planting crops and in the fall, on fair weather days; they want to be harvesting crops. On the other hand, farmers are hard working and skilled operators who know how to maintain and repair equipment."

Harold added, "The number of equipment operators we require and demands by other employers in the area is taxing the operating engineers union to the extent that they are scraping the proverbial bottom of the barrel. The manpower shortage brought some interesting people into our employment. One person came to work who didn't know how to start the equipment he was assigned. He told me, I've been in the union about six months, and I did the training, but this is my first job."

Harold continued to explain the hiring situation, "Several showed up drunk or high and were sent back to the union hall. Three of our new employees are women who out-work many of the men. Two men had physical disabilities that made it impossible for them to operate the hand and feet controls on the equipment. One such person was hired and, given the right assignment; he is one of my most valuable assistants."

Harold said, "On several occasions both unions, the operating engineers and laborers, knowing Aldridge is an out of state employer tried to coerce us into hiring unemployable union member friends and relatives."

Dean noted, "The effect of those and similar adverse situations on us and other company projects will have a negative impact on Aldridge's profits. Here at Trout River there are many unresolved issues, change orders, and claims. Aldridge's financial and corporate future depends on fast and satisfactory compensation for expenses incurred because of delays and added work. Without fair treatment by the Corps, at best, Trout River will be a break even project."

## CHAPTER 53

Dean was alone working on his daily report when the door to the field office opened and in walked Herb Flaherty. Dean was surprised but glad to see him. "Herb! What the hell, what brings you all the way over here?"

Herb answered, "I'm here to see the job, but I want to bring you up to date about happenings within the company. You are a shareholder and an officer of the company. I know you are probably hearing rumors concerning the company's financial health. You have a right to know the facts. I didn't feel right telling you over the phone."

Dean said, "I've heard rumors. Sean, one of the company truck drivers, said he heard there are financial problems. I haven't given much thought to what he said."

Herb responded, "There are some problems. We're working through them. Let's sit down and I'll explain as best I can. "Through 1974 and into 1975 no one but top management knew of the growing financial crisis. Your work here at the dam has not been affected. However, to maintain appearances, we are struggling to meet payroll, pay invoices, and meet bank obligations. The company has about two hundred fifty million dollars of work among the three divisions. Typically the accounting for each division is kept separate. But with the crisis, we are meeting our obligations from any source of income. We're robbing Peter to pay Paul."

Herb continued, "Cost overruns on this project are caused mainly by the deliberate anti-contractor actions of inspector Towelson. The other unresolved issues also have financial consequences. In addition to problems on this project, our financial problems are occurring because of our aggressive engagement in the interstate highway program during the sixties. A lot of the company resources are committed to building highways. Aldridge along with many of our competitors believed the interstate highway program was never ending."

Herb said, "I know I'm rambling but hear me out. In 1970 the federal government, through the Federal Highway Trust Fund, began funneling highway dollars to mass transit, resulting in less funding for fewer highway projects. Mass transit is more railroad than highway and we're not equipped to jump into that venue. More contractors are chasing fewer highway projects and the competition, although good for the highway program, is bad for highway contractors. Our heavy and highway division is invested, both in personnel and equipment, for construction projects where there is more competition chasing fewer opportunities.

While Dean remained silent, Herb nervously continued, "We have pledged, as collateral to our bank, a lot of our equipment. When our bank, St. Louis Merchants Trust, began to see slow payments and a rising debt to asset ratio they reduced our line of credit. In fact, the bank, as is their right, is demanding that we repay more than a million dollars immediately. Without actual notice from Merchants Trust, they are dumping us.

"I and the other majority owners, Shearer and Warden, have no alternative but to seek a new banker. A week ago, on May 9, 1975, we called an emergency shareholder meeting. Robert Warden told us he couldn't believe Merchants did this to us that we've always banked with them. Arthur Aldridge started banking with them thirty years ago. Now, at the first indication of a problem, they don't want to, or won't work with us."

Herb continued his explanation to Dean, "Our division is the hardest hit by the current economic situation. There is no justification for continuing to beat ourselves up in the highway construction market. As discussed at the meeting we need to develop a new financial plan with a new bank. We are going forward with the knowledge that a bank alone won't solve our financial crisis. We need to change our overall business plan by cutting unnecessary expenditures, tighten our cost controls, aggressively collect money owed to us, and sell anything we don't need."

Herb said, "I told the group; during normal times the banks would be beating down the door for our business. But here we sit, helpless, like fish in a bowl. Somehow we need to regain control of our own destiny."

Finally, Dean said, "I'm as guilty as anybody for contributing to the problem. There are a lot of unpaid change orders and claims on this job. I haven't given them my attention. We get along by going along, and we need to be more aggressive. But talk is cheap. I keep getting stonewalled by the resident engineer; he doesn't want to face up to our demands. So the unresolved issues just sit there."

Herb agreed, "You're not the only one. On many of our

projects there are millions of dollars in uncollected pay requests, change orders, and claims owed to us that we have ignored. I'm asking you and other project managers to be more aggressive collecting money that is owed to us."

Dean said, "I hear you. We'll do what we can."

"By the way," Herb said, "There will be another share holder meeting next week, Friday, May 16. At that meeting we'll decide on a new banker. In the meantime, we have to look at every operation within our company and root out waste, sell unneeded equipment, and intensify collecting money that is owed to us. Going back to the bank situation, we have an inquiry from First National. They are not the power they were, but neither are we. If everyone agrees we'll vote to change banks."

Dean acknowledged, "I'll be there."

***

Dean left the job Thursday afternoon and attended the shareholder meeting on Friday at the St. Louis office.

The shareholder meeting began at one o'clock p.m. Victor Shearer was the first to speak to the eleven shareholders. "Thank you all for being here. As most of you know we have been searching for a new banker. My search has produced just one bank that is interested, First National. They have three conditions. First, Aldridge has to divest itself of one million dollars of debt by selling off encumbered equipment. Second, First National will grant a five million dollar line of credit equal to the remaining balance after divesting but we cannot add to the line. Third, and final, all of Aldridge's banking needs must be carried out with First National. The agreement prohibits us from incurring debt from any another source. First National will handle all of our checking, deposits, payroll, and all other banking needs." Two of the minority shareholders expressed concern, asking why there was no concerted attempt to work out a compromise with Merchants Trust. Their objections were quickly satisfied followed by a unanimous vote to change banks.

Before the meeting adjourned Robert Warden asked to speak to the group. He got right to the point, "Our Company is facing the most serious crisis in its fifty-five-year history. Unless we can turn things around, by the end of this year we will be out of money and unable to pay our bills. That's all I have to say."

An emotional shudder and chill went through the eight minority holders. Although most people in the room were aware of certain financial problems facing the company, they did not expect to be brought so abruptly to face the facts.

A lengthy, but fruitful, discussion ensued wherein company problems and causes were aired enlightening those from all three company divisions. Some possible solutions were informally proposed. In the end, however, there was no solution offered to resolve the company's financial problems.

# CHAPTER 54

Work on the embankment that would become the Trout River dam continued. Three feet of select rock was in place for the foundation. A Sixty-foot wide clay core was being placed and carefully compacted to form the impervious core of the dam. Work progressed placing the millions of cubic yards of random earth fill on the upstream and downstream sides of the embankment. A three feet thick layer of rock on the upstream face provided scour protection that would last more than a hundred years.

Every day the Corp's inspection team regularly checked the quality and in place density of thousands of cubic yards of various materials going into the dam. The inspection team became like a part of the Aldridge crew. Each team had become reliant on the other. They communicated, shared information, and they all had to endure the same weather environment. Corps inspector Towelson was not one of the team players. In fact, Towelson was annoyed by the apparent cooperation going on between his inspectors and the contractor employees. If he could, he would create dissension to replace cooperation. Safety was a primary goal.

Since the beginning of the embankment, in June 1972, Aldridge had a trained safety compliance engineer assigned to the project. Jonathan Weller was assigned to assure compliance with the new Occupation Safety and Health Act of 1970, commonly referred to as OSHA. Jonathan and his counterpart on the second shift had dictatorial power over the worksite. In March 1972 Jonathan, along with several other Aldridge employees from other projects, attended four weeks of safety training sponsored by the Missouri Contractors Association. All driven equipment, before it arrived, had backup alarms and certified roll-overprotection.

In spite of many clashes with workers about safety violations, Jonathan was well liked. Every Monday, before they started the week's work, he had a safety meeting with both shifts. During those meetings he stressed safety at work and home. The emphasis was on looking out for each other, telling the foreman of anything that might affect equipment and personal safety, and being alert.

Jonathon became the go-to person for problems that didn't get addressed by management or supervisors. He was the referee for occasional clashes between workers. Jonathan was twenty-three years old; a recent graduate with a mechanical engineering degree from the University of Mississippi. Born and raised in Hattiesburg, Mississippi he never left the state until hired by Aldridge. Raised by his grandmother, he never said why, who instilled him with the need for honesty and directness. Although he was the youngest person on the project, Jonathon didn't waste words. He based his solutions to problems on common sense. Jonathan, although not in a field needing a mechanical engineering education, loved his job and the challenges.

One hot summer day in July 1975, Jonathan reprimanded Hank Meltzer, a dozer driver, for not wearing his hard hat.

He yelled at Hank, "Where's your hard hat? You know that's a violation of OSHA and company rules. Shut your machine down and get off the dozer."

When the man stepped down, he collapsed at Jonathan's feet. Jonathan noticed an ugly gash on the side of the man's head, apparently the reason he wasn't wearing his hard hat. Emergency medical personnel and an ambulance took the man to the county medical center.

Before the ambulance took him away, Jonathon asked how he injured his head. Hank answered, "I had an early morning fight with my wife. She got mad and hit me with an electric mixer. We're having a financial problem that was the reason for the fight. I know I need medical attention, but I don't want to lose a day of pay."

The man was treated and released and was back to work the next day. He didn't say any more about the situation at home.

Similar incidents rarely occurred, but when they did Jonathan was right there to see to the worker's safety and provide council when necessary.

## CHAPTER 55

For three years, since the summer of 1973, Dean and his family had been residing in Clearfield County. They weren't close friends with Wayne and his family, but they had shared time together. A few evenings out for dinner, a couple of weekend cookouts and some hiking about the dam area was the extent of their social contact. In May 1976 as the lake was filling and the project was coming to a close the ongoing disputes about claims and change orders would tax what little friendship existed between the two men.

Before Dean could put his full attention to solving the disputes and claims at work, he had to address a problem closer to home. As the project neared completion, Dean and Diana had a timing problem. Michele, now seventeen, would be graduating from Trout River High School on June 4, 1976. By that time Dean would be permanently back at his vice president position in the St. Louis office. In fact, except for closing out Aldridge's Trout River contract, Dean and the family were ready to move from their Clearfield County rental home in March 1976. The situation caused Diana and the girls to remain in Clearfield County, without Dean, until Michele's graduation.

Dean and Diana, during one of the several trips to St. Louis in February 1976, found the home of their dreams. The home had four large bedrooms, three and a half bathrooms, a three-car garage, and an office for Dean. Located in an upscale area west of the city it was what they wanted. It was scheduled to be complete and ready for them to move in by the end of March. The whole family loved the house and the neighborhood.

Diana told Dean, "I had doubts about the temporary move to Clearfield County. I agreed because we needed to be together and you wanted to finish the dam. But seeing our new home made all the sacrifices worthwhile." Diana grabbed Dean in a bear hug and said, "You more or less tricked and coerced me into the house of my dreams. You're a sly one, but I love you." At the end of March 1976, Dean had to return to the office and Diana had to stay with the girls in Clearfield County. There was a lot of work waiting for him, and Herb was growing impatient. Herb was giving most of his attention to the company's financial crisis, and Dean was needed to manage the company's ongoing work.

Dean and Diana worked out a solution that would keep the girls in the local schools until the end of the current term. Dean would go back to the St. Louis office and live in a motel. Diana would stay in the Clearfield County rental home until school let out for the summer and Michele graduated. The family planned to spend weekends together in Clearfield County.

During the first week of April they closed on the purchase of the new home. Dean had the job of getting all of their furniture and belongings from storage and transferred to the new home. No attempt was being made to organize the new home. Diana and the girls would have that job when they got back in June. Although the plan was the best they could conceive it would be taxing for everyone.

\*\*\*

On March 17, 1976, Aldridge crews placed the last load of soil in the embankment. There were few people there to witness the occasion. Most of the Aldridge employees who toiled, sweat, and suffered to build the Trout River Dam were gone, their efforts not acknowledged and sacrifices not rewarded; their services no longer needed.

Dean arranged for a topping-out party in the testing lab building. It was a small party. The attendees included Wayne, Dean, three equipment operators, one laborer, the project superintendent Harold Schneider, and three other Corps employees. Towelson was gone, already assigned to another project somewhere in Kentucky. God help that contractor. Dean, knowing Towelson was taking money from an unprincipled contractor, had plans that would torpedo his career.

After enjoying excellent barbecued pork and side dishes, Dean and Wayne said their goodbyes, wishing each other good luck in future endeavors. . Dean made an iced tea toast, "Here's to the dam and everyone who will enjoy the soon to be completed recreational facilities. Let us remember the sacrifices made by people who had to relocate to make way for this beautiful place."

# CHAPTER 56

In June 1976 the dam was finished, and contractor employees were finishing a few remaining items and preparing to leave. Corps of Engineers personnel were diligently monitoring filling of the Trout River Lake.

Two properties remained un-acquired. The Olga McCoy shack and the Connors farm.

The infamous, gun toting and deranged Olga McCoy and her son had resisted all attempts by the government to remove them from the property. In 1971 the government acquired title to the property by eminent domain. McCoy had never accepted the escrow held by the court. She refused to vacate the property. The government, with Wayne's advice, avoided eviction proceedings until they no longer had a choice. The dam impoundment was forming and Olga's property was near the shore.

The McCoy property contained ten acres, a rundown shack, some outbuildings, and an old unused whiskey still.

Olga knew no other home; she was born here, and her two boys were born here. Until the government decided to build a dam that would flood her property she planned to die here.

Their primitive living conditions allowed them to be self-sustaining. They heated and cooked using a wood burning stove; they stole electric from neighbors to run a few lights, power the well pump, and heat some water. They lived off the land aided by subsistence provided by county services.

JD Henderson, Wayne's son, now seventeen; and his good friend, Wesley Norton, Raymond and Carole Norton's son, had for six years, used the government-owned property for exploring, hunting, and fishing. They knew the four-thousand acres like their backyard. They also knew to avoid the McCoy property.

Olga McCoy was in her sixties and mentally unstable. She was considered a witch by some and just plain crazy by others. Her son Kenneth, like his long ago deceased father, made a meager living selling illegal whiskey and, occasionally, some marijuana. His market area, also like his father, was in the streets, brothels, and casinos of Northern Kentucky. Government agents killed Kenneth's father in the fall of 1939 during a moonshine whiskey deal that went sour. The unused whiskey still, disguised as a chicken coop, was evidence of the father's long past endeavors.

One day in mid-July 1976, as the lake was filling; JD and Wesley were scrounging around the woods in the vicinity of Olga's shack looking for truffles, a very lucrative hobby. In June the boys made $125 selling truffles. Olga had seen the boys before and resented them being nearby. She was near the end of her ability to defy the government as the rising lake and shoreline edged closer to her home. In her twisted mind, she devised a plan to, in her skewed way of thinking; punish the hated feds by using the boys as leverage.

The boys were about one-fourth mile away, well clear of her property. Olga came out of her shack and wandered toward the boys. "Hey," she shouted, "Cain you kids help me git an animal outta my chicken coop? I think it's a raccoon."

The boys, being somewhat macho, yelled back, "Sure, we can chase it out." The chicken coop as she called it was actually the old whiskey still. Built of solid oak planks, it had no windows.

When the boys innocently entered the so-called chicken coop expecting to find a raccoon Olga slammed the only door shut and dropped a two by four in place securely preventing the door from opening. The boys were her captives, and she illogically planned to use them as leverage to save her property. For several moments the boys didn't understand their predicament until they realized she trapped them inside the old still. They yelled and pounded on the walls until they were exhausted. Olga and Kenny ignored them; the boy's shouts merely bounced off the empty woods.

Nighttime added to the already dark interior of the smelly old still. Olga stayed in the shack while son Kenny was in charge of the captives. During their captivity, he did not give them water or food. They were too scared to sleep. They continued to try to attract attention by pounding and kicking on the walls and shouting for help. At one point, about midnight, Kenny yelled, "Shut yer goddamn mouths, or I'll come in there and cut off yer pekers." No effort was made to calm the boys; in fact, every effort was made to terrify them.

About the time they were lured into captivity, JD's mom, Melissa, called Carole Norton at their new home and farm and asked, "Do you know the whereabouts of JD and Wesley?"

Carole, surprised that they weren't at Melissa's house,

said, "I don't know where the boys are, but now I'm worried. I'll get Raymond and ask him to go over and check around our old farm." It's unlike the boys to go somewhere without leaving a note or checking in with us.

It was late afternoon when Melissa called Wayne at his office. "Honey, have you seen JD or Wesley? They haven't been home all day."

Wayne, somewhat alarmed, said, "I'll drive around the old Norton farm and see if they are in that area. The lake is almost half full, and the Norton farm is almost entirely submerged."

When Wayne arrived in the area of the old Norton farm, Raymond came up to him and in a very concerned voice said, "I haven't seen the boys all day. Wesley is supposed to be at the new farm; he has work to do. He is ornery but never fails to do the things I tell him to do. Sometimes JD helps him."

It was getting dark when a search for the boys started. Two of the construction workers still at the dam joined the search team. The sheriff sent two deputies. A few county residents agreed to help search. About fifteen people began scouring the area around the rising lake. A few poked about in the shallows surrounding the new impoundment. A small group of the searchers strayed near the McCoy place but failed to hear anything. By daybreak they were all exhausted but agreed to continue the search after a few hours rest. The boy's families were panic stricken. Carole Norton was beside herself with worry, "The boys have never been away for more than three or four hours. They would never stay away all night."

The captive boys were tired, thirsty, hungry, and scared of the unknown fate that awaited them. They had been captive for more than twenty-four hours. Olga, who had no phone, decided it was time to make her demand. She had Kenny go to the nearby town and, using a pay phone, call Wayne.

All Wayne heard was, "This is a friend of a homeowner whose place you are trying to steal. You government people need to leave her place alone; just stop filling the lake and ya'll git the boys back safe. Or we'll make a deal. We'll sell if you come up with seventy-five thousand dollars more for the property. Do one or the other, or something bad will happen to the boys. If you buy, by midnight tonight, put the money in a bag and place it in the dead tree on Trout River Drive near Sawmill Creek and leave. No cops." Click, the messenger was gone. The message sent as Olga had ordered.

Wayne immediately called Sheriff Spearman and told him of the phone call. It did not take long for Wayne and the sheriff to narrow the identity of the property owner to Olga McCoy. In fact, her property and the Connors farm were the only ones left. They ruled out the Connors.

Within minutes, Sheriff Spearman arrived at Wayne's office. In spite of the situation, he had to chuckle as he told Wayne, "This beats all. That stupid woman owns the only possible property left. It's like she's sitting on top of her shack yelling, here I am. I've got the boys."

The sheriff warned Wayne and Raymond, "Stay away from the McCoy place. Those people are armed, unstable, and dangerous. When it's dark, I'll take five of my deputies over there and get the boys back. By sneaking up in the dark we can surprise her, her son, and anyone else who might be helping her. One of my deputies, Jake Horner, was a Green Beret in the Army. He'll lead the operation. Mind you, stay away; these are dangerous and unstable people. They're armed and they're druggies. God only knows what they're capable of."

The captive recovery plan was simple. The Green Beret crept silently to the building where the boys were held captive. Kenny was guarding the chicken coop/still. He was almost asleep sitting in a rickety old lawn chair. Jake grabbed him, wrestled him to the ground, while another deputy handcuffed him. He then unlatched the door, let the boys out, gave them some water and hustled them away, warning them, "Get going before Olga comes out!" They were dirty, hungry and thirsty, but otherwise unharmed.

Kenny was handcuffed and awaiting transport to the Clearfield County jail. Olga came running from the shack with the 12 gauge loaded and ready shouting, "Git yer hands off my boy."

A deputy was standing beside the door. When Olga passed through the door, he grabbed her and the gun. Fueled by her rage, she was all one deputy could handle. A second deputy quickly assisted, and the two of them were able to subdue her. The deputy told his buddy, "She's little, and she is old, but man is she strong!"

Sheriff Spearman noted, "Olga screwed up. Instead of quietly taking the generous escrow deposit and relocating she and her son are now kidnappers, two counts, and face serious felony charges. Olga, for sure, will be charged with resisting arrest."

Later after hearings and trials Kenny, because the crime occurred on federal property, was sentenced to six years in a federal prison. Olga was again remanded to psychiatric care and evaluation until the authorities could assess her mental condition. She remained in the care of the state for five years.

The deputies escorted the remaining two adults, identity unknown, off the property. They refused assistance and left the county, disappearing into obscurity. The government had finally heard the last from Olga McCoy.

\*\*\*

The last working farm to be acquired consisted of one hundred sixteen acres, a modest dwelling, and the usual farm outbuildings. The elderly residents, Elmer and Dorothy Connors, had worked the farm for thirty years. They were ready to retire. As soon as they knew the government was going to buy their farm they were ready and willing to sell. Their two adult children had no interest in the farm but had an inflated idea of the property value. The kids control over the parents was the only reason preventing the sale.

Tony Gianconi, a Corps real estate specialist, attempted several times to close the sale on behalf of the government. Gianconi explained to the Connors, "The government acquired your property by condemnation procedures nearly five years ago. That action resulted with the court placing the fair value of the property in escrow."

Tony continued, "The court will release the funds to you when you sign the agreement to sell the property to the government. Failure to comply with the court order will require that we forcibly evict you." He explained, "The fair value of your farm has been increased proportionally to the Norton's and the other owners involved in the eminent domain proceedings."

Two weeks of haggling was required until the Connors finally agreed to sell. Their children were not satisfied with the agreement but acquiesced to their parent's wishes. The Connors signed the sale documents on October 26, 1976; about six months after the impoundment began to fill.

# CHAPTER 57

In October 1976 the contractors were gone, and the public had access to the area. In March 1976 before the government accepted the project, Dean met with Wayne to discuss unresolved issues.

Dean informed Wayne, "We complied with instructions from you and as required by the contract we provided timely notice and documentation concerning many unpaid expenses for owner-caused delays, stop work orders, and extra work. As you know, there are six unresolved issues. There are four delays caused by court-ordered stop work injunctions, a government employee's subterfuge, and authorized acceleration expenses following a flood. There are many other time and money issues for which we will relinquish our rights, provided the six items I just listed are satisfactorily resolved including time and money. It will be a whole new ball game if we have to take legal action to collect our money."

Dean reminded Wayne, "There are one and a half million dollars of unpaid extra work and delays hanging in limbo that you or somebody in Louisville is sitting on. Your chief inspector's sabotage and subterfuge alone has cost us over one million dollars. Every dollar and every day of delay have been carefully accounted for, documented, and submitted to your office in a timely manner. Every page was provided as directed by you and approved by your technicians and engineers."

Wayne shrugged his shoulders and held his hands out when he replied, "Dean, you can't be serious, do you really expect to get paid for all that BS?"

Dean angrily replied, "You are the one who told us to log our expenses, have them verified, and submit a daily report to your office. In good faith, we followed your instructions to the letter. Are you telling me the government is reneging on your promise to pay us? Am I to believe that no one other than people in your office has even looked at all the documents? Are we expected to walk away from here empty-handed? That's not going to happen!"

Wayne again showed a helpless expression, "I'm just following orders. It appears you're going to have to take these matters to the district office."

Dean was furious. He told Wayne, "Okay, per the contract, we submitted all the paperwork and justification with the notices. Just tell me when and where and I will be there. It appears that this is no longer a friendly dispute but all out war. I'm ready. Let your people know that this concerns important issues and represents a lot of money. Make sure the right decision makers are there." Without another word, Dean abruptly left Wayne's office.

Two days later Dean received a letter from none other than the chief engineer, Jordan Lipper, notifying Aldridge that the government has disapproved all remaining unresolved monetary issues. The letter instructed them to submit the required paperwork necessary to close out the project. Lipper also advised Aldridge that the government is withholding final payment and retainer until all closeout documents are received. There was no mention of a meeting, how to resolve the unresolved issues, or plans to address same.

Dean, now permanently in his St. Louis office, fired off a scathing six-page certified letter to Lipper, with a copy to Wayne, reiterating Aldridge's claims for time and money and demanding a meeting for the purpose of resolving unresolved issues. At the advice of the company lawyer, Dean allowed thirty days for a response before Aldridge began legal action to recover and all monies due.

Two weeks later, Herbert Flaherty received a certified letter notifying him that there would be a claims hearing at the district office on May 21, 1976, at nine o'clock a.m. Herb turned the matter over to Dean telling him, "Go get 'em!"

***

Herb and Dean discussed the magnitude and complexity of the claim situation. They decided to obtain expert advice in the person of Barry Thompson, a professional claims consultant. Thompson, a retired Corps of Engineers engineer turned lawyer, was knowledgeable about the inner workings regarding the way claims were handled when dealing with the government and the Corps of Engineers.

The consultant told Dean, "You have a pot full of valid complaints. Keep your cool and state only verifiable facts. They are wrong; they know it, and they know they have to abide by the contract and mandated laws intended to provide a level playing field. If this has to go to the United States Court of Claims, they will get their butt kicked."

Dean and the recently hired claims resolution consultant were at the district office at the appointed time. The meeting was off to a bad start when, upon entering the conference room, Dean observed that Wayne was not there. The chief engineer, Jordan Lipper, explained, "Mr. Henderson is on leave. His chief inspector, Brian Towelson, is here in Wayne's place."

Dean was shocked. He told the room, "Wayne was at Trout River from the first day, he has the most knowledge about what occurred. He knows what caused the added work and the conditions at the time the work happened. I can't believe that we weren't notified of his absence."

Lipper stated, "We will go forward without Mr. Henderson, please sit down."

As Dean and Barry sat, they looked at the others seated in the room. In addition to Dean and Barry who sat at the far end of the table, Brian Towelson sat smug and confident on the center left, Lipper at the head of the table below a giant picture of some army general, and two of Wayne's engineers occuping the right side. Dean noticed Richard Albert, the Corps general counsel, sat on the right side of Lipper. Scattered about the table were two other people unknown to Dean.

All the Corps people had the same stack of documents before them. Dean's stack of documents was three times as big as the others. He assumed somebody had summarized Aldridge's entire package of claims and requests for pay and distributed it to everyone; probably just before this meeting. Barry whispered to Dean, "You have to educate these people. Some of them probably don't even know the location of the Trout River or the dam. You will be the teacher."

Lipper spoke first, "Let's start by discussing the expenses

incurred resulting from the flood."

Dean immediately stopped him, "No, we prefer to start with the worst first, the matter of a government employee in a responsible position falsifying test results and using his superior knowledge and position to delay, hamper and interfere with efficiencies that adversely affected the contractor's expenses and progress. All of which is documented by outside experts, daily project reports, and numerous notices to the resident engineer."

Dean caught his breath and continued, "Until two weeks ago the government never denied any of the requests for time or money. Despite firsthand knowledge by the resident engineer, this person's actions were allowed to continue unabated for six years. As stated in numerous and timely notices, the impact on this item of our expenses totals $1,082,000."

Dean looked around the table. He looked at the consultant who gave him a slight nod. He drew a deep breath and said, "The Aldridge Company doesn't want to take this action. But I believe your goal in having Mr. Towelson here instead of Mr. Henderson is to force a 'my word against his word' situation. To nullify any such thoughts, I have in my hand a notarized statement from Mr. Herman McGraw, president of McGraw Construction Company.

Towelson, slouching in his seat suddenly sat up.

Dean had the floor, "Mr. McGraw affirms that his company built a similar dam in Ohio where Mr. Towelson was the chief inspector. They experienced similar overzealous behavior from Mr. Towelson. The Corps denied McGraw any compensation for the outrageous conduct by a government employee. Because McGraw lost a lot of money and because they considered Towelson's conduct unusual and shameful for a Corps inspector they initiated an investigation into Towelson's past.

Towelson suddenly jumped to his feet and shouted, "These are all lies from a bunch of cry-baby contractors who can't make any money. They try to make up for their stupidity by drumming up claims for extra money. Mr. Lipper you should end this right now!"

Lipper, still in a state of disbelief, said, "Sit down Mr. Towelson, allow Mr. Richardson to continue."

Dean allowed a few moments to pass before he continued, "McGraw discovered that Mr. Towelson was surreptitiously paid by a local contractor to harass, cause extra work, and create havoc during the construction of their project. We know the identity of the contractor who was making the secret payments. We have been asked not to reveal his name. This subterfuge started when the guilty contractor lost the bid for the project McGraw's company built."

Dean confidently continued, "McGraw brought the matter to the attention of the Ohio Contractors Alliance who quietly queried the local contractor in a closed-door meeting. The guilty contractor did not admit to wrongdoing but neither did he deny his actions. It came out during the investigation that the sore loser just wanted to teach out of state contractors a lesson."

Dean explained, "About three years ago we found out that Towelson was accepting money from, at that time, an unknown source. The purpose of the tacit agreement between Towelson and the unnamed contractor was to undermine our progress and increase our costs. However, we didn't have written proof until a week ago. Until now we were unable to do anything with the information."

The Corps employees in the room were obviously unprepared for this sensitive and unprecedented contractor claim directed at a particular Corps employee. Everyone was looking at Towelson who had his eyes fixed on his hands.

Lipper reacted by requesting a copy of the statement and asking the group to take a short break. He remained in the meeting room with Towelson and Richard Albert, the district's legal counsel.

About thirty minutes later they reconvened. Towelson was gone. Lipper was trying to regain control of the meeting. He announced, "We have told Mr. Towelson to leave the meeting but to remain in the building. We consider McGraw's statement an unproven assertion. An internal investigation will be conducted by our legal department. Until then there is nothing we can do."

Barry Thompson, the Aldridge consultant stood and introduced himself, "I am Barry Thompson and for thirty years I was employed by the US Army Corps of Engineers. Many times I sat where you are sitting. During that time I never observed the blatant disrespect shown in this room. You are trying to belittle this contractor and their request to recover expenses that occurred for reasons beyond their control. Aldridge followed the contract and notified the government of unknown and hidden situations, not anticipated by the contract. To add insult to injury they had to endure artifice by a government employee that caused added expenses. They have been very fair, giving the government the benefit of the doubt by leaving out of their claims any ambiguous or unproven expenses including overhead expenses. If we have to take this to the U.S. Court of Claims, we will go back through every detail and nuance of this project. The amount of the claim will double. We'll demand interest, delay expenses, overhead, and profit on every dime we are due. Mr. Richardson has submitted a bare-bones request for some of the money they are owed. Please show some respect. Let's get this done today!"

Dean again took the floor and asked, "Which parts of the delay and subterfuge expenses are in question?"

Lipper quickly responded, "All of it."

"Okay," Dean said, "Do you deny the many instances of your inspector improperly taking samples in order to falsify required government reports concerning concrete aggregate gradation? Towelson's sampling methods and reports were proven false by Mr. Loren Hauser; a concrete expert who, until his retirement, was an employee of the Corps of Engineers."

Dean continued, "Are you aware Columbus testing and Inspection made similar soil tests which their soils testing expert said proved Towelson was purposely demanding over compaction of the dam embankment causing countless hours of added labor and equipment expenses? I don't know what you have in the packet before you, but if you look, I'll bet the damning concrete and soil testing reports are there. In addition to numerous written notice of Towelson's subversive actions, there were even more verbal discussions with the resident engineer. On one occasion Mr. Henderson notified you, Mr. Lipper, of the falsified tests and you suggested Mr Towelson, 'was just doing his job.'"

"Nobody wants this to go beyond this room. The people are here with the authority to resolve all of our concerns. With the preponderance of documentation and the total lack of offsetting documentation from the government, the U.S. Court cf Claims will rule in our favor. Let's move on."

Lipper was finally ready to talk, "What will it take to settle the inspection situation? Dean, what's your bottom number?"

Dean answered, "Mr. Lipper, We are entitled to the amount stated, $1,082,000. The equipment rates were taken verbatim from the Corps published 1973 *Hourly Equipment Ownership and Operating Expense* manual. Labor rates are the same as stated on our payroll records. We added overhead at the rate agreed to at the beginning of the project. We did not add profit. The amount is already bare bones."

Lipper said, "Give us something, we don't want to go away empty-handed either."

Dean contemplated whether to cooperate; he knew Herb had encouraged him to 'get what you can.' He asked, "Give Barry and me a moment."

Looking at the large amount of documents comprising the testing claim Barry quietly said, "I think you should give a little but stipulate that there will be some non-monetary issues come up later."

Dean was ready to deal, "Mr. Lipper we will adjust the amount by twelve percent, lowering the final amount to $952,000. We'll make this adjustment by deducting our overhead expenses, some labor, and some equipment costs. We also stipulate that there are non-monetary issues we will address later."

To everybody's surprise, Lipper offered his hand and said to Dean, We have an agreement, next item."

The group took a fifteen-minute break. When the meeting resumed Towelson was nowhere in sight.

Dean once again took the floor, "There are four documented instances of court ordered stop work injunctions scattered throughout the project. The first, including time to stop and restart, lasted sixty-three working days during which all equipment was, as ordered, by the resident engineer placed on stand-by status. Although we had labor and other expenses, we are requesting reimbursement for standby equipment only. We have not asked for expenses incurred due to seasonal variances delaying summer work until less desirable weather. The expenses are only for standby equipment calculated at the rate published in your own equipment expense manual."

As there was no response Dean said, "Let's get this done. The injunction delays are summarized by number. Number one delayed the work sixty-three work days. Those days multiplied by the cumulative idled equipment standby rate of $302 per hour extends to $152,000. Injunction number two delayed the project twenty-eight work days, costing $67,600. Injunction number three delayed the project twelve work days, costing $29,000. Injunction number four delayed the project forty-seven work days, costing $113,500. The total delay cost covering all four injunctions is $362,100. We are not asking for interest, profit, overhead, lost labor or any other expenses."

It took about ten minutes while Dean and Barry were excused from the room for Lipper and his team to reach a decision. When they are all back in the room Lipper announced, "We have agreement on the injunction delays."

To keep the meeting moving, they had worked through lunch and it was nearing one O'clock, Dean asked, "Can we keep going? There is only one other unresolved cost issue. It is the expense incurred to recover from the flood." It appeared the group was willing to go on. Dean forged ahead, "Within three weeks after the flood our expenses were submitted and, I thought, approved by the resident engineer. Our documented expenses, including agreed overhead and profit, is $102,000. Are there any questions about the cost of this work? No one voiced an objection, so Dean stated, "Okay, we're good on that one too."

Dean thanked everyone for their support and understanding. He wanted to, but didn't, ask what will happen to Towelson. After thanking the group Dean continued, "There are a few remaining items of concern we would like to wrap up while we are here. As explained earlier, to expedite agreement we took the high road and didn't add any additional amounts for profit, overhead, tools, weather, or any other things. Where applicable we included bare equipment and labor expenses only."

Dean looked around the room, "In return we'd like to expedite final payment and retainer. Today is May 21. Is it possible, provided all project closeout issues are addressed by Aldridge and all change orders and pay requests are processed by the Corps, that we can finalize everything by August 1?"

Lipper nodded his head in agreement.

Dean, after being reminded by Barry, said, "Oh, I almost forgot. We assume the change order will include corresponding extensions to the contract time."

Lipper assured Dean, "Yes they will. Now let's go to lunch, I'm starved."

Before Dean and Barry departed, Dean spoke privately with Jordan Lipper. "Mr. Lipper, it embarrassed me and I was uncomfortable bringing to the forefront the Brian Towelson matter. I want you and the rest of the Louisville District to know how strongly the Aldridge Company believes he was acting alone and in no way were his actions a reflection upon the Corps of Engineers. Your organization has the highest standards in the industry. Towelson's despicable behavior was an anomaly. We're looking forward to working together on many future projects."

\*\*\*

When they left the district office Dean felt like a huge weight was removed from his shoulders. They resolved all the outstanding issues for a total of $1,416,100.

Barry said, "You did great in there. You really didn't need me."

Dean said, "I don't believe that, you were my big gun. They knew they couldn't bully me with you by my side. Facts are facts; you're mentioning the U.S. Court of Claims took the fight out of them. But, despite the acrimony created by Towelson, I enjoy working with the Corps. They are honest and hard working. They are also the world's best design and construction organization. I don't fault them for trying to get the best deal for the tax payer's money.

Dean noted to Barry, "They owe us retainer equal to five percent of the contract amount. That alone is $1,837,000. They also owe us $57,700 for our final pay request. With what was agreed today August first we'll receive a check for at least $3,310,800. I know the company needs it."

## CHAPTER 58

During the last six months of 1975 and early in 1976 favorable happenings occurred, some in and some out of Aldridge's control. These occurrences would have a positive impact on Aldridge's dire financial situation.

In the early '70's the Unites States had been shipping vast amounts of the nation's construction equipment production to Vietnam in support of the ongoing war. As a result used construction equipment was in demand and prices were being forced upward. These circumstances allowed Aldridge to gave up far less of their equipment fleet than expected. An auction to satisfy Merchants Trust's demand to repay one million dollars on the line of credit was very successful. What remained of their vast fleet had a higher book value.

The one million dollar drawdown of their Merchants Trust line of credit reduced the total owed to five million dollars.

The increased value of their fleet prompted a decision to sell off via auction a lot of older, unneeded, and unencumbered equipment. An auction in August 1975 resulted in, after expenses, slightly over another one million dollars in cash. This influx of cash was used to ease their accounts payable situation.

The cash crunch caused Aldridge to increase their efforts to collect money owed to them on sixteen public projects.

Their previous profitability had caused project managers to make unnecessary compromises and become lax when negotiating monthly pay requests with owner representatives. There were also several substantially complete projects where all or part of the retainer was past due. No more Mr. Nice Guy; they began taking more aggressive action to get paid. Eventually, this attitude improved cash flow.

Many of their projects had unresolved claims and disputes. There were also agreed to change orders that owner representatives were sitting on for lack of motivation to process the paper work.

Although the matter was finally resolved at the claims hearing on May 21, 1976, at the Trout River Dam, in April 1975, Wayne and Dean were still haggling about one hundred thousand dollars of added cost to prevent a disastrous flood that occurred in June 1974. Aldridge brought the proverbial hammer down on unpaid extra work. In some cases, they employed the services of claim lawyers to convince public owners to pay according to contract requirements.

The result of Aldridge's team efforts to amend for previous lax attitudes added another million dollars to the company coffers.

***

In April 1976 The Corps of Engineers declared the embankment dam complete and began to fill the lake, taking advantage of the spring rain and increased flow in the Trout River.

A lot of incidental work remained; roads and parking, topsoil and seeding being the most important. The last activity performed by Aldridge's employees was placing fifty thousand cubic yards of topsoil six inches thick on the downstream slope of the dam. They subcontracted three hundred thousand square yards of seeding and four miles of paved roadway to responsible local contractors.

In July 1976 Aldridge received the final change order in the agreed amount of $1,416,100. In August, also as agreed, they received a check for final payment including the change order, the final pay request, and retainer. The Trout River Dam and Lake was finished and available for the public to enjoy.

\*\*\*

By spring 1977 at the Trout River Dam and Lake you could see beautiful vistas in every direction. There were three hundred campsites, a beach, boat launch ramps, and miles of hiking trails. For the sportsman, there was fishing and designated hunting areas. To serve the public there was a Corps of Engineers office and an Ohio Department of Natural Resources information station. Nestled in the midst of all the surrounding beauty and amenities was the beautiful twenty-two hundred acre Trout River Lake.

It took one more frivolous lawsuit in 1978 to finally bring an end to the opposition. By then even opponents had to admit, "It looks nice."

On September 29, 1977, the government held a dedication ceremony opening the Trout River Dam and Lake to the public. The US Army Corps of Engineers was represented by, soon to retire, Deputy Commander Lieutenant Colonel Chad Ramsey, resident engineer Wayne Henderson, numerous local politicians, a few State Officials, a couple of media representatives, and a smattering of curious onlookers. All of the politicos were posing and preening for the press cameras. All were smiling and hoping for a chance to make a public statement about their contribution to making the Trout River project a reality. Not among the attendees was biased reporter Roger Wilkins, he had new crosses to carry.

Absent, and not invited; in fact not even notified of the dedication, were the real builders; employees and officials from the Arthur Aldridge Construction Company. Missing and not acknowledged were the men and women who began their day at 5:00 a.m. and traveled to work through a slow moving chain of snake-like red tail lights accompanied by many who believed their destination was more important than the others. After at least an hour of murderous travel, the Trout River workers arrived, depending on the season, at a cold, wet, windy, hot, humid, muddy, dusty, and dangerous workplace. After arriving, in all kinds of weather, they got to ride on benches set in the bed of a pickup truck and took a half mile ride to the work areas. After they worked hard enough to build the assigned project and their skills were no longer needed, they were given a final check, a layoff notice, and sent to look for another project to build where some politician will brag, "...and did you see what I built?"

Long gone are the former owners of the land the government took to create the Trout River Project. Their former homes and farms no longer exist. Their historic schoolhouse and their cemetery are in a new location. It's doubtful that anyone among future visitors to the lake would say, "I wonder what happened to the people who lived here? Thank you. Thank you for giving up your home so I can enjoy this marvelous place."

***

Two years later Wayne and Dean crossed paths. The Corps of Engineers sponsored a major conference on a new concept called Partnering where contractor and owner shed the adversarial relationships that until now dominated the construction industry. Partnering is a written agreement between owner and contractor to work as a team to achieve successful completion of the project. Wayne was a speaker at the conference, and Dean agreed to provide testimony that the concept works. Once again they were working together to achieve a common goal. Upon seeing each other Wayne told Dean, "I bet you thought I was out of your life after I bailed out on you at the project closeout negotiation."

Dean smiled and said, "Yeah, I sure did."

Wayne explained, "My boss thought it would make it easier for both sides if I didn't participate. I believe he was right. Oh, by the way, they sacked Brian Towelson but didn't file charges against him. He had to leave the government with no references."

Wayne and Dean, two bulls in a china shop called the construction industry.

After the Trout River Project was completed Wayne returned to the Louisville District Office and embarked on a career path that would eventually lead him to be appointed chief engineer. His family was happy to be back in Louisville.

When Herbert Flaherty retired five years later Dean became a majority owner and a president of Aldridge Construction Company. His family was glad to be back in St. Louis and in their new home.

# THE END

# EPILOGUE

Aldridge ended 1975 a, barely, solvent company. Company officials were making concentrated efforts to bring the company back to profitability. However, economic factors, excessive overhead costs, lack of a substantial work backlog and a dismal outlook for future contracts caused the three majority owners to hold a closed door meeting on January 14, 1976.

Once again Victor Shearer took the lead, "This meeting, as you know, is to discuss the future of Aldridge Construction. Right now we are solvent. We are paying our bills and making required loan payments. The lack of new work and ongoing overhead expenses, including our salaries, and the cost of completing existing contracts is sucking the life out of our company."

An oppressive silence ensued. Finally, Robert Warden usually the most reticent of the three broke the silence, "Let's face the facts. We are a dinosaur in a race horse world." He looked directly at his partners and friends, "The next six months are going to be the most trying and disruptive in our lives. We might have to close the doors for good."

Herbert Flaherty nodded his head in agreement, "We have no choice, we'll have to liquidate more assets and cut payroll to a bare minimum. We need to downsize, and we have to start now."

A lengthy discussion ensued to indentify necessary financial actions, treatment of laid off employees, and disposition of equipment. Aldridge had annually completed projects valued at about two hundred million dollars. There was still a lot of work on the books.

They put their plans into action.

As work on uncompleted contracts progressed unneeded equipment and supplies were brought back to Aldridge's equipment yard, truckload after truckload. Storage and office trailers, pile driving equipment, cranes, dozers, loaders, air compressors, pumps, scaffolding, off road trucks, hydraulic excavators, loader backhoes, graders, scrapers, and generators. Aldridge sold all unneeded equipment and supplies.

Downsizing included another massive auction that disposed of the latest influx of unneeded equipment and vehicles. An Auction in May 1976 disposed of five hundred thousand dollars of equipment, the proceeds applied to the line of credit. Downsizing required office employee layoffs. Unneeded office and project office employees received a severance package, based on their length of service, including extensions of their benefits and pay.

After completion of several Aldridge contracts, including the Trout River Dam, downsizing, to the extent needed, was completed in June of 1976.

The office and equipment yard were less than their former selves but still substantial. Aldridge still had bonding capability although less than at the height of the company's glory years. They were still bidding and being awarded projects.

What remained of the company, actually more than half of the size at the peak in 1972, was lean and mean. The military might say they were a real fighting machine. The three remaining owners and eight shareholders had experienced a miracle. "Most important," as Herb said at a shareholder meeting in June 1976, "We have learned a lesson. We'll be more careful and alert to what is going on around us. We're not going to be complacent."

Robert Warden had the last word, "Everyone who ever worked for the Aldridge Company can be proud of their accomplishments. Even our failures have been beneficial by teaching us lessons about what pitfalls to avoid. We are at a turning point. We see the beginning of exciting, challenging, and rewarding years filled with unexpected joys and sorrows. We can all be proud of the hundreds of projects and landmarks built, and to be built, with our hands and minds."

# ACKNOWLEDGMENTS

Thanks to Carole, my wife of fifty-eight years. During that time she has learned to expect and tolerate the unexpected from me. She was the one who, after a year and a half told me, "Just finish the damn book." Carole's sister, Karen, an award winning English teacher, put me on the right track with a "D" for my early effort. Jean Marie spent several hours critiquing a later effort, thank you Jean Marie. Jerry, my former boss and early mentor was the first reader. His comments and "commas" improved the entire book. Family friend, Jaci, encouraged me to keep going.

*The Falls City Engineers,* by Leland R. Johnson and written under the auspices of the Louisville Engineers District of the US Army Corps of Engineers, provided helpful information to verify some of my recollections.

This book wouldn't have happened without a prod from our daughter Tami. She asked me to write down some memories and events from my experiences during almost fifty years managing construction projects. I got carried away as memories of the dam came back to me and I fictionalized them into this story. It's been a blast!

# ABOUT THE AUTHOR

DAVID GRINSTEAD is a first-time author. *Behind the Dam* is a story based on a project that occurred early in his fifty-years of serving the construction industry. He began his career in 1963 as a structural design engineer. A year later he became employed as a construction project manager, retiring fifty years later as vice president and division manager of an Ohio construction company having $250 million in annual sales.

During his fifty-year career, he has managed or was involved in more than a billion dollars of construction projects including the dam, pump stations, industrial plants, and water and wastewater treatment plants.

He has served as a trustee for the Ohio Contractors Association as a contractor's representative on the Ohio Laborers Health and Welfare and Insurance Funds and was a director of the Ohio Contractors Association. In 1997 he headed a team that built a 17,000,000 gallon underground, first of its kind, post-tensioned water reservoir, that earned a Build Ohio Award and the prestigious Associated Contractors of America's Build America Award.

He has held registration as a professional engineer in Ohio, Pennsylvania, and Virginia and was a licensed contractor in Florida and South Carolina. In 2006 David was inducted into the Cleveland Engineering Society's Hall of Fame.

He lives in Canton, Ohio with his wife, Carole. They have been married for fifty-eight years.